The Poisoner
First Edition
Copyright © 2024 by I.V.Ophelia

Cover Art:
Photograph: Isabel Malia (@smoltog on all platforms)
Model: Bailey Harris
Hair: Vanessa Luciano
Snake: Baby Noodle (Owned by Lydia Lux)
Editor: Tiffany Tyer

ivophelia.com

DEDICATION

*None of these characters should be held in any high regard, they are
sometimes not even palatable to the most senseless of us. They were
designed strictly for fictional consumption. Eat well, my loves.*
—I. V. Ophelia

AUTHOR'S NOTE

REGARDING CONTENT

This is a Gothic Romance and includes explicit sexual scenes. The book also has elements of horror and mystery, which means there may be descriptions of violence, gore, and blood. These characters may take part in consuming substances that are inappropriate and should not be repeated. Some scenes include light BDSM, which in reality would be performed by experienced partners who have had extensive conversations about trust, consent, and boundaries. There is discussion of sexual assault and an on-page non/dubious consent scene. Not all actions in this book were made for sexual gratification and should not serve as a reference for healthy or realistic sexual and emotional relationships. If you are sensitive to non/dub-con, please enter chapter 48 cautiously.
As always, depiction is not endorsement.

KINKS

Primary kinks include:

Vampires, primal, a variation of knotting, risk-aware consent kink, chasing, biting, hair pulling, blood play, forked/split tongues, light creature features, brat/brat tamer, spitting, predicament, and mutual stalking.

Kinks included, but not necessarily intended for romantic/erotic effect considering their context, though they are worth mentioning:

Dub/non-con, impact play with a whip, inappropriate use of rice, degradation/praise, sadism.

My dearest reader, if you are ever unsure of a kink or what it entails, please research the name to make sure you are going into this with informed consent.

Otherwise, enjoy.

PROLOGUE

Have you ever wondered how long it would take for a lethal dose of arsenic to kill you?

Thirty-five hours, twenty-nine minutes, and fifteen seconds.

I should know. I counted myself.

CHAPTER ONE
THE POISONER

M y heels clicked against the wet cobblestones as I stepped out of the coach. The rain was pouring steadily that night. Heavy water drops fell from the dark expanse above, only becoming illuminated when they passed the streetlamps on their descent. The footman held out an umbrella as I stood there looking up at the white stone apartments. The windows were alight with life, people in every room, and warmth traveled through the many corridors. The shadows of people inside teased the activities that were concealed within. Phoebe's place must have had at least fifty rooms by the sheer size of it. One could easily get lost and never resurface.

"Alina!" Phoebe squealed from the doorway. "Perfectly late!" she quipped. "You wore *black*?"

"Black is suitable for every occasion." I grinned, entering as I greeted her.

"Well, it doesn't have to be *every* occasion, Alina. This is a party, not a wake." My dear friend let out a dramatic sigh, her hands thrown up in defeat. She knew that my tastes were very particular and wouldn't be the first to change my mind about them.

My brow flicked up in amusement at the peeved redhead. "Phoebe, relax. I promised that my attire would be up to the dress code." I slipped off my overcoat, and it was whisked away by one of her beetling staff. I gave her a reassuring squeeze on the shoulder. "Besides, you can never be too prepared. What if a guest brings you to such anger that you smite them? I will be fashionably prepared for the occasion."

Phoebe could not keep up with her irritated facade, and her tight expression twisted into an excited beam. Her arms wrapped around my neck in a tight hug. "It's good to have you back. We have much to catch up on! Even with a year's worth of letters, I still haven't heard much about what little quests you've embarked on!"

"You didn't miss out on much, though I'm sure you have much more exciting stories than I."

"Well, then we must create some trouble now that you're home." Her arms were crossed in front of her, a smirk gracing her dainty, sprite-like features. A strawberry curl untucked from her neat bun, framing her pale little face. Phoebe was one of those girls who had an effortless air to her beauty. Her skin was like alabaster, pale enough that you could see every emotion through the rosy heat that graced her cheeks. Her red hair made her green eyes all the more captivating.

"Then it is trouble we shall create." I smirked back.

Phoebe and I had been friends since before I could remember. We were like two thorns of the same rose, an easy connection between us. Our fathers worked together often in the pharmaceutical industry, though her father had his hands in a plethora of other pursuits. My father was a one-industry pony— he dedicated his life to studying medicine through botany, chemistry, and physiology. I admired him for that. It was a noble profession, and he was able to get far with the investment of Phoebe's father. Sometimes I wonder what else he could have given the world if he had not passed last year.

Losing him broke a part of me that I would never understand. I spent the last year as a hermit on our country estate. With the social pressure of being friends with Phoebe, I could not risk being seen in that state. My father's reputation was the only thing I had left of him, and I would be damned if I tainted it by acting out. I did not expect to return so soon, but I missed the city's life.

I never thought I would be one to miss the nights Phoebe would host, though I might have overestimated how well I could handle this much socializing after a few days of travel. Overstimulating was an understatement when it came to the chaos she could curate.

Everything about her home was large and grand, with an extraordinary decorative staircase that snaked up both sides of the room and conjoined at the top. There were archways on either side and straight ahead under the balcony of the stairs. Dozens of art pieces littered the walls, and rare furniture was scattered about. Some of these pieces would have made the best craftsmen weep in awe. It all radiated wealth and status, perfect for hosting hundreds until they stumbled out at dawn just to repeat it again the following week.

Her hand gripped my arm as she pulled me toward one of the many rooms. The humming of chatter swelled as we neared. Everyone was dressed in silken gowns and tailored suits. The silhouettes were enough to intimidate anyone, even those familiar with the latest fashion plates.

The gown I'd chosen had a simple silhouette. It hugged my waist, aided by my corset, smoothing down the front of my hips before it pooled straight to the floor. The back of the dress slightly bustled before a subtle train followed behind me. The black silk left a slick shine, reflecting the soft ambient light with every cascade and gather. The neckline was low and wide, nearly off my shoulders, adorned with fabric roses that decorated the front of my bust and scattered through the draping. A thick lace choker with a matching black flower was secured high on my neck. Lastly, my hair was half up, with inky ringlets draped over my shoulder. In my hand, I clutched my black feather fan between my gloved fingers, the silk opera gloves climbing up and ending above my elbows.

Phoebe's dress was similar, but was a soft blush pink with white lacy details. She chose a more dramatic corset silhouette that accentuated her breasts in an impressive display. Her gloves were entirely made of thick white lace, and her fan was made of silk with similar decorative elements as her dress. She also chose less modest jewelry, with heavy diamonds kissing the skin around her neck and ears. She shined like fresh dewdrops on the pink roses in her garden. I had always believed she was the most beautiful woman to walk the earth, and she had not proven me wrong thus far.

"Then I heard that Benjamin is here looking for our acquaintance, Mary, which is quite delicious because I heard she may have already taken a lover." Phoebe looked back at me while she clutched my arm, realizing I had drifted off. "Alina, what troubles you? You disappeared in there." She frowned, jabbing her index finger at my temple.

"I am well. I just haven't gotten a routine together," I mumbled, following her through the crowd, our arms looped together. We plucked champagne flutes off the nearest passing platter and drifted over to mingle with the other guests.

Phoebe radiated elegance and hospitality. My own aura had

always been a bit unapproachable, maybe a bit macabre. It was not an issue personally, as I preferred some distance between myself and strangers. I already brought too much attention to myself by existing most days. When I thought about it, seeing what kind of characters dared to approach was amusing.

Phoebe was chatting up some pompous characters I had never seen before. Faces all began to look the same after a while, so I would not remember if I did meet them once upon a time. "This is my dear friend, Alina Lis. She owns the apothecary next to the florists in the West End. She's a sort of scientist!"

I tensed when I realized she had been talking about me. I appreciated her enthusiasm for my profession, but not every man was appreciative of women owning or inheriting property, never mind working in any scientific field. The shop was my father's and was passed to me when he died.

"Nowadays I write for scientific journals about the toxicity of beauty products and offer safer alternatives. If you read the tabloids, you may have read my work." I gave a polite smile, not looking for remarks about women working outside their "expertise." It put men at ease sometimes, to know that my skills involved something more feminine. Explaining myself was exhausting. I would instead dumb it down to keep my peace.

Speaking of peace, there was the matter of the under-the-table products reserved for women looking to eliminate any unsavory characters, bound by marriage or otherwise. My exceptional understanding of botany and chemistry had allowed me to aid in the disappearance of many men—a professional poisoner, if you will. Phoebe didn't know that half of the business existed, but her up-to-date gossip made choosing my next subjects fairly easy.

I preferred not to call them victims. They were anything but.

A poisoner's job was never finished, as a poison could always be better. More refined, purified, deadlier—until you made something new and started the process again. That was why every recipient was a subject, each corpse leaving more flirtatious hints as to how the poison could be improved for the next sinner.

It wasn't long before Phoebe turned her attention to hosting-related endeavors while I spoke, leaving me alone with the crowd.

"Ah, so you are like a pharmacist?" The man's words were accurate, but he turned to his friend to scoff before returning any acknowledgments to me. "Say, what is wrong with the color of your hair? There—on your face."

I pulled a tight smile in response, my fingers brushing over my eyebrow. "There is nothing wrong. It is poliosis. It just turns the hair on the left side of my face white." My voice was kind for the sake of educating, not that a loaf like him would know.

"Surely if you are a pharmacist you must know how to fix an ailment like that."

"It is no ailment, more of a curious biological happening." A deep, steadying breath was drawn to keep myself from falling into more unfavorable expressions. "I prefer to call it a rarity."

Ignorance was expected, and I never blamed them. It is not a choice to be stupid, though I gave my best efforts to be sympathetic. I doubted that it would have been such a talking piece if I were born blonde. Unfortunately, I was gifted with my mother's black hair, which stood out like a melanistic rabbit on freshly fallen snow.

I excused myself from the interaction, swapping out my empty champagne flute for a full one on my way to the other rooms.

There were many repetitive conversations with other ladies about some of my writings, mainly those from the tabloids about beauty regimens. It was nice to know that my work was appreciated, even if the other half was otherwise unknown—for good reason. Someday maybe I would be as notorious as Giulia Tofana, but for now, it was between myself and the women who needed it most. Personal pleasures were like drying flowers, best kept away from the light to preserve their vibrance.

My eyes lifted to take in the new scene in the room. The ceilings were tall, with an impressive collection of paintings climbing up the walls. Mismatched sizes of canvas were placed together in eclectic harmony on each wall. There were portraits, exotic landscapes, beloved animals, and an odd folklore scene here and there. All were displayed proudly in gold-leaf frames. I leisurely strolled through the crowd, my attention jumping from one painting to the next. Rooms like these just screamed *money*.

The trill of instruments tuning up tore my attention away from the decadent display of art. All guests gravitated toward the main ballroom. The wood on the floor was stained with complementing hues of brown and tan, laid out in a convoluted pattern framing the floor. There was a piano in the corner, and some musicians were tending to their instruments. I stood at the edge of the room among many others, anticipating the festivities soon underway. I twisted a strand of hair between my fingers, sipping down the rest of my champagne and nearly spilling it from the corner of my lips.

Slow down, Alina. The night is too young to be this sloppy.

Hugging the corner, I watched the crowd excitedly split into dancers and spectators. I chose to be a spectator this time. There was something comforting about people-watching. I liked to wonder what it was like to *be* different people. My eyes flicked to the assortment of couples swaying and fluttering around each other. Some were seasoned married partners going through the evening's motions, some were magnetic lovers glowing in each other's presence, and then there were the ones meeting eager eyes for the first time, displaying caution and curiosity in each other's movements. It reminded me of different species of birds and how they choose to attract their mates.

The room's temperature was rising, and my head was starting to believe it could float. It was a good thing I paused my pursuit of spirits. The herd of bodies made slipping out and into the next room difficult. I knew there was a lounging area from when I walked through it before.

Why do I do this to myself? I should have used tonight to rest.

I stumbled into the room with two fingers pinching the bridge of my nose, easing the spell of nausea that quickly approached.

A sharp yelp returned some of my sobriety to me.

Two figures were on the chaise on the other side of the room.

A man was seated in the middle of the lounging chair, his knees resting in a wide stance with a woman poised between them. He had a black-gloved hand gripping her neck to the side, his other hand tightly around her arm. He was dressed entirely in black. It made the woman's baby-blue dress jump out against him.

The click of my heels alerted him to my presence.

His eyes trailed across the room slowly before settling on me, no haste to his demeanor. He didn't move, not even a flinch to indicate any remorse for his disgraceful position.

His eyes were a cold, pale gray color. The type that could cut you down with a quick glance. His golden blond hair fell slightly over his face. One might describe an angel in any other situation, though that heavenly warmth never reached his gaze.

I could not remember anything but those dead eyes, leeching any form of comfort from the air between us.

His grip on the woman tightened, and she let out a sob that rang blurry in my ears. All I could hear was my blood rushing through them.

A hungry grin crawled across his sharp features. There were wet crimson trails dribbling down her neck, staining the lovely blue silk of her dress.

I swore I saw a flash of light reflect in his eyes.

Brutish men were no mystery to me. I had come to know them well. But I had never seen one so brash as to rejoice upon being caught. No discretion, an absence of shame.

There was a feral air to his expression before he grabbed her jaw, extending her neck out farther. A red glistening tongue dragged up her jugular. He kept me in the corner of his eye as if to ask, *What will you do?*

I wish I could say that I made that man suffer—that I put his hands in jars and severed the tongue from his mouth. Instead, I did something far worse.

I did nothing.

CHAPTER TWO
THE CREATURE

"Go on, keep squirming. Then I can show you how delicate windpipes really are," I whispered, brushing my bottom lip across the pretty birdie's ear. A satisfied groan escaped low in my throat when my words earned a sob from the frail little thing.

I trailed my lips down to her neck. I could practically feel that metallic tinge in the roots of my canines.

She wriggled one more time before I bit down on her neck, pressing her hips closer between my legs to hold her in place. Heat flooded my throat and warmed my body faster than neat whiskey. I pulled back to inspect my handiwork, edging myself to savor the taste and make my meal last a little longer. Besides, carrying dead weight would be more unpleasant than her current flightiness.

Click.

I *hated* interruptions.

It took a moment to force my attention from the fresh body, and my eyes slowly settled on the figure in the archway.

Oh? I wasn't prepared for another course just yet. My lucky night.

I inspected the body standing in the archway. It appeared much more delicious than the one in my arms.

Her tall, lithe figure was swept up in buttery black fabric. Images of how it would look discarded on the floor immediately made a home in my mind. I would have mistaken her for a shadow between her black dress and midnight hair if it wasn't for that milky flesh. Her eyes were like the tundra ice, unforgivingly cold and vexed.

A smirk crept past my facade, making those pretty lashes of hers flutter in disbelief.

Will she be sober enough to remember me? Was she scared or fascinated? Why was she just *standing* there?

Why was her expression more satisfying than the mouthful I just savored?

My fingers dug deeper into the prey in my lap, eliciting another feeble sob.

A flash of anger graced those bright eyes.

Would she make a similar sound when I grabbed a fistful of black hair? When I wrapped my fingers around that graceful neck? Would she fight me, curse my name like a witch? Or would she cry, begging me to keep going? All questions I would happily seek answers to.

I flattened my tongue on the poor soul's neck, sliding it slow and steady. A trail of blood and saliva painted the canvas of skin.

What will you do now, voyeur?

A fire alighted in her. If I had been closer, I might have been able to smell it radiating off of her like heat on a furnace. My amusement was cut short as she slipped away while I was lost in thought.

What a shame.

My appetite had changed. The meal I just witnessed was worth the hundred inebriated snacks I would catch this evening.

It had been a while since that unbridled, rapidly returning passion for the hunt returned to me. I must have just needed something worth chasing.

Will you have just as delicious an expression when I catch you?

CHAPTER THREE
THE POISONER

N*auseous.*
Alcohol threatened to make a reappearance due to my inability to gauge my own limits. My head swam until memories from the night before resurfaced in my murky brain.

Those dead eyes were still burned onto the back of my eyelids, haunting my nightmares as well as my daydreams.

My stomach finally released some much-needed reminders into the water closet, though all those memories in particular had turned to bile.

The hangover and whiplash from remembering the events made me sick, *disgusted*.

I wish I could say that it was directed entirely at that man, but the guilt weighed on me the moment I left that girl there in the grasp of that human bear trap. My self-preservation overpowered my need for justice at that moment, and I will never forget how filthy it felt.

I had not fully understood what I saw, but knowing that it

wasn't a dream was enough. That hungry look in his eyes could only be described as uncouth, carnal, even.

My fingers gripped the edge of the sink as I hesitantly glanced at my reflection, hoping the image would just jump out and slap me. Dark streams of stray hair were splayed in every direction, knotted from a night of unrest.

Get ahold of yourself. You have work to do.

I was to meet Phoebe today, but I was having difficulty making it out of the confines of the bathroom with this guilty sickness that riddled me.

Alas, I was able to pull myself halfway together by my seams. Moving through the town house, I looked for particular clothing items somewhere lost in the scattered chests waiting to be unburdened of their contents.

Not too long ago, Phoebe and I were racing these halls with our wooden horses, pretending we were adventurers who made this home our very world, with infinite possibilities to explore our imagination.

The Eastwater Manor was my temporary home for now. This place belonged to Phoebe's family. I was merely a tenant until I could acquire something else.

The estate was a beautiful Georgian town house with three stories and too many rooms. It was located at the end of a quiet street, surrounded by abodes just as elegant. A lush walled garden awaited in the back, hidden from neighboring views. My favorite was the humble greenhouse tucked away between the overgrown ivy. I was grateful to be staying in the most excellent area of London. The house was covered in soft creams and whites, and a warm wood lined every banister and corner. It was my favorite place to visit when I was young. Even then, it was just as much of a labyrinth as it is now. Nothing had changed.

I dressed myself in the first sturdy walking suit I could find upon opening my trunks of clothing. My mood was just as grim as my attire. I think a skeleton would look cheerier than I.

My hand traced over the intricate carvings along the banister. The morning light leaked through a unique circular window, watching over the foyer like an eye, illuminating the soft gold-leaf patterns in the ivory wallpaper. The circular window hung above the landing, separating the stairs from the next floor and bringing light into an otherwise dark space.

I rubbed the back of my neck to relieve the tightness of my muscles. The thin black lace of my collar tickled under my jawline.

I approached the doorway to check the mail basket and to open the door for any parcels. The breeze that greeted me reminded me of how close we were to the end of autumn. The trees lining the street were shedding and nearly bare. The bustling of horse hooves and chatter of crows rang with rampant nostalgia for the season.

When I closed the door behind me, the click of the lock echoed back into the home, bouncing around like a rumor against the walls. The sound dissipated once it fled far enough away. A reminder of the loneliness that held my heart so fondly.

"I PROMISE I would have stayed longer! I don't know what happened. A fever overcame me. There was no predicting it!" I smiled sheepishly while tearing off another piece of my pastry.

Phoebe and I met for breakfast at the park to make up for my sudden departure last night. There was a small café with little chairs and tables set outside, a quiet place for people to watch or read. In our case, it was the perfect place for morning gossip.

"I was just glad to receive a call from you, to hear that you were all right. You worried me terribly when you disappeared into thin air." Phoebe huffed but knew she couldn't stay mad. "Did you at least mingle a little? Meet anyone? Any details to spare?"

I shook my head before pausing, remembering the strange creature of a man. My cheeks must have given it away because Phoebe released an excited squeak. Though my flushed state was from anger, not bashfulness.

"You *did*, didn't you? Why didn't you say so?" She squirmed in her chair as if settling down for a long juicy piece of hearsay. "Well?" Her gloved fingers squeezed her teacup in anticipation.

"It wasn't like that," I scolded, though her excitement tugged at the corner of my lips. "It was just in passing. Nothing happened."

Phoebe gave me a displeased look, her nose wrinkling as she did so. Then, something over my shoulder captured her attention, and she quickly forgot her previous interrogation.

Her elegant smile returned. "Look! We caught the attention of an illustrator right over there!" She gestured, tilting her head in his direction as if not to give away that she had spotted the artisan.

It would not be the first time, as our contrasting styles usually caught the eye of the wandering artists of the city. Phoebe was always bright, elegant, and clean. Myself, on the other hand, preferred the dark and ominous.

Due to my work, I had a personal ritual of wearing black. I was the cause of many funerals, such events that I could not and would not pay any respect to—it was only fitting that I always dressed for the occasion. An homage to my peculiar talent. There was no need to change out of funeral attire, as men die every day —a cause for celebration.

As for spiritual reasons, I had none. Black would always be fashionable, mourning or not. Plus, black tended to keep my interactions with people to a minimum, an added gratuity. If anything, I was sure it would look like gloating if the spirits saw me now. A poetic thought.

We sat for a few more moments, allowing the illustrator a chance to get a good look before we embarked on our morning stroll.

"Murder! Body dumped at the docks! Ripper among us! A monster out for blood!" a paper boy shouted, prints and bag in hand, shoving them out for people to view.

I tossed a coin to the boy and snagged a paper, quickening my pace as Phoebe struggled to keep up.

"A body at the docks? Why, that's not news at all." She frowned, trying to peek at the paper as I unfurled the front cover.

"Not just any body," I muttered, mostly to myself.

I could barely make out the face when looking at the illustration, possibly due to the actual corpse not having an identifiable face to begin with. It was a silhouette of a woman wearing an elegant dress.

It might have just been black ink on paper, but I knew I specifically recognized that dress in baby blue.

My fingers crushed the paper between them as I shoved it in a bin while passing by, wiping my hands nervously on my skirt as if to rid them of the guilt that stained them.

My new subject has reared his ugly head again.

Phoebe and I parted ways at this point so that we could embark on our separate errands for the day. My first stop was the florist.

Caldwell's Flora and Botanicals, the sign read.

I've known Mrs. Caldwell since I was a little girl. My father always riddled her with strange requests. Her shop was one of the only ones that imported flowers and plants upon special request. Her husband was well-connected to the freight and import industry. This was a must for my father, who was constantly experimenting with odd flora for medicines, tinctures, and whatever else he was engrossed with at the time.

She eventually became reliant on her for anything I needed for my work until I left the city a year ago. She didn't ask questions unless it was "How much?" or "How soon would you like it?" Over the years, she had grown on me, an extended family of sorts.

"Did my special order come in? The one I telephoned last week?" I asked, looking over the counter at the short, plump woman.

"Alina! Yes. It looks like they sent more than necessary, but I have no use for your odd little plant, so just take the whole bunch!" She bumbled around, pulling up a flat crate and slapping it on the counter. Removing the top, she revealed a generous amount of white snakeroot.

I inspected it, keeping my hands away from the shrubby plant, though it was hard to restrain myself from running my fingers over the lush leaves. It was a rich green color with little white flowers dotting the tops, similar to a hogweed. It was an unimpressive-looking plant, but the chemical inside was something magnificent.

Within this uninspiring weed was a chemical called tremetol. It took a few days for symptoms to register and could quickly bring down men and beasts alike if given enough through subtle means. It was quite a nice piece to hide in the perfume collection for the right buyer.

"It is perfect, Mrs. Caldwell," I breathed. I couldn't hide my grin any longer.

"You and your bizarre choice of flower arrangements. I don't understand it, but it's nice to see you happy." She chuckled. "It's just good to see you back home. How are you settling back in?"

She gave me a look that I had been seeing all too often since my return from solitude. That look of pity, condolences. I was waiting for that shoe to drop when I saw an old face, a never-ending reminder that I'd returned with one less family member than I had before.

My voice turned stiff again. "Thank you again. I'll see you about."

THE CONVENIENT THING about Caldwell's was that it was only three blocks from my father's apothecary, *my* apothecary.

Balancing the crate across my arm, I jammed my key into the lock. When I pushed open the door, a sharp ring of the shop bell trilled.

If I could bottle the smell of the shop into a perfume, my skin would never hold another scent for as long as I was alive.

Inside, a holy manifold of herbs and antique wood scents mingled. Waves of nostalgia greeted me every time I entered. My father came home smelling like the apothecary most nights when it was not the morgue. I loved when the cologne of the domain would follow me home, savoring every moment it stuck to my senses. Because of this fantastical place, his memory would never fade. It was like he was here with me always—in every way but physically when I was in the shop.

Past the dark wooden counter was the back room. I called it my lab, even if it was improper and haphazard. This was where the magic happened.

In the back room, brass instruments that belonged to my father or were retired from the King's College lab were scattered across the extended workbenches. Glass bottles diverse in shape, color, and ounce capacity were stacked neatly under the benches, a layer of dust collecting with patience on their surfaces. It smelled less pleasant than the front of the store, more noticeably of mildew and bleach. The only light came from slender horizontal windows high on the walls that could be propped open for ventilation. Lastly, a simple back door opened to the alleyway where the bins and rats were kept. I used to catch my lab rats out back, but I had decided that I would most likely breed my own this time around for consistency.

As far as anyone was concerned, I studied the toxicity of compounds used in beauty and wellness, giving me good reason to collect the type of plants I do. Most of the academic jargon lost people immediately. Follow-up questions were few and far between.

As I placed the crate on the workbench, the bell at the front door rang already. Unfortunately, I would have to wait to dissect this beautiful specimen later.

Throughout the day, clients wandered in asking about makeup, what to take for which ailment, what plants would make their skin lighter, which made them skinnier, and which ones would make sure their husbands could perform the typical.

I didn't mind any of it. All curiosities about botany made me enjoy this side of the business. I would rather people ask than believe whatever the tabloids told them without a paper backing it. This was why I frequently submitted my own articles. It wasn't hard to dumb it down enough for everyone to understand *X was poisonous, use Y.*

The bell rang all day, but I was excited to hear one particular ring as she entered my shop, Madam Berdot. She was one of my long-term *special-order* clients. All of my clients were appreciated relatively equally, but this particular client was the one I looked forward to after long weeks or months. I had given her a generous amount of the experimental snakeroot poison just the other month through the mail. I used leftover samples my father had hidden away to make something new. She wrote to me a few weeks ago that it was working well, which was why I ordered more of it.

Her occupation came with the unfortunate hazard of dealing with unfavorable men. She owned one of the most established brothels in the city down by the harbor, so it was the perfect grounds for testing whatever solution I came up with, and she would gladly subject especially horrible individuals to my curiosity. My only rule was that she must use it on men of an abusive nature.

"We need to talk," she said abruptly, her eyes shifting to the group of patrons perusing the herbal shelf. Her anxious hands brushed through her frizzy blonde hair, and her emerald-painted eyelids fluttered skittishly toward the front door despite her recent arrival.

"Of course, please." I gestured behind the counter toward the back room to talk discreetly.

She gripped my arm with her clammy hand. "I don't know what happened, but it stopped working."

I arched my brow at her. "That is not possible."

"Well, it is. It was working, I'll give you that, but then it didn't. Do you know how much danger you are putting me and my girls in?"

I lowered my voice. "It is not possible, because it would not have degenerated with time. A small amount of that will bring down a horse. I made sure of it."

"He just got sick, and he came back, and he——" Her voice

hitched in her throat. "I thought maybe I didn't use the correct dosage, but then it just works for some and not all."

"You do not owe an explanation. Let me get you something else. Was anyone hurt? Do you need anything?" I asked, already picking through the thin drawers behind the counter. I pulled out a small vial. "Arsenic. Though if he is an immediate danger, I would recommend faster, more blunt alternatives. Do not take any more risks than you have to."

She snatched the vial from my hand and nodded. Without another word, she left my shop in a hurry. I could not tell if she was upset with me, though I could assume that our professional relationship would be affected by this stumble.

There goes my steady supply of test subjects.

THE SUN HAD DISAPPEARED over the foggy skyline, and the light in the shop slowly dimmed. The glow from the handheld lamp guided me as I closed up for the night. The floors were swept, shelves were faced, and items were restocked before the new day tomorrow. At this rate I would not have time to take apart my new plants.

Until tomorrow, my beautiful specimens.

I turned my back to the door to focus on my one-hundred-and-fifty-drawer apothecary cabinet, shifting through for some loose inventory. I noticed the small leather satchel containing my house-call orders, due to be delivered sometime soon, before I checked to ensure I was not forgetting anything.

A low clicking sound that I couldn't place echoed through the room.

The sound was so amiss that it took a beat to register that it was not some sort of tinnitus rattling in my ear. It was like something had crossed a cicada with the chattering noise a cat made when it saw birds outside the window. A sound of curiosity and predation.

It continued for a long minute that felt eternal.

It was coming from the lab, somewhere far within the darkness that peeked at me through the cracked door.

I debated whether I should snap the door closed or invite the critter in by opening it wider. I decided on the latter. When I did so, the light from the lamp flooded across the dull floor. It illuminated only the dust that fluttered through the air—the curious noise abruptly silenced.

Just a dark, empty shop remained alongside deafening silence.

My brow furrowed as I closed the door, snatching up my satchel and lamp. I would not try to trick myself into believing it was a figment of my imagination. I either tracked in an exotic insect with my fresh shipment of snakeroot or an animal was hidden somewhere in my shop.

The walk home was longer than usual that night. My skin shifted with unease from that sound. It was guttural and unfamiliar, though it did give me some excitement about finding the creature in the morning, whatever it was. I always wondered what I would name a newly discovered insect or mammal.

By the time I arrived at my front door, my legs were worn from all the standing and walking from the day. In the foyer, moonlight greeted me as it began to peek through the window above the stairs, scattering across the neat tiles.

Settling into the living room, I poured myself a well-deserved glass of scotch. One thing about Phoebe's father, Mr. Aston, was that he *knew* his liquor and only kept the best around. He also had a knack for collecting some of the oldest bottles and barrels I had ever seen, based on the last time I saw his collection at their estate in the country.

With the crystal glass in hand, I kicked my boots off at the bottom of the stairs before I walked up. The slow start to the morning wasn't helping the fatigue I was currently suffering. The soreness was more noticeable as I ascended each step.

After the first flight of stairs, an audible scattering was heard.

"*Another* pest?" I groaned.

My weapon of choice was a broom from the small closet at the top of the stairs.

Scritch. Scritch. Scritch.

I peeked around the corner at the end of the hall. Then I waited. It could have only gone left or right. As I leaned against the wall and took another sip of my drink, I listened for the next disturbance.

Scritch. Scritch. Scritch.

Again. To the left was my bedroom. I traced the broom along the carpet to see if I could spot any critters on my way, ready to catch them.

At the end of the hall, my bedroom door was ajar.

It was silent for a moment. The remaining liquid in my cup swayed from side to side, as did my posture. I confidently clasped the broom in my other hand, waiting for the sound to reveal itself again in the dark bedroom.

The door let out a pitchy whine as it revealed the room upon a gentle shove.

There was no use leaving the room so dim if I was to find anything in there.

I glided across the room to turn on a light by my bed. The lamp flickered when I turned the dial, the flame growing lazily to brighten the gloomy room.

Then, there was the sound again. Right behind me.

Not the scratching noise, but that *clicking* from the shop.

Petrified once more, I listened intensely as if to convince myself that I could decipher what it was this time around. It was nothing like I had ever heard before. I had traveled the world in pursuit of exotic plants and animals, and nothing had ever come close to this *thing* I heard.

As I turned on my heels, the noise stopped abruptly. No creatures were in sight. Just a dim, empty room.

I could have sworn that it had been a few meters away, but there was no evidence of anything to suggest such a thing. The only proof that remained was tucked deep into the corners of my imagination, accompanied by the buzz of my poison of choice.

CHAPTER FOUR

THE CREATURE

Isn't she just delectable?

Alina Lis, the savory arrangement spread out before me.

Her thick black hair was scattered across the silken sheets. From the looks of it, she could not keep from tossing and turning throughout the night. Maybe she could sense the presence of a certain predator stalking her cozy nest.

Clever girl, just not clever enough.

I just watched, promising myself that I would behave. *Just this once.* There was plenty of time for play. My hunger had only grown since I finished my last meal in preparation for *her*.

I was a gentleman. I liked to get to know my prey before I ate them. It was only polite. I worked so hard today, following her every move. I read up on her as well, conducting my own research on this fascinating new plaything of mine.

I deserved an up-close-and-personal reward, especially with the amount of walking this woman does. At least I knew that her circulation would be phenomenal with how active she was. I didn't expect half of the things I discovered about my meal today. Miss Lis moved quickly, and some of her errands were hard to understand. There were so many peculiar rituals in her routine. Though the apothecary was an interesting development. I supposed she owned it, since she seemed to be the only one with the keys.

It had been so long since I had stalked anything worth the trouble. To get so intimate with a life ready for the taking. I would be disappointed if she made me work this hard only for her to taste bland. Flavor aside, I nearly forgot how exhilarating it was to chase. I would say the time was well spent. Memorizing her routine, her life, her *scent*. It was like she was mine already. The poor thing was just painfully unaware.

The body atop the bed beckoned me forward, closer to the bed. A delicacy reserved only for me.

The elusive creature's beauty was like a witch must have carved her out from an ancient forest, haunted by spirits of old and harboring centuries of secrets. Not to mention her...*unique* coloring. It was like someone had spilled refined sugar across ground charcoal. Accidental and one of a kind, too much of a shame to waste.

She rustled under the covers and turned away.

Could she feel how close I was?

Close enough to take a bite.

Carefully lifting the silken fabric of the bedding, I hoped to see what she hid under her typical morose attire. I was disappointed to see she'd kept her nightgown on, but maybe it was for the best. After all, this felt *wrong*.

A naked body was no mystery to me, but seeing hers would feel sinful. One must not consume a delicacy with haste. It would be mannerless. Her hair snaked in loose curls over her pale skin all the way past her hips, as if they were drawing a map for the places I wanted to touch. Only the outline of her body was visible as the fabric wrapped around her. Somehow it still felt like I was peeping under a nun's habit.

I tilted my head to the side as I peeked, not wanting to disturb her by lifting the sheets too far from her body. If only she would roll toward me. I wanted to see more. She was purposefully shielding herself from my gaze. *Fine, have it your way, but only for tonight.*

Her scent teased my nose, making me take in a sharp breath.

I lowered to my knees beside the bed, my eyes fixated on the bewitching affair before me. My fingers brushed the hair away from the back of her neck.

I can't help it. Who am I to rob myself of life's simple pleasures?

Leaning closer, I buried my nose in her hair and wrapped a dark tendril around my palm. As I took in a long breath, my senses danced in the presence of her. She smelled like black cherries, bitter almonds, and liquor. There were small notes of something else, something that made my throat tighten and burn. Oh, I just knew she would simply unravel me.

The new innervations put my head in a spell, making sure the memory of her was etched properly into my mind. After all, it was essential to know any prey like the back of your hand, to know them well enough to anticipate their every move. I wouldn't mind knowing this one in any way I could, in due time.

Within the flesh underneath all the motilities, there was something more challenging to place, though I had experienced something similar a few times prior.

Undiluted, potent, untouched. A drop of that sweetness could make anyone go wild with hunger and desire.

She was lucky I found her first, truly.

Anyone else would have torn her to shreds if they got close enough to know.

"Ah…so sweet," I mumbled, my face buried into the crook of her neck.

I was right when I said she was rare. A blood type held by few, but like no other flavor this world could create. She was what we would call a Mellifluous Host—a rare delicacy.

I loved being right.

Her blood had a curious spice to it, adding some tasteful aromatic notes.

She was so enticing like that, her neck poised delicately before my jaws, waiting for me. I could snap it in half with a single bite.

I glanced up at her face. It was so soft, so peaceful. Like a sleeping fawn wrapped in the comfort of the night, confident that they were hidden from the terrors that lurked about in the darkness. She was helpless, innocent.

I ached for her *physically*.

My canines twitched, sore from anticipation, begging to disappear inside the tender flesh beneath me. To scar that untouched skin would be the ultimate aphrodisiac. The same feeling plagued me last night and made an unfortunate mess of my previous meal. I knew she saw my handiwork in the paper that morning. I wanted her to know that it was me.

I shifted where I knelt in an attempt to get comfortable. A low, excited clicking escaped my throat as I adjusted my hips, making my teeth chatter from the chill. That look on her face when she saw the sketch in the paper made me shake with excitement. I wondered if she would make that face again for me. I could not help the chorusing that vibrated in my throat as I thought about it. It was all so exhilarating. Why didn't she ask about me? Not even a mention to the police.

How rude.

She was of the perceptive kind. I would have thought her first call would be to the station or the papers.

What are you up to? Why won't you play?

It was quite frustrating to go through the trouble just for her to ignore my gesture. I did not understand her reasoning. Maybe I just needed to be more obvious. Typically, I wouldn't bother with the extra effort, but she just set me on *fire*. It was impossible to ignore her, but I could not imagine how she managed to ignore *me*.

"I look forward to us, little shadow," I whispered against her ear, tucking a bit of hair behind it before I allowed her one last night of rest. One more night before our games began.

CHAPTER FIVE
THE POISONER

B lood, there is blood everywhere.

  I am on my hands and knees, staring down at my reflection in the thick, sticky liquid.

Why is there so much? Is this my own?

I look up. A black expanse surrounds me, and the scarlet pool spans as far as the eye can see. My body is completely covered in blood from head to toe.

Droplets flood my vision, making it red and blurry. It won't clear up no matter how hard I rub my face. It feels like the more I scratch, the more blood comes dripping down.

"Ah…so sweet."

A blurry figure in the distance speaks. It sounds more like I am underwater. I blink and frantically try to clear my eyes, trying to see what is in here with me.

There's a tall figure, his back turned to me, blood dripping over his lean muscles. He looks like he was carved from stone. He could have told me he was Lucifer himself, and I would believe him. His semblance transcends the realms of humanity, embodying a mystique that surpasses mere mortal attributes.

His head turns over his shoulder to look at me. That familiar smirk matches those dead pale eyes reflecting back at me.

As the corner of his lips peel up into a smirk, that predatory clicking rises in his throat, like some type of demon from a deep circle of hell. Explicitly tasked to torture me.

I stagger back as my vision blurs again. All I see is the predatory reflection of his eyes in the low light as he approaches.

"I look forward to us, little shadow."

The sudden drop of my heart ripped me from my mind and back into reality.

"It's because you're *working* all the time instead of having fun with *me*," Phoebe badgered, tapping the rim of her cup.

"It's not that. I haven't slept well the past few days. Work relaxes me."

"Work *relaxes* you? Please, when has any normal person ever said that and meant it?"

"I mean it!" I laughed, but Phoebe's expression told me she didn't believe it.

We decided to meet at Phoebe's place for our morning gossip session, as the rain had put a damper on our walk.

"Maybe you're not sleeping because there's a ripper running the streets apparently. I am sure you saw the story about the new bodies," Phoebe murmured.

"What new bodies?" I reached my hand out eagerly. "Show me."

She offered up a newspaper printed from that morning.

There were two bodies found in the harbor. The illustration pictured their pale faces and rigid bodies laid out on the dull cobblestones where they were dragged out.

It was notable that the two girls appeared similar. The paper stated they were not related, not even acquaintances. But they looked *so* familiar.

Their eyes were clouded, yet a glimpse of light hues remained visible. Dark, wet hair clung to their faces in disarray.

Another item of interest was the skin on the left side of their faces. It was neatly peeled off from above their eyebrow and through their eye. The exposed muscles and neat borders of the wounds on their faces insinuated that it was meticulously done, methodical, even.

There was no question about who did it, but it made me wonder about the need for theatrics.

This was a message for me. Trust me, it was received. Though the motif to my markings was distasteful at best.

My repulsion must have shown on my face, since Phoebe yanked the newspaper from my clenched hands. "That's enough of the macabre for one morning."

My mind swam with possibility. Would he come for me today? Tomorrow? A fortnight? I was relieved he had not shown himself yet, as I was not looking forward to such an interaction. I could only hope this threat was a stand-alone. Luckily for him, there was no need to worry about the police. He would have to worry about what *I* would do to him, especially if the taunting continued.

Nevertheless, I had to be prepared for whichever scenario he chose. There was no knowing what he would do, but I had a feeling that killing me would be too kind based on this creature's cruel tastes. Putting so much effort into a message would be a waste if he were going to make it quick.

After I parted with Phoebe, I made some stops at the market and the apothecary. The bottles and pieces of metal clinked together in my satchel on the journey home. The dark was not something I was afraid of, but I was not going to put myself in such a precarious situation either way. I closed the shop early to make sure of it.

The continents of my satchel were dumped over the kitchen counter as soon as I arrived home. I could not decide what I needed, so I grabbed a little of everything. Small, oddly shaped vials of varying colors rolled across the wood. Some were clear glass, exposing different colored liquids. Others were dark brown tinted glass for the more photosensitive solutions in my collection. I forgot to label them, so it would be a surprise for both of us if I decided to use them. Other items clattered onto the table, such as a metal syringe, freshly sharpened seamstress shears, and an extra folded barber's blade. I had many knives at home, though you could never have enough.

I had to admit, I caught myself getting almost giddy thinking about what I would be using. Fantasizing about the confrontation. Would he be surprised to learn that his hunt will end with his death? I daydreamed about the look that might cross his face when he realized that he would be pursued back. Should I make it fast or slow? Which reminded me, I needed to retrieve some rope from the greenhouse just in case I got the opportunity to drag it out longer.

The surface of the glass bottles was cool against my fingers, trailing over to the assortment, not sure which one to pick up first. My fingertips had a slight red tint, as I habitually forgot to use my gloves when appreciating my beloved greenery. One of many awful habits.

Phoebe would always scold me and attempt to prescribe her own beauty regimen of beef tallow and other ointments to rid me of the irritation. Luckily, gloves would forever be the norm, and no one had to see my hands for as long as they were fashionable.

I didn't mind. Getting my hands like this had taken many hours of work. It was a sign of accomplishment. My father said unmarked hands were a sign of a man who had not worked for his achievements. He was most likely referring to a future husband, but I decided that it was a standard I wished to hold myself to as well.

My attention was eventually pulled from my trinkets and on to more important tasks for the night. I turned to the doors, windows, and anything that opened to ensure they were locked. I even closed the shutters for good measure.

Maybe it was overkill, but this was no ordinary subject of mine. I knew what he was capable of, but his unfortunate soul could not possibly know the damage I could do in return.

The knives and sharp objects were nestled between cushions and other hiding places. Satisfied with my efforts, I retreated to the bathroom, feeling confident in my fortification. It was doubtful that anyone would break in tonight of all nights, but just in case, I made sure I had leverage over the familiar grounds.

An hour or two was spent easing my tired body in the bath, changing into a soft nightgown, and brushing out my hair when I was finished. After I braided the long strands, I twisted them into a low bun, securing it with something extra special.

The stick securing my hair sheathed a needle doused in snake venom from the *Bitis arietans*, commonly known as the puff adder. Freshly imported. It was a subtle detail I included in my hair as a precaution whenever I planned on making any late-night endeavors. Today was the first time I felt the need to wear it alone in my home.

My reflection threw me an assured smile through the mirror's fog before I pulled on my black silk robe. It was my favorite lounging piece, as it had carefully embroidered thistles woven in purple thread along the shoulders, then down the sleeves and hems.

Sleep wasn't at the top of my list of things to do, so I would rather spend quality time alone. Some leisurely nighttime activity.

I hummed an anonymous tune as I entered the living room. This room had always been my favorite. There was a large stone fireplace with stories of old carved into the mantle. The ominous figures shifted in the fire's flickering light, making them squirm to life to tell their tale. There was no need to turn the gas lamps on, as the fireplace gave a warm enough glow. About thirty minutes remained before the radiance would be reduced to pale embers.

The mood would not have been whole without something for the other senses. I poured myself some more scotch from Mr. Aston's collection.

I delicately placed the phonograph's needle at the edge of whatever recording was already resting on the machine, and it started to play. It crackled to life before becoming a waltz. It was a lovely instrumental piece for a dark and rainy evening.

As the music settled through the house, I tipped my head back and sipped from my freshly poured glass, swaying to the string instruments. I made a small dramatic twirl as I crossed the foyer to the dining room.

I laughed to myself.

How childish, these simple pleasures.

I made off for the kitchen and eyed the bowl of fruit in the middle of the countertop.

Oranges. A rather generous pile at that. They were expensive, but worth every coin. There was just something about citrus fruits. It was probably the way they sometimes bit back at you that I loved the most. It was best to save them for later when the alcohol settled my mood.

Many more moments were collected and forgotten that night as I drank myself into a manic state.

A rustling was heard across the house as I finished peeling the perfectly ripe fruit. A groan escaped me, and I slammed my knife flat against the table next to my highly anticipated treat.

I might have been able to keep out killers, but I was not great at keeping out smaller pests.

With the lit candle, I grasped the holder tight in one hand. I suspected the noise was that critter from the other night or a burnt log finally giving way inside the fireplace.

I crossed the foyer again, entered the main living room, and stepped in front of that grand fireplace. However, when I approached, all the logs had been reduced to ash. Only a few glowing embers remained with no proof of disturbance. My tongue clicked in annoyance as I inspected with my single candle, crouched in front of the pile of dust.

At this point, the darkness had completely consumed the outside world, and the early morning hours had crept up on me. The entire house was turned to shadows.

Losing interest in the burnt pile of nothing, I adjusted the robe tighter around my body. The candle flickered wildly for a second. The flame danced upon the wax. I naively studied it for a second before my skin tingled, announcing the presence of something looming over my shoulder.

Eyes.

The flame snuffed out with a quick puff of air, a muffled hiss as it extinguished.

I yelped, turning quickly on my heel and dropping the holder. It clanged against the floor and spilled what was left of the melted wax.

The phonograph shrieked when its needle was forced off the track, vaguely resembling the noise I had made a moment before.

Finally, surrounded by darkness and silence, I waited.

Breathing in enough air proved difficult. It was like my lungs could not expand enough, leaving me breathless and lightheaded. I was like a bat trying to locate anything out of place in the dark expanse, except without the echolocation, only blindness.

A smoky scent surrounded me. The type of smoke that existed in aged whiskey barrels, exotic cigars, and men who ruin reputations.

Notes of blackberry and bay leaves trailed behind like an aftertaste.

"What a sweet sound you made…"

A smooth voice cut through the air, like a red-hot knife through butter, before it burned the wood of the board below.

My body stiffened, petrified from the cryptic voice that reached out to me. I thought it was best not to respond, granting me extra time to pull my thoughts together.

"Don't be rude. You have a guest. What kind of host ignores a guest twice?" He tsked, and steps could be heard nearby.

"*Guest* is a generous title to give yourself," I scoffed. "It may be in your best interest to stop this childish pursuit if you enjoy your nervous system remaining intact."

"Oh"—I could hear a cocky smirk in his voice—"she not only speaks, she also bites."

"I am sure you would be the type of degenerate to enjoy that," I sneered.

A chuckle could be heard somewhere before it melted into that ominous predatory clicking, like a rumble at the back of a crocodile's throat.

The hairs on the back of my neck did not just stand, but

wanted to rip themselves out of their cuticles and run for the hills. Every fiber of my being wanted to tear itself from my skeleton to escape the presence before me.

I moved to the middle of the room, searching the dark for any moving shadows.

"Who are you?" I asked, my hands warily in front of me to avoid the furniture.

"I am anything you want me to be." His voice manifested next to my ear. "I'll let you decide, one last illusion of autonomy before I *devour* you."

A hand rested on either side of my hips, something like needles brushing against the back of my neck. The sensation made me jump, but it made my body hot with something else I was embarrassed to admit.

"Awfully bold to assume that you will get that far." I kept my voice steady.

"Let's not begin our courtship with lies, my dear shadow." He sighed. "You'll realize soon enough that we are the same. That's how I know that you want to see how far I will get."

"Same? You disgust me. You are a man, a *demon*."

"I am surely neither." He laughed, and something wet slicked up the side of my neck.

I whipped around and wiped the wetness from my skin furiously. "You devil!" I shouted, grabbing the pewter vase off the tea table and slinging it across the room. It smacked against the wall and clamored onto the floor with a loud bang.

A low growl echoed around the room. It was impossible to distinguish where it came from, further disorienting me.

"If you want me to be the devil, how about a wager?"

"I don't gamble."

"Not with money, but you gamble with something else daily."

"It is not a gamble when I know I'll win."

"Do you?" He paused. "Know you'll win?"

"Of course I do. I always do."

"Then what's the harm? Indulge me."

His voice circled me in the darkness like a snake coiling around its prey before that inevitable squeeze.

I could only see a tall black figure moving as he passed in front of the windows briefly.

"If you can get to your bedroom before I catch you"—something tugged at a piece of my hair, a hand brushed against mine —"then I'll leave you alone for tonight." He tugged at the sleeve of my robe like he was inspecting his prize before he had won.

"And if I don't?"

My question was only met with a chuckle. "I'll give you a head start as a gift of good faith." The words came out sickly sweet, slow and tempting.

My legs moved before I could think.

The archway was only a few paces, and I slid in front of the stairs, but I heard his movements on my heel.

I made it halfway up the stairs. Then, a sharp pain in my ankle.

It was not possible that he gave me headway with how fast he caught up.

What a cheat!

A yelp slipped out as I reached for my hair stick. My body whipped around to face him as I fell. I slashed the needle at the man—*thing*—before me. His face was illuminated by the moonlight spilling from the circular window above the entrance.

There was a flash of angelic blond hair, and those pale, dead eyes narrowed on me. The last thing I saw was my needle slashing his cheek before the back of my head met the sharp step of the staircase.

CHAPTER SIX

THE CREATURE

"Well, what does she like?" the plump florist asked.

"I was actually hoping you could help me with that." The healing cut on my cheek felt tight as I smiled. "I believe she is a regular of yours?"

"Oh! Of course, I would be happy to!" She beamed. "What's the name?"

"Alina Lis," I said. The name was almost too comfortable in my mouth. I could just salivate at the taste of it on my tongue.

"Ah yes, she is quite particular." She nodded. "You're lucky I know her taste all too well. Give me a minute to tidy up the back."

I pressed my palms together and gave an exasperated sigh. "You are a godsend."

The stout woman bustled to the back, and I let my smile fall once she disappeared.

The wound on my face was healing slower than usual, but healing nonetheless. At first, I was confused about why Alina would arm herself with just a mere needle. It was rather anticlimactic. It was only after the first few days that I realized she had attempted to *poison* me.

Believe me when I say this woman gave me butterflies in my stomach. Though that might just be internal bleeding. Either way, she had charmed me.

"Mr. Forbes! Please follow me—I think it would be easier for you to pick yourself. I can't bring them all out for safety purposes!" the woman called.

I raised a critical brow, but moved past the counter and around the corner to the back room.

"Everything on the left wall are new imports she placed before her return home. Please don't touch them though—I will gather them once you choose. Give me a shout whenever you're finished!" She gestured to the shelf in the room before attending to the ring of the shop bell.

When I saw the wall of flowers, everything started to make sense.

Every single plant on that wall could kill any average man with enough care and proper preparation.

Could she be the cause of all of the sudden poisonings of men and Vipera? I was starting to think she had more up her sleeve than I initially assumed.

I plucked a stem of nightshade from the vase, spinning it between my fingers. Looking back, it did make sense. A botanist, deadly exotic imports, the apothecary, and the poison needles. She had a purpose and a small fortune to carry it through. The scales were starting to even out, which was not a problem for me. It just meant I was allowed to be a little rougher in my approach.

I chuckled to myself and brushed the bloom of nightshade across the cut on my cheek mindlessly. She probably thought she killed me! Imagining her relief after that night was amusing. It would be even better when I saw her again. Witnessing her confusion and cutting down her ego would be delicious. She might even think herself a poor poisoner when she sees that the venom did not take.

This was the most fun I had ever had on a hunt.

"Sir! I told you not to touch it! The poor girl already ignores my pleas—you'll irritate your skin!" the shop lady scolded, plucking the plant from my hand.

"Apologies. I wanted a closer look," I said. "You seem to know what she likes more than I do. There is too much to pick from. Would it be possible for you to make a few arrangements?"

"Yes, of course! Just let me know how many—"

"As many as you can make. Telephone me when you finish. I will send someone to pick them up." I pulled a calling card from my pocket, handing it to her as I passed.

Ideas rushed to my head every minute after my new discovery. Alina's deadly nature allowed me some creative freedom now that I knew that my toy would not easily break.

I NOTICED Alina's mornings started more or less the same every day. She had a strict routine.

First, she met for breakfast, though she didn't eat much despite the frivolous locations. I assume that she did so for her counterpart, Phoebe Aston. Social circles were small, though their connection surprised me.

Anyway, they always started with breakfast.

Every single morning *almost* without fail. I threw a wrench in that well-oiled machine the minute she hit her head on those steps.

I was glad I did not just eat her then or else I would have been upset with myself for wasting the opportunity for more games.

While Alina was surely bright, she had the worst case of fixation I had ever seen. The minute she opened a book, it was like she disappeared—only a shell of a person. I nearly bumped into her several times. When passing her at the market, I even let her run into my shoulder. She said sorry and did not stop walking.

I will repeat myself: she said *sorry* and did not even *look* in my direction.

Those cold eyes never left the ink on those pages. The only effort she exhausted, aside from reading, was to bite into an apple after she muttered her apology. It was quite annoying actually. I wanted to shove her off the bridge, but she might be more upset about the book getting wet rather than the sight of me.

Most of her day was spent in the shop, making God knew what behind the scenes. I was never interested in the sciences, though I was sure it was all very impressive—as there was a lot of expensive-looking equipment in the back room. They were not new by any means, but looked complicated enough to know that they were not cheap. She was a professional despite the hand-me-down tools.

I could usually watch her from the back room as customers kept her busy in the front. She thought her door latch was faulty, but it was just me keeping the door cracked so I could observe comfortably from her beloved workspace. I was always there. Even when she came to the back to grab extra supplies, I was watching from behind the door.

Once again, it was the worst situational awareness I had ever seen. She was so absorbed in her work that she did not think anyone could get to her, so confident in her abilities that she lost that instinctual fear of what lurked in the dark. She was cocky.

After work, it was up in the air, but typically she always ended up at home before eight thirty in the evening.

Today, she made a house call. It only confirmed my suspicions about her being the Poisoner, since her house call was to the brothel at the docks.

I kept a healthy distance as I followed her dark figure, slipping to the back of the tavern. She was talking with a woman. The light from inside the tavern illuminated the unkept blonde strands of the mistress as they spoke.

Alina handed her a small pouch filled with different-sized vials—she was resourceful in using old perfume bottles. I could only imagine what horrors those dainty flasks held within them. It seemed she was targeting men she found distasteful, which was understandable, knowing how many men of my kind were suddenly falling ill with aches and pains. Though they thought it was a coordinated effort to harm the Nest, which was amusing considering that she had done this entirely by accident and without her knowledge.

Like every night before, she went home after her business was finished. Every step of her routine served a purpose, no room for leisure or pleasure. Even at home, she studied papers or brought her own experiments. The only pleasure she allowed herself seemed to be in booze or baths—of which she had a nasty habit of falling asleep inside of. I did not blame her for doing so. Her routine exhausted even the spectators.

I sat on the stool next to the bath, watching her head lean against the porcelain of her tub. Her damp hair stood out as it stuck to the stark white surface.

No, I did not watch her undress.

I waited for her to submerge herself actually.

It was not the right time to see her like that. I wanted to wait for the perfect time, to see her squirm like a mouse with its tail under my boot.

I was here to observe, much like the first night I watched her sleep. It amazed me how often she put herself in danger, including her interactions with me.

My elbow rested on my knee, propping my chin in my palm. I flipped the barber's blade she'd left on my seat open and closed, fidgeting as I was lost in thought. The peaceful expression on her face made it almost hard to believe she was capable of being a menace.

I wanted to leave her be, but I worried she would drown before I got to do the honors myself. All of my effort would be wasted.

I stood up and walked over to the end of the tub, looking down at the hair draped over the lip of the basin. The stitches on her head held the jagged edges of the wound together. It was slightly raised, still irritated from our fun before. I parted her hair gingerly, careful not to disturb the sleeping snake. It was a larger wound than expected, nearly making me wince at the sight of it.

Humans were so obnoxiously delicate.

CHAPTER SEVEN

THE POISONER

I t had been a week since that night, but I could remember it like it was yesterday.

Or at least I thought it could be yesterday. Had it been a week or two? A day or a few? I tried not to bother myself with any sort of counting while I recovered from my concussion. Trying to measure out dosages was hard enough, never mind keeping track of days.

I wished I could say that it did not shake me, that I was strong and fearless of whatever life brought me. In all honesty, it made me question my capabilities. I had never been so intimate with death in my lifetime, and I did not intend on that kind of proximity again.

The light from that big circular window shone in my eyes that dreadful morning. My hair was matted to the side of my face when I awoke, covered in old blood. The wood of the stairs was now permanently marked with a crimson stain, despite how many times I scrubbed it. That mark on the floor was the only indication that anything had happened that night. Otherwise, there were no signs of break-in or commotion. Even the vase I threw was neatly placed back on the table, a set of red poppies placed aptly inside. A cheeky reminder that I was alive only because he allowed it.

The only reason the police were not informed was because I knew that the man could not have survived very long afterward. The venom would have killed him in a day. There was no cure for snake venom. Not one that was easily accessible at least.

As far as Phoebe knew, I got drunk and fell, which was not entirely implausible. If she knew what happened, I would never get another moment to myself for as long as I lived. She had been checking on me daily, coming to my place for our morning routine to ensure I was resting.

Phoebe had developed the habit of overstaying her welcome. She joined me for every activity, even coming to the apothecary and pretending to be interested in plants to make me feel better. It was amusing, but it made it difficult to consult with my special clients while she was around. Today, she was a specific brand of nervous chatter.

"I think Edith got an invite to the masquerade party. I guess they let anyone in these days," she babbled, trying to fill her boredom with gossip.

"Oh, yeah? Who's that?" I asked vacantly, prompting her to find something to talk about while I took inventory of the shelves. Notes were taken on what was low in stock as I climbed up the wall ladder, step-by-step, until I was at the highest shelf.

Phoebe ranted about the happenings, love triangles, and other side stories she had not gotten out of her system yet.

"I am having an event in a few days. Just something small and intimate in the botanical gardens! It's right up your alley with all your...plant *things*," she said awkwardly, and gestured to the wall in front of her, not really knowing how to add to the topic. She shifted in place as she observed the bottles on the walls, picking at her nail beds.

"You don't have to stay with me. I promise I am well." I threw her a reassured smile.

"How do I know you won't fall off that ladder? Or in the back room with all those dangerous instruments? Or—"

"Phoebe, I'm fine." I leaned down toward her on the ladder and offered my pinky out. "I promise."

She gave me a distraught look before she gave in, hooking her pinkie around mine. "Please just call me if you feel even a little cold. All right?" she pleaded.

Nodding, I squeezed our pinkies together before letting go.

She left me hesitantly as my next client arrived. I picked up a glass from the top shelf and leaned down to hand it to her, rattling off the vital usage information before returning my focus to the stock. The end of my pencil was pinched between my teeth as I wondered whether I should make different-ounce bottles for more variance in quantities.

The moment the bell went off by the door, the air in the shop weighed heavily on me. The hairs on the back of my neck stood erect, and my still-healing head wound throbbed once again.

No. Impossible.

As the thoughts crossed my mind, that *incessant* clicking cut through the air, the vibration tickling my eardrums.

"Do you by chance have anything for snake venom?" a cool voice asked.

I stared at the shelf. My mind immediately went over every possibility of how he could have survived. Each conclusion had a probability of near zero.

"You know, when a snake bites, it is usually because it gave you a fair warning to run." I smiled sweetly, looking down over my shoulder from my place up on the ladder.

I realized that this was the first time I'd gotten an objective look at my attacker.

The blond figure innocently tilted his head up at me, but it did not take a saint to see that the man was dripping in sin. Those same gray eyes peered back at me in what could have possibly been adoration.

God help me and whatever this man was thinking.

I wouldn't lie. He was beyond what I expected. Simply calling him handsome would not do him justice. Every fiber of this man was fashioned to tempt, designed for predation. His sharp jawline and muscular physique were like something only the masters could carve from their imagination rather than coming from reality. His hair was neat and swept to the side, paired with his finely tailored attire. I was almost jealous of the clothing clinging to his body, though I was most jealous of that scarf around his neck— which I would love to replace with my hands.

He approached the shelves, trailing a finger carefully over the countless bottles and studying the little labels, then leisurely leaning down to look at a lower shelf.

How arrogant, the way he was so comfortable in a place he did not belong. Typical of a man.

"Do you know why the mongoose almost *always* wins against the snake?" he asked, not bothering to look back up at me as he crept closer. "The snake believes her bite is the most reliable way to kill, as she hasn't been given a reason to believe otherwise." He placed a hand on the side of my ladder when he finally made it to my side. "The only problem is that the snake could never anticipate that the mongoose has a resistance to her *unforgiving* bite, and has developed a taste for his rival's flesh." He tilted his head, turning his gaze up to me.

"Don't be silly. You are a man, not a mongoose," I sneered.

"Again, I am neither of those things, but I know that

metaphors are hard to grasp for you *scientific folk.*" He grinned, leaning against the shelf as he watched me.

My boots hit the floor as I climbed down from the ladder.

It was alarming how tall he was now that I saw him in broad daylight—at least six feet four. I was a little put off, since I was usually taller or equal height to the men around me.

This must be how Phoebe felt having to crane her neck up at me all this time.

His expression did not waver as I studied him. Blood rushed to my cheeks, as I realized I may have been staring too long.

I turned on my heels, granting myself the comfort of putting the wooden counter between us.

"You almost seem disappointed. That hurts," he said mockingly, gripping his heart dramatically, then resting his elbows atop the counter. While his demeanor might be playful, the look in his eyes was purely carnal, focused on one thing only. "I thought we had such a lovely time."

"How are you here?" I questioned, fidgeting with drawers and their contents.

"Why would I not be, darling?"

"The venom."

"My entire body is made of poison." He laughed. "Or maybe I just got lucky."

"I don't believe in luck."

"There are many things you don't believe in, but probably should." He leaned in closer. A gloved hand reached out toward the side of my head.

I slapped his hand away, and he gave me an expression that imitated some sort of pity, like he was tending to an injured lamb.

"Relax. I can smell how agitated you are from here. I just wanted to see my handiwork again."

"I don't know who you think you are, but I will make sure to liquify your insides the next time you lay a hand on me." It took all my energy not to look away, every single one of my senses lighting up like gunshots in the night.

His stare was intense, something uncanny that made my body scream that I should get away, run, and hide from his view.

My threat only made his smile grow wider. "Sounds like a date."

"What?"

"You heard me perfectly fine." He winked, sliding me a calling card.

"I try to kill you, and you take it as flirtation?" I raised my brow, rotating the paper and glaring at the typeface.

Silas Forbes
Astor Industrial & Petroleum

The name sounded familiar. It was most likely a name that I had heard a few times before at various events and gossip circles. I would not be surprised if I heard it from Phoebe earlier, though I admittedly was not listening.

Of course this bastard came from money. How else could he afford to be so reckless?

"Mr. Forbes." I studied the card.

"Silas," he corrected. "If we are going to become acquainted, I'd rather you not address me like a stranger." He propped his head in his hand.

"What makes you think I want to see you?"

"You're a curious creature. I *know* that you want to. Don't you want answers?"

I raised my brows in mock surprise. "Oh, of course! I shall host an interview in my home with tea and biscuits on the off chance that you do not kill me first! Completely reasonable. *Do you take me for a fool?*"

"Quite the opposite, but I know that your curiosity will eat away at you until your mind is satisfied."

I changed the subject. "You cheated."

"Pardon?"

"Our wager last time we spoke. You said you would give me a head start as a sign of good faith."

"What if I decided to pursue you in *bad* faith?" He cocked his head to the side. "I can't help it. Don't get mad at a Windhound for chasing something that runs."

"Again with the zoomorphism." I rolled my eyes, shoving the card into a miscellaneous drawer before slapping it shut. "If you were an animal, you would be a pest."

"I hope you will wear something nicer next time. I like it when my meals come with those pretty little garnishes." He ignored my previous chide.

I bit my tongue and glared, turning away and forcing myself to focus on another task other than him. He had proved to be quite an irritant already. Maybe if I ignored him, he would disappear—like a boogeyman.

His footsteps receded, followed by the ring of the front door. His presence was pervasive, bringing a stifling air to any room he was in. It even lingered after he left, like a strong cologne.

While his interactions made me uneasy, they made me look forward to the next. I would be lying if I said his departure did not disappoint me.

I wanted to strip that smug look from his face when I eventually found a way to remove his stain from this earth. For once, I had a competent subject, but there was an inconvenient learning curve. Most of my work did not involve a chase, offense *or* defense. Poison was straightforward like that. I would prove every thought that crossed his mind wrong in the coming days, weeks, months—however long it took for him to succumb to me.

Men, they were all the same. This one just happened to have an appetite for these things. It shall be no different than the rest. They all gave in and withered at my will, one way or another.

Brrrrrrring.

I looked up from my book to peer at the door. I heard a rustling and then a clang of the metal letter slot as it slapped shut. The mail had dropped.

Placing my book carefully on the tea table, I set my pen down in the middle to mark my place.

A copy of the *Young Ladies' Journal* was in the basket when I glanced at the letter bin, but nothing worth ringing the bell for.

Unlocking the door, I peered out to see a small rectangular box on the front step.

Gingerly, I collected the box and placed it on the table. I awkwardly seated myself across from it, the box confusing me as I was not expecting a parcel.

It was wrapped in expensive paper and felt light, like a gift. Phoebe would have told me if she was sending something for me, so that was one sender out of the question. The only other acquaintance I knew who might go through the trouble would be Mr. Forbes.

Do I want to open this? What if I pretend I never saw it and throw it in the bin? It is not too late to turn back now.

After several thoughtful moments and eventually deciding

against my better judgment, I unwrapped the paper from the box, revealing a velvet casing.

Christ, I am beginning to think he's less interested in killing me and more interested in courting me.

When I opened it, I saw one of the most beautiful pearl pieces I had ever seen.

The demi-parure necklace was a choker made entirely of strings of seed pearls. The strands were bent and fashioned into rosettes with a gold clasp in the back. It was quite thick, as it had several strings stacked horizontally. As I inspected it closer, I noticed something different about the jewelry.

Usually, a piece like this would have been made of horsehair, something fine but strong enough to hold the most delicate pearls. But the hair seemed finer, and black was an odd color to use when stringing white pearls.

There was a note within the box.

I would have strung them with hair from my last grand gesture, but I thought using yours would do perfectly well, a more personal touch.
—Silas

The realization hit me, and I could feel the bile rise in my throat.

I dropped the necklace and forced my body out of the room, releasing whatever my stomach was holding on to over the tile.

He is the devil. This I am sure of.

A burning, hot anger was building in my chest, making my fingers and toes grow cold as the blood rushed to my core. What could I have possibly done to deserve my own personal demon?

CHAPTER EIGHT

THE POISONER

I clutched the knife in my hand until my knuckles turned white.

Pacing the room, I glanced at the clock again.

One a.m., thirteen hours after our previous encounter.

Sleep was not something that would come to me tonight. Every sound the house made set me on edge, waiting for my least favorite bump in the night to appear. Intuition warned me in every way that something was coming.

That liar promised me a visit. I was not often asked questions I did not know the answer to, but the fact that he survived bothered me. I *needed* to know how. It would only be a matter of time before I found out, and then my anxiety would be laid to rest.

I was unsure when he would come, all I knew was that he *would*. Then, this deadly dance would commence, and I *had* to win. There was no other option. If I disappeared, who would take care of the men like him in this world? He did not deserve to be here, but those girls he murdered did. They had lives, families, aspirations—and he made out like a thief.

My hands and feet were cold, and my body had become clammy from the adrenaline pumping through my tired heart. With the knife still clutched in my fist, I lifted my hands up and down slowly, like a conductor, instructing myself on how to take in air and let it go.

I added extra soap to the bath as well as dried lavender. No herb would be strong enough to calm me, but the effort was admirable on my part.

I set the blade on the wooden stool beside the tub for safe-keeping.

The hot water tingled as I lowered myself into it, forcing the blood back to my appendages. I groaned as the water crept up to my neck. The tension cracked like ice cracking in a water glass when I was finally submerged. It would have been more enjoyable if I was not prepared to run at any given moment. As much as I would cherish the opportunity to lie in the tub for hours, it would be too much precious time wasted.

Despite my efforts, my body betrayed me. It did not take long for my mind to swim, and I drifted into the void as a result.

A thud sent a shock through my heart as I woke. The whiplash from the sudden awakening cast an unpleasant spell of dizziness. My vision darted from the closed door to the clock on the wall.

Three a.m.

You fool, Alina!

I snatched the knife from the stool and lowered it into the water, obscured by the remaining suds. As much as I preferred not to be caught in this state, I might not have a choice in the matter.

The last encounter admittedly made me doubt if I could pull this off without some sort of chemical aid. Maybe if I was quiet, he would skip this room. My candle had already burned out, and

I had not moved in some time. He could not know I was in here. I thought maybe I had a few minutes.

The heavy sound of a pair of boots echoed through the hallway, the old wooden floor whining under each step. My breathing slowed the closer they came. One after the other, leisurely in approach.

To muffle any noise my breathing would create, I placed my hand over my mouth. The sound of steps made it outside my bathroom door, and the knob slowly began to turn.

With a deep inhale, I sank under the water, hoping he would see an empty bathroom and move on. Now was a good time to test how long I could hold my breath. I tried to relax my body under the water, saving any oxygen I could spare as the muffled footsteps sauntered into the room.

My eyes clenched shut as I waited. I think I even caught a little voice in the back of my head praying. The silence under the water was deafening. My lungs ached, screaming at me for air.

Just a little longer.

Suddenly, a sharp pain of hairpulling made me suck in, but my lungs were met with water instead of the air they craved.

My head was yanked above the water as my hands clawed at the leather-covered hand that pulled on my scalp.

I choked out some water and met that familiar feral stare.

"Were you trying to ruin my fun by offing yourself before we began?" he asked, crouching beside the tub. "That's not very sportsmanlike of you." His eyes lowered to the soap suds covering my chest.

I spat in his face.

That only made him tighten his grip. "Don't waste too much energy. The chase is only fun if you are actually trying, dear."

"You creature," I seethed.

"Well, well, that would be closer than your previous guesses!"

A wild smirk, paired with a crazed look in his eyes, flashed before me. I would say he was enamored, but it was most likely the itch to kill me.

He pulled me closer to his face by my hair. "Now, let's get started, shall we? Let's go over some ground rules," he instructed, suddenly letting go of my scalp, causing me to slump upon release. As the man stood, he smoothed the wrinkles from his dark coat and stepped away from the basin. "Get up. Let me see you."

"That's unfair. You're fully clothed." I hugged my body and sank lower into the tub. My fingers graced the hilt of the knife that rested on the floor of the tub under my legs.

"Alina, don't make me ask twice." His face went cold. Nothing in his tone insisted he was joking. "I won't be a gentleman and ask next time."

I took a shaky breath, stalling as much as I could to put off whatever fate I was about to meet. Before sheepishly standing, I clutched the knife behind my back. My hair fell in thick, wet tendrils down my body, thankfully covering my breasts. My legs crossed awkwardly. Everything was too exposed. The soap suds slid down my figure and back into the water from whence they came. My free hand covered whatever it could.

What is the point of this? Humiliation? Sadism? The former and the latter all at once?

He let me squirm there for a long minute, not saying a single word. His eyes crawled over my body at a painfully slow rate. I could not make myself look at him. I only imagined the hungry expression that would without a doubt be present. Or maybe I was afraid of seeing a look of victory, of satisfaction.

Was this some sort of power play? To break me down before we began?

My cheeks burned, hot to the touch. It could have been the

lack of sleep, but I felt like a million little bugs were crawling around my skin.

He finally spoke. "Do you like games? Let's play a game. You hide, and I will seek you out." He moved closer.

"How do I win?" I asked, shivering as the cold air from the cracked window licked my body.

"Hide until dawn. You have three hours until then." He smiled, approaching until we were only a meter apart.

"Will you kill me?"

"No."

"Then what do you win?"

"I get to eat you alive," he said coldly, cocking his head to the side as his gaze ventured lower, watching me shake before him. "Are you scared?"

"I am *cold*," I hissed between clenched teeth, shrinking into myself to obscure his view.

"Is that how you will shake when I catch you? Or will it excite you to be under me in all the ways I plan to have you?"

I swung the knife, aiming straight at his chest.

My wrist smacked against his grip, his fingers squeezing around it.

His expression never faltered, and that wicked glint lit like wildfire. "I was wondering when my little snake would strike." He let me push the tip an inch into his shoulder, then another and another. The white shirt under the dark coat turned wet and black from the wound.

How is he just standing there?

He cracked his neck to either side and leaned in close. Something changed. Blood rushed to the whites of his eyes, filling them with darkness until there was just a halo of a silver iris surrounded by a sea of black. "Our game starts now." He hovered above me. A wet split tongue slid over my lips slowly.

My eyes widened at the man—*Creature*—before me.

My shock subsided when he quickly pulled the knife from his shoulder. I dove under his arm and darted out of the room. There was no time to rationalize what I saw. This was beyond what I could have prepared for. This was never a fair game, and he *knew* it.

I moved light on my feet through the labyrinth of rooms. I made sure not to touch creaking doors and to skip squeaky floor panels I knew of. I managed to grab a robe that I had discarded on a chair to save some of my remaining dignity.

His pacing could be heard throughout the house before it stopped. He was listening for me, waiting for a mistake to be made.

It was hard to move fast without making any noise. A hiding place would be difficult, since it could not be as obvious as the closet. Hide-and-seek might be more difficult than I anticipated.

My weapon of choice was a sharp poker from the guest room fireplace. The first hiding spot that came to mind was to slip under the bed, hidden by the fabric trim.

Crashing, thumping, and rummaging could be heard nearby. That clicking sound erupted sporadically.

It was all starting to make sense. There was some odd comfort in knowing that my methods were not faulty. I just had not considered that he was inhuman, which I would have called myself hysterical for considering even if I did suspect it.

Species developed mutations often, though I would have never expected so many in one organism, a person least of all. His heavy boots moved slowly into the room, stepping from heel to toe.

Calmly, he approached the curtains, shoving them aside as if he expected to find something besides newly disturbed dust. The closet doors were flung open next, and a long pause followed as he stared inside, seemingly distracted by my clothing.

"Your scent is infatuating," he said aloud. "I suspect you'll taste like the equivalent of honeysuckle and cayenne when I bite past your cold composure." He practically moaned, strutting out of view.

I lost sight of the movement, and I could no longer hear him. With what I knew at this point, I wondered if his threats of eating me were to be taken literally.

Hands wrapped around my ankles and swiftly yanked me out into the open.

A scream of pain ripped from my throat before I whipped around, landing a hard blow across his head with the cast-iron poker. The strike was so blunt that his head snapped to the side, giving me a moment of recovery.

As I scrambled to my feet, a sharp crack came from my ankle, rolling it unpleasantly.

I let out another yelp as I was forced back to the ground.

His fingers dug into my leg, flipping me over onto my back as he dragged me across the wooden floor. The wood grated against my skin despite the silk robe.

"That was really good! I am *so* proud of you for taking the hit at least," he mocked, lifting a boot on my chest to keep me down. The poker was ripped from my hands and tossed across the room.

My heart sank as it clamored against the floor, far away from my grasp.

As if my heart had not already labored from running, it was pounding under him now.

His black eyes watched me, burning into my own as my nails dug into his leg.

"I am going to *kill* you," I breathed, hitting his leg. My chest heaved up and down as best it could, fighting to keep that steady rise and fall as I struggled underneath the weight of him.

"Are you done?"

"You can't eat me. People will notice I'm gone and look for me," I said breathlessly. "I won't taste good. I've had long-term exposure to too many toxins. Look!" I pleaded, extending a hand with my fingers splayed to show the red skin from too many curious touches.

"Oh." A smug grin crept onto his face. "Did you think I meant that literally? I guess in some sense it will be, but not the way you think." He shook his head. "Human meat is too stringy. It gets stuck in my teeth," he said plainly, opening his mouth to point at two sets of long, thin canines on his upper jaw.

I blinked in confusion, attempting to rationalize the image I was seeing. I tried to lean up to get a closer look, but his boot still held me in place.

"Oh? Is that enough to convince the skeptic?" He laughed. His fangs were suddenly gone. He stepped back and picked me up.

"Wait—"

He ignored my plea as he sat on the chair in the corner, pulling me on top of him. His legs spread wide, forcing my own to open wider as I straddled his hips.

"I won fair and square." He gave me a cocky look.

"How on earth could that have *possibly* been fair?" I snapped, but I had trouble keeping eye contact in my panicked state.

My mind was still flashing images of the fangs, the tongue, the eyes. Just as I thought I understood things, the less sense it actually made, at least not when I tried to map out the levels of classification for what possible species he could have branched off from.

"Don't worry. As a reward for a truly *valiant* effort, I'll make sure you enjoy it," he purred in my ear. His hands slid up my hips and circled around my waist. His muscular stature made my body feel delicate in his grasp. One squeeze and my spine would snap.

A warm, wet heat trailed across my neck. His split tongue slid over my skin and tickled my earlobe. That all too familiar vocalization of clicks rang in my ear, though I didn't know if that was a good or bad sign. The noise was so complex when it was directly next to my ear, like two pitches harmonized together.

I shied away from his touches, dizzy from the adrenaline high wearing off.

He stayed close to my neck, exhaling against my skin.

I flinched, expecting a bite, but it never came.

Wait, was he…?

"*Stop!*" I pushed on his chest and leaned backward. The blood that rushed to my cheeks was probably noticeable even in the dimmed light. I pulled my robe tighter over my body, aware of my immodest position.

"What? I could be selfish if that's what you like," he suggested, his fingers digging into my sides.

I winced.

He was not going to let me go.

If I have no choice but to be close, then might as well take advantage.

I leaned in cautiously, letting my hands slide down his chest.

Despite my prior prejudices, a heart was beating somewhere in there. It was impossibly fast. Counting the beats, I realized that it must have been around three hundred per minute. That might have been thought impossible, but as of an hour ago, I found that my stalker had some peculiar adaptations. It would have been more exciting if my discovery was not set on eating me.

As my hands crawled higher, I traced my finger hesitantly across his bottom lip, fearing he would bite.

"Open." My lips hovered close as I moved my finger down to pull on his bottom lip.

He graciously complied, tracking every movement closely, like he was waiting to snap if I made any move that did not please him.

My index and middle fingers pushed past his lips, his tongue dancing around them.

The tongue split directly down the middle, producing two independently moving halves. They were flexible and coordinated as his tongue moved along my fingers. He let out a low groan as he sucked on them.

With haste, I hooked my fingers downward, forcing his jaw open.

"Where do you hide them?" I demanded, tilting my head to the side to get a better look. My other hand joined to push his head back.

The Creature pulled back and grabbed both of my wrists.

"What in God's name are you doing?" A look of genuine shock cut through his charade.

"Don't bring him into this. Show me where you hide your teeth. You can't just show me something like that and expect me not to ask questions." I pulled my wrists from his grip. "You promised me answers the other day. You *owe* me."

Now *he* was looking at me like *I* was the crazy one. His brows furrowed. "Fine, but no more fingers."

He tilted his head back slightly and opened his mouth for me.

I would not mind him so much if he were always this obedient.

Both sets of fangs folded neatly against the roof of his mouth, similar to a snake. He let them flex forward, flush against his canines, matching his human teeth seamlessly when pressed against them. Two long pairs of perfectly deadly needles, though the outermost set was shorter and thicker. He kept his eyes on me, waiting for my reaction.

"You have front and rear accessory fangs. Like some sort of cross between a Viperidae and Colubridae," I rattled off excitedly, running my finger along the larger needle, not able to hide a smile as my mind raced from theory to theory. "Are there more of you?" I whispered curiously.

His expression was serious as he searched my face, looking for some hint of my behavior being a jest.

"Why are you looking at me like that?" My eyes shifted between his, analyzing him back.

A low growl vibrated in his chest.

What is it now?

He lost his cocky edge and was dangerously steady.

My breath hitched. I had not realized I was holding my breath—or maybe it was an anxiety attack. I averted my gaze awkwardly, not knowing if feeding my curiosity was the wisest course of action.

The silver halo of his irises studied me. It was like if I made a sudden movement, he would snatch me up and eat me, which was still not out of the realm of possibility. Knowing how much this man liked to hear himself talk, I knew that his silence was unnatural.

His hands moved from my hips and trailed up my waist. Leaning in, he breathed steadily against my neck, seeming to savor the proximity.

My hands pushed against his broad shoulders when his hands ventured too close to my breasts. My body was rigid with discomfort.

He was not letting go. Any struggle made him hold on tighter.

Why is my body so impossibly hot?

"I can't," I said hoarsely, pulling away.

He grabbed the hair at the back of my head, tugging it back to expose my neck.

I was a trembling, flustered mess in his arms, both from fear and shame, but mostly from shame.

My body shook from nerves that left my body more depleted than before. To my surprise, he did not bite me with those terrifying displays of teeth, but he deliberately sucked at my skin like he was trying to relish it before he got a taste.

He left a soft kiss on my pulsing artery, so gentle that I may have even mistaken him for a lover. Then, the warmth of his contact traveled down to my breasts, leaning me forward again as his grip on my hair tightened. A predatory rumble could be heard as he nipped and sucked on the sensitive skin, moving the fabric of my robe away as he worked.

He pinched my nipple between his teeth, and I took in a sharp breath.

A sound that could be interpreted as a deep purr came from him.

It made the tightness in the pit of my stomach knot eagerly.

Are those sounds for me or because of me?

His other hand trailed along my abdomen, working his way lower.

"No!" I snapped, and my hand shot out, digging my nails into the wound on his shoulder.

Not even a flinch became of my desperate clawing. His brow arched at me amusingly, as he leaned up and trailed his tongue up the side of my breast.

I bit my lip, but he gave me no time to think before he sucked, leaving marks as he worked his way to my collarbone. I squirmed in his arms as his hands and mouth explored me, leaving rough marks on my pale flesh.

His possessive touch made me feel ways I was ashamed to admit. Pinches and bites were left all over my torso as he left mark after mark, his sick way of leaving his claim on his catch. He touched wherever he could, poking and prodding to find what made me twitch, though he did not attempt to touch lower again. It was like he was saving the best for last.

A tightness burned in my core. It could be the leftover thrill from thinking I was going to die or because a creature so deadly was deciding that he would rather play with me than eat me. I was flattered, to say the least. I did not believe in heaven, but knew I would not be heading there with the ideas crossing my mind. I was wondering when he would just end it, just sink those teeth into my jugular and end my suffering here.

"Where did you go?" he whispered into the crook of my neck. "You drifted somewhere. I could feel it."

"*Hell*," I answered honestly, my eyes having difficulty staying open.

That earned me an endearing laugh. "Fair enough." He sighed, leaving kisses along my jaw, nipping at my skin, and sucking hard high on my neck.

I did not remember what happened next, because my body was then surrounded by darkness, succumbing to exhaustion.

No. 13.

CHAPTER NINE
THE CREATURE

No words could have described her at that moment.

It was painful to wrap my mouth around her flesh without getting a proper taste. The little sounds she made satiated me far more than her screams. I wanted to devour her until there was nothing left, until she was just a shaking, pathetic mess in my arms.

Alternatively, I wanted to shield her from the world and keep her in my room—like a pet.

There were only so many ways to captivate a thing like me, and Alina succeeded in every way I could think of. To see her in this state, skin flushed with embarrassment, shame, and arousal. My marks painted her body like a canvas, proudly announcing every bad intention so her body knew what was yet to come. Even her skin tasted sweet, exactly as I imagined and more.

As I let go of her hair, she slumped backward. If my arm had not been around her waist, she would have fallen off my lap.

She fell asleep.

How irritating.

Alina's head knocked sluggishly against my shoulder as I tugged her forward. Her peaceful expression was lit by only moonlight from the window, a defeated body collapsed in my arms. I could have taken her then, but for some unknown reason, I did not.

The image before me would be a keepsake in my mind if I let it burn long enough. It almost made me forget that dreadful itch to be angry with her for leaving me for *sleep*.

The night was too short. I wished I had longer. *How terribly unfair.*

I heaved her body up and made my way to her master bedroom, my favorite place in the entire city as of late.

Her living space was so familiar to me that I could paint a mental picture of every object in the room. I knew where she kept her hairbrush, which drawer she put her stockings in, the way she tucked a four-inch barber's blade under the left pillow, and the way she kept arsenic in the side drawer just in case.

I laid her out in the soft, silken sheets. Tonight I was easy on her, but I was pleasantly surprised that she fought instead of struggling. I meant it when I said I was proud, like a teacher who marveled at their pupil. Surely she would only get more ferocious as I subjected her to every bad idea that crossed my mind. It would be quite an exhibit to see how far I could push her before she crumbled.

I wanted to control whatever might move her.

Every inflection, tension, or release. Every push and pull. Every drop of blood or tears.

No exceptions.

It would all belong to *me*.

But for tonight, she earned some peace.

THE THICK SMOKE from my cigarette overwhelmed my lungs, filling them to capacity before being blown back out.

The ships bobbed lazily in the harbor, only illuminated by streetlamps and a stray flame here and there. Bells occasionally chimed as the hulls swayed with each passing wake. It was colder tonight—or should I say this morning? There was an hour left of night cover before the sun would begin to burn the fog away.

My hunger affected my focus more than I cared to admit. I was becoming more irate with every minute that passed.

What the hell was I thinking?

I should have fed on Alina when I had the chance. Made her scream my name and beg me to stop—or beg me to keep going. Either would have taken the edge off this deep-set starvation that held me in its grasp. Everything I fed on had disappointed me so far tonight. I fantasized about how she may have tasted if I had sunk my teeth into her hours ago. Nothing came close to even the scent of her. The perfume clung to the inside of my nose, though it was fading fast, like a dream that did not wish to be remembered.

How could she *sleep* when faced with imminent danger? What an enigma.

And those curious eyes—the way she *looked* at me.

It vexed me.

No one had actively *stuck their fingers in my mouth* to inspect me like some kind of test subject before. A small part of me wanted her to keep going, to explore me like I wanted to explore her. To show her everything she wanted. Would she cower in fear the more I exposed to her? Or would showing more of my creature habits excite her?

First rule of being a predator: do not get attached to food. But what could I say? I was a man of indulgence. She completely disregarded danger as she sank herself deeper in the name of curiosity. It lit something within me. Scaring her was one thing, but I sensed something else when she observed me, like something to be cut open and examined. She seemed almost relieved that I was no mere man.

I might be going about this the wrong way.

What made her tick? It was rare to find someone, a human no less, who held nature and all its creatures in such high regard. Maybe she could truly understand me. I did not know whether to be scared or aroused by her eagerness, especially if I might not keep her around.

But maybe I had to. She was too important to leave to her own devices. She would chase that high of discovery and fall into someone else's hands. That would not do.

Thoughts of other people's hands all over something that belonged to me made my hair stand on end. She was *my* meal. I'd earned it.

Stop.

I was getting too worked up.

Focus. Time to hunt.

I sucked the last bit of life out of my cigarette, stamping it out in the dirt.

A few stray commoners bustled about their early work routines. There was a dark-haired girl who dumped a bucket of questionable substances in the street over by the tavern.

Snatching her was quick. Her body was light like a feather. My hand clamped over her mouth as I dragged her into the alleyway.

Trembling with anticipation, I finally sank my teeth into her. The heat flooded my mouth, and I was overcome by greed, biting harder to satiate the impulse. She cried at the first long set of fangs that punctured her throat. When the second set dug into her flesh, the venom relaxed her muscles, and blood ran faster from her feeble body.

It tasted *bland*, like bread made with no salt. Boiled meat with no herbs. Stale biscuits left in the open air overnight. The dull liquid drained until it ran dry in my mouth.

I forced myself to finish, trying to imagine that it was my dear shadow from earlier tonight. When I closed my eyes, I envisioned that sweet spice that would flood my senses, her thick black hair tangled around my fingers, those blue eyes wide with terror…

My stomach twisted, and I winced in pain. My meal was not agreeing with me, even when I tried hard to entice my appetite. I clenched my jaws harder, pulling a mouthful of flesh in frustration as the body fell.

When released, my prey folded like a sack of flour, a blunt thud on the ground.

I expelled the freshly extracted blood from my stomach, only to watch as it absorbed into the gravel.

Another wasted meal, just like the other three.

It was like the thought of Alina made everything taste bland, leaching all flavor and sustenance from anything I tried to consume. This must be how Tantalus felt—just slightly too far from his fruit.

She has cursed me, vile witch!

No matter how much I told myself she was only a meal, I knew I was lying. These changes were too sudden, catalyzed by my obsession.

For now, sustenance was needed. I would be trying all night long if that was what it took. I just needed more time.

CHAPTER TEN

THE POISONER

M y body ached like I'd slept on gravel. I inspected red and purple bruising as I sat up in bed. There was a mixture of those caused by the chase and those caused by his filthy mouth. Aside from the marks, large scrapes crosshatched from my shoulder down to my lower back from the altercation. Even the fabric of my bedsheets brushing against them produced an unpleasant sting.

"What a prick," I huffed, swinging my legs off the edge. As I put pressure on my ankle, I realized that it would be added to the list of damage he caused, as it must have twisted unfavorably during my struggle. Inconvenient, but nothing I could not walk off.

Placed on the nightstand, there was a single nightshade stem.

Why does he insist on leaving gifts?

Placed next to the bloom was a handkerchief. The white fabric bled red from one of the sides. When unraveled, a brittle, disembodied finger was placed neatly in the silk.

My nose creased at the smell. I was sure there would be a story in the paper about the owner of the appendage in question. No matter, I did not have time for puzzles today. The finger was disposed of discreetly in the toilet.

It reminded me of a cat I once had who liked bringing me dead critters every morning.

As amusing as it was, there was no time to deliberate about the Creature's less than savory habits. I had things to do today.

Phoebe and I were supposed to shop for dresses for her garden party, though I believed she threw it together only to make me feel better.

I pressed on the bruise on my sternum, and memories of the weight of his boot resurfaced. The smell of leather was still fresh in my nose. The marks scattered up my neck, my breasts, my ribs.

However, I could feel my face get hot when I remembered how I reacted to that encounter—I still could not believe I prodded around in his mouth. *How embarrassing.* Sometimes I wished I could turn that annoyingly impulsive side of my brain off. But I could not blame myself entirely for my motives. How often did anyone get so close to a brand-new species? I had to know.

THE DRESS for today was a conservative mourning gown to hide the fresh markings up my neck, so nothing strayed from my typical attire. I rubbed my palm across my sore neck, eliciting a deep sigh. Even though it had been nothing more than petting, he was absurdly rough. There was no need for this crude display.

"Which one? Pink or blue?" Phoebe asked. She peered at me over her shoulder as the seamstress held up two fabrics.

"Why not something different? A mint or sage?" I suggested tiredly.

"Oh, I nearly forgot that greens were an option," she mumbled, giving the seamstress one look before the nimble artist fled to the back to pull more silks.

"Your eyes are red. Are you still not sleeping?" Phoebe went up on her toes to grab my face, inspecting either side. In doing so, she spotted the bright purple and black bruise peeking out from under my high collar. "Alina Katarzyna Lis! What is *that*?" she squeaked, squeezing my face in her bout of excitement.

My eyes were not the only thing that had turned red by now.

"Nothing! *Nothing!*" I tried to hush her.

"I feel so betrayed. You're off conquesting and haven't told me all the delicious details? I am truly offended," she said in faux disappointment.

Her giddy demeanor settled when the front door of the shop rang, indicating a new customer. However, her cast was less than amused when she peered past me to see who it was. The change in her demeanor was as sharp as the first winter breeze.

My brows knit together before I craned my neck to see who could have caused such a drastic change in her attitude.

That devilish smirk appeared before us.

"God must be looking favorably on me today if he placed you in my path," the Creature said as he entered the shop, his tone so sickly sweet that I could feel a cavity forming already. In his hand was the blackened shirt from the previous night.

"Mr. Forbes——" I began.

"Silas," he reminded me, his eyes trailing to Phoebe.

"*Silas*," Phoebe acknowledged him with a tight smile, though she was too expressive to hide her distaste. "What brings you to a seamstress? Do you not have your own?" she asked coldly.

"It is Sunday, Miss Aston. I would not ask good Christians to work on a Sunday!" he replied with a tinge of sarcasm in his tone.

These two seemed to have...*history?*

"Besides, some nasty moth ate through my shirt," he said, holding it up. It had a large black stain on the shoulder from where my knife had pierced him.

My focus landed on the shirt, and when I returned to his face, he was already looking at me. "Was it a moth or a squid?"

He only answered with a laugh before setting his shirt on the counter. An apprentice gathered it quickly.

"Well, it was a pleasure as always to see you, Miss Aston." He gave her a snarky farewell before he turned to me. "Alina." My name rolled off his tongue as he lifted my hand to kiss my bruised knuckle, his eyes not leaving mine.

After a moment's pause to run his thumb over my skin, the corner of his lip tugged up subtly before he pulled away.

As I watched him leave, green eyes burned holes into the side of my face with the intensity of Phoebe's glare.

Turning sheepishly, I came face-to-face with the most aggravated expression I had ever seen on my dear friend.

My shoulders tensed, and I could only muster an awkward smile, wiping my hand on my dress where he'd touched it.

"Please don't tell me—"

"No, it's not—"

"*Anyone* but him, Alina!" she scolded, slapping my shoulder with her gathered gloves. "Promise me you'll stay away from him." Her expression was stern.

"I've tried, trust me. He's like a dog to a butcher's dumpster," I grumbled, scratching my neck again. "It just...happened. It was nothing." I could not say much more about the encounter without her thinking I was a madwoman, but alarming her was the last thing I wanted to do. She would not understand this sick chase I had been stuck in. She did not have to be worried for much longer, thankfully. I just needed a little more time to get rid of him.

Her gaze flicked between my face and my neck in suspicion.

"Ma'am! Your fabrics!"

I was relieved when the seamstress spoke, holding up a few silks for Phoebe to pick from. The tension slowly dissipated as she settled back into her fashionable state of mind.

A string of jealousy wrapped around my heart and pulled me into a knot.

Was he only fixated on me to get back at Phoebe for some long-lost fling? He had been following me, studying my life. I would not be surprised if he knew of my association with the Astons. She had never mentioned him, though I was gone a long time and might have missed some things. I would have thought she would mention a man in her life, since she spared no other details regarding her endeavors. Though I suspected she was unaware of his...*true* nature. If she was, everyone would have heard about it by now. That made me feel that my acquaintance with the Creature was somewhat special.

If I found that even a hair had been plucked from her head, I would be removing his heart and keeping it in a jar on my desk. It would make for a perfect paperweight.

PHOEBE BOUGHT me a few new dresses. She convinced me to get a deep red and a navy evening gown. She said she would deliver them so I didn't have to carry them while on my errands.

The market bustled today, as it was a pleasant afternoon, sun rays peeking through the overcast. It was a little warm in my black attire, but it was not like I had a choice to wear anything else. My neck had turned all kinds of colors from the abrasions of the night before. The markings worsened as the day passed, so I purchased some ingredients for a bruising oil.

With my covered basket, I skimmed over the crumpled list pinched between my fingers. *Oranges, lilies, violets, cherries, castor oil, vinegar,* and *earthworms*—though I had already gathered worms at the park earlier.

A body pressing against my back nearly caused me to drop my basket. A certain Creature leaned down by my ear. "You smell like cherries today. Did you wear that for me?"

"Maybe you smell cherries because you're about to have a seizure. Perhaps the venom did affect you after all," I scoffed, refusing to pull my eyes from my list.

"You know, that cut you left healed quite smooth. Have you thought of working in cosmetics?" he bantered, reaching around to pluck the list from my fingers. He held it above my head as he inspected the handwriting.

"You bug!" I looked straight up, and the back of my head hit his chest.

"This is…quite the list. Has anyone informed you that you're an extremely odd woman, or do they assume that you already know?" He tilted his head down at me.

Reaching up on the tips of my toes, I snatched it back and walked away.

"You always look so disappointed when you see me." He sighed. "Is it because you're hoping one of your little potions will work? I hate to break it to you, but if a knife in me didn't work, neither will fancy tinctures."

"Why did you keep that shirt? It's ruined. You could buy a million shirts." I was still reeling from this morning's encounter.

"Because it's a masterpiece made by my dear shadow. I can't bring myself to throw art away!" he teased. "Besides, then I would have to admit to stalking you. I would much rather make all the excuses in the world to see you," he said sweetly as he walked beside me.

We went down to Caldwell's together, or rather, he followed me.

"Alina! *Oh!* Mr. Forbes!" Mrs. Caldwell said, flustered, brushing off some stray foliage from the counter and smiling nervously. "What brings you two in today?"

The Creature opened his mouth to speak.

"Just the import and a few more items," I spoke quickly, sliding her my list.

How embarrassing that so many people were seeing us together. I knew that Phoebe would chew off my ear on the telephone the following day. Rumors spread faster than steam engines nowadays. The more he was seen with me, the more suspicious I would become when I threw his soon-to-be lifeless body in the same harbor where he left those girls.

Mrs. Caldwell lifted a thin wooden crate from behind the counter, placing it in front of me. Her eyes shifted between us. "So I take it she liked them?" Her eyes landed on the Creature.

"You could say that." He flashed a deceptively sweet smile her way.

"Mrs. Caldwell, I actually have another request. Could you check the back to see if I had any leftover blackberry stems?" I asked, trying to hide my displeasure with him as I spoke.

"Oh! Yes, of course, let me check on that for you." She nodded, turning and slipping into the depths of her shop.

I turned quickly to the Creature. "What do you think you're doing?" I bite out through clenched teeth, shoving a finger at his chest.

"Is it really such a terrible crime to buy you flowers?" A slight twitch of a smirk appeared as he attempted to play the fool. I was sure there were many bad thoughts stewing in that rotten brain of his that I would rather not know.

Mrs. Caldwell returned with my things, and I put the loose flowers inside the covered basket, keeping the lid ajar to let the buds breathe. When I went to grab the box, he snatched it.

"No need to burden yourself with such a heavy box! You should be resting instead of doing heavy work," he taunted. How patronizing.

If my gaze were an arrow, it would be through his head already.

With my sweetest smile, I bid my florist a good day.

When we reached the outside, I snatched my box back. "Don't ever do that again unless you want arsenic in your whiskey," I seethed.

He could humiliate me all he wanted in private, but doing so in public was playing with dynamite.

"Oh? I'd love to see you try." He lowered his voice. "How would you manage that, my dear shadow?"

With a saccharine grin, I stood on my toes to whisper against his ear. "You'll let me do it. You'll beg me to, because I know that you can't bear to stay away. *Isn't that right?*"

He stared momentarily. "Perhaps." He cocked his head at me. "Let me at least hail a coach for you. Can't have you overexerting yourself like *last night*."

My expression returned to its typical stoicism, and I took my time studying his expression. Finally, I backed down and took a step back.

He took that as a truce and waved down a passing coachman.

The Creature's intentions were lost on me. Considering what happened last night, it was all too playful, too friendly. I noticed his gaze lingering on my neck. Despite his words about my own misery when I saw him, he seemed disappointed that he was unable to see his exploits that tainted my skin. I would go as far as to say he was irritated.

He helped me into the cab with my hand in his, leaning down to it in what I thought would be a kiss. His fangs snapped forward and moved to bite a finger.

I snapped my hand away. "You are a *fiend*," I hissed, yanking the cab door closed.

"Only for you." He shrugged.

"That's a lie, Creature. You're *always* a fiend."

The cab jolted forward, and his silhouette disappeared as we passed.

CHAPTER ELEVEN
THE CREATURE

I was starting to think she lived part-time in that shop of hers. I thought she would have left by now. It was three hours and fifty-two minutes past closing, and I had yet to see her resurface from her den. Each day she stayed longer. Sometimes I pulled up a chair at the closed café across the street while I waited to escort her home.

This is taking too long.

I stood from my seat, about to pay her a visit through the shop's back door, when I saw her emerge from her cave.

There you are.

The keys jangled between her fingers as she locked up, giving the door a tug for reassurance.

I began to walk down the street, except she went the wrong way.

When I turned around, she was walking in the opposite direction.

That is not the way to your house, little shadow.

Walking faster to catch up, I followed behind on the other

side of the street. She had a pad of paper in her hand, head down looking at the paper as she weaved through the streets. I began to worry, since she never strayed so far from her routine. I could count the locations she frequented the most on a single hand with digits to spare. Not once had I ever seen her walk this way.

It must have been at least thirty minutes of foot travel just to see her standing idly outside my home.

She was like a tiny figurine before the large, stately manor. It could be a museum with its size paired with the number of things I had collected throughout the ages.

She broke from her frozen state to write something down.

What are you planning, minx?

She paced in front, then snuck around to see if there was a way to peep in. Along the side of the house, she tugged at the service entrance. It was locked, but I made a note to myself to leave that one open from now on. Finding a stray Alina in my home in the middle of the night would be quite a treat.

I hoped she would try and knock, but that did not seem to be in her plans tonight. Then she retreated, back in the direction she was *supposed* to go earlier.

The muscles in my jaw twitched. What was the point of coming all the way out here if she wasn't going to do anything?

CHAPTER TWELVE

THE POISONER

At least twenty glass test tubes were stacked in the wooden holders scattered around my lab. Some were diluted with water at different rates, some were control samples, and others were extras. It was hard choosing which poison I wanted to make, so I decided to make them all. Stocking up on inventory would never be a bad thing, especially now that I had to figure out which would work on this Creature stalking about.

I might have imported too many plants. I only had so much time to make extracts out of them. I doubted I could get through them all in a timely manner.

The clock rang. My pen left a stray mark on my paper in response to the clamor.

Two p.m.

Phoebe's garden party had nearly slipped my mind in the frenzy. She would have my head if I was tardy to yet another event. It was bad enough that I had canceled our morning walk and blamed it on needing time to prepare.

IF EVERY EVENT Phoebe threw was like this one, I would have a lot more fun.

The event was held at the botanical gardens inside their esteemed greenhouse. For me, it was like bringing a child to the zoo. My chest swelled with butterflies, my eyes probably wide with awe. This was the first time I had felt genuine happiness in the past few weeks, out of all the events I was forced to attend.

The glass cathedral towered above in intricate panels. The sky transitioned from blue to pink and red, painting its own fresco for everyone to view through the domes of the greenhouse. This was my personal haven. A chapel of the living world.

The rarest flowers, trees, and shrubs decorated the grand glass fortress. Birds chirped in delight as they fluttered through their heavenly residence. A pang of jealousy hit me when I imagined being a bird living in this protected arboretum, genuinely. Oh, how I wish I could metamorphose into one of those fledglings.

The vermilion evening gown Phoebe picked for me practically glowed under the warm lights and the red sky. She lent me some rubies to match, since I was never interested in keeping any family jewels on me. The only other finery in my home would be the Creature's cruel display of pearls.

My redheaded friend had yet to appear, though I assumed that she would be buzzing about like a distracted bee. That was more than all right with me. It gave me time to relax for once. While mingling with too big of a crowd made me nauseous, it was tolerable when I was in my element, such as this.

One flower caught my eye, a tall green spindle stuck straight in the air like a spear. Its ambiance practically pulled me toward it, begging me to inspect it closer.

The brass plaque read, *The Corpse Flower (Amorphophallus Titanum).*

"Magnificent, isn't she?" a deep Russian-accented voice spoke next to me.

Glancing to my right, I saw an enamored character staring at the odd specimen before us. His soft amber eyes were curious and full of wonder.

I could sympathize with that, especially in a place like this.

He met my eyes before shrinking into an awkward posture, which looked out of place considering his towering muscular build and handsome face. A humble smile tugged at the corner of his lip, dimples peeking through as he adjusted the rim of his wire glasses. He looked maybe twenty-five, two years older than me, in an academic brown suit.

"Viktor Kaskov." He held out a polite hand, his accent sweet and playful.

My brow rose in what could only be a mixture of surprise and skepticism. A man wanted to shake my hand as equals?

Cautiously, I took it, squeezing gently. "Alina Lis—"

"I know! Apologies. I should have prefaced that I am a fan of your work." His eyes were intense, looking deeper than I was comfortable with. "Your paper on the effects of *Ageratina altissima* on the nervous system of vermin was fascinating. How did you think to use white snakeroot as the subject? It isn't prevalent around here." He tilted his head to the side, a few black curls falling out of place as he studied me closely.

Overwhelmed was an overstatement. I was not used to men taking anything I wrote seriously. "I was introduced to it on my travels with my father. He had a fascination with these things." I looked down at my hand clasped between his.

"How interesting. A woman of science and adventure? That is something rare." He squeezed my hand before letting it go. "Have you seen the display of poisonous and carnivorous flowers within the gardens yet?"

"I didn't know there was one. I really should visit more often." I gleamed at the offer.

THE POISONS and carnivore section was separate from the others. I was not certain we were allowed entry. The closed-off conservatory was in a different wing of the gardens.

Larkspur plants lined the walkway, about four feet tall, coming in blues, pinks, purples, and whites. Foxgloves bloomed in tall spears as their little trumpet blossoms opened gradually down the stem. Other flowers on the ground included nightshades, hogweed, oleander, trumpet flowers, and other exotic toxins that I had never seen before. Hung around the edges were pitcher plants, flytraps, and other sticky-looking counterparts, though I was less familiar with cannibalistic flora.

We explored together for a while. Neither of us kept track of the time. This was like my little paradise away from the social hell that awaited outside the doors. Lots of pointing, searching for plaques as we guessed their binomial nomenclature, and stealing a cutting or two while he kept a lookout. I removed my gloves to save them from any smudges of dirt as I collected.

"Do you know how to propagate these? Some I don't think I have seen before." I cupped the little sprigs of plants in my hand like they were gold. We were both seated on the bench before one of the man-made ponds.

"I may have a paper or two. I could send some through the post as long as you can send them back." He grinned.

His demeanor was so warm and calming in a sense. It should be familiar to me.

"Do I have to return them? How cruel," I joked, placing the clippings in my purse.

"Your hands—" He grabbed my hand suddenly. "I'm sorry. I should have done the cuttings for you—they're irritating your skin," he said worriedly, staring at my red fingertips.

I could not tell him that it was because of the dozen plants I had just processed, but his concern admittedly made me blush. Was I becoming bashful? Around a man, of all things?

"No need to fuss over it. They're just sensitive," I assured him, slipping my hand from his, my skin already missing the tenderness. "I...I should be getting back," I said quickly.

"Of course. I am sure you are quite busy." Viktor smiled. "Don't wait for me. I may stay in here for a while. Social gatherings aren't my forte."

He really did understand.

I nodded in understanding. "Well, I appreciated the company genuinely."

"Anytime. I mean it." He winked.

With that, I departed, leaving him alone in the beautiful mirage along with those heavy feelings.

As I advanced through the buzzing crowd, my eyes stayed focused on the plants along the footpath. I crouched down and slid a blade from my sleeve, using it to carve away some more of the stems to propagate later. It felt like I was stealing jewels from a museum, but I doubted that anyone would mind.

Standing again and admiring my new specimens, I tucked them into my clutch and surveyed the crowd.

There was one slightly frantic figure in the middle. It took me a minute to process who it was.

The Creature's head whipped in my direction, his expression angry, like I had been hiding from him purposefully. He was storming directly toward me.

Alarms blared in my head, and I quickly moved through the crowd to escape the main gathering area. People bumped into me, diverting my route as I slipped through the bodies.

"*Move!*" I hissed.

Off to the far side of the greenhouse, there was a door with a *No Patrons* sign on it.

The door was almost latched shut behind me when it was shoved back open, only slamming shut when the predator entered behind me.

"Where do you think you're going?" He flipped the lock on the door.

"Your conclusion is as good as mine." I stood my ground.

We had stumbled into a nursery. The room was small and made of old, foggy glass. Wooden shelves held a mess of small planters containing a diverse selection of seedlings. It was at least quieter than the central area.

My attention wandered to the small plants, and I was tempted to take a few.

"Look at me." The Creature stepped in front of me. "Let's not get distracted so early." His smile was nothing but sarcastic, irritated, even.

"What is it now? Can't I just have one night to myself?"

"I let you have a few nights to yourself." He stepped forward.

I stood firm in place. I would not let him intimidate me.

"As if I were to believe you weren't watching me the whole time. Do you ever take a day off? Perhaps find someone new to play with?"

"We are far past that, my shadow." He chuckled, hanging over me like a gallows. His fingers smoothed over the side of my face, and his other hand trailed down my arm toward my balled-up fist. "You're lucky that you're delicious. I don't usually let prey suffer for this long."

His finger trailed across my cheek, then his thumb pulled down on my bottom lip.

My teeth clamped down on his finger.

He shouted in pain while I made for the door, but his other hand grabbed me by the back of my neck, pinning my chest against the wood of the door.

"*Alina.*" He clicked his tongue in disapproval. "What have we learned about running?"

"Find another damsel." I spat some of his blood from my mouth.

A burning festered in my throat, making me squirm under his grip. The pervasive sensation got stronger. It was like a hand was closing around my throat while I was forcibly fed hot embers.

My breath quickened, and I let out a cough. A whimper accompanied it when I failed to clear it. A bitter metallic taste took over my throat.

The Creature turned me around to face him. "What did I tell you?" He tilted his head to the side. "Did I not say I was made of poison? I thought you would have surely taken that part seriously."

My eyes watered, and my fists had balled up in his shirt from pure desperation. Another labored gasp was taken in vain. The burning was unbearable, like trying to rid my throat of hot coals only for it to spread farther.

What is this?

Admittedly, as a poisoner myself, I had never thought I would be the one to be poisoned. The past few weeks had been full of many firsts. How poetic that I die the same way I reaped.

He lowered his face to mine, and my body protested the proximity.

"Do you trust me?" he whispered against my lips.

"No." My voice came out as a weep. My sight was blurred from tears, and I gripped him tighter to steady my dizzy spell. The air was being cut off from my lungs, and they struggled to expand.

"Find it within you to do so, just this once," he whispered.

He grabbed my face with one hand, jolting it toward him. His lips found mine, and I could feel his tongue slip inside my mouth. The kiss was soft, despite his voracity.

I refused to return any such gesture, but then the burning slowly dissipated. My body forced my mouth open to take in air, and he wasted no time seizing the opportunity. A gasp escaped me as my throat loosened, making our kiss deepen.

The Creature picked me up and pushed me onto the workbench, gardening tools clattering to the ground.

My breath hitched at the sharp movement, our lips hovering earnestly over each other. If the room had been dark, there would be static electricity trading flashes of light from the tension between us. My hands were riddled with tremors from shock.

He almost killed me. *Again.* And nobody would be left to blame but myself, as much as I would want it to be his fault entirely. *The Poisoner Who Poisoned Herself.* I could see it on the headstone now.

He was generous enough to let me catch my breath. How humiliating.

I did not have to look at him to know that an undoubtedly coy look would be present as he watched the color return to my face.

"You know, you're quite cute when your lips turn blue." His eyes glanced from my lips to my eyes. "I can understand why you prefer to execute people this way."

There was that dreadful pang in my gut. The knot formed low in my abdomen as I entirely took in the position I was in.

This Creature was poised above me, hungry and waiting. His hips were pressed between my legs, his hands steadying my tremors.

It could have been the adrenaline, or it was a manifestation of my own hunger. I did not know how to explain it. It was like a jolt of lightning had shot through my body. Why did he make me feel so *hot*?

"What little thoughts are smacking against the inside of your skull?" His pupils were constricted. The air about him was as dangerous as the still air before a storm.

"No…thoughts," I mumbled, refusing to look at him.

"You seem upset."

"I am."

"Oh, that won't do, then, will it?" He leaned down, biting gently on my ear as he pressed his body against mine.

My hair had slipped out of my neat bun when his fingers tangled through the midnight strands. He hiked my dress up to expose my legs, using his hips as a barrier that kept them from closing.

"Wait—" The words fell short before he sucked high on my neck by my jaw. A cold, leather-covered hand traced under my dress and crept up my thigh. I tried to clench my legs closed, but he was in the way.

"Behave," he breathed into my neck. "I am trying to be nice. Let me cheer you up."

My skin was on fire wherever he breathed, touched, sucked.

Any thoughts about my rigid ethical compass slipped away and spun out of control. He was purely magnetic that way.

As much as I hated him for making me feel like this, for him, of all people, he could have anything he wanted. Why bother me? Why must he be so stubborn and fixated on the one who wanted to kill him?

"Remember how my tongue felt on your fingers that night?" he asked against my neck, placing another mark on my neck above one of the nearly healed bruises.

I nodded and turned my face away in embarrassment.

He responded by pulling away.

A disappointed knot formed in his absence. I looked down and saw those broad shoulders between my legs. My eyes widened, but my reaction was delayed by a warm, wet sensation against my skin.

"*No!*" I snapped, but he reached up and gripped my thighs, my legs resting on his shoulders. He pulled my body closer to the edge of the table.

His tongue traced up and down my labia lightly, teasing around the area before I could feel myself throbbing in anticipation, twitching at any stray movements. His tongue dampened the surrounding skin. Fingers played with the hem of my silk stockings as his focus was dedicated entirely between my thighs.

"*Let go!*" I grabbed him by the hair, yanking his head up.

His now-black eyes peered up at me through his blond lashes before his face lowered behind the bunched-up dress, ignoring my protests.

A long tongue danced playfully between my legs before prodding gently to ask for entrance.

If I bit my lip any harder, it would have bled. Though I did not think he would mind that either. It was getting harder to muffle the sounds my throat ached to make. What kept me from saying no? Whenever I thought to tell him off, I was distracted by the feeling of his tongue teasing me. My fist still held on to his hair, but I was unsure if I wanted to push him away or pull him closer.

Slowly, he pushed his tongue inside until his lips could suck on the surrounding area, coaxing a soft gasp from me.

This was new to me. In the many times I'd tried to seek pleasure from a man, it never came close to something like this. The tightness forming at the bottom of my abdomen made me pant, struggling to catch a full breath. The windows began to fog around us in the small glass room.

His mouth vibrated against my skin when a low clicking emanated from his throat.

I lay back on the table, letting go of his hair, as I was unable to support myself as pleasure rippled through my body.

He shifted by standing up, my legs over his shoulders, so that he was in full view, but so was I. He glanced down at me while he lapped between my thighs, using one of his hands to play with my clit.

My cheeks were now red from embarrassment *and* from the blood rushing to my head from the position. My nails dug into the table's surface, desperately trying to find something to grab.

I could only manage to glare at him. If I let him derive too much pleasure from this, he would begin to think he'd won.

"Oh, if this isn't the most beautiful view"—he flattened his tongue against the wetness coming from me—"then I don't know what is." Without another moment wasted, he slipped that devil's tongue into me again, reaching deeper than I would have expected anyone to.

I yelped, arching my back.

He gasped against me as he moved his tongue, flexing it

forward and curling to hit that forbidden spot that was not often found.

"*Silas!*" I whined, closing my eyes tight as he moved inside me.

Calling his name made him physically tense, his movements becoming more ravenous.

There was not much more I could take. My abdomen was so tight that I could combust from the heat. The end was coming on fast. There was no stopping the wave washing over me.

The orgasm ripped through my body with such intensity that I swear even *he* could feel it move through me, clamping around his tongue. It rolled through me in waves, each time less intense than the last, before it left my body and took any remaining tension with it.

My body went limp, and my chest rose and fell with a dizzy pant. The corset was not helping me in the slightest to regain my breath.

He slipped that unforgivable tongue out, slicking over his lips in response. "You know, you taste better than I imagined." He smirked. "But all those lovely sounds really made it an experience," he teased.

"I cannot...wait...to *kill* you," I breathed, letting my head fall back with a thud against the table. I just needed to close my eyes for a minute.

What have I done?

"Is that any way to thank me?" He dropped my legs, pulling me back up to a sitting position, my thighs shaking. "If you'll let me do that, why not let me have a different kind of taste?"

"I have to get back—"

"What's the rush?" he asked, leaning in. "Why not just stay here all night?" He pressed his hips between my legs again—an awful insinuation.

Sickening.

"You're delusional if you think that will happen."

"I saved your life and tasted both of your sweet lips tonight. Anything can happen."

I lowered my gaze in embarrassment. In anger and in haste, I pushed myself off the table.

"Red looks good on you," he said, "especially when it is blood rushing to your face." He laughed, but I was already out the door.

I tied my hair back up again and used the previously secured ribbon to tie it into place. What a mess this was.

My shaking hands fidgeted with my ribbon in an attempt to tie it in a bow before my face smacked into a hard chest.

"Miss Lis!" a nervous voice bumbled. "I am so sorry, I should have seen—" Viktor placed his hands on my shoulders, looking down at me with those sweet brown eyes. His expression twisted in concern when he saw the state of my flustered face. "Are you all right? You look a bit drained," he said.

"Yes—yes, it's all right. I just needed a break!" I exclaimed nervously, itching to get as far away from that room as I could, my legs still quivering. "How about we dance? Yes! Let's dance. Come!"

My hand was clasped in his as we moved through the foot-paths into the main event area. Some string instruments lit the room with a comforting spirit among the low ambient light. The sun had set, and a few stars littered the dark sky on the other side of the glass ceiling.

It was best to be surrounded by people, as I wished not to grapple with my thoughts for the rest of the night. I plucked a champagne flute from a passing tray, and I let the cool liquid slip down my sore throat in a single swig.

Viktor looked perplexed as I dragged him with me.

We joined the crowd that occupied the floor, and I clung onto this new figure of mine like a life preserver on a sinking ship.

"Miss Lis, are you sure everything is all right?" he whispered, resting a hand on my waist and taking my hand in his.

"Yes! Fantastic—everything is great!" I forced a smile, peering over his shoulder skittishly like I might fly away at any sudden movement.

He did not press the subject any longer but pulled my body in gently with a reassuring squeeze of my hand. The gesture calmed me slightly. At least Silas could not make a scene in front of everyone. Not here. I lowered my head to Viktor's chest, and he rested his chin on my head in response.

"Miss Lis—"

"*Alina.* Please just call me Alina," I mumbled into the lapel of his suit.

"Alina," he corrected himself, playing with the sound of my name on his tongue. "Do you want me to escort you home?"

"*Please.*"

THE DOOR UNLOCKED with a heavy click, and I looked back at Viktor.

He was standing on the first step, looking up at the town house. His deep eyes looked like they were eating up the details, taking it in completely.

He reminded me of myself—how he studied everything like it was holding secrets.

"Would you like to come in?" I offered, opening the door wider for him.

He pretended to contemplate it, giving his chin a few taps. "I don't know… That's a really hard decision. What if you turn out to be a witch?"

"There are worse things out there, like alienists." I winked.

He tucked his hands in his pockets, giving a shy glance at his shoes. "As much as I'd love to, I must go. I am rarely even out this late."

"Suit yourself." I shrugged. "Ring me some time, will you?"

"I can do you one better." He smiled sheepishly. "I'll send those papers you asked for."

"We have a deal, as long as you put yourself through the post as well."

"I'll see what I can do." He laughed.

With that, we parted ways for the night.

CHAPTER THIRTEEN

THE POISONER

One by one, I plucked the single stems of lily of the valley that trailed through the home. The delicate stalks held fragile white bell-shaped flowers in neat pearls along its length. It would be counterproductive to play along with my Creature's sick games, but he knew I would not waste perfectly good blooms.

When I awoke that morning, the trail started at my bedside and ran through the hallways, down the stairs, and finally ended in the kitchen.

The light filling the room from the window illuminated small specs of dust that stirred upon my arrival. The light swept across the floor and the table, where a pile of a mysterious fibers was placed.

It did not seem to be anything much. From afar, it looked to be a pile of wool discarded on the table. As I approached, the wool texture slowly morphed into fine hair, spun into flowers and leaves that were fashioned into a wreath. Some areas of the hair were tinted red in messy blotches that did not seem intentional, but were residual from the mess required to gather the materials.

Placed in the middle of the wreath was a rat. It was splayed out on its back, a neat Y cut into its abdomen with the skin peeled back—no head. Everything inside was where it was supposed to be, except the heart was pinned above where its head should have been.

There was no need for a note. I knew that it was from my favorite pest.

I wish I could compliment him on his creativity, but alas, this would be one I could give to the birds.

I carefully picked up the wreath of hair. The fine strands still clung onto the oils of their past owners' scalps. I could feel it on my hands. I plucked the rat heart and put it back inside the carcass, caressing the little body carefully before heading out the back door.

All was quiet at dawn, though a chorus of croaks erupted once I stepped out into the backyard. The only things from him that I kept were flowers. The rest I gave to my raven friends, who had taken up permanent residence in my garden. I tossed the carcass out in the grass, and the fowl enthusiastically hopped toward their meal.

Over by the greenhouse, I hung the wreath on the bird feeder, hoping the other nest makers could make use of it better than I could. He was being wasteful at this point. Every time he left a gift, I tried to find a way to reuse it if possible. Though it was harder to do so with body parts. The only safe place for them was buried under the flower beds to be eaten by the grubs.

I was just thankful it was not something messier, as I did not have a maid on my books. Not that I could ask someone to tidy up human limbs.

"And did he make his intentions clear?" Phoebe prodded, leaning against her knees pulled up to her chest as she sat beside me on the couch.

We were settled in front of the fireplace. Crystal glasses of sweet booze kept us company.

"No, though I wouldn't have minded if he did." I blushed, taking a shy sip from my cup.

"I love it when this happens! I should be a matchmaker. It is like everyone finds a lover at my parties." She giggled. "Will I get to see both of you soon?"

"I am unsure. He promised he would send me some papers. I am hoping he leaves a calling card in the parcel as well." I shrugged, finishing off my glass before holding it out to Phoebe.

"This is so exciting! We can pair up and go to the museum, a fair, or maybe a live show?" she rattled off, lifting the decanter and pouring me some more.

"Sounds like a good time." I smiled. "What about you? Anyone new?"

"Same old. I fear I may never find someone as interesting as you or I, and I won't settle for someone boring." She paused before a nymph-like grin appeared. "Though that won't stop me from taste testing."

"You would run them dry with your parties—wallets and wine cellars."

"Is that not what a husband is for?"

"Touché." I shrugged.

I pulled the blanket over our shoulders, sliding closer so we could fit comfortably underneath.

"Have you been smoking?" Phoebe asked.

I shook my head. "On occasion, but not recently. I don't prefer the taste."

"Huh." She picked up my braid and brought it to her nose. Then she leaned into my neck and inhaled, scrunching her nose. "It smells like smoke."

"Odd." I raised my brow, lifting my hair to my nose as well. "Wash day was two days ago. It could be from walking outside."

"I thought so. I never took you for the type to pick up smoking. Though I can imagine you drinking things you shouldn't." She laughed.

"Right." My lips tugged into a brief smile as I stared at the plait pinched between my fingers.

"How about we wash now? I can help—let us go!" she slurred, kicking her legs off the couch and dragging me to my feet.

"That's unnecessary! I'll do it tomorrow!"

"It'll be like old times!"

"We were five! I don't think we will fit in the tub now."

Her grip did not ease up on me, pulling me the rest of the way to the bathroom. One thing I missed were our sleepovers. Phoebe and I did not keep anyone else as close as we were, as we were glued to each other's sides most days. I wondered what she did while I was away. I was half expecting her to make more friends other than just myself. In a way, I was relieved that we could pick up where we left off so seamlessly.

"Looks like you made out like a bandit at the market today," she commented, placing her drink down as she picked at the upside-down bundle of lilies drying on the door.

"There was a special price. I couldn't say no," I lied, then turned to the porcelain basin.

I wobbled over to turn on the water, but the water sloshed oddly, indicating something was in the basin.

Rats. Two—no, three—dozen rat carcasses were piled at the bottom of the tub. They were all opened up like the one before. The water pushed them against each other as they rolled and bobbed like a morbid cranberry bog.

I gagged and held my hand over my mouth.

"Do you need me to hold your hair?"

"No! No, Phoebe," I rushed out. "Just…can you run and get me some ginger?"

"Are you sure I—" She stepped toward me.

"No! Quick! Please go grab it!" I shouted.

She scrambled out the door, off on her mission for a spice I did not have.

As I leaned over the tub, my hands gripped the edge in anger. That was enough. He could subject me to whatever game he wanted to play, but I would not allow him to traumatize my dear Phoebe. She was a gentle soul, and I would not allow him to be so careless. At least the ravens would be happy.

I unlatched the window above the tub. It opened to the backyard. It was more convenient to let the birds in than throw the mice out.

Instead of ravens, there was a more unfavorable Creature standing in the middle of the garden.

He was silent. All he did was smirk with his hands shoved in his pockets.

My tongue clicked against my teeth in disgust as I turned away from the window.

I locked the bathroom door on my way out. It was tomorrow's mess for me to worry about.

"I'm feeling better now!" I shouted for Phoebe, running down the stairs quickly and going to the back door to check the locks.

When I peeked out the window, no figures were waiting outside.

CHAPTER FOURTEEN

THE CREATURE

Today, she scurried like a manic shrew, blindly gathering herself for whatever hole she was about to dig for herself.

Every day, her objectives might as well be cast in steel, but today she was on a different kind of mission. Perhaps my gifts inspired her to break from her unrelenting daily pattern.

I waited in the shadows of her hallway, tucked away as she moved around her bedroom. I could see her through the slightly cracked door, her figure fluttering in the candlelight.

She did not bother to turn the gas lamps on, which meant she would be leaving soon.

My back was pressed against the wall next to the door. Backlit by the candlelight on her vanity, her form began to shed some layers.

She struggled with a few buttons on the back of her high neckline. I wished so dearly that I could help her strip faster. She finally popped them out, undoing the rest painfully slow. She slipped the dress down to expose her undergarments. A sheer white corset cover and underskirt hid the rest of her. A peek of black cotton stockings appeared as she adjusted her garters, tying a small pouch under the skirt. She slipped that familiar needle into her hair as she twisted it up.

For me?

She dressed in what I called her working attire, which was a wool walking skirt and simple blouse. The last garment piece was a pair of muddy boots.

Those were her walking boots. She must be working tonight. Typically, she brought a satchel with her for deliveries, so she was lighter than usual. I was curious to see who she was going to meet. After she was finished, she flung the door open and walked right past me.

There was that nasty preoccupation again. Poor thing.

THE WALK along the winding streets began to look *familiar.*

She was coming to see me.

I watched intently as she moved closer to the home, inspecting the exterior again. I'd left the service door unlocked, though she did not bite. Instead, I watched her crouch down and pop open the cellar window, slipping inside through the basement.

Finally, a proper move.

I'd wondered how long she would let me flirt before she struck back.

Moving around the side of the manor, I stepped up on the stone edge to get a look inside. She moved about, rifling through my things to find the perfect place to set her trap.

It was like watching an animal in their natural habitat—

seeing exactly how they worked when supposedly no one was watching.

It was not long before she wandered into my study. She left the door open, so I had a full view of her pouring one of her vials into my decanter.

How cheeky of her. I think it is time I "came home."

Approaching my front door, I unlocked it slowly so she could gather herself. When I twisted the doorknob, I was greeted by the warm light of my home.

For a place I spent the least amount of time, it sure was spacious. It was put to good use for gatherings and other selfish purposes, but otherwise it was like a maze. Most rooms would have a thick layer of dust if I did not employ maids. Upon entering, a large foyer and two sets of stairs joined to form a middle balcony above the room. To my left was the living room, and to my right was my private study. Directly in front of me was a hallway leading to many rooms that usually remained vacant.

A flash of movement disappeared around the corner, as well as the accompanying sound of footsteps.

How flirtatious.

I dropped my keys on a small table next to the entryway, letting them clamor loudly when they smacked against the wood.

A soft shuffling was heard.

There was no particular purpose to my direction as I wandered through my home. Slowly, I took each step, wondering if I was getting warmer or cooler with each move.

When I entered the long hallway leading to the rooms on the first floor, I caught a scent.

The deep chittering sound from deep in my chest bloomed with excitement as I followed, just far enough behind her so she thought she was doing well at this game. I could hear her shuffling through the connected rooms on the left side of the corridor.

I followed the scent closely through one of the lounging rooms, then to a connecting one.

There was a brief flash of a shadow from under one of the doors.

There you are.

As I made my way down the hall, the scent got closer and closer until I reached the room she was hiding in. I did not go in. She was right next to the door on the other side. I leaned against the wood, quietly taking in a breath. I could smell her fear—the sweat dancing across the back of her neck, the heat that would undoubtedly be burning her cheeks.

Rushing such a special occasion would be a waste. I had been waiting so long for some effort on her part. The windows on the first floor could not be opened, so she would have to come out eventually.

I stepped back from the door, walked down the hall, and stopped at the end.

I'll wait.

It took everything in me to push down that involuntary clicking that wanted to burst through my throat. It hurt to hold it back, but seeing her emerge would be worth it.

Like clockwork, it took twenty minutes for Alina to calm her heart enough to make her next move. I could smell every pulse that coursed through her veins. The adrenaline was a spicy tinge to her typical aroma.

The shadow slipped out, looking at the opposite end of the hall first—a dead end. Then she turned her face toward me.

Her expression made me salivate. Those blue eyes narrowed at the sight of me. A flash of horror graced those delicate features before her mind was lost in calculation, putting up an impressive facade to hide the terror that lingered under her skin.

What will you do now that you've been caught on your own terms? You started it this time. You will have to forgive me for what I do next.

The low chorusing vibrated from my throat and deepened in my chest cavity as it became hungrier, *coveting*.

Instead of panicking, she stood straight and moved to the middle of the hallway, fully in view.

There is no use in hiding. What is next?

She stood there, her eyes scrutinizing me from head to toe, assessing her options. There were none—not many at least.

Removing my hand from my pocket, I checked the timepiece on my wrist. I was not particularly curious about the time, but I was sure it was like an eternity for her. Every moment that I did not move or speak, I could feel the trepidation festering inside her, even if she refused to show me. I would grant her five more minutes, and then I would force it out of her.

"Three twenty-six," she said.

I glanced in her direction.

"The time," she clarified.

"I gathered."

"How many more minutes before you move?"

"I thought it was clear that I was waiting on you. This is your game, dear."

"Don't call me that."

"Darling?"

"No."

"Stubborn thing." I clicked my tongue at her, tucking my hand back into the pocket of my trousers. "What will it be?"

During our banter, she had let her hair down, which only meant one beautiful thing: *needles*.

She pushed through one of the doors. I assumed that she

would try her luck at going around through the connecting rooms.

She was slippery, but I was faster.

I kicked open the third door, hitting her with it before she could exit, and she fell back.

"I'm tired of this game." I stepped toward the weak body on the floor. She clutched that same needle in her hand. It made me feel all nostalgic when I remembered the tingle of the poison inside of it.

"Don't lie. You love games," she sneered.

"Of course, but I would rather you think it through more meticulously next time." I smiled, stepping closer.

She scurried back, but I stepped down on her skirt and leaned over her.

"Let's play a new game, my choice this time."

She kicked out a boot, and I grasped her by the ankle.

She swung her arm and buried the needle in my calf.

I twisted the ankle sharply inward. The yelp that came from her just exhilarated me more, edging me further.

"I think it's time we had a drink together. You like drinking, don't you?" I yanked the needle from my leg and tossed it away.

She did not answer, her shoulders tense.

"I will take that as a yes." I grinned, then dragged her harshly across the floor by her ankle.

"No!" She thrashed and kicked. There were pitiful attempts at grabbing furniture, hallway corners, doorframes, anything she could. She even grasped at the rug, her nails leaving trails of disturbed fibers all the way to my study.

"Unhand me!" she shouted. "I'll scream!"

"This isn't your town house. The only one you'll be screaming for is *me*." I dragged her through the large double doors. There was a tall arched window behind an intricate executive desk, books covering the walls. Overall, it was a standard study—not that I used it for anything.

Today, though, it would be of great use.

I shoved her in front of the desk but left the doors open—an escape route, just out of reach.

She winced, glaring at me with fire that could have only come directly from the Phlegethon itself.

"Relax. It's just a drink," I said innocently, moving to the corner to fill two glasses. Whatever she spiked my decanter with had no scent, but I was sure she would tell me what it was with a little pressure. I returned to her, leaning on the front of the desk. She did not move from her spot on the floor.

How obedient.

I brought my own glass to my lips, parting them as I breathed in the burning scent. I snapped a side-eye at her. "You know, you should have the first drink. It's only polite that a guest enjoy anything first."

I lowered a glass to her, but she shook her head.

"Alina Lis is refusing a drink? Now I know that something must be terribly wrong." I gave her a look of faux concern.

"I prefer a different mood for drinking."

"Tell me, Alina, did you tamper with my bourbon?"

"No."

"*Alina,*" I warned, "don't lie to me."

"I'm insulted that you assume the worst," she replied playfully.

I leaned forward, towering over her delicate frame. "Are you willing to give me your word?"

"I give you my word."

"And what do you swear on?"

"God."

"No, it has to be something you care about." I cocked my head curiously. "How about your life?"

Her lips pressed into a fine line.

I have you now.

"Let's test this theory." My grin widened. I tipped my head back and let the poisoned liquor flood my mouth. I swished the liquid to gather the taste. Then I peered down at her.

Her eyes softened, watching with an unmistakable vivacity that she had shown many times before. An expression of hope, even if she had not meant it to be read in such a way. That glimmer of curiosity was always brighter than her facade, possibly the only honest thing about her.

I grabbed her by the face. The pads of my fingers pressed into her cheeks, forcing her mouth open as her hands gripped my wrist, digging her nails into my skin. I squeezed tighter to force her jaw to open wider for me.

I spat the liquid directly in her mouth, pressing my hand over her mouth before any more could spill from the sides of her lips. "Now swallow," I said, leaning closer, my voice lowered.

Warm breath quickened through her nose as it fanned over my hand.

Her eyes grew pink as the tears welled up. I would like to pretend that it was from fear, but I knew that it was because the alcohol was burning her mouth the more she held it in.

"What? It's not poison, correct? Why all the fuss?" I asked her, removing my hand slowly from her mouth.

She held it in on her own.

Genuinely, I wondered what she would do. Would she end it here or subject herself to more of my torture?

After another moment, she opened her mouth and spit out the liquor, gagging slightly as it soaked the front of her skirt and shirt. She spat several times on the floor, attempting to rid her mouth of the numb feeling.

"That's what I thought." I sighed, circling her.

Her white blouse became more transparent, allowing a small, damp window to view her breasts, pushed tightly against her by her corset. It was a shame she wore anything underneath at all.

"What do I do with you, hmm?" I asked. "How about another game? I'll give you a second chance to take control of this mess you have made."

"No more games."

"That's not up to you anymore." I hummed, ideas swarming from the depths of my imagination. "Get up."

CHAPTER FIFTEEN

THE POISONER

His eyes held something sinister. An idea danced behind those devilish eyes.

I slowly rose to my feet.

"Elbows and palms on the desk," the Creature crooned, tipping his head toward the desk.

"Why would I do that?"

"Don't you want a way out?"

A breath came out shakier than I would have liked, but I forced my body to comply. I bent over the desk, my elbows and palms pressing against the dark wood. I could only focus on the intricate details carved into the surface.

The wet fabric clung to my chest and thighs, reminding me how sticky and cold I was. The cuts and scrapes tingled against the liquor-soaked fabric.

My legs wavered. It could have been from anticipation, or maybe it was from the high of the chase. I would have described it as anything except fear, though that certainly played a part.

He stepped to the other side of the desk.

"If you lift a single elbow or palm," he started, tucking some hair behind my ear, "I will kill you. Do you understand me?"

"How do I win?" I glared, my palms trembling against the desk.

"The prize is that you get to choose when you die, and I will make it quick, a kindness not afforded to many," he said sweetly. "Remember, palms and elbows." He tapped the wood of the desk twice before turning on his heel.

He left me there.

Bent over his desk.

Shivering and alone.

THE NIGHT CREPT by like a slug across a block of salt.

Slowly, the morning light loomed over me in a blanket of light. I gave up on holding myself up. It would not be so bad if I just laid my head on the desk. With heavy eyelids, I finally allowed myself some rest as the fear of the demon somewhere in the house faded from my mind.

"Good morning," a low voice whispered in my ear. Silas's voice sounded like it was still waking up. It echoed in my head as he spoke to me. My eyes did not open until his hands were placed on my hips.

"What are you doing?" I tilted my head to peer over my shoulder.

"I'm being polite. Do you not say good morning?"

"You know very well what I am speaking of."

"Oh." I could hear the smugness in his tone. "Do you mean this?" His hands moved lower, reaching down to hike up my skirt.

"You filthy pest!" I gasped, squirming in place, but my heart leaped when I realized I had almost moved my arms from the desk. I glared over my shoulder. "You're cheating again."

"If I remember correctly, there was only one rule." He leaned over me and pressed his chest against my back. He moved his hand between my thighs, gently playing with the hem of one of my stockings.

I wanted to clench my fists, but that would mean moving my palms. He was toying with me, hoping I would move.

He would not dare do anything. He could fondle me all he wanted, but I was not moving

His fingers moved higher on my thigh. The touches reached the opening in my underclothes, leaving soft traces along the sensitive skin.

I flinched, but I did not move from my place.

"Am I making you nervous?" he asked, breathing deep as he buried his face in my hair.

"I'm not nervous," I croaked tiredly.

His other hand gathered the hair at the back of my head, pulling my head back so he could reach my ear. "Oh, my dearest Alina...I want to do such terrible, sickening things to you. I hope you know that."

His hot breath tickled my earlobe as that bizarre tongue reached out, extending so that he could lick my cheek, probably to taste the sticky bourbon left over from the night before.

"I do not fear you."

"*Liar*," he whispered. "You're practically vibrating beneath me."

"I'm cold. You wasted perfectly good liquor."

"You did that on your own when you spat it out. You should have swallowed. Then you wouldn't be in this position." He sucked softly on my neck. "I wonder what you will taste like after marinating in fear. How much longer will you make me wait, you cruel thing?"

"An eternity—whatever that means for you."

"Very well." He sighed, releasing me and backing away. The Creature returned to my field of vision when he reached the other side of his desk, leaning back in the leather upholstered chair. The light from the window behind made him look like a vision from heaven, though I knew better than to trust a pretty halo. His head rested in his palm as he observed me silently, exactly like he did when he caught me in the tub. He wanted to watch me squirm, but I wouldn't allow him the pleasure this time.

I simply laid my head back on the desk, closing my eyes for more rest. He would have to rip me off the desk if he wanted me to move. Patience was something of a virtue of mine. It was only a matter of how much he had left.

CHAPTER SIXTEEN

THE CREATURE

I had never met such a stubborn woman.
Leaning on the doorframe, I tapped my foot against the floor as I checked my watch. She had been in that same position for at least twelve hours. Despite her depressing and grim attitude, I feared that she might actually want to live this time.

This was all wrong. She was not cooperating with how things were supposed to go. Why could she not play the games as intended from the beginning? It would never have gotten this far.

For some reason, when I threatened to kill her hours ago, it did not taste right in my mouth, leaving the words sour on my tongue.

When I imagined my hands squeezing the life from her, pulling her flesh between my teeth and relieving it from her bones, it did not bring me the pleasure I originally anticipated. It left me numb. I felt nothing, no matter how I imagined it.

I was beginning to realize that my obsession with her was not due to *that* kind of hunger. Her liveliness, stubbornness, sharp tongue, and wit was what I craved. Her disregard for risk, the way she pursued me back, our morbid flirtation back and forth was what I looked forward to the most. No matter how good she might taste, I could not have that sort of fun with a corpse.

As I stared at her from the entryway, she was no longer standing, just lying on the desk, knees buckled. I supposed I never said anything about her having to stand.

I approached her at the desk, tilting my head to see her face. She had a peaceful expression, like a cemetery statue. I must have worn her out if she was comfortable resting in this state.

I leaned in, resting my forehead against her head as I breathed in. It did not matter that she smelled like a drunk tossed out of the tavern in the early morning. It was amusing, comical considering her own habits. As I retreated, something else tainted her scent.

I narrowed my eyes at her, leaning back to look at the floor. The vermilion rug had changed color. There was a darker red patch under her boots. I could have mistaken it for a shadow if I was not close enough to see what it really was.

She'd pissed herself.

That brat.

"Alina!" I shouted.

She flinched awake. Her pupils tightened when they landed on me, making her eyes impossibly blue against the red of her tired eyes. "Yes?" Her voice cracked.

"Get out."

"No."

"Game is over. Just go."

She did not seem convinced, raising her brow at me.

"I mean it. My appetite is gone," I growled, walking away from the study and to the service door. I opened the latch with a loud click and flung it open. I waited, but she still did not come.

"*Alina!*" I shouted again. "Before I change my mind!"

Still no response.

"For the love of all things horrid," I grumbled, storming back down the hall, but she was gone by the time I returned.

Then I heard the service door slam shut down the hallway.

That little minx.

CHAPTER SEVENTEEN
THE POISONER

I was not superstitious.

Upon my father's grave, small flowers grew.

They say that if you were a good person, flowers would bloom on your grave. If you were a bad person, there would only be weeds.

I still believed it was a tale that people told themselves to make them feel better.

My body ached like no other. I was falling apart at the seams. My body had old and new bruises and scratches from my many encounters with that animal of a man. On top of the physical ache, my muscles strained from sleeping so long bent over a desk and not moving an inch for hours upon hours. It was still unbelievable to me that I'd escaped with my life by being too odd or too much of a nuisance on several occasions.

I knelt before my father's grave. Even his headstone was as intimidating and imposing as he was. It was a tall, dark carved stone of something like granite. His death mask was placed in the middle. Though even at "rest," he was stern and focused. I learned just how permanent those creases in his face were after he was laid to rest. It was a shame that he was not buried next to Mother, but they disagreed on where they wanted their final resting places to be.

Jacek Aleksander Lis
April 1845–January 1889
"It's better to have a sparrow in one's hand than a dove on the roof."

It was his favorite saying. A frequent phrase he used to repeat to me, enough that I could hear it in his voice as I read it. It was often relevant to my ambitions. He constantly warned against taking on more than I could, critiquing my ideas for being too grand, vague, and unachievable.

"I'm sure you're thrilled to see me, isn't that right, Father?" I winced, as if he would answer. I knew he would be disappointed in me if he saw me now. It had been over a year since I saw him at the funeral before hiding away in the countryside. "My delay will be worth it. A lot has happened since I arrived."

We—I—spent the next hour talking, just out in the open. He was the only person I could tell everything to, as the dead rarely passed judgment. It was therapeutic, but a bit pathetic on my end. The deceased were the only ones who would understand my troubles.

"Phoebe and I are still friends. I'm in the old town house now. I've collected a few more friends—maybe an enemy or two. You always said those go hand in hand. A natural balance, though I don't know what I did to deserve this one." I laughed, picking at my red fingertips. "Before you ask, no husband yet."

I took a deep breath, my throat clenching from restraining the grief.

"I've discovered something," I started to say, plucking a flower from the grave and twisting the stem between my fingers. "I think I can study them. Make something good out of it. A new creature. He's…fascinating. Something I've never seen before." I gulped, my eyes stinging. "I wish you were here to help me. I don't know if I can do this on my own. When you left, it was like my Library of Alexandria burning. I don't know what I don't know. It's like the more I learn, the less I know. I hate it," I mumbled, tilting my head back to beg the tears to go away and to reabsorb into my eye sockets. The overcast screen of clouds hung low above us.

Thick drops of rain started to plummet from the gray expanse. First, a few, then many. Before I knew it, the water would soak me. It was an unusual rain, heavier drops than usual. Another tall tale would say that meant death was near as well. I supposed death would always be near, my closest companion. The stray cat that purred against my door, knowing me as a reliable source of food.

My knees ached from sitting for so long when I finally rose to my feet. The blood returned to my legs in a tingling rush.

"Let us do this again, on a happier day," I said, tossing the flower back onto the bed of foliage.

The rain reminded me how cold it was getting already. Autumn was ending quickly. Even in my black attire, there was no stopping the cold from penetrating my bones, my mind, my perpetual state of being.

Walking through the foggy path, I saw a few magpies settling in and a cat or two running through the graves for cover. The fog danced in their wake, curling and disappearing into the air.

There must be a storm coming if even the crows had nothing to say.

Aside from the rain, the cemetery was a forbidding type of beauty. Centuries of secrets tucked away under the ivy-ridden floor, forever to be kept in their crypts. This cemetery enjoyed the cover of trees, like an arboretum of sorts. In life, my father would forage here, since there were not many places to do so that were close to the city like this.

The statues stood tall, looking down on me with pity as I passed. The angels' eyes were always a bit stern, despite their elegant forms. They were judging me, looking down on me. That was why some of my favorite statues in the cemetery were those of dogs, horses, and one sleeping lady basking on top of a tomb.

As I passed a dark footpath, low, harmonizing clicks penetrated the thick fog. The thin air allowed the sound to travel like the light flashing across the sky.

Not now.

Moving down the footpath and through a covered bridge in the cemetery, I hid underneath the ivy that hung in front of the forgotten catacombs. Thunder rumbled across the sky, giving a low vibration to the walls. The trees outside began to thrash, picking up their pace as they smacked together in a chorus of cracking, smacking, and swishing.

If there was more clicking, I would not hear it between the sounds of brewing weather, but I did not wait to find out. Under the bridge, a path of catacombs opened up, a cedar tree growing from the top of the structure in the middle. It was a circular sunken path that went all the way around the tree, lined with many doors to private tombs and stairs to the upper level, dividing the circular structure into quarters.

Tall sprigs of spiny bear's-breech grew along the path,

neglected by the groundskeeper. It was a tall plant with small fruits, something resembling olives placed neatly up the spine. The leaf edges bowed into tight spikes.

I ripped one out of the ground, pricking my hands in the process. I did not bring anything sharp, so this would do just fine in a pinch.

Footsteps echoed from under the bridge, so I ran up the stairs to get to higher ground, ignoring the cold air that bit at my skin and the chafing of my damp mourning gown.

I peered from above, crouching low, watching that blond Creature move into view. Another set of clicks could be heard as he walked underneath me. He kicked the wall in frustration, muttering and running his hand through his wet hair.

As I leaned on the edge of the higher ground, some dirt crumbled from the edge and landed on his shoulder.

His head snapped up, and we both froze for a moment. Like we were holding pistols to each other's heads. We were both still. A snap of lightning lit up the sky, and his eyes flashed their reflection back at me, a perfect analogy of how intense his stare truly was.

The stalemate was broken when he moved quickly for the stairs.

I stumbled back and ran toward the tall, house-like tombs littered through the cemetery like a miniature town. The sealed doors gave no leeway as I tugged on each handle, desperate to find one left unlocked. I ran through the headstones, jumping from bed to bed as he neared in my peripheral vision. I climbed on top of the mossy sarcophaguses, ascending higher up the steep hill before reaching the next landing.

I stopped at a crossroads. My throat burned from exhaustion, my pause granting me little relief in the panic. The crowd of imposing statues surrounded me like a jury, and my executioner was close behind. Pieces of wet hair slapped against my face as I turned, glancing at each of the paths. There was no road that seemed better than the next, all equally dark and unknown, as the rain muddled everything in the shadows into one.

Only then did a flash of lightning clue me into which path *not* to take. The light illuminated a tall figure in the middle, approaching with a calculated steadiness that could only have come from something truly cold-blooded, ready for the kill.

The path I chose did not matter, as long as it was not his.

I cut across the stretch of graves. Small, humble headstones were kicked over as I hastily ran without regard for the disturbed souls beneath my boots.

I lost sight of him, but as I approached a large tomb, two clasped hands carved above the frame of the doorway read, *We shall meet again.* My hands met the doors for only a moment.

My body was jolted forward, crashing through the doors, and strong arms wrestled with me on the floor. I grabbed both ends of the bristly plant and pushed the sharp weed up against his throat, keeping him far enough away where he could not bite.

He hissed at me, baring his fangs with such violence and anger. It made me realize how his threats to kill me could very well be honest, and he would not break a sweat. This was a predator through and through. I had no reason to expect anything human from him. I would be a fool if I did.

I used all of my strength to push the thorny shrub against him. Black blood began to trickle from his skin as he pushed harder against it. I brought my knees up and kicked outward, shoving him back to allow me to stand again, but his persistence knew no limit.

The thorny stalk slashed across his face when I swung, cutting his skin, but it did little to faze him.

His eyes were blackened and narrowed at me as he lunged again, grabbing me by the neck and forcing me backward.

The back of my knees hit the edge of the stone sarcophagus, and he slammed me down against it, my head hitting the stone as I went down. The wind was knocked out of my lungs from the sheer force.

I dug my nails into his wrist, gasping for air. My heart banged against my ribs, threatening to make its own escape if I was not going to be able to run. His grip tightened, pinning me to the slab below.

I tried to raise my knee again, but he kicked my legs apart, firmly placing himself between them.

"Let go!" I tried to shout, but his grip was cutting off my voice.

Then he tugged my dress up with his free hand, yanking my leg over his shoulder.

"*No!*" I screamed. My eyes widened, and I fought against him, grabbing at anything I could. Tears welled in my eyes. This was the first time I found it within myself to be terrified of him. There was nothing I could do. He would do it, and I would be too weak to stop him.

He slid his hand higher up on my neck by my jaw, forcing my neck to extend, opening me up to his mercy. He was close enough that I could see his fangs twitch at the sight of my pulsing neck. He was shaking like a rabid animal, ready to tear through whatever he could catch.

"*Silas!*" My plea came out as some sort of cross between a scream and a sob, unable to decide if I wanted to die fighting or frightened.

He paused, his quaking body hovering above me, eyes fixated on my neck. His wet hair left waterdrops on my face, mixing with the fresh tears.

It was like hearing me cry his name snapped something in him, but he could not decide how he felt about it. The look on his face was harrowing. He was livid, frustrated, or conflicted—whatever it might be, he was not going to tolerate me any longer.

"Say it again."

"S-Silas…" I swallowed hard, a lump forming in my throat.

"Not like that." His voice shook.

"Please don't—" I squirmed. Hot tears stained my face and pooled in my ears, but I kept a stern expression as long as possible.

He moved close, our noses almost touching. It was like he was looking at an enigma, not recognizing me in this state.

"Again," he said, his voice low.

"*I hate you.*" My voice cracked, and my throat was starting to ache from anxiety and the pressure of his fingers.

"Again," he demanded, burying his face in the crook of my neck, pressing his hips tighter between my legs and letting his long, needlelike teeth brush against my skin.

"*Silas,*" I choked out, "*I'm not ready—please.*"

This is the end, isn't it?

His head tapped against the stone next to my head in annoyance.

"I can't do this," he breathed, letting my leg slide off his shoulder.

He leaned back, studying my pitiful state. When he released my neck, the blood rushed back to my head, and I groaned, relieved to finally breathe in the damp air. I closed my eyes and coughed. The rush of fresh air irritated my throat as I greedily tried to suck in anything I could. I waited for whatever came next, but alas, the other shoe never fell. The presence against me vanished, and the air became lighter in its absence.

When my eyes opened, I only saw an empty tomb. The metal double doors slapped lazily together as the gloomy tantrum of weather continued, unaware of the commotion under it, not one blond devil in sight.

CHAPTER EIGHTEEN
THE POISONER

"I overslept. No, Phoebe, please calm down. I just drank too much. I wasn't feeling well. I promise everything's fine!" I pleaded with her, clutching the telephone tight as I leaned against the wall.

"Don't lie to me! I called and called until I realized you weren't even home!" she cried. "I was going to file a police report when I didn't hear from you!"

"Phoebe, it's all right. I'm telling you I am fine. I was visiting someone, it took entirely too long. Then yesterday I went to see my father. I just lost track of time."

She took a shaky breath, but took no relief when I mentioned I had company. The tension hung between us even through the phone.

"You can come over if you'd like? I could use some advice on something," I offered.

"Advice? On what?" Her interest was piqued.

"I...um." I paused for a minute. "I ran out of clothes to wear."

"I will be there in thirty." She wasted no time, hanging up the phone with a click. It did not take much to convince Phoebe to visit, *especially* if clothing was involved.

I leaned my head against the wall next to the phone, letting out a long, exasperated sigh. Today would be long. I could feel it.

Most of the morning was spent scrubbing my skin, not just because of how disgusting I felt but because the poisoned scotch from that night had formed a pink rash that appeared the next day. I slipped on the lightest, least itchy dress I could find, one of Phoebe's silk tea dresses that she'd left behind at some point. The soft texture soothed my irritated skin. It was like a friction burn over the front of my body.

My plan did not just fail, it blew back in my face faster than poorly packed gunpowder. He didn't have to do much, as the humiliation was all due to my lack of foresight. He found me too quickly. He must have watched me climb inside his house, possibly watching me poison his decanter as well.

How amateur.

He was livid when he told me to leave. It made me smile, knowing I was at least a nuisance to him. He might have caught me, but I won. I was still *alive.*

My smile faltered as I realized he would probably be coming for me soon. He certainly seemed determined previously in the cemetery. Why he did not end me there was my only question. It was possible that he would not be so playful when he returned. It was a good thing Phoebe was coming over. I should suggest that she stay the night.

The ringing of the doorbell made me flinch.

That was quick. I swore she just hung up!

I swung the door open to see a tall figure holding a few stacks of books and a satchel.

My sweet Viktor, how terrible your timing is.

"I thought it was best to deliver directly, as they are loans, but then I couldn't decide which ones, so I brought them all. Bound and loose-leaf." Viktor peered shyly over the rim of his thin glasses. "I'm sorry—I should have telephoned you, but I regrettably did not grab your calling card."

"No! No, it's perfectly fine. Please come in," I said quickly, glancing behind him for any more unexpected visitors. Thankfully, none.

"It is bigger on the inside," he commented, balancing the books in his arms and looking up at the circular window above the staircase.

"It is not mine," I said, locking the door behind him. "I'm just occupying a friend's spare."

"You are friends with people who have *spare* homes? Like extra carriage wheels lying around?" he teased.

"I know, it all sounds quite frivolous when I say it like that." I scratched at the irritated skin of my palms. "Let me take some of those off your hands. Come." I slid some of the books into my arms, beckoning him toward the living room.

The living room walls were lined with bookshelves, and a rolling ladder rested in the corner so that I could reach the top shelves.

"On the tea table, if you would," I instructed, sitting down with the books as I inspected the spines for their titles and volume numbers.

"I assume that the books don't belong to your friend either?"

"No, this is my collection. Most of it passed down from my father," I said, not taking my eyes off the papers until he sat next to me on the love seat.

He reached into his satchel, pulling out three unbound papers a few inches thick.

I gleamed when he handed them to me. Carefully, I read

through the titles. All of which were writings in current botany journals detailing new flora, guides, and other chemistry involving natural toxins. The only gift that could come close to this would be three dozen oranges.

"Will these be fine?" he asked, looking over to see which one I was flipping through.

"These are *perfect.*" My excitement radiated, and I wrapped my arms around his neck, squeezing him in a tight hug. "Thank you, Viktor."

His hands hesitated, reaching out and hovering above my waist, before he allowed them to wrap around me and return the gesture.

The front door lock clicked, the door flinging open.

"So I have a few options, but I couldn't find many colors that you wouldn't gag upon seeing—" The fluttery redhead let herself in with the spare key, glancing over at us from the foyer and peering into the living room. "Oh—am I interrupting?" She wiggled her eyebrows suggestively at me.

"No—No, Phoebe." I blushed and let go of Viktor, smoothing my skirt before rising from my seat. "This is Viktor! The one I met at the botanical gardens—"

"Yes, of course! I wouldn't assume that it was any other Viktor." Phoebe laughed and reached out her hand. "Phoebe Aston, pleasure to make your acquaintance."

He stood to meet her, and he made Phoebe look even shorter when he stood above her, taking her hand and shaking it. "Pleasure is all mine—if you ever are looking for locations for events, I have a few connections among the museum curators if you're interested!"

"Of course I am! Here—take my calling card." She shuffled around in her clutch before handing over a blush-pink card with her name and number.

He nodded and took the card, slipping it into his jacket pocket before lightly patting it. "I will ring you with anything I find."

Phoebe peered past him to look at me, raising her brow. "You must be desperately low on clothing options if you wore *white* for once."

"I can leave you two be—it seems like a very important matter." Viktor rubbed the back of his head.

"No! Stay!" I smiled. "The more the merrier! I've had such a long few days. It's nice to have company," I said, though I wouldn't admit that it was because I was afraid. I needed witnesses. My Creature only bothered me when I was alone, rarely showing up with others present. He could be here already, waiting for them to leave.

"I BURNED THE COFFEE. I hope you like it black," I slurred, wobbling over to Viktor as I set the cup on the table.

Clothing was scattered across the chairs, the couch backings, and in a disheveled pile on the floor as a result of all three of us deciding to drink and critique Phoebe's curation.

"You made it exactly how I like it! I prefer it more burned actually!" Viktor's accent thickened when he was drunk. He guided the cup's rim to his mouth, drinking the coffee with ease. He smacked his lips mockingly. "Delicious! Don't worry, it adds more flavor."

Viktor had convinced us to drink vodka rather than dark liquor tonight. He was fairing just fine, but Phoebe and I were pink in the cheeks, giggling like schoolgirls as we aimlessly picked through clothes.

I laughed at him as I walked over to Phoebe, who held up another dress.

"What about this one?"

"Viktor, is blue a yes or no?" I asked, turning toward him as I held the dress up to my body.

"Any color would look just fine." He sighed, leaning back as he reclined on the love seat, though his legs were too long and hung off the arm.

"That's not true," Phoebe scolded. "Nobody looks good in orange."

I rolled my eyes and handed the dress back to her.

When I turned, the darkness of the foyer was ever imposing. It was endless, expanding on forever if I did not let my eyes adjust.

That was when I saw him—that unmistakable outline of a body by the kitchen window across the hall. I was right about him not interacting when people were over, but now that I knew he was here, I could not let anyone leave.

I was still angry with my Creature.

"Let me see that one." I pointed lazily at a red dress.

"Red? Are you sure?" Phoebe mumbled.

"Why not? I'm feeling a little adventurous," I joked. "Viktor?"

Upon hearing his name, he sat up like a puppy, standing at attention.

Viktor watched curiously, that same wonder in his gaze, like how he'd looked at the plants in the garden. He was holding *me* in the same regard. It was a new feeling, knowing that two men were looking at me like that, though I was sure I would be getting grief about it later from one in particular.

Phoebe held the red dress against my skin, trying to see how it would look before deciding if she should let me try it on.

"What do you think of red?" I asked Viktor.

He kept his eyes on mine, not even bothering to look at the dress. "Nothing could compare," he said simply.

"You didn't look."

"I don't have to." He grinned.

"Cheeky." I flicked a brow at him and glanced behind me, the familiar specter displaced from the spot he was before. A victorious smile spread as I turned back to Viktor and Phoebe. "You both should stay here tonight. I fear I have developed a habit of injury when I'm inebriated."

"It is amusing that you thought I wasn't going to stay with or without your permission." Phoebe laughed, gathering my previous dress and handing it to me.

"Shall I let you two go, then?" Viktor asked.

"No, you'll sleep here too. Besides, who else will carry me up all those stairs? Surely not Phoebe," I joked.

"I'm afraid that would be improper, but I know that Phoebe is stronger than she looks. I am sure she could do it easily." He laughed, standing from the couch and stretching. "I will see myself out—but I will telephone you in the morning to see how the hangover is faring."

I did not remember him leaving, but I remembered Phoebe closing the door behind him. Then the two of us stumbled up to the third floor to my bedroom.

I rolled onto the bed in my dizzy state.

Phoebe tugged the sheets away and crawled in with me.

"So?" Phoebe hummed, rolling onto her stomach beside me in bed. "Keeping that one around?"

"Maybe." I rolled my eyes at her. "I haven't decided yet."

"What makes you hesitate?"

I shrugged. "It wouldn't be fair. My attention is split."

Her grin faltered. "Who?"

"Nobody."

"Who is it, Alina?"

"No one."

"I surely hope that it is not a certain *S* name."

"It might be. What is it to you?" I lifted my head and turned over to face her on my side.

Her delicate brows knit together. "I don't want to see you hurt is all," she said as she touched my cheek gently, running her finger over my dark lashes before trailing over to the lighter ones.

"You have nothing to fuss about. I can handle any man that throws himself my way."

She smiled briefly before hugging me close, resting her head on my chest.

I paused, looking down at the redhead. It must be the emotions running high from the liquor. I hugged her back and rested my chin on her head.

My sweet Phoebe, you worry for me too much.

I COULD NOT SLEEP. My rash had begun to burn with every friction between the bedsheets. It was upsetting that I could not simply take off my skin and wash it like a soiled dress.

The only relief I could think of was to draw a bath again.

The water was like heaven. I sank lower until the suds were up to my chin. The way it lapped at my wounds and caressed me. Who needed comfort from another when you could just soak alone in the bath? The buzz in my head was pounding. I should have drunk more water in my pursuit of spirits.

My head rested against the side of the tub. I clutched the

edge and leaned my head against my arms, hiding my face as if to ground myself. Lying on my side, I curled up against the rim of the basin. The remaining light from my candle strained my eyes despite it being but a small glimmer.

I must have dozed off, floating in and out of sleep as my nauseous state threatened to make me lurch every now and then.

A hand gathered my hair away from my face. I made another gagging sound and groaned. Phoebe must have heard me.

"I am fine… Go back to sleep. I am fine, just…" I curled my knees closer again, trying to breathe deeply as I kept my eyes closed.

Deep breath. You're not going to get sick. You're fine, I chanted to myself.

Calming fingers brushed through my hair, dragging gently along my scalp as my hair was gathered back and laid over the edge of the basin, out of the water in case I *did* get sick.

"Please go. I don't need you getting sick as well if my afternoon drink makes a reappearance. No more vodka for us," I whimpered, my forehead still against the cool surface of the tub. "Hmm…that's nice," I whispered. Relaxing at the touch, I leaned into the palm that caressed my scalp. Having my hair played with was one of my favorite feelings.

Then the tingling on my scalp stopped, and my hair was set back down.

The sound of retreating footsteps was followed by the deafening scent of smoke and metal. It hit my senses like a crop on a horse's hindquarters.

My eyes snapped open, and no one was there, but the smell remained.

I slowly turned. The water in the basin was a thick, opaque crimson.

Hesitantly, I lifted my gaze. A girl was slumped over the opposite end of the tub. Her sticky hair clung to the side of her lowered face and stuck to the side of the tub as she hung loosely over the rim, her arms extended down into the water. Between her arms, a wet piece of paper was stuck to the porcelain, right below her bleeding neck.

The ink was blotched and runny from the dampness, expanding in the paper fibers like veins.

Red does look good on you.
—S

I swallowed hard, unable to focus on anything else aside from the words bleeding together on the pulp of the paper before they became illegible blobs.

An eerie chittering sound echoed through the house, calling out for me in the darkness, though it was rhetorical, not expecting me to answer the call.

CHAPTER NINETEEN

THE POISONER

C *hop.*
     I swung the ax down, lodging it in the stump.

Unlike Phoebe, I did not feel the need to hire a full staff to keep up with the home. When the only occupant was myself, it was more embarrassing to have a staff. I did everything myself, which I was used to from my solitude. My father used to let me split a log or two while he showed me how to maintain our cottage in the countryside. I only needed to cut some smaller pieces for the woodstove, as the ones I'd bought were more fitting for the large mantle.

Another thing about not having a staff was that no one would question you when you had to add more peculiar duties to the list.

Chop!

I swung the ax down on the arm where the elbow was connected, splitting the limb.

He had never left me with an entire body before. Burying it

whole would be cumbersome. The appendages would find a home fertilizing my hydrangeas. However, I let the ravens take what they wanted from my pile before I laid them to rest in the soil.

The autumn air was cool against the sweat accumulated across the back of my neck and forehead.

There was a taut pinch in my abdomen, and I used the propped-up ax to lean on the hilt. Eve's curse had visited me a bit early this month, I suspected from the stress of having a *psychopath* on my heels. No wonder I was so bleary. The pain was getting worse when I was not in a consistent state of lukewarm discomfort, which was almost worse than brief bouts of pain in my womb.

After the splits were placed in the firewood box in the mudroom, I hoisted the ax over my shoulder as I trudged back inside. My boots were wet from the grass, leaving marks across the floor, but I was too lightheaded to fuss about it. The white blouse I wore was a mistake, as it was covered in scuffs of dirt at this point. Thank goodness my skirt was black. I did not need two stained garments. The labor for today was finished. Laundry would be an issue for a later time. My muscles ached for a warm bath, with no burden of extra work to pull me from my relaxed state.

Every step up the stairs made me feel like I was carrying some gravitas burden. I swore I heard my joints creak during the ascension. At the end of the second-floor hallway, a shadow at the opposite end insinuated that someone was waiting around the corner.

Today of all days?

He had some nerve showing up after that scene in his house, the tantrum in the cemetery, and leaving me a body to dispose of on my own. I would *not* allow him to disturb me in my limited time of peace.

With careful pursuit, I let the ax slide off my shoulder.

Thwap!

The blade smacked into the wood of the wall next to his head as I turned the corner.

His eyes were wide. I might have actually caught the elusive Creature off guard. He glanced at the ax and then back at my face. *Genuine* surprise.

"Marry me," he breathed.

"Get *out!*" I yelled, yanking the blade out of the wall and sending splinters scattering across the floor.

"Not when you flirt with me like that." He backed away a few feet before stopping, a taunting instigation.

I swung again, the weight of the ax too slow to catch him when he was attentive, missing him.

Another swing. He ducked before it could meet that smug face.

"Oh, you're really teasing me now." He grabbed the handle between us, headbutting me in the face.

The pain shot through my head, and I let go of the ax, stumbling backward and hitting my head on the floor.

When I looked up, he was hoisting the ax over his head, directly above me.

I shrank and covered my face.

Thud!

No pain followed the sound.

My arms slowly fell away, the ax buried in the floor to the left of me.

He was staring, waiting for me to realize he had not killed me.

"I can appreciate a good fight. You know, I thought you were only an underhanded type of woman. It's good to know that you can strike too." He stepped past and crouched beside my head. When he knelt down, he placed his hand on my forehead, wiping some blood from the cut he created when his head met mine.

"That was juvenile." I glared up at him.

He licked the blood off his finger. "Worth the headache." He moaned. "Silas, one. Alina, zed." He made a zero shape with his fingers.

THE NEXT DAY was no different.

I bounded down the hall, slipping on the edge of the rug before picking up my pace again.

Silas was not too far behind, his boots smacking against the creaking wood.

I snatched a metal-tipped pen when passing by a writing desk, the only item I could use as a weapon on such short notice. It was better than having to use my fists.

The heels of my walking shoes hit hard against the floor. It was too late to be quiet. We had passed the silent portion of our chase hours ago. This was the longest I had been able to elude him so far. I skipped several steps on the stairs to get down to the second floor.

Suddenly, there was a tight grip on my hair, pulling at my scalp.

Oh no—

Silas wrapped my braid around his palm and drew back hard.

I screamed as my back smacked into his chest.

"Silas, two. Alina, z—"

"One!" I shouted, and shanked the tip of the pen into his thigh, relieving the pressure from my scalp.

I was unsure if the following animalistic noise was from pain or arousal. I would rather not dwell on it.

Jumping down more steps and hopping over the railing, I made for the back door leading to the garden. I was halfway across the grass to the greenhouse before a force toppled me to the ground.

We rolled a few yards from the impact, tangling with each other. Scratching, biting, and gripping.

The only pause we had was when I stuck a small, rusty potting shovel against his neck.

The only thing he could do was keep me in place by straddling me.

Finally, a stalemate.

Our breaths could be seen in the afternoon air, mingling in a singular puff of vapor before it disappeared.

He was angry, but tired at least.

I was grateful for that, as I was suffering the same exhaustion from this waltz.

"When…will you admit…that I won't yield?" I breathed, my red fingers gripping the handle of the shovel, pushing it against his skin.

"You will," he exhaled wearily. As he caught his breath, he leaned back with his hands on his hips, looking down at me as if to decide where we would go from here. The overcast light made those cruel gray eyes look even brighter—more calculating.

I would be seeing those eyes every day that week, hoping the last time I saw them would be on a silver platter.

He shoved my chest into the wall of the hallway outside my room, kicking my legs apart with his boot.

"What we have here?" He pressed his hips against me, one hand firmly gripping the back of my neck.

He'd caught me while changing today.

I only had on a thin white petticoat skirt and a sleeveless corset cover. It was a little more exposed than I preferred, nowhere to hide anything sharp.

Silas lifted my skirt from behind, staring at the bare skin. He grabbed one half of my backside and squeezed.

I flinched at his touch. A hot dribble ran down my leg.

"Oh, I feel like I've just found gold at the end of a rainbow," he said sweetly. "Now this is making a bit more sense. Why didn't you tell me it was your *strawberry week*?" His words were childish, mocking.

Don't be such a child.

He let it fall down my leg, blending into the red Persian carpet as it met the floor.

"Ah, how inconsiderate of me to pursue you in this state!" his voice rang in my ear. "But first, if you want any relief, release that thing in your mouth," he demanded, holding his gloved hand out in front of my mouth.

I gave him a long, seething glare over my shoulder before slowly spitting a small glass vial into his palm.

"I knew there was something in there. It's not like you to refuse a good banter," he teased before pocketing the vial and removing his glove with his teeth.

"What are you doing?" I demanded, pushing my palms

against the wall, but his grip on the back of my neck held my cheek against the wallpaper.

"Being a gentleman, of course," he said low in my ear as he gathered the fabric of my skirt, exposing me in the front. The warmth of his fingers danced along my pelvic bone before cupping between my thighs.

"*No!* Stop that!" I fussed.

His index finger gently pushed against the entrance of my vagina.

My breath hitched, and I pushed back against his chest. This *animal* was touching me during the worst time. How could he possibly think this would make me feel better?

His finger slipped inside easily, lubricated by the fresh blood.

"Silas, *please* take it out," I pleaded, my body rigid from discomfort, both inside and out now.

He added a second finger and moved them tenderly inside, flexing against the swollen parts of me.

My body let out a sharp tremor, my head flinching back.

"There you go. Let me in," he whispered against my shoulder, gently gracing it with kisses while he stroked his fingers inside me.

I would never admit it, but it felt good—*really* good.

It was like the sore parts of myself were melting in his hand. While the idea was uncomfortable and unthinkable, the endorphins were doing wonders for the pain in my abdomen, like a release of tension that I was never sure how to deal with, if not with laudanum.

"*Disgusting.*" I couldn't disguise the gasp when he picked up his pace.

"You? Never," he said sweetly in my ear, his breath fanning across the back of my neck.

He quickened his pace. Everything inside me was so sensitive, like it was waiting for a release like this.

My head jolted back against his shoulder, and I let out a labored breath, unable to focus on whether I wanted to kill him or give in.

He stepped back, walking us backward until his back hit the opposite hallway wall. His other hand cupped my breast as he held me against him. He hit someplace deep inside that begged for more.

"*There*," I gasped, gripping his wrist as his fingers stroked against my insides.

"There?" he repeated, but he moved his fingers slower.

I groaned and scowled up at him.

His smug expression peered down at me before he turned his face into my hair, seemingly basking in my flustered state.

"Finish what you started," I warned, my nails digging into his hand as my hips rolled in his grip.

"If that is what the *princess* wants." He let out a soft chuckle.

He curled his fingers, the methodical strokes making that familiar knot grow tighter in the pit of my stomach, sure to hit that same spot I begged for.

Relief and pleasure dulled the throbbing pain little by little before I forgot it was even there in the first place. All I could focus on was his fingers inside me—the new ache that was forming.

As I got closer to what would be my sweet release, I bit my bottom lip, not willing to give him the satisfaction of any sounds that I would make as the orgasm rippled through my body.

A low vibration came from his chest as my body melted in his arms, before pulling his fingers out to inspect their scarlet coating.

"Does the point go to you or me? Is this a draw?" He hummed, licking his fingers clean.

"That is revolting." I grimaced, ignoring his question.

"Blood is blood." He smirked. "I will take anything you give me—*anything.*"

THIS GAME WAS BECOMING ARDUOUS. It consumed all my time and energy, day and night.

He'd corralled me to the attic this time.

I stood on the small balcony, knife in hand. It was the only thing I had not thrown at him that night.

His tall form appeared in the doorway of the attic entrance, and he lunged forward.

I held the knife up to my throat.

He practically skidded to a halt, dead in his tracks.

"What are you doing?"

"Ending this."

"You are bluffing."

"Am I?" I trailed the tip between my breasts, pressing against the skin to coax out a thin stream of blood.

"Stop—" He inched forward.

I MOVED BACKWARD, bumping against the short railing and faltering.

Strong arms pulled me roughly from the edge, holding me against him, though the tip of my knife was now under his chin, teasing the flesh of his neck.

"What was the score again?" I put pressure on the blade against his skin.

"Five–eight, your lead," he mumbled.

"Yield, or I will throw myself off the roof when you're not looking."

"I yield," he said quickly.

A satisfied smile curled at the corner of my lips.

"Will you put that down now?" He raised a brow, glancing at the knife.

I reluctantly pulled it away, but so did he.

"Have you had enough of the fighting? Shall we try something different?" he asked, leaning on the railing beside me and pulling out a flask.

"I am tired of you," I said simply, eyeing his flask as he took a swig.

"A celebratory gift?" He offered it to me.

He'd kept me busy enough all week that I did not have a moment to sleep, never mind drink. I took it from his hand and drank a few gulps before handing it back. All that excitement was making my abdomen cramp up again, like someone had punched it. I would have assumed that Silas was the cause, except he never hit me during our little games. Which was odd now that I thought about it. He only wanted to chase, catch, release, and repeat.

"You know, if you just gave in, I would be worshipping you right now instead of chasing you," he whispered in my ear. "Though it is rather exhilarating when you play hard to get."

"I am not playing," I said flatly. "I don't trust you. There is not one tender bone in your body. What makes you think I would ever entertain a sadist like you?"

"Not one bone?" he asked innocently. "You're a woman of

science. Doesn't it flatter you that something superior wants to have you?"

"Superior?" I challenged. "If I remember correctly, I won."

"Because I *let* you," he stated simply.

"Is that what that was at the cemetery? Letting me win? Or was that a surrender?"

He fell silent, his expression unfaltering, but I could see his body physically tense.

How interesting. Could I be witnessing remorse? I had truly seen it all if that was the case.

No. 15.

CHAPTER TWENTY

THE CREATURE

T oday, I found her in the greenhouse.
The gravel crunching under my shoes gave my position away outside the doorway.

"Silas, the greenhouse is glass. I can see you."

"I wasn't hiding."

I was hiding. I assumed that she was not paying attention. Turning the corner, I leaned casually against the doorframe of the entrance.

The greenhouse was small, but that did not stop her from putting as many plants as she could inside. It was an impressive collection, but I knew better than to get close to anything she kept around.

Alina was sitting in the corner of the bright glass room, a book clutched in those elegant fingers. Today, she wore white. It was less kept than her normal stuffy attire, showing off her lovely neck and that pale skin that flushed at the slightest temperature change. The light attire made her eyes flash an impossibly light blue, like I was looking into ice covering a lake, but even colder than that. I wished I had spent even the smallest amount of time as a painter to solidify this moment, as if no one would believe the sight of the specter before me.

She would make the most beautiful apparition, already haunting every corner of my mind.

Her nimble fingers flipped another page. In her mouth hung a cigarette, unlit.

"You know, the enjoyable part of smoking is lighting the cigarette." I approached cautiously, though she did not look to be in a running mood this morning. I was close enough to have caught her scent clearly without the adrenaline and blood clouding it.

She smells like black cherries and cyanide.

"I ran out of matches," she said simply, flipping a page.

"Is that why you don't seem in a rush to escape? You were banking on me having a light?"

"Yes." She used her mouth to tilt the cigarette up to me, not peeling those eyes from her book.

I reached into my pocket and pulled out my mechanical lighter, flicking the wheel to spark a flame.

She finally pulled her attention from her literature to lean in, puffing the cigarette as the tip cherried. It was easy to fall for those misleading lips—so soft, but hiding a sharp tongue like no other. My urge to rip her apart faded every day I pursued her, but I was sure her urge to dissect me and jar my insides grew in tandem.

As she pulled back, I dragged another chair out to sit at a safe distance, lighting my own coffin nail against the cool air.

The morning air nipped at my face in contrast with the bitter smoke. It was no wonder why she liked it out here. Birds fluttered about their waking hours, and the dew coated the greenhouse glass, giving a soft glow to the humble workspace.

I would bother her, but she was so bewitching like this—absorbed in herself, confident enough not to flee, but intelligent enough to have several weapons hidden on her person no doubt.

Against my higher urges, I chose to let her be, to admire her in the open for once.

CHAPTER TWENTY-ONE
THE POISONER

"This one looks like you." Viktor pointed at the piebald fox, taxidermized in a fierce stance with its jaws open wide. The specimen had a darker coat, with flecks of red peeking through the undercoat. Seemingly random splotches of white took over patches of the hide.

"And this one looks like you." I pointed to a four-eyed grub preserved in a jar of ethanol.

He frowned. "Well, I thought the fox was cute."

"Who said I didn't find the bug cute as well?" I gave him a mocking smile, continuing through the exhibit.

Viktor had asked if I wanted to see the temporary oddity exhibit that was traveling across Europe. I was impressed with the skillful articulations, though I was unsure if the exhibit was real, exotic and domestic animals with all their deformities and uniqueness proudly on display for our viewing pleasure.

My favorite was the two-headed calf. She was quite beautiful. They'd positioned her in a way that she would have looked upon birth, eyes closed and curled up. How peaceful she was. If I spoke above a whisper, I feared I would wake her.

Viktor found more interest in the wall of spines, organized by color. He was studying to be an orthopedist and was currently researching more about the human spine. How charming it was when his eyes lit up upon closer inspection of the vertebrae— brown, white, black, even green spines on display. I was almost afraid to ask where they got so many, but they claimed that they were left over from cadavers used for science and education. Whether I believed that answer or not, it did not matter. The bones were here regardless.

A long glass display caught my eye. There were three shelves, with skulls varying in shape, size, and features stacked neatly in a line. I eyed each of them until I reached a particularly odd piece.

The jaws were propped open, a long fang exposed, the other tucked against the roof of the mouth.

Maybe the displays *were* genuine after all.

"What have you found?" Viktor rested his chin on my shoulder to see it from my point of view.

My vision shifted from the skull to our reflection in the glass. I tipped my head, touching my temple to his. "Do you think it's real?" I asked.

"I don't know, though I wouldn't bet my last coin on it."

"Do you think something like that could exist?"

"There's not really much point in wondering."

"Humor me. How do you think an irregular human could live without being noticed?"

"Like many creatures, in plain sight perhaps." He glanced at my face instead of my reflection this time.

"Perhaps," I mumbled, moving away from him and the display to continue on.

The exhibit became less interesting the deeper I lost myself in thought. From what I had seen so far, it was possible to have a poison and a cure come from the same body. I only got a small, rather literal, taste of that at the botanical gardens. It gave me an idea, a terrible one, but I had two people to convince if I wanted it to work.

"Viktor, do you know anyone in phlebotomy?"

"I might. Why?"

"I may need some tools."

CHAPTER TWENTY-TWO

THE POISONER

A loud bang at the front door rattled through the house, bringing my consciousness abruptly back to earth. My groggy eyes peeled open, my vision struggling to clear.

"Who in God's name is even up this early?" I grumbled, kicking away my sheets and draping a robe around myself.

The sun had barely risen and fog clung to the windows as I descended to the foyer. By the time I grabbed hold of the cold metal doorknob, something was sticky under my feet. My face twisted in disgust at the consistency, and I stared down at the floor.

A pool of crimson slowly leaked from under the door. The red color crept up my nightgown and robe as it was absorbed into the fibers. The bile rose in my throat before it retreated after I took several deep breaths.

It took quite a bit of effort to pry the door open. For some reason, it was heavier than usual.

Peering out, my eyes landed on a body. A thick metal spike

was stuck through the head and pinned it to the wood of the door.

The body belonged to a short woman with frizzy blonde hair, maybe around thirty years old. Her pale eyes were decorated with a familiar green pigment.

My hand slapped over my mouth, and I shut the door. When I heaved my body weight against the door, my knees betrayed me and I slid into a crouched position behind the door.

I could not breathe. I would not breathe.

My chest was going to crush itself under the force of my asphyxiation. I told her not to bother with the poison if it was just going to end up like this!

The realization hit me like a hangover at dawn. While my tinctures had taken many lives, I had never actually seen the bodies that lay in the aftermath. Not often did I stick around to make sure my poisons worked, because there was no reason to doubt them in the first place. My work was secondhand most of the time, my poison floating around with whoever paid for it. Maybe that was my mistake, but it did not matter now. The only time I saw a corpse of my own making was an accident, and it was not nearly this gratuitous.

THE POLICE TOOK forty-five minutes to show up, at least thirty minutes too slow for my taste.

The police would not have been my first call, but I had no choice due to such a public display. If I tried to hide it, I would be lighting a fire underneath myself. Why would Silas break his pattern just to put me in the spotlight like this? He would surely find a knife in his chest the next time I saw him.

The morning was spent on endless questions by detectives and providing identifying information about who the body belonged to. No one would have identified her if not for me. The cautious exchanges of glances from the coroner's team made me feel uneasy, like they knew that this was my fault. Their accusing eyes scrutinized me as I answered.

You're being paranoid. Deep breath, deep breath.

I had to talk Phoebe off a metaphorical cliff when I explained the situation. She was so shaken that she would not let me take my own cab, insisting on sending her own. It would probably be outside the shop in an hour or two. I was to spend the next week at her place, just as a precaution.

Why would he put something like that on my doorstep? Did he want me to be in the spotlight? Or was it because I was not paying enough attention to him? It would not be a surprise if this was his childish response.

An innocent woman was murdered because I *failed* her, painting a target on my back with her blood.

Phoebe's place was no less grim than my town house or the shop. The day was hollow and dull as the hours crept away from me. They say time is a thief, but I say time, he is an escapologist. No matter how hard you tried to hold on to it, no matter how hard you tried to tether yourself, it would always slip right through your fingers.

My friend forced oranges and other pleasantries onto me to make me forget, but nothing could make me swallow the sour taste of my guilt. Despite what my friend might think, no amount of tart sweets could fill the void. A thick fog followed me that I could not wake up from. All I could see was the blood pooling under my feet. Scrubbing myself could not wipe away the shameful tar that stuck to my insides.

The sun rose and fell like any other day, and I returned to my creature habits of cuddling up with a cold glass of whatever was available. The warm embrace of liquor was the only thing that could settle my nerves.

The sharp trill of Phoebe's landline made my head pound. I leaned against the arm of the chair, massaging my temples, as Phoebe scurried to answer the phone.

"Did you find—" She paused as a voice spoke on the phone. "Why would I tell you that? She is— No—" Phoebe huffed and turned toward me, holding the phone to her chest. "Alina, it's for you."

My brows pinched as I rose from my chair, holding the glass close as I approached. I pressed the phone to my ear. "Hello?" I mumbled.

"*That* excited to hear my voice?" Silas laughed through the scratchy earpiece.

"Piss off." I hiccuped, my shoulders slumping forward as I turned my back to Phoebe. I could feel her eyeing me, even as she retreated to the living room to grant me some privacy. I knew my dearest friend well enough to know that she would be eavesdropping.

"Pleasant as ever," he remarked. "Why aren't you at your home? Hiding away, are we?"

"Hiding? You nailed a corpse to my door," I whispered as low as possible, my hand cupping the phone.

"Hmm...no, I think I would remember that. I'm actually quite upset that I didn't think to do that."

My limbs ran cold as I clutched the phone, my shaky hand clutching the phone became numb as I was sure every drop of blood in my body had pooled at my feet, and my heart threatened to drop through the floor from its heaviness. "Do you mean to tell me that it wasn't you?"

"No. Though with the rate you've been poisoning people, it doesn't surprise me in the slightest."

"Nobody knows that it is me."

"None that you know of. Your antics didn't work on me. I'm sure they have failed on others," he said, though his tone lacked concern. It sounded like he was insulting my skills. While it hurt to hear, it was unfortunately plausible. "Don't beat yourself up about it."

"I'm not. I am thinking," I mumbled, finishing off my drink.

"How about you come and pay me a visit?"

"It's midnight."

"That hasn't stopped you before."

"Is there a catch?"

"Why? Do you want there to be? I can make one up if that's what you'd like—"

"I'll meet you, but not for leisure. I have business to discuss with you."

"Business?"

"A proposal."

"Oh?" I could hear the smirk in his voice through the phone. "Consider me intrigued."

"No tricks," I warned, hanging up on him, slapping the phone against the receiver, and turning back to Phoebe. "I'll be back."

"You're going out? Why?" she asked, panic in her voice. "It is late. You should stay *here*."

"I have something to do. I'll be back before dawn."

"Alina." She grabbed my wrist. "What did he want?"

"Just a concerned citizen." I tugged my wrist away.

She followed me as I rushed over to the entryway, tossing on a jacket.

"*Alina*," she repeated, her fine brow twitching as her expression twisted into a worried pinch.

I raised my brow, waiting for another plea.

She stared away for a moment, just to avert her eyes. "Just… please be safe out there. All right?"

"When am I ever unsafe?" I grinned. "You worry too much. I will be back before you know it."

IT WAS unnatural to arrive at his front door, ringing the doorbell like any civilized person. No smoke and mirrors, no sheathed daggers, no traps. A simple, modest announcement of my arrival. Though it seemed he left the door open for me anyway.

The imposing wooden doors croaked as they were pushed open. Only a few remnants of light remained inside the dwelling, a few gas lamps along the walls, with the exception of the majority of the light coming from his study.

The doors closed softly behind me before I followed the long carpet of light leading to the room.

Even with such terrible memories of the office, I might have liked to stay here under different circumstances. His collection of books far surpassed my own, for which I harbored intense envy. It would take an eternity to read them all, and I would gladly confine myself to finish in a timely manner.

The Creature was nowhere to be found, but oddly enough there was no impression that I was not welcome. With the calmness of the scene came a small, pinching feeling of dread deep in the pit of my stomach. Fighting or fleeing was not something the body could turn off, and I was painfully aware that the plan was foolish, ill-fitted at best. But unique problems required modern solutions.

My fingers dragged over the spines of the books one by one. At least twenty layers of shelves must have climbed up to the high ceilings. It seemed unlikely that the top shelves were ever touched based on the thin layer of dust on the books at eye level.

Poetry filled the easiest-to-reach shelves. Some history, philosophy, and law texts were poised a little higher. Many appeared to be first editions, which made me want to cease touching them for fear of agitating the delicate bindings.

"If you don't make an attempt on my life tonight, maybe I will let you borrow one."

I glanced at Silas over my shoulder and gave him an unamused glare.

He leaned against the entryway, supposedly having been there for several minutes. His attire seemed relaxed, a few buttons undone on his shirt as well as his sleeves rolled up his forearms. Pushing off the wall, he approached the other end of the bookshelf, trailing a finger over a couple spines before plucking one book from its place. He began to walk toward me, examining the first few pages to make sure it was the book he was thinking of, then held it out to me. "I think you'd enjoy this one."

I threw him a suspicious stare before I took the book from his hand.

"*Fear and Trembling*," I read the title. "Is this a joke?"

"It is philosophy, so sometimes." He smirked. "You seem like an existentialist to me."

I peeled the book open, the pages fluttering as I flicked through. If this was some sort of cruel humor, I would not know. I snapped it shut and clocked the new decor on the floor before his desk.

"New rug?" I raised a brow.

"Yes." He grimaced, moving past me to his decanter. "I would offer you a drink, but I haven't finished your homemade concoction yet."

"Why didn't you dispose of it?"

He lifted a shoulder and poured himself a glass. "It has a nice tang to it. Bites back a little." He took a sip as he moved to his desk, sitting on the front of it as if to wait for what I really came for. Though his expression held some reservation. "You wore red," he commented.

He was right. A red pomegranate salve painted my lips. I had to keep myself from biting my lip. "Not for you."

"Then who?" There was a slight smugness to his tone.

"Myself," I said.

"If that is what you think, so be it." He shrugged. "Now, I am more interested in a certain proposal you mentioned earlier."

"Don't worry, it's a modest one." I reluctantly peeled myself away from the bookshelf and toward the middle of the room.

"I think I would need to hear it before agreeing to such a statement." He sipped the poison from his cup, those striking pale eyes stalking me over the rim of the glass.

I pressed my thumb into my other palm, fidgeting. Why was it so embarrassing to ask?

"You said you 'can't do this,'" I started. "In the cemetery."

"Did I?"

"Yes, it was the last thing you said to me that night."

"If you say so." He stared. "What of it?"

"You were going to eat me."

"I never said that."

"By the sight of your teeth twitching, I beg to differ." I stepped closer. "I'm not angry with you, not entirely. I assumed that it was something you couldn't help."

"Are you calling me an animal, Miss Lis?"

"I have worse names for you—but nevertheless," I continued, stopping in front of him, our eyes level with one another. "I'm prepared to offer you a deal."

A softer rendition of his predatory clicks emanated from him, but it sounded muffled, like he was trying to hide the fact that I had piqued his interest—or his appetite.

"I want to trade," I said firmly. "Your blood for mine."

"You want...*my* blood?"

"Yes, I want to study you," I said plainly.

"Why would I let you do that?"

"Because you're hungry. You're not eating."

His brows furrowed, and he sat up straighter. "Nonsense."

"I had spent many nights wondering why you would be so wasteful. I assumed that you were feeding well with the number of bodies you were leaving around until you interrupted my visit to my father. Then I saw how truly exhausted you were. You were *trembling*. Every part of you wanted to do it, but you didn't." I paused for a moment, thinking carefully about my next words. "Then, you said you couldn't do it. It had me wondering, why don't you just kill me? Why do you act like you need permission?"

"I don't."

"Then why?"

"Tension spoils the blood."

"Liar." I poked my finger into his chest. "Tension doesn't spoil the blood. You want to taste it paired with *pleasure*."

He averted his eyes, refusing to answer like the stubborn child he was.

"Please feel free to contest if it isn't true. Unless it is due to a change of morals, *Creature*? What happened to wanting to kill me and ravage me for your own uses? Have you grown a heart as fast as you healed the wounds I have left on your body?"

He was unwilling to look at me.

"Answer me, you vile thing!" I shoved his chest with both my hands. "Why did you stop?" I shouted.

He snatched my wrists, yanking me forward, our noses nearly touching. Every tense muscle, every tic in his jaw, every stern expression concealed words left unsaid—I wanted to poke and prod at every single one of them.

"Why haven't you killed me yet?" I asked shakily. "Why did you hesitate?"

"You ask as if you were hoping I would." His eyes narrowed dangerously, and I could feel a vibration against his chest. He was holding back so much—I feared he would combust. "Like you would not mind dying if it meant your assumptions would be correct."

My chest rose and fell quickly despite my attempts to appear calm. It was becoming harder knowing our proximity—the danger of being within biting distance of a thing that could not help himself any more than the next savage animal.

"You want to know why I haven't killed you yet? My mouth runs *dry* when I think of killing you. I didn't understand it. It frustrated me for a long time. I would usually be skipping *heartbeats* at the thought of ripping through something as divine as you." The darkness in his eyes had disappeared when he looked back at me. It was replaced by pain. "It would not be the same. I wanted to hear you dedicate your cruel words only to me. I didn't care if you were yelling at me, screaming at me, telling me no…as long as it was for me. Soon, I didn't want you to leave. When I was away, you danced around my mind like a man's deepest regret, ferocious and intoxicating. You want to know what I want? I want *you*, Alina. *All of you.* Every hair on your head, every tear, laugh, and scream that rips from your delicate vocal cords will all become *mine*."

This was one of those times when I forgot whatever clever thing I had to say next. The simmering anger inside me mingled with a knot I did not want to acknowledge.

"You are a cruel, wicked thing, Silas Forbes," I bit out.

"There. That's it." His hand shot up and gripped my jaw, squeezing. "I want to taste every venomous word performed by your lips until you have to invent new ones just for me."

"You are just hungry." I gulped. "You think you want me, but you want to feed. I have no qualms with that. Just don't pretend it's anything more." I pried myself from his grip, backing away. "Take my deal, or leave it. That is the only way you will continue to see me."

"How often?"

"Excuse me?"

"How often do I get to see you? Under this proposed deal, of course." He stood from the desk.

I retreated farther. "Once a week."

"Seven days a week." He advanced.

"Twice a week." Another step back.

"Four."

"Three. I can't bear to see you more than that." My back hit the wall.

"I can work with three." He rested a hand on the wall beside my head as he leaned down. "How often will you make an offering to me?"

"You get blood when you give blood. In my lab."

He stared up as if to consider it, sighing when he finished weighing his options. "Where do I sign?"

I swallowed the lump forming in my throat, glancing away.

"You trust me enough to settle this over a handshake?" He raised his brow. "You're a poor businesswoman."

"I'd rather there be no paper trail detailing our odd exchange," I muttered under my breath.

"Since you think me a devil, how about we seal it accordingly?" He grinned, leaning closer than before. If I flinched, our lips might touch.

"No."

"Allow me at least one simple pleasure," he groaned.

He grabbed my face again, making me flinch as he pulled it toward him. He finally closed the space between us and captured my lips with his own.

While Silas was possessive and bold, his kiss was soft, and the lingering scent of smoke and blackberries added that extra edge that sent me somewhere else far away. He was just as intoxicating as the lingering taste of bourbon.

When I opened my mouth to breathe, he took the opportunity to deepen our kiss, gently running his tongue over my bottom lip, begging for entry.

He cupped my cheek to pull me into him, the other hand snaking around my waist as if afraid I would slip away, as was often the case.

A soft moan escaped me. The sound only encouraged him, as he undid my coat and let it slip off my shoulders. He tugged open the buttons down the front of my blouse, exposing my neck.

"The pomade was a nice touch. You should consider being more subtle next time." He took my bottom lip in his mouth and sucked on it. That devilish tongue wiped the red tinge off his lips, peering off in the distance as he tried deciphering the taste. "Cyanide? Really?" He tsked as if I should know better.

"You have to at least admire my persistence." I shrugged.

"You are a woman of many admirable qualities," he whispered, kissing me again, sucking and biting at my lips as if he wanted to taste more. "It's a nice flavor on you. I want more." His tongue glided down across my jawline, the movements of his lips against my neck becoming greedy.

"I want to hear you beg for me," I breathed. "On your knees, preferably."

"Why would I beg when I could just make you melt with a single tongue-lashing between your legs?"

I pulled a small blade from the hem of my sleeve.

He eyed me cautiously.

I scored it across my palm, letting the blood trickle from the fine lines on my hand. "Consider this an advance."

His knees practically buckled, his chest pressed against my lower abdomen, and his eyes held an unwavering focus on my hand. When he reached for my hand, I slapped it away.

"Uh-uh! How do we ask for favors?" I was almost satisfied with the image before me. Blood trailed down from my hand to my elbow and dripped onto the floor as I held it out of reach.

His jaw twitched with every precious drop wasted.

"Beg," I repeated.

His glare burned hot as he held my gaze.

It was amusing to see it all unfold. If only I had known that I could have done this sooner, maybe I would have had more fun with him by now. Taming beasts was easy if you dangled their reward just out of reach.

"If you're going to compare your nasty impulses to the likes of dogs," I purred, "then you better bark."

To my surprise, his hands slid up my legs under my skirt, and he nipped tenderly at the skin of my abdomen. He rested his chin on my sternum as he looked up. *"Please."* His words rolled off his tongue like honey, a toxic edge to his voice. The malice was building inside of him. I could feel it in sparks as I rubbed against his nerves like two pieces of flint.

What a sight to behold!

I lowered my bloodied hand over him, just above his face so he could see the droplets pooling on my palm before they threatened to fall.

He leaned up and dragged his long tongue across it.

I had not realized how long it was, which explained many sensations from previous encounters. The pain of the cut faded and tingled at the touch of his tongue, like there was some sort of numbing agent within his saliva.

His eyes turned black until only a crescent of silver blue peered up at me. My working theory was that these creatures' bodies sent blood to their eyes when they were aroused by prey or other stimuli to aid their sight while hunting. Butterflies formed in my stomach thinking about every time it had happened when he laid his hands on me.

He cupped my hand with his own, holding it closer as if it were going to be taken away before he finished savoring it. He sucked on the wound greedily until that tingling reaction numbed my entire hand. When he pulled his bloodstained mouth away, I could see that his fangs were barred, unable to help themselves from reaching forward.

"Restraint looks good on you," I said. His eyes flicked up at me in annoyance.

My bloodied hand swiped across my chest, the warmth dripping down between my breasts.

Silas lifted me by my hips as he stood, pinning me up against the wall. He dragged his tongue across my chest, teasing a nipple with his tongue as he cleaned away any trace of red.

A satisfied hum bloomed in my throat as I wrapped my arms around his neck. "See what happens when you say please?" I taunted, tugging his hair to make him look at me.

"Let me feed from you," he whispered.

"You just did—"

"No, I want to try here," he said against the crook of my neck, leaving a soft bite on my skin.

"You haven't earned that yet."

"How cruel." He let out an exasperated sigh as if to contemplate if it was worth edging himself on like this.

Our breathing began to synchronize as our bodies pressed tightly against one another. It was undeniable that we had been avoiding the tension that bloomed between us. It was intoxicating enough that we both needed a moment to collect our bearings.

I spoke after a long moment. "Why do we do this, Silas?"

"Why do we do anything?" he said against my neck, gripping me tightly as he rested his forehead against it.

Seeing any tenderness from a thing like him was strange, especially for something like me.

CHAPTER TWENTY-THREE
THE POISONER

This evening I was meeting an old friend of my father's, Dr. William Hayes. He was a professor at King's College and consulted at nearby hospitals. A peculiar man, to say the least.

His tall and lanky figure could be seen from afar, resembling a scarecrow that deterred the park pigeons. He sat in the folding chair at one of the metal tables, carefully unwrapping a piece of hard candy.

"Dr. Hayes," I greeted him.

"Alina! So nice to see you again!" He beamed, standing to hug me. "What has your little brain been working on lately?"

"Little things here and there." I sat across from him.

"Butterscotch?" he asked, offering me a neatly wrapped candy. I shook my head. "I always keep some on me for the children at the clinic. Makes the bloodletting go a little easier." He sighed.

"I wanted to ask you something," I started, unsure how to explain the situation. "I'm developing an antidote to a new toxin."

"What kind of toxin? What are you trying to cure?"

"For a toxic type of blood. I have a sample of the blood and a counterpart that neutralizes it. Is there a way to replicate that but catalyze it so it neutralizes and unravels the toxin's structure itself?"

"Could be, especially if you have that other counterpart sample," he said steadily. "Where did you get this?"

"It's not important. But I do have another question." I rubbed my palm nervously. "Hypothetically, do you think it would be possible for a human's body to become poisonous? Like how some plants are entirely toxic from blossom to root?"

"Hypothetically, anything could be possible," he said pointedly, "unless there is more to your question."

"Well, maybe it does sound a bit outlandish when I say it that way," I mumbled. "Anyway, do you think it would be possible to get me into the lab at the college? I would only need it for a few hours a week if there are any vacant labs."

He paused as if to check a schedule locked away in his head. "I could make some time. But let me check for sure once I get back to my office. I can telephone you if I find any vacant blocks for the semester, if that works?"

"Yes! Yes, that would be amazing." I smiled. "Do call on me if you find any gaps. I'll take any."

"Of course, anything for Jacek's little girl." He patted my hand before pausing. "How have you *really* been? Since the incident?"

I swallowed hard and glanced down, giving an unsteady laugh in response. "Unwell at best. Empty at most," I replied, squeezing his hand back.

"You would tell me if you needed anything. Anything at all, right?"

"Of course," I lied. The professor's eyebrow ticked up in suspicion, but he did not press.

"All right." He pulled a tight smile, which was a lot coming from a man who was as stern as the clergy.

"Alina?" an accent pipped from behind me.

Dr. Hayes's eyes narrowed at me and then at the man behind me.

I turned around and smiled. "Viktor! What a pleasant coincidence. How have you been?"

"I am well. I'm surprised to see you here with my professor." He laughed.

I stood up to give him a tight hug.

"Shouldn't you be in another class by now?" Dr. Hayes raised a brow at him.

Viktor gave a cheeky grin before raising a shoulder. "Perhaps. At least it's not your lab." He looked back at me. "Besides, I was on my way to you, Alina." He held up a black leather gladstone bag.

"You brought it!" I gasped, leaning close so he could pop open the bag to show me its contents.

"I borrowed it from the lab, so please bring it back in one piece." He glanced nervously at Dr. Hayes.

"Don't look at me. I'm not in charge of equipment inventory." Dr. Hayes shrugged, standing up and buttoning his jacket. His tall figure loomed above both of us. "I'll be getting back now. I will send word soon about your lab time," he said to me, then turned to Viktor. "I trust I will see you in lecture tomorrow? Unless you plan on skipping that too."

"I'll be there." Viktor smiled sheepishly.

"Have a good rest of your afternoon," Dr. Hayes said. He gave me a farewell hug before tipping his hat then stalking off. As he passed, the pigeons flew off in unison, scaring away the critters in his path.

"How do you know Professor Hayes?" Viktor closed the bag and clasped it.

"He was a friend of my father's," I said. "He is usually the one to lend me papers."

"Ah, I see I have competition, then?" he joked.

"Yes, I have a queue of men extending down the street waiting to give me papers on germ theory and whether or not evolutionary theory holds any weight." I rolled my eyes. "Walk with me?"

"It would be my pleasure." He held his arm out to me.

There was no rush to get home despite the quickly cooling weather. The company was enough to keep me warm.

"What are you looking to do with this contraption anyway?"

"I have found someone with strange blood. I want to study it," I tell him truthfully. "I was happy to have a willing participant."

"I guess they must be willing, especially if you want to use this on them. Bless their soul," he said sarcastically. "Do you want me to show you how to use the apparatus? Can't have you torturing the poor soul."

"Is this your way of asking to be my lab partner?" I grinned at him.

"I wouldn't be opposed to helping, but you're doing the writing."

"Deal."

"WILL IT HURT?"

"Possibly. There's only one way to know. If you're going to use this on people, it's important to feel it," Viktor explained.

"Do I get to stab you too?" I joked nervously, staring at the long, curved needle in his hands.

"As a reward, maybe I'll let you." He smirked, tying the tourniquet around my bicep.

"How kind of you." I shifted in my seat at the kitchen table.

The blood transfusion apparatus was a tall graduated cylinder with a flared base to keep it upright. Two long tubes were secured at the base with long, curved needles at their ends. For the extracting and movement of blood, hand pumps on the side were squeezed to create suction for siphoning blood from one person to the other. We would use this one way, since it was the easiest way for me to measure and collect the blood.

"Ready?" He peered at me from over the rims of his glasses, positioning the needle at the crook of my arm.

"Mm-hmm," I mumbled, unable to look away.

He pushed the needle carefully into a vein. I was hyperaware of my veins pulsing against the tourniquet and the sharp pain entering my arm.

I flinched, squeezing Viktor's knee as I watched it go in.

"You don't need to watch."

"I do. How else will I learn?"

"Fair." He twisted a dial on the apparatus before squeezing the pump. The blood slinked through the foggy tube and filled the glass about five milliliters. He pressed his thumb on the punc-ture and removed the needle. "See? Simple." He kept his finger on the wound before wiping it with a cloth.

"I was expecting something more from the contraption." I laughed, looking down at his hand holding my arm. A wave of heat hit me suddenly, nausea rushing over me.

"Alina? You look pale—"

I rushed to the sink, throwing my head over to heave.

Viktor was already behind me, rolling up his sleeves quickly and gathering my hair at the back of my head so it did not mix with anything unsavory.

"This is why they tell patients not to look." He tried to lighten the mood. "It's just adrenaline."

"Yeah," I groaned. I could feel the heat subsiding, but the whole ordeal had caused me to work up a cold sweat. I hung over the sink and shivered as I waited to see if anything else would come up.

"How about we take a break, yeah?" He smoothed the stray hair from my face and peeked over my shoulder to check on me. I could feel his hand brush against my neck as he continued to move away any flyaway hairs.

I nodded, afraid of heaving again if I opened my mouth.

"How are you feeling?" Viktor checked the temperature of the cloth he had placed on my forehead.

"You don't need to fuss over me," I mumbled as I lay on the couch, book in hand. I glanced up from the words on the page.

"You scared me there. I thought you were going to faint." He sat on the floor by the other end of the couch. He adjusted the pillow under my ankles before he settled again, picking his notebook back up.

"I am not sick." I laughed, tapping the back of his head with my foot.

"You are the only thing worth fussing over." He smiled, making delicate pencil strokes in his notebook. It occurred to me that he was not writing or annotating.

"What do you have there?" I put a ribbon between the pages of my book to mark my page as I leaned up.

"Nothing to be concerned about." He shielded the paper from me, turning his body away.

"Give it here!" I crawled over and plucked it from his hands.

When I saw the sketch, it was a charcoal drawing of a woman reading. I could only assume that it was myself. He'd somehow even captured my markings. I thought this was the first time I'd seen myself candidly. "I thought I would look meaner when no one was watching," I joked.

"You only look mean when people *are* watching." He took the notebook back from me.

"I didn't know that you were an artist." I lay on my stomach to watch him sketch over his shoulder.

"I am many things. I've had many years to practice the arts in between studies. I get bored easily when auditing classes that I'm already familiar with," he said. "Information gets repetitive the more time you spend at different colleges."

"What other mediums have you dabbled in?"

"All of them. I have always been told I am gifted with my hands." He smiled over his shoulder. "I enjoyed the theater and painting the most though. What else is there to do when you have nothing but time?"

"You say that you are an old soul. You look like you are barely twenty-five." I tilted my head at him.

"They said something similar when I posed for an illustration class once." He grinned, turning the page of his notebook and starting a new sketch. He began sketching a cute critter, some-thing like a ferret.

"What is that?"

"A sable. We have a lot of them at home in the wild. They make for soft coats."

"How morbid," I scolded.

"It is true. Anything that cannot be kept as a pet is usually a pelt." He filled in the beady eyes of the critter on the page.

"You never talk about your home." I studied him rather than the drawing this time. "What is it like? Do you have a family?"

"I am from a small village originally," he said. "Otherwise, there is not much. It is a cold and formidable place."

"What brought you here?"

"Business. I came for a work opportunity."

"You are working while studying? An apprenticeship?"

"In a way, yes."

"We should visit the fine art wing of the museum next time you have a free day. I think you would be inspired." I laid my head down on my folded arm. He was so rigid when focused, yet his hand was light and relaxed as he sketched.

He flipped the page, turning to sit facing me from his spot on the floor.

"What are you doing?"

"Museums don't inspire me quite like they used to. I've seen every painting they have. It is old to me."

"There are thousands of artworks in those archives." I cocked a brow. "You couldn't have possibly seen them all."

"Maybe." He shrugged. "But why would I go see those masterpieces when there is one right here?"

I grinned at him and tossed one of the couch pillows, hitting him in the head.

He laughed, adjusted his glasses, and continued.

I lay there studying him. His hand moved nimbly across the paper. His grip on the pencil was firm but skillful. He swapped a few times between two different pencils, smudging the sketch with his finger and erasing parts of it.

"How does it look?"

He turned the notebook toward me, and I gingerly held it closer. There was that familiar face again. Maybe I was a narcissist for enjoying this type of attention, though I did not see the harm in this particular instance.

"If you keep drawing me like this, people may actually think I am pleasant."

"You are pleasant." He smiled. "I don't know why you think yourself to be some distasteful spirit."

"That is because you do not know me yet."

"I know you well enough if I am spending my *only night off* extracting bodily fluids and using you as my muse." He leaned back on his palms as he sat.

Night.

It was *nighttime*.

I sat up quickly and glanced at the timepiece on the wall. It was nearly seven thirty at night.

"Apologies. I didn't realize that I'd kept you so long," I said hastily, though I was more worried about him meeting my other admirer. I fear what would happen if my Creature saw another man in my home. I did not think his reaction would be any different than how he expressed his frustrations typically. What a mess he would make out of Viktor.

"It is no trouble." He stood up, rolling his shoulders tiredly. "Do you have a curfew?"

"No, I just remembered I have an early start. I did get a lab time secured. Will you be free on Wednesday?"

"I can be free for you." He winked, gathering his satchel.

"I will hopefully have samples. I will let you know how I do with the extractions." I walked with him to the door, trying not to act too flighty. "Five o'clock on Wednesday. Got it?"

"Got it." He tapped his temple. "I will remember."

"Perfect." I smiled, leaning up to hug him tight. "Good night, Viktor."

I watched as he walked down the steps of my town house, only faintly illuminated by the streetlamps, before he became another shadowy figure in the street.

I closed the door and locked it behind me, sighing as I went back to the living room and plopped on the couch. He left his notebook on the tea table. Opening it again, I stared at that last sketch of myself. I was clearly having an identity crisis. I did not recognize myself if I was not scowling. Walking over to my bookshelf, I placed the sketch on the eye-level shelf. I tilted my head as I backed away, admiring the new piece of art. Maybe this was the first of many. I did not collect art, but maybe I should start.

CHAPTER TWENTY-FOUR
THE POISONER

T his was a bad idea.

My chest was tight, threatening to crush my ribs as the hour neared.

The clock only served to heighten my anxiety instead of ease it. Each time I checked, it was like less time had passed than before. The timepiece hand crept sluggishly toward that number three, slower than cold molasses.

Was it a mistake to make a deal with a demon like him? He was unnatural, a menace. It would be absurd to expect him to act decently enough to hold a deal. My word wasn't much stronger than his, as he had already spat it back in my face, *literally*.

As of now, I believed it was safe because I had something physical to offer him. I thought the proposal went well, considering he could have cut me down right then and there in his home.

Rosiness burned in my cheeks and ears as I remembered our exchange, our less than formal "handshake" to seal the deal. I rubbed my face in an attempt to make the color retreat.

My lip had endured abuse from chewing it all morning, remembering the ghost of him there.

No, not him. Never him. Don't let your mind wander like that.

A cringe clamped down on my body as the bell chimed.

"You're late." I slammed a drawer shut as I brushed away my previous thoughts.

Silas stopped at the door, checking the timepiece on his wrist. "It's exactly three."

"On time is late." I could not help but grin.

"What have you done with my disagreeable Alina? If I didn't know any better, I would say there was a spark of excitement upon my arrival!" He spoke with a sarcastic tinge. "Perhaps tomorrow I shall also believe in God!"

"Humorous as usual. Lock the door and flip the sign. There is much to do," I directed.

"I am also going to have your undivided attention? Oh, I must be truly special." He flicked the lock and carefully turned the wooden sign, marking the start of our first *physical.*

"THAT'S NEW." He frowned, staring at the blood transfusion apparatus that stood erect on the workbench.

"It is, but that is for later."

"I thought dinner was on you?"

"*Later,*" I repeated, gathering some other tools before we began. "Take off your coat and roll up your sleeves."

"Straight to business, efficient as ever." He shed his coat and laid it neatly across a vacant bench.

"Feel free to get comfortable. You can stand or sit." I grabbed a stethoscope and my workbook.

Silas opted to lean against the table, his arms crossed in front of him as he watched. He appeared calm, but an edge about him waned on the side of caution as he observed the many tools that must have been alien to him.

I set the buds of the stethoscope in my ear. I gestured for him to uncross his arms, and he reluctantly did so, his hands gripping the edge of the table he was leaning against. I placed the stethoscope against the cotton shirt, painfully aware of how it clung to his torso. His heart was just as quick as last time, impossibly fast. I counted as I watched the timepiece ticking on my wrist. He averaged two hundred and thirty beats per minute based on fifteen seconds.

Plucking the buds from my ears, I jotted down the number.

"How am I doing so far?" He leaned over to see what I was writing.

"Horribly. You should be dead with these numbers," I said plainly, "but we already knew that."

"Fair." He shrugged.

We circulated through all the typical physical tests—blood pressure, reflexes—and we ended by checking his mouth, which I was most interested in.

"Open." I held up a glass probe.

"What would that be for?" He eyed my stick.

"To poke around," I huffed. "Just open."

He sighed and obeyed.

I flattened the glass rod against his tongue, pushing down so I could see inside.

His tongue twitched, and the two independently moving pieces of the split end curled in discomfort. It was amazing how it went unnoticed until he made them move apart from one another. No one would suspect this peculiarity unless they were looking hard.

I grabbed his jaw and tipped it up, looking at the roof of his mouth. The light from the small window allowed me to properly see it now. His fangs were folded neatly against the roof of his mouth, though I could see the muscles at the base that allowed them to flex forward. I could also see something like holes in the roof of his mouth along the edges.

"What are these?" I poked them with the rod.

He physically flinched, not something I expected to be sensitive. He pushed my hand away.

"It's for scents." He grimaced.

"Like a Jacobson's organ?"

He looked at me blankly, lifting a shoulder up in ignorance.

I quickly moved back to my cabinet, shuffling through the many jars and vials. I picked one from the back and moved to the other side of the room.

Silas glared at me, frustrated at my lack of explanation, as he stared at the corner I stood in.

"Tell me what you smell and when you catch the scent," I instructed, popping the cork off the jar. "Now?"

"No," he said.

I took two more steps forward. "Now?"

"No."

I began a steady approach. "Tell me when, and I will stop."

He was silent.

I moved closer and closer until my knees knocked against his. I lifted the jar up to him. "Nothing at all?"

"Almonds. I could smell it six paces ago."

"Why didn't you say anything?"

"I wanted you closer." He smirked, tilting his head down at me. "Are we done yet?"

"Are you trying to flatter me into ending early?"

"Very likely observation."

"One more thing, then you can have your reward." I picked up a glass vial with cloth stretched over the opening.

His eyes narrowed at it before flicking back to me. "What is that for?"

"Venom. You have at least one set of fangs that contains it, correct?"

"Possibly," he said prudently.

"I promise we are almost done for today," I pleaded with him.

He grumbled before opening his mouth again, flicking his fangs forward for me. They were trembling, hoping to sink themselves into something. It was like they had a mind of their own.

I leaned in close, and our chests brushed against each other. I lifted the vial to the shorter, outermost set of canines. As the snakelike tooth sank into the cloth, venom sprayed spontaneously before slowing to a steady drip. The liquid had a golden tint, like watered-down amber.

Every muscle in his body felt taut, but I did not have to feel it to see how they strained during the process.

His eyes were closed now, and he seemed slightly flustered. Was it uncomfortable? Was his mouth that sensitive?

When I finished, I reached for a cork to plug the vial.

"There, easy." I grabbed the tourniquet.

"Yeah, for you," he growled, running his tongue along his teeth before tucking them back away.

It brought me joy, granting him some discomfort. It was only fair.

Silas's demeanor was bleary, burned-out. Maybe this was karma for depriving me of sleep for weeks. His gaze was glued to the wall like he was second-guessing his decision.

I took my place next to him at the edge of the table. Two

glass containers capable of holding five hundred milliliters of fluid were placed neatly beside the apparatus.

"Give me your arm." I snapped my fingers and held my hand out.

He rolled up his sleeve a little higher, offering his thick arm to me. His lean forearm exposed several veins, so it would not be hard for me to find one.

The tourniquet tightened around his bicep, pushing on his veins to get them to bulge out a little more. I held his arm closer to inspect them.

Viktor made it look so simple, but I would not let it intimidate me.

Silas watched my movements cautiously, but he had no choice but to trust me. On second thought, if he did not trust me, he could snap if I poked him the wrong way with the needle. It did not stop him from doing that to those girls in the river.

The long, curved needle lined up with a vein at the crook of his arm, pressing into the skin. As I squeezed the pump, the liquid came out *black*. Unsure if it was just the lighting or if it was actually black, I studied it as it sluggishly crawled up to the glass cylinder.

"It worked." I bit my lip in excitement.

"Have you not done this before?" He lifted his eyes in brief horror. "You are using me as a test rat?"

"I thought I was very clear about that when I said I was going to study you," I said sweetly. "Besides, he only taught me how to do it last night."

"*He?*" His eyes narrowed.

"Yes, *he*. Viktor. My lab partner." I poked my finger into his chest. "If you kill him, then you go back on our deal. I need his help. Promise that you will not murder him."

He grumbled something under his breath.

"I want to hear you say it, Silas." I kept my eyes on him.

He averted his gaze.

"Silas!" I put pressure on the needle.

"Fine!" he hissed. "I won't."

"You won't *what?*"

"I won't kill him."

"Or maim?"

"I won't maim or kill him."

"I'm glad we are in agreement." I let a pleasant smile grace my features, which only infuriated him.

As shown previously, I put pressure on the puncture before pulling it out.

I took the apparatus and emptied it into the glass jar. I began to write on it with a black wax pencil.

"What are you doing?" he asked, removing the tourniquet from his arm.

I turned the glass toward him.

"Creature" Sample #1 was scribbled on the glass.

"You would not want to mix them up, would you?" I grabbed a rag and wiped the puncture on his arm, guiding his free hand to hold the gauze. "Now, just let me clean this, and I can do it on myself—"

"Don't put that thing near you." He grabbed my wrist. "I can do just fine without it."

"Don't be hasty." I glared. "I do not trust you to take the same amount."

He eyed the jar of his blood, then back at me. "I can measure out just fine in my head."

"That's precisely *why* I don't trust you to do it," I snapped while trying to twist my wrist from him.

"If we are going to see each other more often, isn't it a better use of our time to learn to trust each other a little?" He flashed a grin, the clicking sound starting to vibrate in his throat as his eyes locked with mine. "Let me prove it to you. Let me take a bite."

"What about the venom?" I asked nervously.

"It's not that kind of venom." He smirked. "It would be a mistake not to use it."

"I don't want you to use it," I told him firmly.

"Do you trust me?" he asked, pulling me in and swapping our places. His body pinned me to the edge of the workbench, casting a shadow over me as he loomed with my wrist in his grip.

The last time he asked me that, he saved my life. Even so, the question still troubled me. I shrugged, feeling the blush creep up my cheeks. Here he was, asking me permission again. The action alone earned him some trust, just a *small* amount. I gulped and nodded, signifying that he had my blessing.

His eyes clocked my wrist, studying the veins, similar to how I studied his. Those wicked needles flicked forward, quivering at the sight of my flesh. He was surprisingly expressive and simple to read, unlike human men. If you were ever close enough to see him, he showed you exactly who he was and what he was think-ing. You could likely predict what would happen next. It was like reading an animal's body language—tried, true, *honest*.

He leaned in and embedded both sets of teeth into my wrist swiftly, as if not to let me dwell on the pain.

"Ouch, Silas!" I winced, but he bit down harder, causing my knees to buckle slightly, but his arm circled around my waist to catch me. I watched his Adam's apple bob as he swallowed slowly, feeling the fluid pull through my wrist. Then, a wave of numbness overtook me. The same tingling from before pricked along my wrist until I could no longer feel any pain, just pressure at the puncture sites. Another feeling lingered, not just the absence of pain but the feeling of elation. It was hard to describe other than referring to drugs, though I was sure it was something that tricked the nerves into thinking this was not a painful endeavor.

His eyes closed again, but the slight crease between his brows insinuated that he was attempting to stay focused. Was he actually keeping track of how much he was taking? I took a shaky breath, trying not to let the adrenaline crash sicken me similarly to the time before.

He let out a groan against my skin. I could feel more pressure on my wrist, and I shivered. Then he pulled away, his face flustered as he licked my wound. His tongue slid slowly over the punctures as if to linger a few moments longer before he had to let me go. However, it looked like he considered going back on his deal just for another taste. The red tinge on his lips was wiped away by his tongue. Sighing, he leaned his cheek against my palm, peering down at me. His skin was warm against my touch, though it was tempered by the numbness in my hand.

"What?" I frowned.

"Am I not allowed to look at you?" He turned his head into my hand. "You know, I thought I tasted something off about you before."

"How so?" I raised my brow.

"Your taste, it gives it away. You're Mellifluous."

"Pardon?"

"A Mellifluous Host."

"You are saying words, and I still don't know what they mean."

"It's a type of blood, a mutation," he said. "It means you taste good. Sweeter than usual." He chuckled.

"Thank you…I think," I mumbled, pulling my wrist from his hand.

"People pay good money for blood like yours," he said,

moving his supportive hand on my waist higher as he leaned forward.

"Is that right?" I pushed against his chest. "Are you saying I should be making you work harder for it?"

"Don't be cruel." He chuckled, kissing my neck and pulling me closer. "Let's go somewhere, escape this little cave of yours."

"I have work to do."

"Do you ever *not* work?"

"You're beginning to sound like Phoe—"

"Never mind." He pulled away, rolling his eyes.

Looked like I hit a raw spot.

I pulled away quickly to gather my things. My hand struggled to pick up my notebook due to the numbness in my arm, though I could scoop up most of the things to bring them to the far corner desk.

I was not looking, but I knew he paused. His stare bored into the back of my neck. I wondered if he would say something, but when I turned around, he was gone.

"You're welcome, you plague," I grumbled.

The blood in the glass was like a thick ink in the dim light. It moved slowly around the bottle as I tilted it. I was becoming feverish thinking of all the tests I could run. Which one did I run first? What would I make of it? What other properties did the blood hold? Why was it *black*? The excitement was barely containable.

My thoughts could not be translated into writing fast enough. I made sure to write down the date and approximate time of the draw. I spent hours designing and daydreaming, and my eyes did not seek rest until dawn broke through the fog of night, working until the morning light crept through the windows of my shop.

CHAPTER TWENTY-FIVE

THE POISONER

The college lab was everything I dreamed it would be. It buzzed with an enchanting chaos, featuring a delightful blend of dark wood cabinetry and brass instruments—some of which I had never seen before. There were about a dozen dark wood desks with shelving separating them into halves lengthwise, holding many jars and tools. Everything was organized into drawers or on the tops of the tables—pipettes, syringes, glassware, probes, and cotton pads. Larger instruments were littered throughout the desks, some in their places on the wall and some out in the open from prior students' use. It was like peeping through someone's window, looking at unfinished experiments or those about to start. The entire scene appeared frozen in time, capturing the moment when the students had last left off.

Today the lab was deserted, entirely mine to occupy.

"This brings me back to when Jacek and I snuck into this lab as students." Dr. Hayes chuckled. "Though we had less amicable goals, such as lighting things on fire for a good jest."

"It's odd hearing stories about him being fun." I smiled.

"Though I will never understand a man's natural desire to make things combust."

"An enigma." He shrugged, leaning against one of the desks and putting his hands in his pockets. "You will have to collect your things and bring them back each time. You aren't technically supposed to be here, so you can't store anything."

"That's all fine with me. What time did you say?"

"Three on Mondays and Fridays, five on Wednesdays."

"I can make that work," I mumbled, distracting myself with the far wall lined with glass and wood cabinets. The array of items within this enchanting wonderland surpassed my comprehension, leaving me both intrigued and overwhelmed.

Through a door at the top of a half flight of stairs there was a nice viewing area to observe the entire lab. Underneath it was the professor's desk, where Dr. Hayes had student-authored papers scattered about. He'd taken a break from handing out marks to give me a tour.

"Everything you need should be in here. Standard tools will be on the workbench. You can work at any vacant spot as long as you sterilize it afterward," he instructed.

I nodded as I peered through the glass of the cabinet. Every chemical I could think of could be found labeled in alphabetical order, lining the cabinet from top to bottom. Much like the gardens, I could spend hours only looking.

The door to the viewing area snapped open, and a familiar dark-haired puppy appeared.

"Alina! How did the apparatus work out?" Viktor grinned, rushing down the stairs to come face-to-face with Dr. Hayes.

"L—ook who it is." Dr. Hayes drew out the *L* a bit too long.

"Did you forget my name?" Viktor's eyes narrowed at him. "I know I am a bit quiet in your class, *which I attend*, but surely you haven't forgotten?"

"Of course I haven't forgotten." Dr. Hayes squinted at him. There was silence for a minute between the two.

"Viktor." He raised his brow. "It's Viktor."

"Right, Viktor," Dr. Hayes said slowly, going to sit at the desk at the front of the room. "How could I forget?"

"Easily, clearly." Viktor returned his attention to me. "So? How did it go?"

"It worked exactly as intended. Thank you." I smiled sheepishly, nervously rubbing my bandaged wrist.

"What happened?" His eyes filled with concern as he snatched my arm and held it up.

"Nothing! Nothing happened. I tried to use it on myself—for practice," I lied.

"I can show you again if you need."

"No! That will be unnecessary." I pulled my wrist back. "But I do have samples to look at. Join me?"

"Samples from what?"

"An...animal."

"You don't sound convinced."

"I don't know yet. It's something new." I cleared my throat.

I hoisted my satchel onto one of the workbenches, extracting several individually corked vials containing blood samples. As I reached for the last venom sample, I stared at it at the bottom of my bag. I did not know why I hesitated, but deep down, a subtle inner voice urged me to keep this particular sample to myself, reassuring me that no one other than myself needed to know. Besides, the venom was the least deadly sample of the bunch. I needed to see the blood, which was the whole reason for this study in the first place.

"The sample has odd properties. Black in color, thick, and seemingly poison through something other than bacterial infection," I explained, focusing on the vials.

"What are you looking to do with it?" Viktor asked. He furrowed his brows as he lifted one of the glass flasks, watching the liquid move.

"I want to see how it works, break it apart and see if I can use anything in it. I must get another sample, but the creature's saliva neutralizes it upon contact. First, I need to know how potent it is." I leaned against the table, watching him study the odd fluid.

"So, a poison *and* an antidote?"

"Possibly. I may need to titrate it—I have some guesses about the compounds in the solution. Then, I would probably find the lethal dose. I might be able to bring my own rats," I mumbled as I ran the tests in my head. At the end of the day, I would just have to play with it and see what happened.

"It's your experiment, just let me know what you need. I could navigate this lab with my eyes closed."

"Please don't!" Dr. Hayes piped up from his desk at the front, his eyes never leaving the paper he was marking with a pen.

Viktor and I shared a grin before gathering the samples.

CHAPTER TWENTY-SIX
THE POISONER

"Do you remember when we corralled about a dozen rats into the house when we were little?" Phoebe sipped her unsweetened tea from her side of the couch, poking me with her foot to get my attention.

"I believe we put them in the brass tub on the third floor, or am I remembering incorrectly?" I pushed her foot away. We were huddled on the couch by the fireplace mantle in her estate. Living so close to the friend I could never bear to stay away from was nice. Always a short walk away.

"Yes. I only remember that it was above the first floor because we ran down the stairs impossibly fast when they found them." She laughed.

"I couldn't believe it took the household three days to find them. I still remember the screech of your governess—I thought the kettle was ready." I shook my head. "How old were we? But five years?"

"Maybe six." Phoebe chuckled. "I couldn't believe we didn't

get bit by one of those things. Poor creatures had to endure our games of house."

"Ah yes, our little family of rats."

"Playing house sounded more fun back then." Phoebe sighed. "Now it's like waiting for the inevitable. Especially when men become less interesting by the year."

"I'm sure it isn't so bad, as long as the children resemble their mother," I joked. "I can't imagine what kind of mayhem our children would get into."

"No trouble of the good sort." She shook her head. "Speaking of"—she scooted closer and set her teacup down on the table—"tell me about your date at the lab."

"It wasn't a date!" I blushed. "But it was fine. We have been spending time together here and there. I asked him to be my lab partner."

"And what did he say to that?" she pressed, eating up every word I offered to her.

"He said yes." I couldn't stop the smile from creeping onto my face. "He is going to help me with some things I'm working on."

"I can hear the bells now!" She smirked. "Will we be able to go on a date together if I bring someone? Oh, how fun it would be! Please say yes!"

"Of course." I yawned. "I'm sure we could all find something to do."

"I already have ideas." She grinned but noticed my exhaustion. "Are you still not sleeping well?"

"No, it's been the oddest thing. I have been going to bed early, but I'm troubled by unrest or bouts of sleep paralysis." I sighed.

"Let us try something," she said suddenly, scurrying to a different room.

Phoebe was one of those people who liked to play caretaker despite some inexperience in anything medicinal. She tried to make everyone feel at home, bending to everyone's beck and call. A people pleaser, even if it was to her detriment.

"I was prescribed this for a toothache." She brought over a bottle and handed it to me. "Take a sip."

"What is it?" I uncorked it to smell.

"Cannabis. It isn't the worst when it comes to taste. I prefer it to the others. But it is supposed to help with all sorts of things, sleep deprivation included."

"Ah yes, I am familiar," I mumbled, taking a few long sips before returning it to her. The flavor was sweet and earthy, with a bitter aftertaste biting at the back of my throat. I only hoped it would act fast so I could forget the aftertaste.

MY FINGERS COMBED through the long strands of my hair aimlessly. As I passed the kitchen table, I snatched an orange, happily peeling my treat as I went back to my guest room. On the way upstairs, I grabbed a journal that Dr. Hayes had lent me, a publication about germ theory.

It was interesting to think about small, bug-like particles that could cause decay in different body parts, similar to a toxin. It was not new by any means, but the theories under this broad umbrella were entertaining hypotheticals. Dr. Hayes said I must return the journal in a few days, which did not give me too much time to enjoy it.

With the journal tucked under my arm, I continued up the stairs to my guest room with my half-peeled orange in hand.

My guest room had the most elaborate bay window with a

spacious sitting area to curl up in. The perfect reading nook. I settled in comfortably as I continued to peel my snack, discarding the peels on the side table next to my candle. As I took a bite of orange slice, a red flickering caught the corner of my eye.

My heartbeat was in my ears again. It hurt with every pulse. Ignoring the voice in the back of my head, screaming that I was not safe, was becoming increasingly difficult. It was apparent that privacy was no longer expected in my life. No matter where I went, he would always be there waiting.

"Were you going to just sulk over there until I noticed you?" I spoke, reluctantly pulling my attention from my fruit.

The cigarette embers glowed brightly for a moment before fading. A cloud of smoke blew through his nostrils as he sat back in the chair in the corner. "You never noticed me before." He ashed the cigarette in the decorative vase on the side table.

The glow reflected red in his eyes, similar to a cat when it peered at you in dull light. It would be sinister if I was not fascinated by it. The more I observed him, the more I wanted to dissect him and get lost in the details. To open up his chest cavity and pull out all the parts, numbering them one through seventy-eight, assuming that he had no extra organs.

His tastes were similar to mine—always adorned in black. Though I suppose that was to blend into the cover of night. He wore a simple black shirt with the first few buttons undone and the sleeves rolled up his forearms. Only then did I realize he had red stains on his arms and hands, as well as smudges of red by his neck, like someone had put up a fight not too long before.

"You look revolting." I plucked another orange slice. "It must be exhausting being my least favorite nocturnal companion—"

"Stop." His voice cut through the room. We were on opposite ends, but his voice was clear and stiff, his fingers rising to pinch the bridge of his nose in annoyance.

He was bothered.

A wicked glint crept into my eyes when I realized I was under his skin. Something had happened, and he needed me. Why else would he come in any civilized manner—or rather, more civilized than usual? What a delicious opportunity.

"You are going to give me more." He took another long pull of his cigarette, tilting his head back to let the smoke rise and disappear into the dark ceiling.

"What makes you so sure of that?"

"Because I said so."

I let out a loud scoff.

"Quid pro quo," he suggested.

"Are your answers worth trading?" I stood from my spot at the window.

It could be possible to tease out exactly what I wanted. He would not kill me. He would have done so by now if that was the plan. If it was a game he wanted, I would play. He said it himself: he liked my company, but I knew that tonight he was here because he was hungry. Despite the signs of his catch in the wild, his rigidity told me that he was anything but satiated.

I closed the distance between us, his eyes following slowly until his head tilted up at me from where he sat.

"What is it you want?"

"To feed."

"You look like you already ate." I crossed my arms.

"I need more of you." There was an irritated bite to his words. "It wasn't enough."

My breath hitched slightly. "A need or a want?"

"Need. Nothing else is working," he sneered, his free hand running through his blond hair, wiping some of the blood through it. He discarded his cigarette into the vase when he finished.

"What if I say no? Would I get to watch you perish?" I laughed.

He stood suddenly, making me stumble back. "You don't want to see what happens if I reach that point." That low primal clicking emanated from deep in his chest. "You're familiar with my handiwork, no? Need I remind you by leaving some more souvenirs in your home? Or shall I provide a demonstration right here?"

I backed away, but he stepped closer. He kept going until I was back at the window, falling into the seat when the back of my knees hit the edge of it. I flinched, and my eyes widened with the memory of him at the graveyard flashing before my eyes.

The Creature leaned over me, resting his hands on the bay window cushions on either side of me.

"You are very capable, Alina. I trust that you will make the right choice," he whispered as the whites of his eyes filled with black. He brought a hand to the base of my neck to pull my face toward him. I heard a deep breath before he paused, tilting his head and leaning in. "It will only hurt for a second…"

"No biting!" I gave him a harsh shove.

A muscle in his jaw twitched.

"*But*," I continued, "I will trade you for something."

His brow twitched. "Trade?"

"Yes. You said quid pro quo before, did you not?"

"I did."

"Humor me. Maybe you will get a small taste if you behave." I smirked.

He hesitated for a minute. Those vulturine eyes searched my face for any hint of a trick. "Deal," he finally said, his body shaking. The tremor was so subtle that it almost went unnoticed.

This was a bad idea, right? I could not help the itch in the back of my head telling me I shouldn't, but this was the perfect time to ask for favors. He was hungry, irritated, and impulsive. All of the best ingredients to get in one's head.

I patted the spot on the bay window cushions next to me, scooting over for him.

He sat down next to me, leaning against the opposite side of the nook. The candlelight flickered across his sharp features, making them shift as the shadows danced across his face.

I mirrored him, leaning against the wall as I squinted at him.

The blood on his forearm was red, so it was not his own. My brows knit together in frustration. Must he always be so gratuitous? Was there no civilized way to feed like we did at the lab? It was possible he simply could not be bothered to care. Or perhaps it was something he could not help.

"You know, there's no need for your childish game. I am willing to do this again. This can be mutually beneficial. I am not above a good bargain." I searched his expression for any kind of reply.

"Look who wants to strike deals now. Was I not a devil to you weeks ago? A *creature*? Suddenly, you seem to have a roster of bets to make." His eyes were either dark or simply tired.

"Maybe it is *I* who is a devil." I sat up and crawled closer. "I may be just as deadly as you in a fair fight."

"I would believe it. You are gifted—just ignorant."

"Not for long." I hummed. "I want to know more."

"What is it you would like to know? I am an open book for now." He sighed, leaning back against the wall.

"Were you born like this?"

"Yes, but not all of us are," he answered. "Why do you kill people?"

"I poison men of an abusive nature," I corrected him sternly. "Do not say it like what we do is the same."

"You find me abusive?"

"Silas, you *eat* people. Yes, of course I would consider you abusive." I shook my head at him. "What did you mean by not all of you are born this way?"

"Some are born, and some are made. It's a bit complicated." He shrugged.

"Indulge me." I moved closer so I could lean on the same side of the nook as him.

"I was born. Two full-blooded Vipera can conceive, but it is difficult—"

"Vipera?"

"Yes, one of the less offensive names for us through the ages," he clarified. "Anyway, while conception is difficult, the efforts are worth it, since we live until we starve to death or have our heads taken off," he continued. "The ones that are made are not as sturdy. It's part of how the blood works if you die while the venom is inside you. It corrupts every part of your body as it poisons you. The difference is that corrupted humans get their life span cut in half, since they don't have the natural capabilities to handle it for very long."

"So, I could be one of you if I died after you bit me?" I glanced down at my bandaged wrist.

"You would have to die within six hours of being envenomed," he explained, "but yes, you would turn, but you wouldn't be corrupted."

"What do you mean by that?"

"You are what we call a Mellifluous Host."

"You mentioned it, but it doesn't quite answer the question."

"Hosts are just a by-product of our species diverging. That is why their blood is the richest, most sustainable. You are technically just dormant. So we believe somewhere along the way this random mutation made it possible for us to evolve."

"Dormant?"

"Hosts have all the parts. But the body thinks of them as extra organs—I don't remember the name."

"Vestigial organs," I responded quickly, as my eyes widened in wonder. "So you're saying the venom makes the body recognize them in its panicked state before death?"

"Sounds right. I don't know many technicalities about it, but yes. You would not be distinguishable from those that were born if you turned."

"I don't have extra teeth," I pointed out.

He leaned over and tilted my chin up. "Open. I'll show you."

The blood rushed to my face, remembering his grip on my jaw the past few times, but I opened up to him. It was a good time to practice trust.

He placed the pad of his thumb on the roof of my mouth and pushed.

"Ow—" I muttered around his finger.

"Feel this?" He guided my hand to the spot he was pressing on.

I smoothed my finger over the top, feeling a protruding V on the roof of my mouth. I nodded.

"They're under there." He removed his finger from my mouth.

"Everyone has that." I frowned.

He grinned and shook his head. "You clearly haven't stuck your fingers in enough mouths, if that's possible," he teased.

"I should have poked you harder in yours," I grumbled.

"You didn't answer my question," he insisted. "Why on earth would you become a poisoner? I'm sure not many people tell their parents their lifelong dream is to become a killer."

"My father taught me most of what I know, though I doubt he could have predicted how I would use that knowledge now." I rubbed the back of my neck, flattening my back against the wall as I got comfortable, our shoulders touching as we were confined to the cozy nook. Maybe I would have felt threatened if this were weeks ago, but his presence now was different. Like a crackling bonfire. Dangerous—but *oh so warm.*

"But what made you do it?" he asked curiously, watching me.

"I don't quite know when I started. I guess I've been doing it for a while—" I sighed. "It started out harmless. The other children in the neighborhood would tease my dear friend Phoebe. Bless that poor child. She didn't know how to stand up for herself. Always afraid to make the first move. They pulled her hair and tripped her in the street. So one day I borrowed some chemicals from my father's work desk. I didn't know what they did or what they were for. I couldn't read yet. I only meant to make them eat something distasteful—I put them in their midday meal at grammar school." I shuddered.

"What happened?" His eyes were intense but teasing with something like curiosity.

"Two of the boys got sick. The last one went west." I swallowed.

"You killed him." He didn't state it as a question.

"Yes. I didn't mean to. That was one of very few accidents in my lifetime." My voice grew quiet, like my subconscious was telling me to stop talking.

"What made you do it again?"

"People needed me. First, it was friends, then friends of friends, and eventually through the grapevine."

"Did you ever do it for yourself rather than others?"

"I didn't dare to help myself until it was too late and I got lazy. A miscalculation. One I can't come back from, and I'll be making up for it every day I'm alive."

"Does it eat away at you inside?" he asked, though there was no humor in his tone.

"Every day, like ants digging tunnels—only sometimes I wonder when they will eat away at my nervous system, so I don't have to feel the emptiness when they are done." I pulled my knees up to my chest.

He sighed and draped an arm around my shoulder, pulling me in and resting his head on top of mine. "There are worse things out there than you. Like myself. So take some comfort in that."

"I don't, but thank you," I whispered.

"Does Phoebe know?"

"I never told her. She thinks it was karma." I leaned my head into his shoulder.

He did not ask me to be anything that night. Not his meal nor his conquest. He did not ask me to be strong or to be smart. He basked in the presence of just *me*. There had never been a comfort like this, not in a while and certainly not while someone else was present. How ironic that the only man who could comfort an aching soul like me would be the worst one I knew.

I awoke the next morning curled up in the nook, a wool blanket draped over me, and not one Creature in sight. The only proof of him was the lingering scent of smoked bay leaf that clung to my hair and a bloom of oleander tucked behind my ear.

CHAPTER TWENTY-SEVEN

THE POISONER

"There you are, my bitter flower. Have you been hiding?" Silas crooned, stepping into the back room.

"The only thing I wish to hide from is cleaning duties," I mumbled, scrubbing some of my tools in the sink. It was full of beakers, flasks, stirring rods, petri dishes, and other things I had dirtied in the previous weeks.

He stalked over to me, poking at random instruments as if to pretend he only had a casual interest in walking in my direction.

You are not clever, Creature.

He came up behind me and gripped the sink on either side of me, looking over my shoulder to peek at the contents.

"What are those?" he sneered.

"My tools."

"What did you use them on to get them in that shape?"

"Leftovers from when I had to break up that body you left draped over the tub like she was a discarded linen." I rolled my eyes, pushing back against him. I held one of the long bone saws up to his cheek.

I neglected to include the other half of the sink, which contained old, used saw parts that were meant for butchers but were probably for something like water fowl and big game birds instead of humans. One side of the sink contained the smaller items that were previously detailed. Some were antique tools that my father had kept hidden for amputations: mallets, curettes, bone nibblers, big sheers, and scalpels.

"You owe me a new blade. The bones wore this one down." I lowered the instrument back into the sink.

"I take it back. I may be the one who has to hide from you." He moved away to go lean on the table. "How will you torture me today?"

"Just samples—no torture."

"I was looking forward to it." He sighed in disappointment.

"Apologies for not having anything crueler in mind."

"You are forgiven," he responded with a small grin.

I grabbed some freshly cleaned flasks and moved next to the apparatus.

Silas had already started rolling up his sleeve, knowing what was coming.

"I'm going to need a different sample this time," I said as I tightened the tourniquet around his arm, teasing the veins to find one to poke.

"Is that so?" He raised his brow. "Does that also mean I get more samples from you?"

"No."

"How is that fair?"

"I didn't say it was, but I'm not giving you more blood for a sample of spit." I rolled my eyes.

"Open your mouth. I can give you some right now."

"*Silas*," I warned, shooting him a glare as I slid the needle into a vein, pumping the apparatus as it pulled the blood.

"How else would you like it?"

"In the glass, preferably." I reached over and handed him a glass vial.

"That's not as exciting as my first offer."

"Can you cooperate? For once?" I asked tiredly.

He mumbled something, but I was distracted by the ringing of the shop bell.

"You didn't lock the door on your way in?" I pulled the needle from his arm and slapped a cloth on the puncture.

"I must have been *so* excited to see you that I forgot," he replied mockingly.

"Stay back here. I'm not finished."

"I'm hungry," he hissed impatiently. "Where are you going?"

"To receive clients."

"How long will that take?"

"A minute, several hours, all day—if you had just locked the door, I wouldn't have to receive anyone at all."

With that, I pushed open the door and greeted my clients. I left it ajar so I could hear if he tried messing with anything he shouldn't. I stood at the tall wooden countertop that stretched completely across the room. The cabinetry facing me must have held over a hundred drawers. I never bothered to count. I only knew where I kept everything.

"Do you have anything that can ease stomach pains?" a woman asked. She had come with her companion.

"Aside from ginger, there are a few things I could prescribe. Could you tell me a little more about the pain?"

As I was trying to be attentive to my patron's needs, a rustling of my skirt caught my attention. I glanced down to see Silas sitting between my legs with his back resting on the cabinet drawers facing me. He leaned forward only to disappear under my skirt.

"Is something the matter?" the patron asked.

"No! Apologies—I thought I saw a *rat*." I smacked the side of Silas's face with my knee as he continued his ruse. "Please continue."

"It started a few days ago—" The client began giving me an unnecessary story for her pain that did not seem relevant to its description. With Silas between my legs, it was hard to focus anyway. He began licking and sucking the skin around my thighs and working his way up, but never actually getting near the place between my legs.

"And the pain?" My voice shook. "Is there a particular sensation you can describe to me that could help me prescribe something?"

"Needles, it feels like needles," she explained.

That was when he did it. He sank his fangs into my thigh, piercing the flesh and holding my legs in place.

"*Oh*," I mumbled. "Have you tried cannabis? Or laudanum? It is said to ease…nerves. Nerve pain is what it sounds like." I swallowed hard.

"Miss Lis, are you all right?"

"Yes, I am well, just deep in thought about what could possibly be the cause." I smiled weakly. Silas bit down harder, and I bit my lip, finally feeling the wave of numbness over the area from the venom. Why did it feel so good? It was like morphine. But I could not ignore the stars in my vision.

"You look pale," the companion mentioned worriedly. "Should we come by later?"

"That…might be a good idea. Would you flip the sign on your way out? I must be coming down with a fainting spell."

"Yes, of course! We will drop by tomorrow. Do get some rest!" The woman looked strangely at her companion before they left the shop.

When the bell rang on their way out, my knees finally gave out, and I fell backward onto the floor, pressing my back against the cabinetry on the other side of the narrow walkway behind the counter.

He followed me, and the clicking made his mouth vibrate against my skin, sucking at my thigh as my legs shook in his grip.

I pulled my skirt up, and he glanced up at me from between my thighs, his eyes narrowed in annoyance as I took away his dark cover.

"What are you doing?" I asked, but he only answered by yanking my thighs toward him, making me slouch against the drawers of my cabinet. I could see the blood start to drip past his lips as he fed.

I slapped my legs together sharply, the force making him unlatch from my leg. Though it made his teeth widen the punctures on my thigh as they ripped from the skin. The blood dripped down between my legs, staining some of my undergarments in the process.

"You've made a mess," he huffed, licking over the wound to stop the bleeding and chasing the trail of blood with his tongue between my legs, lapping at my skin.

"Get out," I snapped.

"I'm not finished." He glared.

"Why must you be so difficult?" I pushed his face away and stood shakily.

"Because I know that you like it, deep, *deep* down," he teased, rising to his feet in tandem.

"*Pest.*"

"*Vixen.*"

"I will see you next week."

"No, you'll be seeing me before then. Remember? I get three days." He winked.

"Right," I grumbled to myself. "Run off, then, I have—"

"Work to do," he finished for me. "I know."

CHAPTER TWENTY-EIGHT
THE POISONER

Twenty glass test tubes were stacked in the wooden holders scattered around the lab. Some were diluted with water at different rates, some were control samples, and others were extras.

The rats from this morning's catch dug and scratched at their cages. Each one was separated into its own box.

With clean syringes, I filled each one with a control and three diluted samples in each, plus one fully concentrated sample. Carefully, each rat was injected between the shoulder blades. Two more repetitions were made, recycling the motions. Fifteen rats in total.

My pen quickly moved in confident loops, detailing the observations and injection times. Later, I would check on their progress.

"What if you added less solution B and tested with a larger blood volume?" Dr. Hayes asked.

"We did that already. It doesn't seem reliable enough to give the same output. I think both solutions are unstable," I said, watching half the blood cells burst under the microscope. The past few tests had given no reliable answers aside from the blood becoming damaged.

"And you already added a catalyst?" Viktor asked, leaning over my shoulder.

"Yes, this is the sixty percent solution," I mumbled, dialing the microscope closer to observe the cells.

Several students started to file into the lab carrying books, equipment, and bags—our cue that our lab time was over.

"How about a break?" Dr. Hayes suggested. "You've been at this for hours. It is safe to say we can put it down for a while."

"You're probably right." I sighed, leaning away from the viewfinder and flipping my notebook closed. "I need a drink."

"Lucky for us, I might be able to help with that." Dr. Hayes laughed.

"So then Jacek and I told the dean the next day that the lab must have had rodents that knocked it over and nearly set the lab ablaze." Dr. Hayes laughed, pouring himself more bourbon.

"Please tell me he didn't believe a word you two fools said." Viktor cradled his glass between his hands as he drank.

"It is surprisingly easy to ignite things." I shrugged, sipping the honey-colored liquid from my glass.

Dr. Hayes had some liquor hidden in the bottom drawer of his desk. It was nice to sit around and talk, nowhere to be. It reminded me of when my father would have people over and I got to listen to all their ramblings about work. Many times, Dr. Hayes was there, among others. I missed the laid-back atmosphere, just colleagues conversing instead of socialites talking at each other. It was less exhausting knowing I could let my guard down with them. It made me feel warm inside, and that wasn't just because I was drinking liquor.

"Alina?" Viktor nudged my arm from where he sat next to me. We were in the two chairs in front of the desk, with Dr. Hayes behind it.

"Hmm?" I looked down at his hand on my arm, then at his face.

"Are you all right?"

"Yes, just nostalgic. Sometimes memories can be a little much. I get lost in them." I finished the liquid in my cup.

"Apologies. I sometimes forget." Dr. Hayes smiled sheepishly. "Sometimes there will be exciting moments, and I think of writing to him before I remember…"

"A few months after he passed," I started, "I would call for him, making breakfast for us before it dawned on me that I'd made too much for one person."

"He would be so proud of you, Alina," Dr. Hayes said.

"I am not so sure. You know how he was. Not very generous with his affection." I laughed before feeling Viktor's hand smooth over my shoulder in a comforting gesture.

"Excuse me for my boldness, but how did he pass?" Viktor asked.

Dr. Hayes tensed and looked in my direction. I did not know why everyone danced around the subject, as if I would cry whenever my father was brought up.

"An accident in the lab," I said simply. "His assistant was clumsy. He died of some sort of exposure."

"That is unfortunate, especially for an experienced chemist." Viktor tilted his head. "Did the coroner say what it could have been?"

"No, I did not read the report."

"I see." Viktor squeezed my shoulder gently. "Well, do not doubt yourself on the account of ghosts. You have much to be proud of."

I shrugged and put my glass on the desk, pushing it toward Dr. Hayes with two fingers. He poured me another, and we all shared a silent moment.

"To ghosts and whatever poor soul they choose to haunt," I muttered, raising my glass lazily before downing the bourbon, relishing the burn in my throat. The men followed suit.

"What is next for your experiment?" Viktor asked. "You have been working without rest."

"I do not know. I was hoping more questions would reveal themselves to me as I worked."

"Whatever it is, let me know if you need more time. The new semester will begin in a month," Dr. Hayes said.

"Right," I mumbled.

ALL WAS GOING WELL until we approached the end of the week.

The smell of rot hit my nose the second I entered the King's College lab. The cause was no mystery. My rats from the day before had met the same fate they always did. What happened to me in the greenhouse nursery would repeat for weeks as I tested the blood on rats. No matter how I changed the formula and dosage, it always ended the same.

My hand rubbed the front of my throat, remembering that burning.

The rat carcasses were bloated, and their eyes looked like they had been liquified before the flies had gotten to them. All subjects that received the blood had met the same fate.

My face twisted as I dumped one of them in the bin while holding a rag over my mouth and nose, an attempt in vain to block out the wretched scent. One cage down, fourteen to go.

As I observed one more closely, I realized even the rats that did not receive any blood were in the same condition. There must be some sort of cross contamination.

The lab was free the entire day today. While I would have liked to say the time was spent being productive, it was not. I sat in the room and stared at the wall, eyeing the samples or ignoring the pile of metal tools waiting to be cleaned in the sink. I wasn't able to finish the rest of the cages in my depression.

My forehead rested in my shaky hands.

Get ahold of yourself!

I pressed the palms of my hands into my eye sockets, seeking some relief from this migraine brought on by my unrest.

"Alina, I got the—*oh my*." Viktor barged into the lab, but as soon as the scent hit him, he had to lean against the railing of the observation balcony to steady himself.

"I know, *I know*," I groaned, throwing my hands up. "They all ended like that! I only gave them a drop! Just barely!"

"That is horrid," he mumbled, going down the steps and over to the cages, covering his mouth with a handkerchief from his jacket.

"I don't understand. Based on the lethal dose, this should have only made them ill. I was going to test possible antidotes on them to see if they survived the process." I frowned. "None of this makes sense."

"I don't know what to tell you." He sighed. "Maybe it isn't possible to receive it without the effects taking hold."

"I'll keep looking at it. No more rats for now." I sighed, picking up one of the cages to look closer at the small corpse.

Something was working against me. I did not know what powers were at play, but none of my conclusions or calculations aligned with the outcomes. I did the math myself. I even had Viktor and Dr. Hayes proofread my work. It should have gone as planned. What was I missing?

CHAPTER TWENTY-NINE
THE POISONER

My spine ached with the kind of pain that I could expect from landing in a bush of roses, thorns and all. My eyes opened before my body finished waking. Paralyzed on the bed, I blinked away the blur to be met with a headache and shifting shadows.

My fingers curled weakly as the room cleared and took shape. The numbing stillness faded slowly, allowing me some movement.

As I sat up, pain pinched my back again, and I let out an audible groan.

Something shifted in the corner of my vision.

Past the end of my bed, the door to the hallway was wide open. Nothing but darkness was past the rigid frame. My doors were always closed at night for one reason—my least favorite apparition.

"Silas?" I called out.

Silence for a moment. It was almost worse than him replying.

"I know you're there," I said into the dark void.

One, then two dots of light reflected back at me, hovering in the dark.

"Why can't you just show up during the day? Preferably while I am awake?"

One of those reflective dots lowered, a head tilt. Then they straightened again, slowly lowering until they were low to the ground. The dots got smaller, retreating into the shadows.

"Silas!" I shouted, leaping out of bed and stumbling. I did not remember any amount of poor rest that made my body ache this much. My head throbbed lightly from every thud of my feet against the wood. "Where are you going?"

I followed along the hallway until I reached the end, a door ajar there.

A knot was forming in my stomach, not the kind I would like. The house had never been this still. The air was heavy, much like it was the first time my Creature visited me. This time was different and unfamiliar to me.

Past the door was a vacant room.

The creak of the hinges sang a tale of how long it had been since it was used last, crying out from being touched after all this time. There was little furniture, only a few pieces, and a mirror draped in fabric. Ghosts of where frames once were burned into the walls, leaving a pale outline of memories stripped from the room. All these details were insignificant next to the grand gesture gracing the floor's middle.

The moonlight was like a spotlight in the dark, illuminating a simple wooden chair. The contrast was too stark to make out the details due to my headache. The outline was all I could see for now.

As I rubbed my eyes, I noticed a faint puddle of sleek wetness forming under the chair.

My eyes adjusted, then I could see the source of the peculiar puddle.

Resting upon the chair were one, two, five arms.

All missing their original owners.

The limbs were carefully draped, each hand over the arms and cushions, resting against the chair's back. They had soaked through the upholstery and started leaking onto the floor. Each hand had several heirloom rings on it.

My stomach squirmed inside my body, threatening to release on the floor beside the doorframe. His gestures were not getting any more romantic than the last. I wished he would give me flowers and call it an evening. I feared I would be a skeleton when my Creature was done with me and his disgusting gifts.

My HYDRANGEAS HAD TURNED pink with the number of body parts that I had to bury. The ravens helped with some of it, but they left bits behind for the grubs, so I had to ensure they stayed buried.

I patted down the soil, making sure nothing would peek through as nature took its course. The ground would freeze soon, so it would not be a worry for much longer.

Speaking of worry, today was a big day. I wanted to try fresh samples, so I invited Silas to the college lab. Even though he agreed with no protest, that nagging voice poked and prodded at my nerves.

I was unsure if the hesitancy came with me being formally seen with him in public or because he would undoubtedly meet Viktor. I had no loyalty to either of them, but my situation was unique—and I would probably upset one or both of them just by introducing them. It was also possible that they could get along, but that was unlikely, considering the nature of my golden-haired Creature. No matter the outcome, I needed them both if I was to continue my research.

CHAPTER THIRTY

THE CREATURE

"This is certainly a step up from your cave." I stared up at the large archway that led us into the courtyard.

Grecian-style architecture made an imposing statement as it towered above the square. I had not seen the King's College campus since its conception, though it was the perfect place to hide bodies when it was built many years ago.

"There was no longer a point in using old samples. It's easier just to bring you here," Alina said quietly. Her slouched demeanor made her appear shorter, weaker.

She clutched her satchel strap and twisted it between her hands. The crease between her brows might become permanent if she continued on like that.

I stepped in front of her, her head bumping into my chest.

"You're distracted."

"I'm just thinking is all," she muttered, trying to move around me.

"Which is *distracting* you." I blocked her way again.

She let out a heavy sigh and tipped her chin up at me, a tight tic in her jaw.

"Are you…*all right?*" I asked, the words not feeling natural. The texture of the words felt awful. I wanted to spit them out. However, I was making an effort to behave well and be *kind*.

The bitter taste was worth it, as her eyes softened but also held some confusion, mostly heedfulness. Any change in her mood other than seething anger was a win in my books.

"I am well, aside from the arms I had to bury this morning." She threw me a side-eye as she passed.

"Right." I nodded as if I understood her euphemism, though I did not. I had come to terms with the fact that I might not be able to understand *all* of her quirks.

A tall echo bounced around the hallways as bustling students scurried around. We must have arrived between periods because there was far too much scuttering. The farther we moved into the building, the stronger the scents of stress and desperation.

I did notice the wide eyes as we passed. The whispers that bounced around us.

Under normal circumstances, I would say they were looking at me—but I knew that was not true. They were looking at *her*.

Alina was not one to shy away from the looks. I liked that she was unapologetic about taking up the room. Either that or she was suffering from that infamous myopathy and did not notice the curious eyes to begin with. In every room she entered, she did not ask for attention; she demanded it. Her pretty face was only the surface of it. The air around her became sharp like a barber's razor. She was always calculating—like a bird of prey. It was absurd to remember how I called her a fawn when I first met her. We both knew that describing her as anything meek or small would be a horrible lie.

We finally reached the lab. Unlike the hallways, it was empty except for a few students gathering the remainder of their things from the workbenches. We descended down a short flight of stairs from the viewing area and down to the main floor. This was exactly the type of place I expected her to spend her free time. The space was much brighter with larger windows, much cheerier than her cave.

"I am afraid to ask what sorts of experiments you want to do that require any of these instruments," I mumbled, spinning a dial on one of the tools. They were more like torture devices, which made my blood flow to surprising places at the thought.

"I just need fresh samples," she repeated dryly before opening her journal and setting up her notes.

She seemed less excited to experiment today, but not on my account. Her scent was off, less sweet than before. It was like someone forgot to add salt to a broth. She just smelled watered down. I could not judge her paleness well, but she did seem to have a less rosy undertone today.

I felt a pinch in my gut. My appetite had had enough teasing for one morning. I pulled out a cigarette, flicking my lighter to burn the tip. The tobacco was the only thing holding me over for now. Without it, I wasn't sure where I would be, hopefully not biting into something less than savory.

"Silas!" she scolded me.

I frowned and leaned on the side of a workbench. "What?" I mumbled with the tab between my lips.

"No smoking! We are in a proper lab. You can't just light whatever you want in here. There are combustibles."

I held my hands up in surrender and plucked the cigarette from my mouth, going to put it out in a small glass dish.

"No! Those were just cleaned." Her jaw clenched as she paused her journaling to watch me.

I squinted at her and went to ash it on the floor, though her eyes told me that it was the wrong move.

I let out a sharp breath from my nose in annoyance, opening my mouth and putting the cigarette out on my tongue before hovering it over a garbage receptacle. "Can I throw it away in the bin, or is this also a *special* science bin that you need to keep clean?"

She rolled her eyes at me and returned to her task.

"Make the draw quick. You just made me toss away my breakfast," I grumbled, sitting beside her on one of the stools.

"Arm." She held her hand out without looking at me.

"'Please, Silas. Thank you, Silas. How are you, Silas? You look so handsome today, Silas,'" I teased, rolling up my sleeve and putting my arm in her hand.

Alina's touch was always cold. Do not misunderstand, it was a pleasant sensation, but I thought I ran too hot, temperature-wise. Even hotter after feeding. Her fingers on my skin were like ice, a simple chill to calm my ever-heated nerves. I often imagined them touching places that ran *hotter* than the rest, but I kept those images to myself.

She wasted no time, an efficient little bee she was. The tourniquet was tied and looped around my arm, and her long, nimble fingers pushed the curved needle under my skin. This part always excited me, possibly because I knew I got to feed after. She got quicker every time she did it.

"Oh, a present for you." I hastily pulled a flask from my pocket and slapped it on the table.

"I don't need booze right now, though I may take you up on it later." Her eyes dialed in on my arm and the apparatus, though I saw a small tug at the corner of her lips.

"I wish it were liquor. No, it is saliva." I gave her my cockiest grin.

She looked at me, then at the flask. "You filled an entire flask with your spit?"

"I didn't have anything else to put it in. You asked for it last time, and I took a bite of you without asking. So I decided to give you the extra sample you asked for. We are even now."

"You don't get to decide when we are even." She tore her eyes from me and lifted the full flask. "But fine, we are even," she mumbled.

She almost seemed impressed as she picked up the flask. It took a while to fill. It was admittedly the oddest thing I had given her, and that was saying quite a lot. The difference was that she actually wanted this oddity.

She pulled the needle from my arm and wiped the puncture. My stomach fluttered from her touches—but mostly because I was hungry. *So* hungry. I'd stopped eating anything else once I sunk my teeth into her. She was the only one I wanted to...

"Alina!"

Who in the living hell was *that?*

A tall, dark-haired man with the most foolish wire glasses rushed down the stairs, elated at the sight of *my* shadow.

She was smiling at him. So bright and full of life. I could even see a small tint of pink dust over those ivory cheeks. I only now realized how much geniality she kept far from me. She only reserved her coldest for our time together.

Looking at her, I could feel something inside me snap—or maybe it was a tooth cracking from clenching my jaw.

I hated it.

I wanted to crush her in my palm like a lightning bug and watch the light go out.

The man approached. His body went rigid, those dark eyes clocking me.

"Silas, this is Viktor! I told you about him the other day," she said, an accusatory look in her eyes as if to add, *The one I told you not to kill, remember?*

Her voice was muffled by the sound of my blood rushing. I could only see red.

"Yes, I remember." I stood up and circled the desk, holding my hand out to him. "Silas Forbes."

"Viktor Kaskov." He gripped my hand.

Mr. Kaskov stood about my height, our eyes level. His demeanor was friendly, but my spine itched at the contact. I might be biased, but I already *hated* him. His energy didn't match. His scent was metallic, like wet brass, the smell of warm wood and spicy leather attempting to overpower it. What did she see in this fool?

Alina picked up the apparatus and moved it to the back of the lab, away from the two of us. It was a mistake to leave us alone.

"How do you know, Miss Lis?" Viktor asked, leaning against the opposite desk to watch me like I was some thief in a bakery. While he appeared cordial and friendly, there was an unmistakable accusation in his tone.

"Courtship," I said, my eyes tracking Alina across the room.

"So she is—"

"My intended," I said flatly, looking over at him. "Why so many questions?"

An amused scoff came from Viktor. "Because I know that is a lie. She has no interest in men, of all things. If you know her, you would at least know that." He laughed, flashing a dimpled smile at me. "How do you *really* know her?"

"Can't fault a man for trying." I answered him. "We run in similar circles."

"That seems more plausible than courting."

"Even so, I have better odds than you."

"Are you certain of that?"

"I am *absolutely* certain."

"We will see."

Our banter was interrupted by Alina's reappearance, this time with her journal and no torture devices. She looked sickly. There was red around her eyes as if she had been rubbing them.

"What brings you to the lab?" That thick Russian accent cut through my thoughts. His haughty tone was grating against my eardrums.

"Alina tells me she might have a study for me to invest in." I politely smiled, but I couldn't help a small sneer. "Not unlike my father, I like to put bets on many horses. Pharmaceuticals are almost as good as property nowadays."

"That's good news!" Viktor was trying too hard to keep up an elated facade about my being here, which brought me some joy. "You must be excited." He looked at Alina, his eyes drifting over her.

Watch where you linger, boy.

"Yes, it's all very exciting," she said, though she'd stopped watching us. Her eyes were closed as she pressed her palm into her eye.

"Alina?" I leaned over. "What is it?"

"Jus' a 'eadache," she slurred, her body suddenly tense.

"Alina!" Viktor shouted as her knees buckled.

I wrapped my arms around her, slowly lowering her to the floor as her body shook violently. Her skin turned almost a pale yellow, and her eyes rolled farther back than I thought possible. I held her head on my lap as Viktor turned her on her side. Muffled sounds came from her as her head was forced upward so forcefully that I could see the veins in her neck throb.

"She's having a seizure," Viktor said quickly. "Don't move—I'm getting Dr. Hayes."

Her spasms began to slow by the time he left. It was only around thirty seconds, but it felt like *so long* while it happened. Feeling her body tense like that in my arms made me realize how tightly I held her.

She slowly stopped moving, her breathing returning to its peaceful rhythm. It was like nothing had happened, peacefully asleep as she was now.

I stared down at her, the pink returning to her cheeks and the blue of her lips fading now that she was breathing steadily. The only things still shaking were my hands. I lifted one to inspect it. The tremors jittering and vibrating from my fingers through my arm were as involuntary as the clicks in my throat.

I wiped the cold sweat from her forehead, moving the stray hairs that stuck to her cheek as I watched her seemingly return from the dead. Perhaps I should stop jesting with her about being a specter, or she might decide to become one to escape me.

"I will not forgive you if you die without my permission," I whispered. While it was supposed to be a joke, it was also truthful.

CHAPTER THIRTY-ONE

THE POISONER

M*y room. I see my room.*
An invisible gravity holds me down like a heavy blanket.
My eyes are wide open, and I see the chair in the corner of the room.
Just breathe.
A prickling gnaws at my spine, and a dreadful draining overcomes my senses. The only thing I can manage is to wait for it to be over.
Just breathe.
It's the feeling of being helpless while your mind plays tricks on you. My only issue is that some shadows in the corner could be real.
These spells are getting more frequent. All I can do is hope they pass quickly.
I awake in worse shape than before I rested. Every single time.
My body so desperately wants me to stay awake.
As if to warn me that if my eyes close, something worse is yet to come.

Lately, no matter how much time I spent away from Silas, I felt even more exhausted. Sleep paralysis visited me every night and refused to permit me a simple night's rest. Of course, when a

Creature was not bothering me late at night, my body must make up for it by doing it itself.

A migraine shot through my head like an arrow through the eye, making a feverish nightmare out of my waking moments as well as my sleeping ones. The nights were so rough that even my lower back was suffering from some type of abuse from my unrest.

My fingers picked at fresh produce and flowers at the market. Normally, it would be therapeutic for me, but the throbbing in my skull made the colors too bright, the world around me moving in a delay as I walked about. My fingers pinched between my brows, and I rubbed over the right side of my face, hoping to ease the pain. I steadied myself on the edge of the vegetable crate when a wave of nausea overwhelmed me. A cold sweat was forming at the back of my neck as I fought the invisible ice pick in the side of my face, further debilitating me.

Someone pulled me from my stable support, and I leaned into the familiar form.

Blackberries and smoked bay leaves. There were no witty remarks this time, just an arm around my waist. "What are you doing? You're usually at the shop by now." Silas frowned. "I waited for hours. Where were you?"

"Apologies. If I knew that my stalker had hoped to see me, I would have rushed!" I gritted my teeth, feeling an uneasiness.

He blocked my path and tilted my chin up to inspect me. A gloved hand cupped the right side of my face, shielding it from the light.

I eased into the hand as I watched him through the glow of white lashes on my uncovered eye.

"You know, your marks really bring out the ice in your eyes when you're irritated," he teased, but he tensed after speaking, his eyes narrowed suspiciously.

"What?"

"Who have you been seeing?" His voice was cold. "Have you been seeing him?"

"What do you mean?"

"You're the most capable creature I've ever met. Don't pretend to be dense." He pulled me away from the bustling crowd and into a quiet alley between two shops.

My body slouched against the wall when he let go. "I don't have time for this."

"It is all over you. The scent." He squinted at me. "Is this what you do when I leave you to your own devices?"

"Even if that were true, I do not belong to you." I clenched my teeth, massaging my temples. This interaction made me want to slam my head into the wall. Anything to get away from the pain. My eyes closed in an attempt to ground myself.

Betrayal was how I would have described the look on his face, but I knew that would require feelings and a willing participant. My chest burned. I was not sure what he thought I'd done, but I could see that something was bothering him enough to think I had crossed some boundary.

As much as I would love to tell him that I had bedded every man in his social circle to get back at him, I'd been too sick to even eat like a living person. All this told me was that he had truly given me time alone.

When I opened my eyes again, he had vanished without a word.

What an insolent child.

THIS NIGHT WAS no different than the others. The pain persisted at an uncomfortable rate. It only got worse every hour, rendering me useless in the confines of my dark room. Only a modest amount of relief was returned to me when my curtains no longer had to fight the light from sneaking inside my room after sunset.

No position was comfortable. Nothing could relax my tension. The pillows were too soft or too hard. The sheets were an insufferable middle temperature, sticking to my clammy skin. The cold sweat made any loose hair stick to my skin, making the flyaway hairs protrude in awkward positions.

I could feel the bed dip down while my face stayed buried in my pillow.

I had a visitor.

His smoky scent troubled my senses and made the nausea return.

My hand gripped the barber's blade under my pillow.

Silas moved some of the wet hair from my face, but I kept my eyes closed.

"I can hear the pulsing of your heart. You can't pretend to be asleep," he whispered against my ear.

I glared over my shoulder from my fetal position. "If you can pretend you're a gentleman, then I can pretend to sleep."

"You wound me, my dear." He clutched his chest mockingly. "My heart is yours to do with as you please! Even if you are to run blades through it!"

"Must you be so melodramatic? Are you not the one that eats flesh and chased me like an animal through this very house?"

"Whatever do you mean?" he gasped. "That is the height of romance!" His expression darkened as he got closer, climbing over me. He threw me a puzzled look. "Why do you smell like that?" His nose wrinkled in disgust.

"Like what—" My words were cut off by his hand grabbing my face, forcing it in his direction.

The swift action prompted my arm to swing out at him with the barber's blade, cutting the pillow in the process, and feathers trailed in the wake of the deadly swipe.

The blade cut his shoulder before he slapped it away, cutting his hand as well. The razor clattered on the wood floor as he pinned both of my arms above my head.

"Get off!"

"Is it him?" he shouted at me, his eyes becoming dark.

"Who?" I choked back, bucking my hips to try to get him off, but his weight held me down. My vision trailed from the pain of my migraine, his blurry figure impending above me.

"Don't lie to me." His voice was strained. "I can smell *someone* all over you. Is it that lab partner? Someone you met elsewhere? A tavern fellow perhaps?"

It was exhausting being labeled only by the ownership of another man.

I spat in his face, and he froze, letting go of one of my arms to wipe it off.

"You know, I've been easy on you. I thought we were getting to know each other. Such a shame," he said, his voice lowered, grabbing me by my arm and yanking me off the bed. "If you want this to be transactional, then fine. You will let me feed willingly in exchange for me not taking it myself." He shoved me forward away from the bed.

His words cut through my skin and made me shiver.

"I am in no condition for you to feed from me." I rubbed my wrists.

I almost preferred him before. This change was frightening. A shooting pain hammered at the inside of my skull, and I gripped the right side of my head again, letting out a loathsome groan.

"That is not my problem," he hissed. "Come on, Alina! Where did all that nerve and valor go?" He circled me, taunting.

"I need water," I croaked, not taking my eyes off of him. I did not have the energy for another one of his games or tantrums. I had to put distance between us. "I need bandages as well, especially if I am to accommodate your carefree feeding style." I glared.

"Fine, fetch them." He waved at me, pulling a fresh cigarette from his pocket and seating himself in the chair in the corner. "I trust that I don't have to tell you what happens if you run, correct?" he mumbled, letting the cigarette hang on his lips as he set it alight. The flicker from the flame reflected strikingly off his sharp features.

With a nod, I steadily moved out of the room, the air lighter as I got farther from him. I did not understand why he kept mentioning another man. While I wish I had the company of someone who was not an all-consuming psychopath, there was no one else. I was a shut-in. He should know that. Which was what made this whole situation even more odd. I had not seen the lab or Viktor since my incident. All of my interactions were reduced to telephone calls.

The kitchen had no light, not even from streetlamps, as I had closed my shutters earlier. The candle in the middle of the counter was lit to aid in my rustling through the drawers.

An instinctual pitch nagged at the back of my head and warned me of danger. I examined the syringes and knives in the drawer. I wrapped my fingers around the handle of the long meat-carving knife. Maybe Silas had decided that he preferred not to wait and was going to just finish me here. Everything in my body told me to ignore the looming presence in the corner.

Something wasn't right. Nothing about this was right.

A sickly-sweet smell surrounded me, reminding me of the first time I smelled embalming fluid in the lab. My hair stood on end, and my heart would soon be punctured by a rib if it beat any harder. I turned my head to catch a glimpse out of my peripheral vision.

Two dots of blue light peered at me from the corner, but this wasn't my regular phantom.

If I ran, would it chase me?

Admittedly, my first thought was to run to the other dangerous creature within the house. This must be why he thought he smelled someone else on me, because someone else was *here*. The question was for how long?

I closed the drawer slowly as I gripped a knife and a syringe, trying to be inconspicuous and not let the thing in my kitchen know I had spotted it. It was extremely hard to walk when you were trying to convince yourself to act inconspicuously and to travel at a calm pace.

Between the pounding in my head and the heartbeat in my ears, there was only so much I could focus on. Stars appeared in my vision. I could throw up. I was stuck between being killed by the thing in my house or by the predator who waited for me upstairs, an impossible situation. It was like I had to pick between butchers. It was just a matter of which one had the sharper knives.

My steps up the stairs were slow. How fast was a normal pace? Was I moving too slow? Possibly too fast? The shadow moved out of the corner of my eye, looming in the kitchen's entryway. As I ascended, Silas's figure appeared at the top of the second flight of stairs. I stopped where I was.

"I thought you had run. Turns out you decided to turn into a sloth. Where is that pep in your step from our first encounter? Surely the red stain on the stairs would inspire some quickness to your pace," he joked, glaring hungrily in my direction.

"I-I don't remember," I said shakily. My anxiety was restricting my breath. "You must be thinking of *someone else*."

He looked offended at my words. "You mean to tell me that you memorize every binomial nomenclature of every plant, but you don't remember our first night together? You would make a poor romantic, Alina," he said cruelly.

How did I let him know without saying anything? I didn't plan on being slaughtered by either of them today, but he was my best hope between the two.

I smiled shakily. "Silas, *my love*, please can we settle in for tonight? I am very tired. You must be as well." I attempted to take a deep breath, but it just turned into a swallow, every word taking precious air from my lungs under the weight of the panic.

Alarms must have been ringing in his head, his cold demeanor becoming apprehensive.

Out of all the adaptations I wish he had, I would have hoped for some form of telepathy. "We have both had such a long day. Maybe we should spend some time together. *Just* the two of us." I broke our eye contact only to shift my gaze toward the kitchen and then back to him.

A shattering noise exploded in the kitchen.

Silas's eyes flicked toward the sound, then slowly moved back to me. There was no telling what he was thinking, but it could not have been pleasant.

The kitchen was empty when we entered, the remaining pieces of a wineglass scattered across the floor. We didn't speak, not even a glance in each other's direction.

The silence was painful. Not a word was said the rest of the night.

S‌ILAS WOULD NOT LEAVE. Ever since that night, he'd been like a leech firmly attached to my side. Not one single moment to myself.

What was worse, not being able to sleep from the fear of the unknown or having my every move openly watched? For goodness' sake, he would not even let me bathe without him sitting in the corner. If it was not for my protests, he would watch me sleep from my bed. It was like I was a child who could not be left to their own devices. It was infuriating, and it only made me loathe him more.

Everywhere I went, my hellhound followed.

He gave me space when I interacted with customers at the shop, but that was about the only privacy I was allowed. I figured he did it to avoid people getting distracted by the celebrity in their midst, but the rumors were already spreading. He was always with me, so naturally people speculated. Whenever a new rumor surfaced, I could count on Phoebe to tell me about it over the phone or at the shop. I was not allowed to see her much either. Excuses after excuses were made to keep it to phone calls or drop-ins.

"No, I told you nothing's happened. I've been commissioned for something I can't say," I lied, hanging close to the telephone on the wall.

Silas was in the corner, glaring out the window, his leg bouncing nervously as I chatted with Phoebe.

"I told you he isn't any good," she muttered through the static. "He's caught up in all sorts of bad business. I don't care how good the sex is. It isn't worth it!"

"How would you know?" I jested, though I was curious about her answer.

"Alina! Disgusting! I do not know him like *that*! Though we have had some displeasing encounters. I am always the one people complain to when he misbehaves!" she explained. "I never understand why girls keep returning to that he-devil. He is shameless!"

"I get it, I get it." I looked back at him, his mind lost in that blond head of his. "We should get away to the country this weekend. What do you say?"

Silas's eyes snapped to me when he heard my words.

"You don't have to ask me twice!" Phoebe squeaked. "Shall we head to Sussex?"

"Yes, maybe we invite a few people? Have an intimate gathering? Something relaxing and fun," I said, as if trying to convince Silas that it would be fine and that I would be surrounded by people. Not that I needed his permission, but it was more my way of asking him to keep some distance.

"I'm on it. I'll ring you in about an hour with the details. I'll get tickets for the train. Oh, this will be so good for us!" She hung up the phone in all the excitement.

"I don't think it's a good idea," Silas said from the corner.

"Why not? I get away from the city where my *other* elusive stalker is wandering, with witnesses and an overbearing friend to keep an eye on me. What more could you want?"

"You're not leaving my sight."

"You're not going to stop me," I countered. "You know, you make many empty threats. While you have given me a concussion and an interesting collection of bruises from our encounters, you never deliver on your ferocious little fits where you threaten to eat me." I laughed. "What a poor predator you are."

"Is this your own suicidal way of telling me that you want me

266

to hurt you?" His brow raised. "I knew that you were insane when I decided to pursue you. I never pegged you for being that kind of maniac."

"It wasn't a challenge, but it brings me to my point that you can't stop me, you won't stop me, but I trust that you will be in the shadows whether I ask you to leave me alone or not." I threw him a sarcastic smile before it dropped. My head still pounded like it had been the past few weeks, but it was dimming. I closed my eyes and rubbed my face, turning on my heel to walk away.

"Where are you going?" He tried to move in front of me, but I pushed past him.

"Medicine" was all I muttered, stalking over to the kitchen. "I know that you have some separation anxiety, but you don't have to follow me everywhere."

"Clearly I do, *my love.*" He tossed my words back at me, a toxic edge to his tone.

My shoulders tensed in embarrassment. I did not need reminders.

Clearly, he was amused by my reaction.

Even though it was nighttime again, the town house was brighter than ever. Silas had turned on every gas lamp to leave no corner dark. I thought it was for his own peace of mind rather than mine.

In the kitchen, I rummaged through the cabinet, pulling out a jar of ghost pipe tincture. They looked like little white flowers despite being a type of mushroom. They had extremely powerful pain-killing qualities. I usually made a liquid from them every few years. To my dismay, there was not even enough to numb a mouse.

Leaning against the counter, I pushed my palms gently into my eye sockets.

Silas came up next to me. "What is it now?"

"Out of medicine." I sighed, defeated. At this rate, I would never get rid of this perpetual slump. The most ironic part of this was that I hadn't even consumed a drop of liquor these past few weeks, because of the pain. How unfair.

"Why don't we try something?" He traced a finger over my shoulder.

"No amount of fondling will cure a migraine," I said flatly, keeping the pressure on my eyes.

"You'll never know if you don't try." He shrugged. "I meant something else, but maybe we should try that too, to be thorough."

I pulled my hands from my head to stare at him, raising my brow to ask him to elaborate. He was being obnoxious, but my current state did not allow me the privilege of being picky about remedies.

He touched my chin and lifted it, his lips hovering above mine.

My body flinched at his touch. No matter our history, I could never anticipate whether he would be rough or gentle with me. It was like a changing wind, unpredictable. While he might not kill me, I would not put it past him to hurt me if I upset him enough. The more I learned about what he was willing to do, the more I feared him. As the fear festered, so did my desire to push him to his limits. Not my wisest instinct, I must admit. His intentions were something I needed to figure out if I were to manipulate the situation in my favor.

His tongue snaked out of his mouth, and instinctively I pulled away. His grip on my face tightened. "You have a headache, yes? Let me gamble on it." He smirked, the two split ends of his tongue twitching readily.

Considering his offer would not be the craziest thing I had done thus far. If anything, it would not hurt to try, though it would leave a bit of a bruise on my ego to give in to such a request. It was not outlandish to think if he could stop me from poisoning myself, he could also cure a phantom migraine. I reluctantly leaned into him.

"Open your mouth for me." He used his thumb to pull down on my lip.

I hesitantly gave in.

He locked his lips with mine. His hand moved to the back of my head to support it, and he ran his wet tongue over my lips, politely asking for entrance.

I grimaced at the moisture and wiped it off.

"Suck on it." He tilted his head at me.

"Excuse me?"

"My tongue, suck on it." He grinned wide. "Remember when you bit me?"

"Oh, I remember perfectly well." I glared.

"Well, how else will you get a taste of relief? I could also just spit in your—"

"Not necessary. Let us get this over with."

This was an odd method. I would rather he just spit in a cup.

He leaned over me, sticking his long tongue out of his mouth, the two split ends curled at the bottom and hanging above my lips.

I felt an embarrassed flush appear across my face as I opened my mouth.

As I went up on my toes to take his tongue into my mouth, he jerked it up out of my reach.

"You rat, are you just pulling my leg?" I hit his chest.

"No, I just wanted to see you like that a little longer." A handsome smirk graced his face. He offered his tongue again.

I reluctantly leaned up and took the tip of it into my mouth. I sucked on it gently, which prompted a sound from Silas.

Did he just whimper?

I studied his reaction through my lashes, his attention dedicated only to me.

He held me closer and leaned down, allowing me to take in more.

Our tongues mingled with each other restlessly. I sucked on his again, biting it softly when it ventured too close to the back of my throat.

He looked flustered at the motions.

I hated that he was right about his saliva being the miracle cure for migraines. I could feel the throbbing dull as the minutes passed. As my mind cleared, I wondered more about his tender reaction.

Could it be that their mouths were more sensitive because it was the only place that held an antidote to their own poison? This discovery was prompting a rather salacious curiosity.

I pulled away, and his tongue slipped out of my mouth, returning from whence it came.

"Come. I want to see something." I pulled on his arm.

Leading him into the cozy glow of the living room, I stopped in front of the mantle. It was crackling with a small fire, lighting our figures in the night.

"Down," I demanded, pointing at the floor.

"I don't think so," he said stubbornly.

I leaned in, playing with the edge of his shirt. "Do you expect me to climb you? Get on your knees, Silas."

His eyes widened at my demand as he slowly complied. The expression on his face was full of intrigue. This view of him was nice. He sat on his knees in front of me, at my disposal.

I ran my thumb over his bottom lip before tugging at the

corner of his mouth. I brought my face closer, leaning over him. "Open," I breathed.

He leaned up to kiss me, cupping my hand on his cheek with his own. It did not take a skilled interpreter to see how much he wanted this, how hard he was restraining himself as our lips met.

I pressed my tongue to the roof of his mouth. His tongue cradled mine, asking for more, to feel more, to taste more.

As our kiss deepened, I put my arms around his neck, lowering myself onto his lap as he sat back on his heels.

Reluctance was apparent between the pleasure and the restraint he so obediently practiced. It brought me joy knowing I could make a creature like him mewl for me, beg for me without a single word.

He parted our lips again to look up at me. I knew he wanted to say something but struggled to find the words. He leaned up to continue the kiss, but I pushed against his chest.

"I want something."

"Anything," he breathed, his hands sliding up my back.

"I want to see more."

He studied me. "Does that mean we can try something else? Since you are so keen on *observation* tonight?" He'd already slipped the top half of my dress off my torso.

Considering his words, I was unsure what else he would want to try. I did not believe I had seen anything past his forearms. Imagining him without his clothing did give me some excitement. I would not mind seeing more, for *educational* reasons, of course.

Even when I remembered how rough he was with me in the past, I wondered what he would be like when he used that aggression in more agreeable ways.

I realized he could probably pick up on my arousal when he licked his lips. His hand cupped my face and then moved to the back of my neck, jerking me forward so that I lay on top of him. His lips were greedy, pulling and biting at mine.

Grinding my hips into his, I gasped. I could feel that he was already stiff. Judging from the bulge, my body had not known pain until the day he decided to use *that* thing on me.

My hands wandered to his shirt, unbuttoning it down the front. He looked up at me as he began to leave marks on my neck, along my throat, and then between my breasts. Marking was a common theme with him, it seemed. The shirt soon slipped from his form. I ran my hands over him, reading his defined muscles like braille, trailing the unexplored territory.

A deep, low clicking sound escaped him. At this point, I was unsure if this nonverbal communication was one of endearment or predation. Maybe it was just from any sort of stimulus that caused arousal, like how some cat species use prusten communication to chuff at each other or how bats chatter in the night.

I lowered myself between his legs on the floor. As I began to undo his trousers, he grabbed my hand. Instead of letting me continue, he just stared at me. Why did he look so worried?

"You've denied me every step of the way. Are you sure you want to do that?" He looked at my expression, carefully analyzing it.

"I'm curious," I whispered. "What are you afraid of?"

He took a shaky breath and traced a finger over my brow before cupping my face. "I'm afraid that I won't stop."

Not knowing if the admission was genuine, I could at least appreciate some display of vulnerability from him. The thought of someone not being able to hold back their carnal craving for me made my heart lurch to my throat.

I ignored him and leaned down, pulling away his trousers and working at his underwear next.

When I pulled out his cock, it practically rushed to meet me. I could see why he was nervous.

The hesitation was not due to size and girth. In those respects, he was beyond what I could have imagined. It was remarkable really. I was afraid to put a number on it because admittedly I had not seen anything so...*large*. It only made sense that he was not human. It would be the only explanation for the display before me.

I bit my lip and looked up at him.

He was watching me still. He was waiting for a reaction—anything from me. Was it possible that he cared what I thought?

I turned my attention back down to his length and left lingering touches there with the tips of my fingers. It was inhuman in stature. I was impressed, to say the least, though I thought it would be more like torture to put that thing anywhere near a vagina.

I leaned down and pressed my lips to the head, flattening my tongue along the slit. He shuttered, and I could see him blink out of his trance.

My hand moved along the velvety length, and I ran my tongue down the side. A wetness had already dripped from his tip to meet my taste buds. The taste mixed in my mouth as I licked, finally putting the tip in my mouth.

He grunted, and his head fell to the side, watching me work in the warm light. The sounds he made were enough for me to feel that tightening in the bottom of my stomach. He pushed deeper into my mouth, touching the back of my throat, and almost prompted a gag.

He flinched at the sound before relaxing again.

Why is he so flighty?

I pulled him out of my mouth, letting the spit pool at the head. I used it to slick down the rest of the length. Upon inspection, I saw something off. I knew he saw the moment I noticed it because he physically tensed.

Along the underside of his cock, close to the base, I could see a pattern. It looked like three V shapes stacked upon each other, measuring a half-inch long each.

Much like his fangs, he had folded spines under the base of his cock. They were almost perfectly matched to his skin, except the black gradient at the sharp point, like small porcupine quills. They folded flush to his skin. I could not even feel them when touching him.

"What's this?" I ran my finger over them.

"I wasn't going to." He flinched again.

"What are they?"

"I don't use them." He looked away. "I did not want you to think I would use them—"

"What are they for?" I asked once more. "Don't make me repeat myself again." My eyes narrowed at him.

"They're for…" he mumbled, something I could not hear.

"I didn't quite get that."

"*Mating.*" He kept his eyes averted. This was the first time I'd seen him *blush*.

"Are you telling me that you have spines?" A wicked smirk crossed my face. "Like a cat?"

"I don't know." He glared at me. "They have always just been *there.*"

I had to admit, this new feature made me wonder what else his body did when he *mated*. It was common for some mammals to possess spines like these to make sure their mates did not escape. The spines would hook into the flesh of their counterparts. Now I was quite curious about what adaptations the females of his species had to tolerate such cruelty.

Mating. The word was sending my brain deep into a primal gutter.

I returned to my former position, wrapping my mouth around his length.

He gasped and grabbed a fistful of my hair, but this time, he pulled my head off.

"Why doesn't this bother you?" he asked, concern twisting his sharp features. His breathing had picked up, and his chest rose and fell quickly.

"You're fascinating." I beamed, slipping his member back into my mouth.

His grip on my hair loosened as he let out another soft groan, savoring every sensation. Even with his tip at the back of my throat, it was still only halfway in.

I tried to go deeper, moving my head up and down.

I used my tongue to explore the smooth, salty surface. I lifted my eyes to him, but he was not looking. His eyes were closed, and his head was tilted back. His hips matched my movements as I swallowed him.

Our pace quickened, and his thrusts in my mouth got rougher, needier. His cock smacked the roof of my mouth before slipping down my throat.

I let out a gag as he quickened, gathering my hair back as if not to obscure my task.

Suddenly, a warm rush flooded my mouth, and I choked.

He immediately let go of me. "I'm sorry, I'm sorry." He panicked, sitting up quickly.

I spat on the floor and let out a few more coughs. I peered down at his cock. Those same spines were now erect. They hooked out like barbs, presumably to keep it inside whatever it was buried in upon release. They quivered, flexing out as if upset that they did not get to hook into anything—their only purpose. I saw something dripping from the spines as well, an amber liquid mixing with his cum.

"They have *venom* too?"

"It's for the pain. The spines, they inject something for the pain, I think," he said quickly, sensing the questions brewing in my mind. "I don't really know the specifics. I just know they're similar to the ones in my teeth," he admitted.

"How considerate." I crawled next to him to face him. "What else can you do?"

He gave me an annoyed look. "Nothing you need to be concerned with."

"What if I fucked you? Would that"—I gestured downward—"not be something I would need to know about?"

"I told you already, I've never used them." He glared. "As cruel as you think I am, I would never do that to a human."

"But you would do it to something else?" I suggested.

"Oh no, I am just saving it for someone *special*," he said, a mocking edge to his tone, pulling up his trousers and buttoning them again.

I sighed and rested my head on his shoulder, looking at the fire dying in the mantle.

The tips of his fingers trailed up and down my back as we sat there.

There it was again, that warm feeling. It was not natural to feel this for the person capable of killing you. The danger might have been the thing that made it feel so much more intense. It could be some sort of Stockholm syndrome, but I had never met a man so interesting. It only made sense that he was not even human—I was not easily satisfied or entertained like this.

"So how old are you?"

"I thought women, of all people, would know never to ask that." Silas laughed, trailing his fingers through my hair as I basked in the warm water between his legs, my back resting against his chest.

"I don't think the rules apply to those who are hundreds of years old, or that's at least what I gathered when you started to talk about the black plague." I looked over my shoulder at him, blowing a handful of soap suds in his face.

He rolled his eyes and gathered my hair in his hands, beginning to plait it slowly.

"You know how to braid?"

"Of course I do. I have sisters."

My eyes widened. "There's more of you?"

"They are nothing like me, but I remember some from when I was young who taught me, and then I also taught one of the younger ones."

"That's…quite sweet actually." I smirked. "I can't imagine you as an older brother."

"I'm the eldest of my father's spawn."

"Are you still close with them?"

"Just one. The others have spread themselves worldwide, not heard of in some time."

"Will I get to meet her?"

"Why do you talk to your father's grave? I thought you didn't believe in the supernatural." He changed the subject.

"I thought you to be impossible, but here you are," I replied, rubbing the skin over my collarbone mindlessly. "You said earlier that you were born, correct?"

"Yes," he said slowly, curious about where I was going with my question.

"The spines," I started. "Do they play a role? You didn't explain the reproduction process."

"I didn't think I had to." He grinned, placing the braid over my shoulder and wrapping his arms around my waist. "The spines are meant to hold you in place," he said against the crook of my neck.

"Hypothetically, if we did—"

"No. Vipera cannot breed with humans."

"Oh," I mumbled, leaning my back against him as I watched his hands.

"But," he began, "if you turned, that would be different. Only because you are a Host."

"I see." I trailed my fingers along his forearms.

Silas let me absorb the new information and began to smooth his hands over my back, massaging my tense muscles. He made his way down to my lower back and pressed.

I yelped when he pressed on my lower back, and I whipped my head back at him. "What the hell?" I growled.

He looked at me surprisedly and held up his hands. "I didn't do anything!" he scowled. He gently moved his hands back over the spot. My skin crawled at the touch. "Is there some injury I don't know about?"

"I don't know. It's been hurting for a few weeks now."

He pushed my torso forward so he could inspect it further. His body tensed as he ran his hands over my spine.

"What?" I looked over my shoulder.

He reached over the tub railing to the side table, grabbed a small hand mirror, and pointed it at the spot on my back so I could see.

Two vertical punctures lined up with my spine on the lower vertebrae, still irritated as if only days old.

My blood ran cold, and I shot him an accusatory glare, but Silas looked just as angry as his eyes fixated on the punctures.

This wasn't from him.

"You're leaving tomorrow. I can escort you to Miss Aston's place." He placed the mirror on the side table before getting out of the tub. "You are going to get on that train with her as soon as possible. I will purchase tickets for an earlier train for both of you." He wrapped a towel around his waist, leaving me more confused than I was before.

CHAPTER THIRTY-TWO
THE CREATURE

There was no doubt in my mind who had been feeding on Alina. Only one Vipera that I knew of preferred feeding off of spinal fluid. I had assumed that he at least had more important things to do than play with my shadow.

A man by the name of Luka Novikov, *the Fixer*.

It was his signature. It only became known since he had a habit of taste testing the targets of situations he was paid handsomely to fix. A frequent name on my father's payroll.

Not only were his methods cruel and torturous in nature, but one's name in his books meant death was near, and it would not be quick. I was unaware that my father had hired him to find the Poisoner, but I suspected that it was the only explanation for him setting his sights on Alina.

He knew, and he was closing in on a delivery date.

That would explain his scent all over her. He had been feeding on her in her sleep for days, maybe weeks.

Luka was a madman. He was responsible in part for many atrocities throughout history. Luka was always whispering in the ears of depraved humans in power. He'd used their insanity to feed himself for decades. Many older Vipera had fostered Luka as a protégé, setting him loose to wreak havoc on whoever displeased them until he eventually turned on them or found a new master. Though once he was out of his cage, there was no knowing what other chaos would befall the situation and what he was paid to fix. I had even heard that he did not bother to use his venom on his victims, a brutal and senseless act of violence.

How could I let this happen? This was why it was best that I stay in *close* contact with my little project. She would hate me for it, but she could not possibly imagine half of what that man would do to her before he handed her over to my father. Deliberate, yet accidental, poisoning of people in the Nest would not be taken lightly.

My ever-talented Alina, if only you knew how good you really are.

Anxiety amplified with every tick of my timepiece. The train arrived at the station. I could spot my raven-haired fixation standing on the platform.

It was not hard to spot someone who looked like they were always in mourning, especially someone with such a unique face. I always wondered why Alina did that. It was creepy and off-putting, but I found it endearing. My favorite shadow, always hiding from the world in the most interesting corners that no one bothered to look at.

She was like a comet that appeared only every hundred years, fierce, bright, and devastating to anything in its way. It only made me want to hide her away from everyone. To take her someplace where she could feed her curiosity without interruption or judgment, only to see the light return to those unforgiving eyes.

She wore a dark-blue walking suit with black fur trim on the sleeves and collar. She had matching black fur on her hat as well.

It looked like she also chose to wear emeralds in her ears today. She was talking to my least favorite church bell, Phoebe.

Phoebe wore something pink. I did not bother to look too closely. I was unable to stop eating up the sight of Alina, tracking her as she entered the train car.

I entered one car down from them to keep my distance. While I said I would leave her alone, I would not let her out of my sight. Ever.

The two sat at one of the tables with singular seats by the window, their bodies facing one another.

Though I remained around the corner, I took a seat at the end of the row so that I could see both of them. At least I could observe them from a distance. Alina was facing away from me, chatting with her talkative companion.

Phoebe's eyes met mine as I stared. I gave a cheeky wave before she turned her attention back to Alina. She was not going to tell her I was there. She knew better. Her defensiveness regarding me was amusing. It seemed like fate that we shared the adoration of the same curious creature.

CHAPTER THIRTY-THREE

THE POISONER

"Is this new?" My eyes scaled the large brick country home.

"Relatively. Father bought it a year ago. He wanted a change of scenery." Phoebe paused. "This isn't far from your family cottage, no?" she asked, but bit her lip, realizing she shouldn't have touched on a sore subject.

"Yes, not too far, maybe thirty minutes."

A year was spent away in that formidable place. It was the only home I thought to go to escape the world that I knew would be watching. I was well aware of how close we were to it.

"Let's get you settled inside, then." She smiled, motioning for her footmen to bring in our trunks, and looped her arm through mine.

The Caldor Estate was something truly bewitching. The giant crosshatch windows stretched from floor to ceiling, cathedral-like. It was an older building, but its beauty held many stories of its creation and craftsmanship. It was an old English house, its architecture laced with historical details. It was hard not to feel like royalty walking through the grand halls. Out in the back of the house was a four-season conservatory, with a glass hall that led to a grand circular room with a green stained-glass dome. Comfortable furniture adorned the room, making it the perfect place to lounge the day away, no matter the season. The upholstery was a sage color to complement the stain of the glass. Potted plants were scattered around the room. I could live here forever if Phoebe let me.

"Is everything all right? You know that you can tell me if you are not well." Phoebe's voice pulled me from my thoughts.

"Yes, I'm fine. Why would I be anything except fine?" I gave her a tired look.

"As hard as I've seen you work, I've never seen you look this drained." Her dainty brows knit together. "Is it Silas? Is he bothering you?"

"No! No, it's all right. A little sleep paralysis is all. I think I've just been sick," I reassured her.

We took our time having lunch and walked through the gardens. There was a beautiful gazebo on a peninsula surrounded by a man-made pond. Many willow trees and tall pond flowers surrounded the area. It would be the perfect picture if two white swans were swimming about.

Phoebe's friends arrived around midday. We all gathered in the cozy conservatory as the evening went on. I knew a face here and there, but not many. I stayed in place on the couch, just observing for now. Background noise and the sounds of the chattering environment were perfect for letting my mind wander, slipping into a deep dissociation. Phoebe had sunk her talons into some poor, handsome soul off in the corner, so it looked like I had the night to myself.

"For someone who hates parties, I sure do see you at a lot of them." A charming accent cut through the voices surrounding me.

Viktor and a couple of his friends approached, and he plopped himself next to me on the love seat. His peers sat in the two chairs across from us.

"I didn't know that you were coming." I smiled tiredly. "How have your travels been?"

"Oh, I was just tagging along." He gestured to his companions. "These are my peers, Nikolai and Boris."

I tilted my glass at them in a welcoming gesture. "It's very nice to meet you. Do you study with Viktor?"

Nikolai glanced briefly at Viktor before looking at me again. "Yes, we have known him a long time. Long enough to know he doesn't study," he joked. It seemed both men shared accents similar to Viktor's.

"What's wrong with your face?" Boris asked abruptly, leaning back in his chair with a twisted sneer.

"Boris—" Viktor's tone snapped in warning, then he said something in Russian.

I clenched my teeth together. "Nothing is *wrong*. It's poliosis. It affects the pigment of hair and skin," I said matter-of-factly, taking a slow sip of my drink.

Viktor snapped again in Russian, and Boris laughed, shooting off some sort of comment that I could not understand before his head tilted back to me. "Is it contagious?"

"I would have thought a medical student such as yourself wouldn't be this featherbrained." I clenched my jaw. "Are you sure that it is Viktor who doesn't study?"

I turned to Nikolai. He was trying to hold back a laugh before cocking his head at his companion as if to ask, *You're really going to take a beating like that from a girl?*

Looking over at Viktor, I saw that something had changed in his face. He looked impossibly stoic, like Boris was on some thin, quickly crumbling ice.

Boris got up, not bothering to continue the conversation.

"I better go console him while he dresses his wounds with bourbon." Nikolai sighed. "It was so pleasant meeting you." He gave me a warm smile before nodding politely at Viktor.

"I am so sorry. You know how some men can be," Viktor reassured me, leaning his arm on the back of the couch behind me. "What brings you this far out?"

"Just getting away from the noise is all." I shrugged, inspecting the liquid in my cup as I tilted it. "It's nice to see a familiar face."

"I am happy to be a light on the footpath." He leaned in as we people-watched.

A phonograph hummed a tune while murmurs brought the night to life. Sounds of clinking glasses and laughter littered the air.

The ceiling became more interesting with each passing moment. Even with the stained glass, it was easy to see the stars due to the lack of light pollution. It was beautiful, reminding me of my time in solitude. I could feel a grip on my chest as my heart weighed on me, feelings of the past pulling it down. I'd spent many nights looking at the sky, talking into the abyss to pass the time.

Eyes were on me.

Viktor had been staring at me through lowered lashes. He leaned in and kissed me, his touch so tender.

I melted into him without thinking, savoring the soft touch.

He pulled away briefly, running his thumb over my lashes as he cupped my face. "You are so beautiful when you look out at the universe. I wonder what it would be like to be looked at with such adoration as you do at the unknown," he whispered against my lips.

"Viktor, I—" My heart could just shatter at his words,

knowing that it would never be something in the realm of possibility. Why did it feel like I was betraying Silas just by hearing it? "I can't," I whispered.

His amber eyes looked pained, but he nodded like he knew my reasons. "I know." He pulled away. "It would punish me every moment it went unsaid." He sighed, standing. "I hope you enjoy yourself tonight. I leave for the city in a few days. Will I be seeing you around?"

"I will be here." My face reddened because he just returned a sad smile. "We still have a few more things to finish in the lab."

He lifted my hand to his lips to bid me goodbye. He took a moment to linger, seeming to savor any contact he could. "Then I will see you soon."

He left me on that couch to let my thoughts ferment inside my already weary head.

Guilt, longing, and neediness surrounded me like ghosts clutching on to my soul. A phantom pain. What if I was letting Silas ruin something that was meant to be? My feelings for both were entirely different, but I could not help the hollowness in my chest. The only thing I could do was fill it with something else, preferably the sweet numbness of scotch.

CHAPTER THIRTY-FOUR

THE POISONER

The crisp morning air was enough to wake my senses. A thin veil of fog settled on top of the pond and extended out to the tree line over the field, waiting for the sun to evaporate it. The sky held a soft blue and purple glow, and a few darting birds crossed the canvas before us. Blackbirds could be heard as they woke their fellow woodland creatures. It was perfect. This place was a haven.

"We should go to town afterward to grab something sweet. I know the most perfect little bakery," Phoebe chattered almost as much as the blackbirds as she squeezed my arm.

"I won't say no to sweets." I took in a deep breath of crisp air as I consumed the smells of autumn approaching.

"How was it last night? I saw that you snuck in a little treat for yourself over on the love seat." She smirked, seemingly overjoyed that I did something other than sulk alone in a corner.

My heart did that funny thing again, leaping up into my throat. I tried to forget. I needed to forget both men before I could rationalize any feelings I had for either of them. "I don't feel like talking about it if you don't mind."

"Wait, what happened? Did I misread?" She stumbled over her words. "I thought you—"

"He kissed me. I told him I wasn't interested."

"He is just your type! Why would you say no?" she gasped. "He's studying medicine. He is into all those weird little science things. I met him at the garden party! He was so sweet looking for you! Your own Prince Charming!"

"What?" My eyes narrowed at her.

"He was looking for you—"

"No, the other thing."

"I met him at the garden party?"

"I thought you had known him before that. You didn't invite him?"

She looked at me worriedly and said, "No, I assumed that it was someone you knew, since he knew your name and said he was supposed to meet you there."

"Phoebe, I met him the same day you did." I frowned.

"Maybe he is just a fan of your work."

"I guess that could be. He did say that he read my journals." I sighed. "I'm sorry, Phoebe. I don't mean to scare you. I must be coming down with some sort of paranoid fit." I laughed nervously, walking with her down to the gazebo.

The flowers around the edge of the pond were wilted. I momentarily stopped to look at them before seeing inky liquid in the clear water.

My gaze trailed farther into the brush, seeing two pale eyes staring back at me. The kind of sound that escaped me must have resembled something unfamiliar, as I could not remember the type of shriek I made. My first instinct was to grab Phoebe by the face and cover her eyes, backing her away from the water's edge.

"Don't look, don't look." My voice shook as she tried to remove my hand from her eyes.

There was a head in the pond.

Boris's head.

THE DISCOVERY MADE the morning awkward as people woke up from their drunken slumbers. As news spread, suspicious looks were traded among attendees. The weight of what had happened hung in the air like the blanket of fog outside. Phoebe had disappeared into her chambers. I assumed that this had been hard on her. I wish I could have covered her eyes quicker after I spotted it, sparing her the image. What good was I if I could not even spare her from the horrors that followed me?

There was only one person who would be bold enough to do that, and I was cross with him at the moment. Especially finding out in this not-so-subtle way that he was still watching me. Was this a warning? Did he see what happened between Viktor and me? My only hope that he might not have seen was the fact that Viktor's body was not in the pond as well.

Retreating to my room, I grounded myself with calming breaths and pacing. A heavy heat plagued me despite my dress being a thin silk tea gown with little extra weight to it. I pinned my hair up into a bun so it was not adding more to the calidity.

A sad-looking reflection in the mirror returned my gaze. The cold blue of her eyes was pale, and she looked like she had seen a thing too many in her short time on earth. I did not recognize myself anymore. So much had happened since I returned. I wondered if staying out in the countryside would have been better. Maybe it was selfish of me to return to civilization. I was a hazard to everyone around me.

By later that evening, the tension had never eased. My depression slowly fermented into something new: rage. I'd already made it perfectly clear that he needed to leave me alone for my own mental well-being. It was like he was dead set on making sure I never knew peace.

Some of that rage was pointed at me. I felt terrible for giving in to Viktor's advances and kissing him, but I wondered if things might have worked out between us had Silas not gotten his hands on me. A typical, boring, wholesome romance. Something that blossomed sweetly, a stable life. At the same time, I might become depressed if I ever settled down, especially now that I knew how exciting it was to be with Silas. As obsessive and scary as he was, he lit something deep inside me that was impossible to ignore. I might just be addicted to the adrenaline high.

My dinner went cold. As much as I wanted to eat, my appetite had dissipated. My frustration with the situation manifested as tears when I excused myself from the crowded table. I was the reason for too many innocent deaths. At this point, I wondered if it would ever be near the number of guilty souls I had taken.

I choked back my feelings until I got behind the safety of a closed bedroom door. I pushed it closed and rested my forehead against the wood. A frustrated sob welled up in my throat as I tried to collect myself, gently tapping my forehead against the door.

"You look absolutely radiant when you're angry," Silas whispered against my neck.

Something else took over inside me, like snapping a violin's bow when the pressure became unbearable. I turned around and delivered a crisp slap across his face. I must not know my strength, because he stumbled after the loud crack landed on his cheek.

"You are the *worst* at following directions! I have known *children* with better impulse control than you!" I scolded.

"I can explain—"

"What is there to explain? You cannot just *kill* anyone who insults me! If you killed every man who said similar things to Boris, I think half of the men I've met would be in the Thames by now!"

"I will not allow anyone to speak to you like that." His eyes narrowed. "Did he not deserve it?"

"I am perfectly capable of handling him myself. If I wanted him dead, I would *do it myself*." I rubbed my temples as if to avoid working myself into a migraine. "Do you forget who I am? You put me at risk when you try to handle things for me. Since when did you decide that I can't handle myself?"

He drew closer to me. "You can handle yourself, you say? Are you so sure? Because if my memory serves me correctly, you seem to get yourself into entirely too much trouble." He loomed over me, the air thick between us. "I couldn't stand how *pathetic* you looked when you cried on those steps, begging me to save you from the monster in your kitchen."

My mouth gaped open, unable to find the words to throw back at him. There was only contempt.

He sighed and shook his head. "*No*, no, that's not what I wanted to say."

"I think you've said enough," I breathed. "Leave."

"No."

"Silas, I *will* scream."

"You won't."

I took in a deep breath, and he slapped his hand over my

mouth, muffling the screech I summoned from every drop of anger I held within me.

"For Christ's sake, Alina!" He yanked me away from the door and shoved me onto the bed with such force that I hit the headboard with a bang.

"Get away from me!" I screamed at him, scrambling up until my back was pressed against the headboard. I gripped the throbbing in the back of my head in an attempt to ease the pounding. Choking back tears, I tried not to show that it hurt or that he'd startled me.

"Are you done?" he asked tiredly.

"Are you?"

"Depends. Are you still angry?"

"Obviously."

"Then no, I am not finished yet." He crawled toward me on the bed.

My foot extended to kick him, but he caught my ankle, forcing it back down. His body towered over me as I lay beneath him.

Usually, he would try to snake his way out of conflict by touching or kissing, or sucking his way into getting me to calm down. Not this time. This time, he lay down and pulled me into the warmest embrace that had ever taken grasp of my body.

My breath hitched as his arms wrapped around me, one hand on my back and the other holding my face into the crook of his neck. Tremors took over my body as I tried to convince myself not to cry.

Don't unravel—don't do it in front of him.

The silence made me angrier, but I could not help but melt. He was intoxicating, my worst addiction. My head buried farther into his neck, his strong arms around me. A hand caressed my head, smoothing my hair back. His chin rested on top of my head. This must be what it felt like for a fly in the grasp of a Venus flytrap, slowly dissolving until nothing was left to give.

"I can't stand when you cry," he said quietly. "The smell burns the inside of my nose."

The comment made my lips pinch into a brief smile, but I could not hold it in any longer. The tears just came as quickly as my feelings were changing.

He pulled away to peer down at me, using his thumb to wipe away the wetness from my face.

"I love your eyes, even when they're red from tears." He placed his hand on the side of my face. "I have never seen someone look at something as wretched as me only to be left in awe," he whispered as he rested his forehead against mine. "For that reason, your eyes will always be precious to me, in any form. I want nothing more than to climb inside your skull and see the world as you do."

It took a long moment to process his words. They were overwhelming me in ways I didn't know how to react to.

"Silas…"

"I have not known fear until I met you, Alina," he interrupted me. "Do you know how horrifying it was to see you on those stairs and wonder what could have possibly scared you enough to cry out to *me*, of all things?"

The pain in his voice was desperate, begging for me to understand him.

"I realized that it wasn't you who scared me the most," he whispered finally against my lips, looking at me through his lashes. "What scared me is what would happen to me without you."

Did he mean that?

I looked at the world with endless awe and romanticism, but I had never considered that someone could look at me the same way—to be someone's unknown, begging to be explored. That someone could take delight in piecing together my very being. I could feel the tears rising in my eyes again. This was all too much.

"I want to go home." My voice cracked into a whimper despite my efforts to remain steady. "Please take me home, Silas."

"*Shh.*" He pulled me in tighter, like I would slip away if he let go. "You just have to be here a little longer while I figure this out. All right? Then I'll take you anywhere you ask of me," he said softly, pulling the covers over us and holding me tight.

I was wrapped in a cocoon. His smokey scent became a comfort rather than a warning. Those notes of blackberries and bay weighed on my senses before calming them. His embrace was no longer predatory, even though every logical part of my brain said it should be. This *should* terrify me. It should make me want to kill him, but the urge was fading every time he held me in his arms. No one had ever killed for me, and it was becoming harder to stay angry at the gesture. No matter what my ethics said, I found it romantic. However, I did not appreciate him handling things for me. I would rather do my own dirty work.

I did not know if he slept at all that night. All I knew was that he never left my side.

That was all that mattered.

CHAPTER THIRTY-FIVE
THE CREATURE

Watching her through the night while she was cradled in my arms felt wrong. Sometimes she would shift, and I would think to let go of her and flee before remembering that I was not in her chambers in secret. She was in my arms because she wanted to be.

When she yelled at me last night, I felt a constriction around my stomach and chest. It was not at all pleasurable like it had been many times before. The entire situation stressed her to the point of lashing out. She had become more unstable as the days went on. There was no doubt that her mentality had suffered in turn. I'd assumed that a country getaway would be relaxing, but it had made her decline faster than I thought. The way the gravity around her was heavy, more so than normal.

She needed to be alone. I needed to take her away. Socializing was not good for her. She needed a place to unravel.

When I finally pried myself away from her that morning, other guests were already awake, and a few gentlemen were scattered about the lounge drinking morning tea and trying to absolve their drunkenness. One dark-haired figure on the couch, in particular, pulled my attention.

"This seat taken?" It was more of an announcement that I would be sitting, not a question. I did not care for this fool's permission.

I took the seat across from our dark-haired acquaintance.

"It is now," Viktor said with a tight smile. "What brings you to this specific corner?"

"Why, I thought the company would be pleasant!" I said sarcastically.

"Late start to the morning?"

"Ah, well, departing a lady's chambers too early would be improper. I thought I'd bring her breakfast." I smiled. "No one to keep *you* in bed this beautiful morning?"

"You're quite sharp for just waking up." He ignored my previous comment, sipping his tea and glancing at the unbound stack of papers on his lap.

"Who said I went to sleep?" I smirked. "Some of us are kept occupied throughout the night."

"Was she also aware, or do you like it while she sleeps?" His eyes darted in my direction.

"Is that what you tell yourself? To make you feel better about being rejected?" I smiled innocently.

"You're on thin ice to begin with."

"Pardon?"

"No matter." A smile returned to his face as he handed me the stack of papers he had been annotating. "Give these to Alina when you head back up, yeah?" He stood and patted me playfully on the cheek before leaving the lounge area.

What on earth was that? Thin ice? With whom?

The papers in my hand looked to be a lab report. Not something I tended to read for fun, but then I saw her name on the front, right next to *his* name. It was a sickening reminder that I was not allowed to kill him, no matter how infuriating he was. I could only hope Alina would tire of him soon and he would fade into the background. She was like a cat, playing with many interesting things until she grew bored. Viktor was no different. She would be rid of him once she was done with her research.

CHAPTER THIRTY-SIX

THE POISONER

The winding trails of the Caldor Estate held some of the most beautiful scenes. They cut through endless fields that turned from wildflowers to golden grass in autumn. The ones that led into the forest went over creeks with thick trees in between, perfect for clearing the mind. The sunsets always lit the leaves on fire in a golden glow late in the day. The main road leading into town was on the other side of the wooded area.

The old English town looked frozen in time, not excluding the shops, taverns, and markets. It was perfectly quaint. Even at its busiest, it was quieter than my favorite market in London.

Phoebe and I arrived on horseback. There was a fox hunt later on, but other than that, it was a perfect leisurely day. We thought spending some time away from the crowd might be nice. It had been awkward between us since we found Boris. I made Silas promise no more surprises unless absolutely necessary. I warned him that he would cause me to fall ill if he kept leaving me with dead things. He was reluctant, but agreed.

Although Phoebe didn't know it, Silas had decided to stay at the estate with me. As they say, it was better to ask for forgiveness than permission, and Phoebe did not need to know why he was *really* there.

I told him he was not allowed to be seen too close to me if we wanted to keep a low profile. More attention was unnecessary as we figured out who my second stalker was. He was reluctant to leave me alone, but he needed to give me some space to keep more rumors from spreading. There were already so many from when he would not leave my side back home.

So far, Phoebe had informed me that people thought we had an arranged marriage, that I had fallen pregnant with his child, or that I was a witch because a man like him could not possibly want a woman who had a nontraditional lifestyle and a pedigree. The stories had become our new form of entertainment. Phoebe seemed less irritable about the whole thing, as I assured her that our relationship was professional.

While Silas's and my relationship was complicated, I found myself hating him less and less, especially after last night. Unfortunately, I had seen every side of him, yet I was still helpless to keep myself from certain feelings. I would like to say maybe my presence had changed him, but I might be getting ahead of myself.

I needed him whether I liked it or not. I knew he wasn't telling me everything. Something was wrong if he was genuinely worried. Stalking out of amusement had turned into stalking out of necessity recently. How did I always manage to attract the strangest men?

"You know, there's a patron gala when we return to the city. Father is lending some of his collection to the museum for a new exhibition," Phoebe chattered excitedly. "I'd love for you to come! Everyone from the museum will be there. I am sure my father could recommend you if you make any contacts. Many men from the natural sciences department will be in attendance." She wiggled her eyebrows at me suggestively.

I rolled my eyes as I adjusted my grip on the reins of my horse. "I will go, but not for that." I gave my horse a nudge with my heel to speed up.

"Don't you care about finding someone? You could ride off into the sunset while you talk about bugs or whatever you science folk use for small talk!" She laughed, pushing her horse forward to catch up with me.

"There are more important things to chase than men. Men are plentiful. It is not hard to find them. Sometimes they even find you."

She shook her head at me as we rode up the path, approaching the estate.

The men were warming up their horses and playing a friendly polo game in the back courtyard.

I could see a flash of golden hair on a chestnut stallion bolting toward the ball, his strong arm smacking it hard with the stick, his body practically leaning sideways off the horse. The ball smacked the net. Some cheers and groans chorused as Silas yanked on the reins, turning around. He spotted me off into the distance, giving me a smirk before he circled around to the other players.

I could feel Phoebe's glare already.

"What?" I smiled sheepishly.

"Strictly business?" She raised her brow.

"Yes, strictly business," I reassured her with an unconvincing smile.

"I wasn't aware he was on our guest list," she said through

clenched teeth, "and I made the list myself. Unless I am missing something."

"He said he came with Jonathan, the one who works for one of your father's acquisitions," I lied.

She looked like she considered the possibility but was ultimately unconvinced.

I WAS reluctant to look in the water, not wanting to see any more unsuspected eyes peering back at me.

Tea was being served in the gazebo for the ladies in attendance. It was a nice day for fresh air and leisurely activity. I looked down at the honey-colored liquid in my cup, pushing my spoon around, stirring the fragments of leaves at the bottom.

"Is it true?" a voice spoke out.

My mind was pulled from my trance as I looked up to see many sets of eyes now on me, waiting eagerly for a response.

"Apologies. I was lost in thought. What was it?"

"Silas Forbes," one brunette pipped. "Is he everything they say he is?"

"What might they be saying he is?" I sipped from my cup.

"They say he's quite gifted in the...carnal subjects." She smirked, and others joined in a cheeky array of giggles.

I had a tense expression on my face. "I wouldn't know. Mr. Forbes and I are not involved other than business." I set my cup down and glanced awkwardly at Phoebe, who refused to look in my direction.

"What project has he commissioned you for? A dog rig?" one woman teased boldly.

"Clarissa!" Phoebe snapped. "I expect more from you, but

you look like the type of mug to know a dog rig when you see one. What's that saying? 'Looks like a duck, quacks like a duck'? How predictable," she spat. I swore her tongue could cut up a woman faster than even the most esteemed butcher.

"It is all good fun, Phoebe." Another woman sighed.

"Do not pretend you asked in good nature," Phoebe sneered.

The table was silent, everyone glancing between the two.

"If rumors are something that you would like to believe, then be my guest to do so," I spoke finally, rising from my seat to excuse myself.

I placed my hand on Clarissa's shoulder in passing, my lips to her ear. "No amount of insult will be able to make you feel better about a man like him preferring a woman with a bit more… substance." Malice lingered in my words, leaving them all with that as I headed back to the house.

It might not have been wise to feed into the rumors about Silas and me, though it was not like I could make them disappear either. What was one more rumor? No one knew which one to believe anyway. Someone had also spread a rumor that it was confirmed from the horse's mouth that we were courting, though it was not from mine, that was for sure.

THE LOUNGE AREA was warmly lit, the tall windows painted with strokes of rain pouring down against the glass. The sound could lull me to sleep as I sat alone on a decorative chaise. I had not seen Phoebe since the garden. I imagined she was displeased with me at the moment. Eyes shifted at me nervously as people bustled about, drinking and coming together to continue their hearsay.

The energy of those shifting gazes changed when a tall figure moved through the crowd, seating himself next to me.

"Now, why would a pretty girl like you be sitting by herself? It sounds like a waste of good company," Silas whispered playfully.

Curious glimpses were stolen by the people around us, but I could only look at him.

"Well, I figured it was the best way for everyone to keep their heads," I said sarcastically, clinking my glass against his before letting the rest of the scotch slip down my throat. "People are avoiding me like the plague."

"Oh, that is because I told them that you were carrying my demon spawn and also secretly engaged to me." He smirked.

"So you heard the rumors too, I take it?"

"Of course! I started a few of my own. I felt like I was missing out," he joked. "Half of them did not sound terrible."

"I like the one about me being a witch. I think it was the one with the most conviction. The apothecary? Are people losing their heads? A devilish man following me around like my personal henchman? I would say that it is a very strong possibility."

"Well, you have certainly bewitched me." He laughed. "Any more tricks up your sleeve? Any of your special *potions* left to try?"

"Keep it up and maybe I will make one just for you. *Again.*"

"I quite like your poisons. I have acquired a taste for them." He leaned close to my ear. "It is not the only thing I have developed a taste for."

"Shouldn't we be keeping our distance?"

"You know very well that I couldn't do that any more than I could be a vegetarian." He slid his arm behind me to rest it on the back of the couch. "How about we go somewhere more intimate?"

"People will notice," I mumbled into my cup. "They'll talk."

"They already are, so what's the point?"

"Are you suggesting that we court publicly?"

"Why not?"

"You don't think it would be bad for your reputation?"

"You're intelligent, a uniquely skilled killer, and beautiful beyond my wildest imagination. I think you would be good for my bloodline."

"Very funny," I scoffed. "Be careful. One might say you almost sound sincere."

He leaned back in the seat, eyeing the people fluttering about.

"You know, I've never felt the need to keep humans around. They're so frail and needy." He kept his eyes on the crowd. "Many people like myself, including my father, keep them as pets often. Especially ones like you."

I watched his steady expression, but he did not look my way as he spoke. He then took my hand and stood up, pulling me toward the back of the room.

"I always thought it was senseless to possess something so delicate that could break if you used it the wrong way. I couldn't understand how that effort was worth a meal that you could find out in the open and dispose of later. There would always be another." He pulled me out the door and ventured down to the pond, away from prying eyes. "Now I understand what it is to become obsessed, devoted to possessing someone. Enough to fight the urge to lock you away so no one can set wandering eyes on you again."

There was something bright in the look he gave me that would have me believing that his last statement was not a joke. I had watched the obsession fester inside him since the moment we met. I knew how far he would go because of me, but how far would he go *for* me?

"Why are you telling me this?" My voice was strained.

Frost began forming on the grass as we walked along the edge of the pond. The conservatory glowed a bright orange over the dark blue surrounding the night.

"Just in case you needed convincing." He looked at me through those angelic blond lashes, running his finger down my arm before intertwining our fingers. "I want all of you, not just blood. I want every piece of flesh that clings to your bones and more. I want to own every expression that crosses that pretty face. Every hair on your head belongs to me, no part of it untouched by my hands."

"I don't belong to you," I reminded him.

A smirk crossed his lips when I said that, like it was a challenge. A carnal expression graced that striking face. "If you believe that, then maybe you are a fool after all, Alina," he said smoothly, taking my hand and lifting it up to spin me around. He crossed it over my chest and held me against him, his other hand wrapping around my waist. We could hear the muffled sounds of music in the distance. His breath fanned over the back of my neck as he kissed the skin softly, swaying with me as he caressed my body.

His obsession was worse than I thought. I assumed that it was caused by my supposed special blood he talked about, but now I knew that it was so much worse. He would never leave me alone. He did not care if the public knew. It meant cutting me off from everyone else. If intimidation failed, I knew he would not hesitate to deliver body parts to my door if any man tried to move on what he thought was his.

"You are the fool if you think I could belong to anyone." I

unraveled myself from his arms, but he pulled me back in. He dipped me low with a tight grasp.

"You say that, but there will come a time when I ask you, and you will say yes." He pulled me up to where our noses touched.

"That is quite a fantasy you have." I raised a brow. "Unlikely, I fear."

He chuckled and cupped my cheek softly, lovingly, even.

"We will burn that bridge when we get to it, my shadow."

CHAPTER THIRTY-SEVEN

THE POISONER

"I take it you liked the pastries?" Phoebe hummed.

"Anything with citrus, you know I can't fight it." I bit into my fourth tart of the morning.

Breakfast was enjoyed outside along with the other guests.

As I stared down at the pastry, I lost my facade, the smile dissipating like a flame on a wet wick. So much energy was dedicated to *looking* happy instead of actually being happy. The weight of my situation was stealing my appetite and dragging my mood down every time I remembered it. The sensation always came on so suddenly.

"Morbs?" Phoebe asked once she noticed my demeanor.

"Morbs," I answered.

I was lucky that Phoebe understood my moods, like she could read me faster than her tabloids. As a socialite, one had to get alarmingly good at reading people.

The brunette from the other day, Clarissa, glared in our direction and whispered viciously among the other debutantes. So young and high-strung. It was hard to blame them. I was the same not too many years ago. They were settled on a picnic blanket by the pond with their parasols. Though I did not have to be good at reading people to know she was not my biggest fan, I could expect a slur of nasty rumors in a few days' time.

I had not seen Silas all morning, which was odd because he usually made himself known as often as possible. All that talk about possession last night. His cocky attitude was insufferable at this point. Could it kill him to be pleasant for once?

My thoughts were interrupted by the thud of hooves pulling a carriage up to the front of the estate. I glanced at Phoebe, but she just stared at the carriage, seemingly not expecting anyone.

That was when that familiar flash of blond appeared, stepping out and surveying the early birds. Those gray eyes finally fixated on me, prompting a handsome smile as he approached.

"Aston," Silas acknowledged Phoebe, but did not take his eyes off me. "Alina, we have an appointment."

I looked over at Phoebe, confused, and she looked back at me equally as perplexed, a worried tinge on her face.

"What appointment?" I glanced back up at him, his shadow blocking the morning sun.

"One that you won't want to miss." He held his gloved hand out to me.

"Why must you steal my friends whenever you find yourself bored?" Phoebe grumbled, and took a sip of her tea, glaring at Silas over the rim of her cup.

"Steal? You give me too much credit." He rolled his eyes at her. "I will return her afterward...maybe."

I took his hand and stood. "What about my things?"

"You won't need them. I'll have them delivered back to London," he answered, beginning to lead me away.

Phoebe and I shared unsure looks before seeing the other

guests staring. I knew that word would get back to every tabloid in London by the time I returned.

He politely gestured for me to enter the coach before following suit. The coachman closed the door securely before the vehicle lurched forward.

We sat across from one another, silent.

The car was furnished in dark leather with red lining. The outer parts were painted a sleek black with gold detailing. Not once had I ridden in something this expensive before, but I would rather ride miles on the side saddle than trap myself in here with him. Though it was a bit late for that.

"Where are we going?"

"So many questions." He leaned back. "You act like I am abducting you. I'm trying to be kind."

"You? Kind?" I laughed. "I don't think you do anything without a purpose."

"You're right." He tapped his shoe against the floor of the cab. "I am clearly trying to trick you into leaving the pretentious parties and useless conversations about diets that you *so clearly enjoy* so that I can have you selfishly to myself," he said sweetly.

"Well, the birds will have a field day with that stunt. You knew that those girls would talk." I glared, nervously picking at my nails.

"All part of the plan." He grinned. "I told you, I want everyone to know, whether you want them to or not. You will play the part if you know what's good for you."

"Why do all of your confessions sound like threats?" I fixed my eyes on the passing scenery.

He paused for a moment as if to ponder my question. The silence went on for a while. He might have given up on a proper answer as we spent the ride just looking out the window, stealing cautious glimpses at one another as we traveled.

After a long journey, we arrived at a different estate. It looked more like a castle the closer we came. Many carriages were parked in the side lot, and horses were being tended to. We arrived in the front and stopped, the door opening for us upon arrival.

Silas stepped out first, offering his hand out to me.

I reluctantly took it and looked up at the structure before me. It looked less like a home and more like a fortress.

Silas tried in vain to hide any smugness in his visage.

What in the world is he up to?

As we approached the tall entryway, someone checked our names before letting us in. There were mainly men bustling about, talking, flipping through papers, and pointing at the many displays scattered along the hallways. In certain rooms, there were presentations with spectators. Some women were here, but they all looked to be accompanied by a man not too far off.

Excitement melted away any prior aversion.

He'd taken me to a *private* exhibition.

"Why?" I turned to him.

His eyes had been fixed on me since before I looked, fully attentive to my every move. "You get that light in your eyes whenever you look at something you're curious about. I wanted to see more of it." He shrugged. "You belong here, not in a stuffy house surrounded by people who don't understand you."

Blood rushed to my cheeks. There was no hint of mockery or sarcasm in his voice. I might be able to trust that he was being sincere.

CHAPTER THIRTY-EIGHT

THE CREATURE

People clustered around the different displays around the domain. Everyone was so hungry, eager to absorb every word and dissect everything they spoke to one another. Small mechanical models of inventions and pending patents were demonstrated and pitched between many patrons. Places like these were where business and science intersected.

While it was all very fascinating, nothing could keep me from studying her. I had never seen her this animated before. It was like life had returned to her recently depressed demeanor. Every unhelpful thought left her head and was renewed with questions brewing faster than a teahouse at four o'clock. Those pretty blue eyes looked like they could not consume the information before her fast enough. It reminded me of how she'd looked at me that night, demanding to see where my fangs could have possibly gone. I swore she would have dissected me right then and there, and maybe I would have let her. This was why I could never dream of staying away from her.

"Alina!" A Russian accent cut through the crowd.

Not him...

She turned her head to see who was calling. A wide smile broke across her lips, and her arm slipped from mine.

I turned to see *Viktor*. His amber eyes looked soft as he approached until then they fell on me. A sinister glint sparked before it disappeared as quickly as it came, and he turned his attention back to my dear shadow. He wrapped his arms around her in a hug, a smirk on his face as he looked at me from over her shoulder.

I will cut that smug look off your face and wear it at your funeral.

"Had I known that you were coming, I would have made an itinerary for all the lectures we should attend," he spoke sweetly to her, enticing her with familiar speech. "Have you seen some of the upcoming patents in the pharmaceutical section yet?"

"We just arrived!" Alina said excitedly before she looked back at me, a concerned look on her face when my demeanor changed. "Silas was kind enough to bring me," she awkwardly introduced, circling back to my side.

Good girl.

"Would you like to join us, Viktor?"

No.

"Of course!" Viktor smiled, joining her on the opposite side.

"The more, the merrier." I forced a rigid smile, but my attention stayed on him.

As we circled to what looked like the biology segment, I noticed some illustrations of plants and some bottles lined up by one of the displays. There were some inelegant men in very questionable fashion in deep conversation about a diagram while holding tinctures.

"Alina, head off that way. I think I will stay behind," I told her, plucking a pamphlet from the table at the room's entrance, placing it in her hand, and guiding her forward. She glanced in annoyance at me, but soon found her attention on the many enticing distractions.

Viktor went to follow her, but I grabbed his arm and pulled him toward the wall, away from the crowd.

"Let her be," I warned.

"What is it? Afraid she may disappear with me if you lose sight of her?" Viktor teased, leaning against the wall as his eyes followed her.

"I have full confidence in her ability to navigate a crowd without getting kidnapped by her creepy peer."

"Kidnap? I was thinking of asking her nicely to come with me. Just because *your* mind is in a gutter doesn't mean mine is as well," he mocked. "I can be quite charming when I have to be."

"Off-putting is more like it."

"I get that you are upset. There is no need to take it out on her though. We are working together whether you like it or not."

"What do you study anyway?" I mumbled. "I find it hard to believe you are a student."

"While I am flattered that I do not look like the scholarly type"—he laughed—"I am studying orthopedics."

I raised my brow at him.

"The study of bones. Though I find my calling in the spine." His stare burned into mine as he paused, a devilish smirk creating a dimple in his cheek. "Spinal fluid is almost as valuable as blood to the body, you know."

It's him. It's Luka.

I departed abruptly, pushing through the crowd until I found my shadow gathered by some plants. They were in the middle of a discussion, but I didn't need her spending a single minute here. If only I had known that the danger had followed her despite my efforts to create distance between her and those looking for the Poisoner.

"Alina, we are leaving." I grabbed her hand and pulling her through the crowd and away from the presentation.

"What was that? You don't need to be rude." She glared at me.

"Apologies. Can't help myself," I muttered distractedly, pulling her to the exit.

Over my shoulder, I could see the third person in our little relationship. Those dark eyes followed us out of the crowd from the corner of the room, though there was no expression of contempt. He raised a brow at me before checking his timepiece mockingly. Luka Novikov turned his back and disappeared into the crowd.

I pulled her into the first coach parked out front.

"I thought we would spend longer," she complained.

I pulled a long rectangular wooden box from my coat pocket, holding it out to her, which made her lose her train of thought completely.

"Open it," I prompted her.

Her fine fingers held the box so gently. She hesitated, possibly due to the other times I'd left "gifts." Though the real gift from those was her reaction.

The box was only twelve inches long and made of dark wood. I had to call in a favor for this, but I knew she wouldn't genuinely like anything else.

She unlatched the box and opened it gingerly. Around eight small vials filled with liquid were nestled into the box's velvet. "What is this?"

"Eight of the deadliest venoms this world has ever known," I answered her. "I have friends in interesting places. I thought maybe you could use them in your research." I leaned over her as we sat side by side, peering at the box's contents.

She looked like I'd given her a ring and gotten down on a

knee. Delicate fingers traced over the vials in awe. Something in her eyes told me that she was taking in the moment. Nothing could break her focus. She closed the box, latched it shut, and held it close to her chest. "Change the address. I want to try something." A vile grin pulled at those pretty lips as her mind raced.

Call me lovelorn, but I adored this woman completely.

"You don't have to ask me twice," I said, hitting the wall of the coach to change course.

CHAPTER THIRTY-NINE

THE POISONER

"Please! Just try it. You said that it wouldn't work. I just want you to tell me how it feels, maybe how it tastes?" I whined.

"I didn't think you would want to use them on me. I thought we were past this," he groaned.

Several metal spoons lined the tea table as we sat on the floor. Cushions and old fur blankets were piled under us as we lingered near the steadily warming fireplace. We'd come to my family's cottage. It was not small, but still about ten rooms. It was a bit of a backtrack, but the closest place we could go. Most of the furnishings and mirrors were still covered in sheets. It brought back old feelings from worse times, though any ghost of the past had disappeared now that I had company.

I held a spoon up to him. "You said that it won't kill you, so why the hesitation?"

"You know, I am starting to take this personally." He rolled his eyes.

"Don't be a child. Try it!" I frowned, pressing the tip of the spoon to his mouth.

He reluctantly opened, and I shoved it in.

With my pen in hand, I awaited any insights.

His face twisted at the taste, and he smacked his tongue against the roof of his mouth. "It tastes like…nails."

"Nails? Do you mean the pain or the taste of metal?"

"Both." He grimaced. "Remind me never to let you cook for me." He took a sip of my scotch to wash it down.

"I can cook just fine. Just don't vex me, and I will exclude the cyanide." I finished jotting down my note before picking up the next spoon. "Now this one."

"We have tried four already," he protested.

"Be a good sport." I glared. "You agreed to be my subject," I said pointedly. I leaned in and whispered seductively in his ear, "Now open up."

He sighed and leaned forward, closing his mouth around the spoon and swallowing again. He clenched his eyes shut and winced in disgust.

"If there is a God, I don't want to know why he would create that." He choked, downing the rest of my scotch to clear the taste.

"That was mine!" I grumbled. "Now tell me how it tastes."

"Like rotting flesh left outside on a summer afternoon."

"Do you think I could…" I trailed off momentarily, thinking about how to phrase my request.

"Could what?" He propped his elbows on his knees so his head could rest in his hands. His eyes followed my pen strokes.

"I want more samples," I said plainly.

"You can drain me like a leech. It won't matter to me."

"No, not blood," I suggested. "Other samples."

"Oh, *please* go on." He smirked. "I could think of a few to give you now." A light clicking sound came from him. He *literally* purred.

I shot him a warning glare. "Not like that," I mumbled. "But I will need samples from your…other fangs."

"Ah yes, and you gave me a generous reward for letting you observe that, if I remember correctly." He played with the sleeve of my chemise.

"Maybe I could do it again if I trusted your commitment." I put my pen down. "Maybe we could strike another deal."

"You have my attention."

"You said before that you want not just my blood but everything," I started, turning toward him so I could gauge his reactions. "I don't want to give you any of that without the same in return."

That only made his cocky grin get wider. "What are you proposing?"

"Access to my body in exchange for yours," I stated. "I can have any sample I want. Flesh, blood, and any organic matter that I request. No exceptions. That way, we don't have to keep bartering."

He leaned in close as I spoke. "And when do you suggest that this deal begin?"

My words caught in my throat, reluctant to manifest. "Now," I breathed.

I searched for a reaction, but the blood that filled the whites of his eyes indicated that he was keen on accepting.

He yanked my legs out from under me, and I fell back into the assortment of fur and cushions piled beneath us.

The only thing he wore was his trousers, his lean body exposing every line of his physique in the warm glow of the flames. He was built like any apex predator should be. The sheer power he held, but never used fully on me. I wondered sometimes how much he was holding back.

He spread my legs before him and pushed the fabric up my thighs, then over my stomach, my chest, and finally, my head. "Are you sure you want this?" His eyes flicked up to my own.

I nodded.

"No." He hooked his thumb in the waistband of his trousers, unbuttoning and slipping them down. His thick cock was gripped in his hand as he pulled it out, smoothing over its intimidating form as he looked at me as if he was waiting for me to protest. "I want to hear you say it. Do you want me?"

"Yes." I swallowed, not knowing where to focus.

He leaned down between my legs, and I propped myself up on my elbows to watch him, his tongue flattening between my thighs, and I shuddered. He lapped and sucked at me as he moved his hand along his length, seeming to savor this as long as he could.

"I thought you were going to feed." I flinched.

"I will," he mumbled between my legs, looking up at me. "But you said I could have it all, and that is exactly what I will be taking."

My chest tightened at his words. He moved up to kiss along my abdomen, between my breasts, then to my neck, sucking at my skin before moving his mouth to mine. His hands touched everywhere he could, leaving nothing unexplored like he'd promised so many times before.

I put my hands on his torso, feeling the warmth emanating from his body, then another kind of warmth between my legs.

He slipped a single finger inside of me, gently pushing in and testing the waters.

The kiss was so tender, so careful that I could only return it with the same softness. Playfully nipping at his lip, I ran my tongue along his. I let it tease the roof of his mouth every now and then, running it over the hidden fangs there. I was already slick between my legs from his avid touch.

He groaned as he added a second finger, curling it inside me and making my back arch against him. Slowly, he moved them inside me before building up his pace and intensity. He looked at me through lowered eyes as he deepened our kiss, using his other hand to stroke himself.

Slowly, he prompted a third finger, spreading them gently to ensure I could handle something a little thicker. I flinched at the addition but wrapped my arms around his neck, holding him close. When he removed his fingers suddenly, I could not help a disappointed whine.

"Don't get ahead of yourself." He kissed my shoulder. "Unless you want me to break you."

"Don't flatter yourself," I whispered, though I was almost hoping for him to try.

He pressed the tip of his cock against me, lining it up with my vulva.

I glanced down to look, but he grabbed my face and made me look at him. "Don't. It'll hurt more if you do that." He quickly locked our lips as he pushed slowly inside.

My yelp was muffled by his mouth. I squirmed beneath him, and his hands gripped my waist, digging his fingers into my skin.

"*Silas*—" No other words would come. Not one coherent thought crossed my mind.

He pushed until he hit the back. I could feel it with a sharp sting. Tears welled in my vision, and I tilted my head back. I had never felt something so full inside me. The heat was doing little to relax my tension. My body was struggling to adjust, and I was afraid to move. Against his advice, I looked down. He was not even fully inside yet.

Dear God, how is this sustainable?

I was unsure I could take any more, even if I wanted to. It relieved me when I remembered the dangerous spines on the underside of his base. It made sense now how he was not able to use them on anyone. I did not think it could reach if he tried.

After a long pause to allow me to adjust, he pulled out, then pushed back in steadily.

My breath hitched in a whimper as I hid my face in his neck.

"Relax." His voice strained as he rolled his hips, pulling out slowly before burying it back inside.

"*It hurts,*" I cried softly, my legs shaking.

"I know, I know," he soothed me. "Let it out, *cry* for me." He picked up his pace. The wetness slicked down his cock and allowed his movements more ease.

As he thrusted, I could feel myself slowly getting used to the girth, allowing him to bury deeper with every movement, though the pain did not go away. I would not complain. I found that the pain was part of what made it feel so intense.

I fell back and gripped the fur blanket beneath me as he lowered his hips between my legs. He kissed and sucked at my neck, leaving sweet nips at my skin. Once again asking for permission, his eyes looking up at me expectantly.

"Please…" I begged.

Upon hearing my pleas, he let his fangs flick forward, hovering over that hot spot on my neck. He either hesitated or had trouble doing both at once.

"*Please,* Silas." I craved him. "Bite me."

The sensation of needles piercing my skin was quick and sharp. I cried out.

The pain was worse than I thought. My veins were on fire,

accompanied by the feeling of long puncturing teeth buried deep in my flesh.

A low growl escaped him as he fed. My blood was rushing from inside, escaping me in a draining sense. My body shuddered, in shock at the pain that was gripping my neck. His jaw tightened. My mouth fell open, unsure if a moan or a cry would come out if I allowed it.

A wave of something washed over me when he clamped down harder. It was not unlike the numbness after alcohol against a fresh wound, followed by the fervor of drunken delirium. Opium, absinthe, cocaine, nothing compared to whatever high came from the bite. The pain slowly faded from my neck, but I could feel everything else more intensely than ever.

His thrusts became harder, sending an electric pang up my spine every time he penetrated me.

Tears streamed down my face from pure ecstasy. It was like morphine was replacing the blood I was undoubtedly losing. My entire body was overwhelmed with quakes.

He let go of my neck, blood dripping down his chin as he licked over the wound, pulling me up into his lap as he sat back on his heels. He shoved my hips forcefully down on his thick cock.

I shouted and threw my head back, steadying myself as I dug my nails into his shoulders, my hips grinding against him. It was like I was chasing a high, wanting to be completely submerged in him, no matter the risk of drowning. I craved to be filled with him in every place I could, wanting more and more of it. Before I knew it, I was taking in his full length.

"How does it feel?" He mocked my tone from earlier. "Describe it to me."

"*H-hot,*" I stuttered. "*I'm burning.*"

"What else?" he murmured into my ear, forcing my hips down again.

I let out a lustful sob, dragging my nails across his skin.

"Don't say that it hurts. I know that's not what you feel," he crooned.

My mouth hung open, but I failed to produce any answer. It was hard enough to form thoughts. It was cruel to ask me to think at a moment like this. I rested my forehead against his, giving up on finding my voice.

He let himself slide out, lifting me up and flipping me on all fours. He lined the tip of his cock up with my entrance once more, but stayed perfectly still. "Beg for it."

I glared over my shoulder. I lowered my torso so my face was touching the ground, pushing my hips back on him.

He pulled it away again.

"Uh-uh! You should know better than anyone how we ask for things." He smirked. "I want to hear you beg."

"*Please*," I pleaded. "*Please*, I…need it inside. I feel so *empty*," I whined, glancing over my shoulder from the floor. "I want to lose my voice by the time I'm done screaming your name."

There was a psychotic glint in his eye. He had been waiting for this, to see me like a cat in heat. This was exactly what he meant when he said he wanted to possess everything. The last thing was my damned mind as he drove me off the cliffs of insanity. I did not care as long as he gave me what I craved.

He failed to hold back any longer, thrusting his length fully into me, the position letting him reach deeper than I thought possible, and my relaxed state welcomed it to the hilt.

I flinched and gripped the fur blanket on the ground before me to keep from heaving forward from the force.

He thrusted with such vigor, it made me question whether or not it was possible to bruise the inside of my body. His rippled body towered over me, turning me into a panting puddle on the floor.

I feared his voracity would make me melt in more ways than one.

He hit that deep, hidden spot over and over as my body became numb from pleasure. All I could feel was him. Every thrust, touch, and grab. Every sensation made me lose my mind further. The sounds that came from my mouth surprised me, as I had never heard such vile noises in my life.

He turned me over, wrapping my legs around his waist. His face looked flustered but determined. One might assume that he looked like he was still holding back.

Not if I could help it.

My hips rolled into him, and I moaned, letting my mouth drop open to say something, but the only thing I could manage was his name.

His movements got rougher, hungrier, and desperate. He was coming close.

I could feel it.

His full length slammed deep inside me, all the way to the hilt. A smirk slipped across my lips as I moved my hips against him, meeting his movements. My eyes met his briefly, begging him for more.

"Don't look at me like that," he said breathlessly, his skin glistening in the warmth. "I won't be able to stop."

I gave him a drunken smile, high from venom and lust. "Then don't," I moaned, making sure to meet his gaze as I gripped one of my breasts, using my other hand to touch myself above the place he was penetrating.

His breathing picked up, and he thrust harder, lifting my hips to penetrate deeper.

"*Silas!*" I yelped, my legs gripping around his waist and clenching my eyes shut.

He leaned over me and wrapped his arms around my waist.

With one final shove, he pushed as far into me as he could, holding my body down so I couldn't squirm away.

An acute pain pricked the inside of my vaginal wall.

"*Stop!*" I cried instinctually, but the pain faded as fast as it came. All I could feel was a periodic throbbing of his cock, and the feeling of his hot cum dripping out.

My breathing came quick, unaware of how much energy I had used for this endeavor, our chests rising and falling against one another.

His embrace tightened as he hid his face in my neck.

"You…"

"I'm sorry," he whispered, kissing the skin on my shoulder and up to my neck, his fingers tangling in my hair and keeping me in place, pushing his hips firmly into mine.

"You said you wouldn't," I breathed.

"*I lied,*" he said lowly.

"Why?"

"Because you are mine." Clicking bloomed in his throat like a purr, his cock still pulsing inside me. He leaned away to meet my gaze. The air around us was intoxicating. My consciousness swirled in a dizzy spell.

I had a hard time keeping eye contact. He grabbed my face and made me look at him.

"You said they were supposed to be for your—"

"Mate," he finished, resting his head against mine.

"But I'm—"

"You are now." He gave a satisfied hum.

"Since *when?*"

"Since *I said so.*"

"And when was that?"

"The moment you tried to poison me. The *first* time. I think the choice is fitting."

"You were serious about that bloodline quip?"

"What reason would I have to joke?" He chuckled. "Though as much as it would delight me to introduce you to my bloodline, we both know that wouldn't work, *scientifically speaking.*"

"Then what is the point of such a gesture?"

"So your body knows its place."

He switched our positions so that I lay on top of him, my hips still straddling his, waiting for his spines to retract from inside me. I peered down and saw small amounts of crimson mixing with the semen that pooled out.

"What did I say about looking?" He grabbed my chin.

"How long until they let go?"

"Thirty minutes. An hour maybe."

"An hour? No wonder you never use them. Who would want to be stuck with you for an *hour*?"

A chill shot through my spine the more I thought about the pain, the memory of it fading quickly from my mind and being replaced with a vehemence more intense than the last. It was like I'd drunk laudanum ten times over the recommended amount. Morphine paled in comparison to whatever was in those spines.

He pulled one of the fur blankets over us and held me close. The fire cracked and snapped, dying down to a simple glow of embers.

Was he insane? Is this why he wanted permission? While it was a bit of a blind side, I was flattered. It was humbling for a creature who'd spent all his life with no interest in this sort of thing just to choose me, the woman who had tried to kill him on multiple occasions. Maybe that was why he liked me. I couldn't be sure. All I could focus on was the warmth of his body and his hands holding my waist as I faded into the sweetness of the night.

I SAT in the bay window of my old bedroom, the stained glass propped open so I could see out into the front yard. A long dirt trail extended far into the fog, lined with thin trees along the path. The air smelled like snow. Winter was nearing fast. By now, every blossom must have died in my greenhouse as well as my pink hydrangeas.

"What bothers you at the witching hour?" Silas's deep, barely awake voice whispered, slipping behind me in the bay window nook to cradle me from behind.

"Everything."

"Have the ghosts been bothering you?"

"Just one."

"Hopefully it is I that you refer to."

"Unfortunately not."

"Tell me."

"I spent an entire year here, alone," I told him. "It is bringing back some unfavorable memories."

"Is this where your accident happened?"

I looked over my shoulder at him with tired eyes. "What do you mean?"

"You said you made a mistake. One that haunts you. It does not take brilliance to piece together that it happened where you locked yourself in exile."

"Why would you assume that?"

"Because you punish yourself when you do wrong or see it.

I've watched you do it. Your exile was your punishment to yourself."

"I do not."

"Lie to me all you like, but please do not lie to yourself," he mumbled, tucking some loose tendrils of hair behind my ear. He leaned back against the nook, wrapping his arms around my waist as I sat between his legs. He kissed the back of my neck sweetly. "Now tell me about it."

"It was a mistake. It wasn't the right time." I picked at my nails.

"Speak directly." He placed his palms over my hands and intertwined our fingers to negate the fidgeting.

"I poisoned my father's assistant." I hesitated.

"Why was that?"

"Issac lived with us while my father studied out here. It is closer to Oxford. That is where his assistant worked. They were studying something new. My father didn't talk much about it," I began, and he let me take my time with it.

"I slept upstairs, he took a spare, and my father took his own room." I gulped. "It was too late. I feel I acted too slowly. I was too unaware, not vigilant enough. I should have woken up before. I don't know why I didn't. I wish I hadn't woken up that time. I almost feel that it would have been better, less damage not to know." My voice wavered.

"Alina." Silas's voice rang low. "What did he do to you?"

"I woke up. I didn't tell my father, but I should have. I don't know if he would have believed me. I convinced myself that it could have been a dream, that it was my own manifestation and maybe I wanted it—"

Silas turned me around, grabbing my face with both hands so that he could see my eyes, which must have been pink and glassy. "Did he touch you?"

"He had me that night while I slept, and the night before, and the one before that, for who knows how long." I shook under Silas's grasp. "I put arsenic in the wine." I sobbed.

"Shh...do not cry for him," he whispered, kissing each tear as it escaped down my cheek.

He pulled me into a tight embrace, pulling my knees up so he could hold me in his lap. I had a hard time calming my breathing. My chest tightened whenever I tried to take in air. The warmest embrace from the coldest creature I knew was my only solace.

"You did what you had to do," Silas said firmly, kissing my head. "Do not fool yourself into thinking what you did was anything other than necessary."

I nodded, wrapping my arms around his neck and burying my face in his chest to hide my shame. His words were encouraging, but they did not shake the deep depression and hate I held for myself for what I did and what my choices led to afterward.

CHAPTER FORTY

THE POISONER

The amount of time I had been spending in the lab was embarrassing.

Though I decided to conduct some tests in my back room rather than the college. Silas had been asking to meet at the shop instead. I supposed the only things I needed at the college at this point were Dr. Hayes and Viktor, though there were some things I could do at home.

Silas insisted that I stay with him at his estate while the danger was still present. Though I hardly left my lab, sometimes falling asleep at the desk so that I could continue working for days on end.

I did not remember when I last opened the apothecary, fully returned to my hermit state. A spell of compulsion had led me down a path of tests and experiments with the number of samples Silas handed over, keeping me occupied for however many days I had been at it. The time was lost in my manic state.

From my notes, I could see that his rear fangs contained a painkiller, a muscle relaxant, and an aphrodisiac.

His blood was similar to snake venom that burns away at flesh and causes swelling, though I was already painfully aware of that.

Then there was the golden liquid from his...other fangs—his spines. From Silas's own knowledge and from my experience that night, it contained some of the same properties as the venom in his mouth.

When I tested it on female toads, they laid eggs the next day. Every single time. I tested it on ten different toads. It was potent in a hormone of some sort, and my theory about it being for reproductive stimulation was correct. It made me nervous initially, only to remember he said that it was impossible without being one of his kind. As far as I knew, I was safe.

My cheeks grew hot when the memories flashed before me. I leaned against my desk and slumped in embarrassment, covering my face as if there were someone to judge me for it.

Mate.

Why was it so shameful to remember it that way, knowing everything I did about his biology? It was getting me flustered every time I discovered a new use for the chemicals in his body. I wanted more of it. I wanted it again and again until I forgot how to speak. However, I had barely recovered from the last time, as the soreness made sitting uncomfortable.

With a deep breath, I straightened myself out, beginning to look at my solution sample again. I had been testing it against the blood to see how it worked. Upon purifying it, it neutralized most of the blood and even broke it down. The reaction was unstable, so results ranged from slow breakdowns to making the blood cells burst entirely. It restored my faith in my abilities despite the upsetting test results from the college lab.

My heart had become conflicted over my special poison for people like him. I had not bothered to ask how he felt about it, because I did not know how I felt about it myself. I would not use it on him. No, I would use him for my purpose, if anything. But I apparently had another secret admirer to worry about. A phantom pain throbbed in my lower spine. Such a violation was unthinkable, knowing that someone was stealing from me something more precious than gold: my autonomy. Unfortunately, not the first time.

That was unacceptable, so I would be ready the next time that shadow stalked into my home. They would all be sorry they'd laid a finger on me, as I would cut it clean off. There would be no hesitation this time. Silas would have to forgive me for the atrocities I was about to wreck on his kind. He was the reason I was able to do so after all.

My body ached aside from the punctures.

I mixed the samples from the spines and teeth and distilled them until I got at least one vial of pure venom. The amber liquid left a golden reflection on the table as the light passed through it. I picked at my bottom lip as my mind slipped to more taboo questions about its usage. There was no knowing if it could be used medicinally or recreationally without someone to test it. If I was so confident in my work, I should test it myself.

I grabbed a clean needle and a torniquet from one of the drawers and sat in front of the small glass tube on my workbench. My thumb popped the cork off of it, and I dipped the syringe into the venom, slowly drawing it up into the glass cylinder. Inspecting the liquid, I rolled up my sleeve in preparation. Only fifteen milliliters in the needle, which I would expect to be the amount in me that night, though this would be more concentrated.

Flicking the glass and expelling a few drops from the tip, I pressed the needle into my arm, slowly puncturing my vein. A numbing sensation of relief tingled when it emptied into my arm. I leaned back in my chair and wearily placed the syringe on the counter.

My body and mind were as light as pollen in a summer breeze. Trains of thought disappeared as quickly as they surfaced, just a flash of feelings rather than material thoughts. It was like lying in a tall-flower field on a perfectly sunny day with an exceptional temperature. Like watching clouds travel across the sky as I listened to the grass rustle in a calm breeze. Was this peace? I was so happy that if I died right now, I would be perfectly satisfied. In fact, if I were on the edge of a cliff, I would leap off just to make sure it was the last thing I felt.

The ringing of the shop telephone yanked me violently back to reality.

I slowly sat up, colors becoming a little brighter, the world moving a little slower as I walked over to the phone. When I lifted my hand to grab the receiver, I could see my hand trail slightly with a faint outline of chromatic aberration around it.

"Hello," I said quietly.

"Did you get back safely? Where are you? I want to see you tonight," Phoebe's melodic voice chirped through the phone.

"I am at the shop. I had a sudden inspiration," I said. "I will not be home tonight."

"Where are you staying if not your home or mine?"

"I am staying with Silas," I said slowly.

"With Silas." It was not a question, but more of a statement of disappointment.

In my fog I forgot to reply, letting the statement hang loosely on the line.

Then, she hung up.

CHAPTER FORTY-ONE

THE POISONER

"What is the point of bringing food if you do not eat?" I mumbled, taking a bite of one of the finger sandwiches while I annotated my book.

"I can't taste anything," Silas commented, looking out over the park as he took another drag of his cigarette. "I could eat it, but it would be the equivalent of uncooked rice powder."

"Then why do you smoke? Or drink?"

"I can only taste things that are burnt or bitter. Like coffee, liquor, and the like." He lifted the cigarette in emphasis. "Oh, and meat. The more raw, the better."

I lowered my gaze to my book, thinking about his answer. We decided today that we would go to the park. Since the word was out, there was no need to hide our familiarity. I loved my lab, but sometimes it was too stuffy.

There were eyes on us at all times, even if they attempted not to see us. Too many strangers greeted us, some of whom Silas knew, but the rest were a mystery to us. Sometimes I forgot that Silas was some sort of celebrity, being the founder of his own company and using his wealth for philanthropic and business endeavors. Not to mention he was considered one of the most eligible bachelors within our social circles.

While I usually had a counterpart dressed in pink when I visited the park, sitting next to Silas made me realize that our preferred way of dressing matched a little *too* perfectly.

We'd brought a blanket and a picnic basket full of little things to eat. His legs were extended and crossed in front of him. He was dressed in black with a high collar that buttoned down the side. He also wore circular tinted sun spectacles to shield the rare London sun from his light eyes.

We had put our blanket in the shade, so I was fine without any accessories. Today, I wore a black walking suit with a high neck, though it wasn't anything different from what I usually wore, so the new markings on my neck were not an issue.

Now that I thought about it, we did look like a matching set —how annoying.

"Did you really have to wear black?" I grumbled, eyeing his clothing.

"Of course. How else will we convince the children that we are phantoms that haunt the park?" He rolled his eyes and leaned back on his elbows. "I do not like the rules regarding colors."

"What do you mean?"

"I think too much is dedicated to different shades. They all look the same."

"Can I ask you something?" I squinted at him.

"Of course."

"Are my books the same color?" I held up two books.

"Yes."

One book was magenta, and the other was orange.

"Are you color-blind?" I asked him amusingly.

"No," he mumbled, squinting at the books. "Maybe. I do not know."

As he squinted, the blood filled the whites of his eyes, and they darkened as they looked at the books. "Ah...they are different colors."

"Does the blood flow to your eyes help you see better?"

"Yes, I can see more clearly, more textures, and obviously I can distinguish between more colors."

"How do you differentiate between the colors normally?"

"Practice, subtle differences, or learning typical colors from what other people say they are. Most of the heightened senses overwhelm me most of the time if it is not to hunt. Too many colors and textures at once. It is just a headache at that point."

"Fair." I nodded, jotting something in the margins of my literature.

"Quid pro quo," Silas spoke up.

I raised a suspicious brow before nodding in acceptance.

"Your father," he started. "You avoid the subject whenever someone brings it up."

I tensed, my pen strokes in my book becoming more aggressive. "Because there's nothing to tell."

"How did he die?"

"Hazard of the job. Tell me about your social structure. Are you pack animals or individuals?"

"Both. What hazard?"

"He was a chemist. I don't know, must have touched something that he wasn't meant to touch," I answered. "How can they be both?"

"We have Nests, Dens, and sometimes we just keep to ourselves. Personal preference." He took another drag of smoke. "Did you see him die?"

"Yes!" I choked, swiping his cigarette from his mouth and

taking a long drag, flicking it away when it burned the tips of my fingers upon finishing. "Enough about him, please." I sighed.

Silas looked at me for a long moment. It looked like he was going to say something, but he didn't.

"What's the difference between a Den and a Nest?" I asked, not taking my eyes off my book.

"Social class and money," he answered cryptically.

"That's not an answer." I glared.

"Dens are like taverns. Food, a place to sleep, everything a humble man would need." He looked at me over the rim of his tinted glasses. "They are typically for the corrupted and those born to lower classes. It is a community effort just to keep the places running, and people will do it because it's a necessity. An unorganized free-for-all filled with the most impulsive people you could imagine."

"Corrupted?"

"Yes, humans who were corrupted by venom. Keep up, darling," he grumbled. "Nests are something like that, except they're more like tight-knit explorers' clubs, exclusive and often limited to those of higher class. You have to be invited."

"So the difference is if you're rich or poor?"

"Not necessarily, but it does tend to work out like that, doesn't it?" He shrugged. "No, Nests are run by families that have known each other since before even I was born. They pool their resources and share only with their small entourage. A Nest is like a general label for connected families under one estate."

"Do you have one?"

"Yes."

"Where is it? What families?"

"I can't tell you that." He laughed. "If anything, it's for your own sake that I don't."

"What do they keep there?"

"Pretty little things like you," he teased.

"I am serious."

"So am I. They keep Hosts there. A quality collection is a must." His eyes trailed over me. "I'm actually surprised you hadn't been snatched before I got to you."

"Take me to one." I snapped my book shut. "I want to see it for myself."

"You want to go to a Den?" he sneered at the thought.

"Yes, and a Nest."

"You will be going to neither. Do you hear me? Do not seek them out," he warned.

"Do not speak to me like I am a girl. I can handle myself." I pointed at him with my pen as I tucked my book under my arm.

"Alina." He grabbed my arm. "Promise me."

I mumbled something begrudgingly, twisting my arm from his grip.

THE ALLEYWAYS of the docks were gloomy as usual. Nearly every news clipping contained some sort of incident from down here. It made sense that this was where a Den would be. It was a familiar hunting ground for me. I'd suspected for a while that one of these back-alley holes would be a Den. I'd narrowed it down to a place by the harbor, not too far from the brothel.

Rest in peace, mistress of the house.

Based on the papers, bodies were suspected of being dumped around this area. No one bothered to follow up, as the victims were typically women with promiscuous lives. Always sought out but never looked for afterward.

I approached the alley where the entrance would be, as there was also one at the front of the building. Some figures were looming outside, cooling off in the night air with a quick smoke. I wore my best impression of working-class clothing, a simple long-sleeved blouse with a brown skirt. Though I wore it higher on the waist, even the tops of my boots could be seen at this hemline. How embarrassingly improper.

Shoe polish stuck to my eyelashes and brows, hiding the white hairs that would give me away as anyone in particular. My hair was worn down as well. It was like walking around in sleeping attire. Entirely too vulnerable.

Moving past the figures who leered in the dark, I knocked on a wooden door, and it creaked open. The noises from inside spilled into the alley, as well as a dim red light.

"Business?" a gruff voice demanded.

"I'm a...Host? I'm a Host," I said unconvincingly.

"You don't sound so sure, love."

"It...it's my first time." I lowered my voice. "Please let me in." My voice shook as I glanced at the figures looming in the alley.

The door opened wider, granting me entry.

"Thank you," I breathed. The tension thickened as I moved farther into the Den. It was crowded in the skinny hallway, with many rooms only blocked by thin curtains as I passed.

Movement and small snippets of images caught my eye as I passed. In one room, a woman was in a chair, letting three, four, maybe five men latch on to her and feed. It was hard to see in the dim light. In some rooms, I could see pipes being passed and sluggish bodies sprawled into piles around one another. It was worse than I would expect even a brothel to be. So unsanitary and taboo, but maybe it only seemed that way to me because I did not consume human flesh to survive.

At the heart of the building, there was a large room with a

sunken lounge in the middle. The platform was lined with a perfect-fitting seating area where a group was occupying it. Along the sides there were stairs leading up to a viewing area around the edges. The place looked like it had been a run-down theater, repurposed for the formidable.

Topless women with fresh blood trailing down their breasts from their necks walked through the tables as if to collect new clients. Their long legs moved slowly, and they were only decorated in stockings and a corset, though it looked like they were used more as decoration than functionality. Privacy was optional when feeding, since there were couples scattered about, tangling with each other. All seats were occupied and covered with Vipera and Hosts. The sounds of laughter, drunken men, and sucking filled the air, weaving its way around the crowded area.

I was a fly on the wall, clinging to the outer edge of the Den as I only observed. I rubbed the back of my neck and was surprised to feel my own skin for once. The blouse I chose did not have a high collar and exposed down to my chest. I realized how much I missed my armor, the garments that kept me safe and hidden. The clothes that made people turn the other way when they saw me.

While the activities were chaotic, it was primarily a positive environment. There was no need to hide anything, and everyone involved acted like they were in a club. How odd it was for everyone to be so relaxed, though I was sure the substances in those pipes helped.

The thought had seemingly hexed my surroundings. Something was unfolding down by the lounge area in the middle.

The men whistled one of the feeders forward, and some mumbled words were exchanged before the woman got down on her knees. She looked in rough shape. She was pale, thin, and had a deadness in her eyes that made me feel a chill in my core. Three men crowded around her, circling her like dogs.

The situation slowly demanded the room's attention, and the others fell silent, watching as if they knew what was about to happen. No one seemed bothered. It was more like the dimming of voices before a show would start.

The three men lunged but were obscured when a hand slapped across my eyes and a strong body pulled me back.

A scream was cut off abruptly before a thud was heard. Then, the sounds of ripping began.

I panicked within the arms holding me and clawed at the hand over my eyes, my body trembling from the noises alone.

"Don't look," Silas whispered in my ear, holding me tight against his chest. "This is why you can't venture into treacherous places like these without me." He rested his head on my shoulder. "The people who live in these places would make me look like a saint."

"Let me see it," I whispered. "I must know."

The wet ripping noises continued, but no one else seemed to make any commotion.

After the noises died down, the regular clamor of the crowd returned to how it was before. Silas's hand fell away, allowing me to observe the aftermath.

Nothing could have prepared me for the sight. It reminded me of how they performed dissections in universities, except I had only seen illustrations of them in books.

The woman's body was flayed open, her chest cavity torn and the flesh peeled away from her body like a flower. Her rib cage was cracked open and posed like open jaws toward the ceiling. Nothing was inside. It was empty.

Her head laid limp. I wished I could imagine that it was painless, but her broken-jawed expression told me otherwise. It was clear from her oddly angled neck that it was not a clean break.

"Alina, look at me," Silas whispered into my hair, but my eyes stayed glued to that spot on the floor. The gravity of my situation weighed on me. My stomach churned, and barely any thoughts formed cohesively.

If this was what the corrupted did, a mental picture of what Silas's Nest would do when they found me entered my mind. What if they realized I was here? What if they all found out who I was? Silas had said my poison was on its way to infamy within these circles. What happened when they found out? My body was shaking hard, my fingers and toes getting cold from the panic.

Sharp teeth sank into my neck, and I flinched, digging my nails into Silas's arm that was wrapped around my waist.

"Ouch, Sil—" He bit harder, and I yelped.

He fed more aggressively, his other hand possessively tangling in my hair, pulling my head to the side so he could have better access. It prompted a whimper from me, and my body stopped shaking, his venom calming my electric nerves. He must have sensed my panic, fearing I would make a scene.

He let go of my neck and lapped at the spot. "Let me know when you've had enough."

THE CREATURE

ONE DAY, maybe I would understand why she did this to herself.

She looked like she was on the brink of either passing out or throwing up, and for once, it was in spite of my toying with her.

My arm held her up as her breathing steadied. She had to look at that abomination on the floor below us to prove a point to herself. There was no doubt that she would use this to fuel her vendetta against anything she found unjust.

The more I learned about her, the more I realized she thought she could save the world. Her rigid routine and pious beliefs were to torment herself as punishment for not doing more, for not knowing better.

Someday she would learn that no matter what she did, she could not save every fawn, and she could not smite the wolf for eating. Whether she liked it or not, it was the other side of the natural order that she held so dear.

I licked my lips and wiped away the remaining taste of her. It seemed to have calmed her, but I could see in her far-off gaze that it would not be enough to pull her from this spiral.

"Let me know when you've had enough," I said cautiously.

"It will never be enough." Her words were barely above a whisper. "Nothing I do will be enough."

I glanced at the scene below being cleaned up, the body being scraped off the wooden floor. The blood added a slick gloss to the dark stain of the wood.

"Then you have your answer." I sighed, scooping her into my arms and walking toward the back entrance. Her head rested on my chest, not one sound from her. I had hoped that allowing her to sneak away and see this place would discourage her from taking on these excursions alone, but it might have done much worse than I intended.

CHAPTER FORTY-TWO

THE POISONER

I didn't remember the last time I ate.

After a few days of testing the venom on myself, I noticed my appetite shrinking. It was like the disappointment of returning to reality made me feel like doing anything was useless. Nothing was ever satisfying enough.

On the bright side, my skin was soft, my body more rested, and the aches and pains had dissipated. This could be used in so many wonderful ways, and it motivated me to keep going. How ironic that a creature so vile could produce something that could ease the pain of others.

I could resume special orders to existing clients soon. Overall, things seemed to be calming in my life again.

Even the wallpaper became more interesting every time I was supposed to be doing something else, such as getting a good night's rest. Every time I tried to sleep, I found myself jotting down notes in the dreams themselves only to wake up quickly and write those thoughts down before they evaporated.

There was no telling how many nights I had spent at Silas's

estate. Losing track of days was an unfortunate side effect of the venom in such a concentrated form. Even with this slight disadvantage, what a relief it was to feel removed from my body, as passive as flowing water in a river.

A walk around Silas's garden was the best way I could manage my unrest. The cold air brushed at my skin and pinched my face. Midnight dew seeped into the fabric of my gown, and my hands could not find anything to do except pick at my nails. The garden was barren of any flowers by now, but the greenery still provided a comforting shadow to hide under. With the witching hour upon me, I accepted that sleep would not visit me anytime soon.

A crackling of the phonograph cut through the air, and the soft hum of a waltz was heard from the living room window. When I turned, the window was illuminated—open to let the swell of music float leisurely out into the backyard. The warm glow from the inside lit the grass in a tall window of light stretching out across the grounds. The soft playing of the piano paired with the rising and falling of the waltz pace was so fitting as of late. A dance was the perfect way to describe it.

A hand smoothed along my waist, and my Creature circled around me.

Silas's hand brushed against my cheek, his thumb smoothing over my skin. His eyes were soft, a calm about them that reminded me of the forest before a heavy rain—a stillness that was serene, but a warning to those who knew what it meant.

I leaned into his hand briefly but slipped away to move around him in return, though he refused to turn his back to me, following my movements.

He stepped closer, touching along the underside of my arm to extend it out, taking my hand gently. His other hand was at my waist.

His hand in mine, our fingers looped together so softly. They fit like pieces that were carved from the same stone. If I had asked myself a few months ago if these hands would be caught being so tender, I would have said that the wool had been pulled over my eyes.

We stepped in the rhythm of a three-four signature as we danced in and out of the light from the window littering the garden.

He was graceful, though I was sure he had had many years of practice. His movements with mine were so smooth that it was like we could go on like this forever, stuck in one fluid moment that seamlessly blended into the next.

He leaned down as he moved, like he wanted to be closer, pulling my waist closer until there was no more room between us and our dance was no longer able to continue. His craving for closeness overpowered the desire to keep going, like it was too much to ask for both at once.

I tilted my head up at him. Our frosted breaths intermingled as we stayed like that, savoring the moment.

We were nobodies at that moment. I was not the daughter of a chemist, a botanist, or a killer. He was not a creature, a cannibal, or a man.

I stood up on my toes to interlock our lips, kissing him sweetly. He let out a soft sound, a sweet gasp of longing, as did I. His arms encircled my waist as mine snaked over his shoulders, entangling my fingers in his soft golden hair.

If he were something to be consumed, I feared I would not savor him and would selfishly eat him first—no time for saving the best bite for last. Only the need to have him remained.

THE CREATURE

THAT WAS the first time she'd kissed me. *Truly* kissed me.

I had not realized until that moment that I always moved first. It would be a moment I would savor, hoping to remember every detail. The tingle along my scalp spread as she entwined her fingers in my hair.

I wanted more than to have her close. I wanted her to crawl under my skin and make a home out of my rib cage, for my heart would only beat for her. Not even a single pump of my atria was allowed if it was not for my dearest shadow, my chosen—my *Alina*.

My hands slid up her spine over the neat buttons along her neckline, popping them out of their loops one by one, though it was hard not to be hasty. One thing she had certainly exercised within me was patience.

She leaned back, pulling me over her and making me lower her to the ground. Her lips tasted so sweet, so *alive* against mine. She had tasted like many things I would learn to love. It used to be the smell of cherries that I enjoyed the most, or the bitter almond taste that I soon learned was cyanide, or the pollen of formidable flowers of the day. Now, it was the taste of her name on my tongue or mine on hers.

Her hands untangled themselves from my hair, and a low groan escaped her as I feasted on her lips, biting gently on her bottom lip when I would break briefly to breathe. Her dainty fingers tugged at the buttons of my shirt.

I slipped her gown off her shoulders and farther down her

torso, exposing her breasts to me. I ran my hands over them. I adored how they fit perfectly in my hands, made for my touch only. Her body was meant to be held by my hands, to be taken by only mine. If I had carved her from clay with my hands, I would be afraid of touching her again, fearing the perfection I had created—I imagined that was what God felt when making her, if he existed at all. I was so enamored. She had me understanding why people believed in such things.

I was too impatient for her to undress me. She only got a few buttons undone before I pulled away, tugging the dress the rest of the way down her body. She pressed her knees together in an attempt to hide from me.

I undid my trousers and touched myself along my shaft. It was becoming painful to deny myself any relief as I looked down at the body splayed before me. She covered her chest with her arms.

"No," I begged. "I want to see you."

"I am cold," she whispered, but I knew that it was not that.

"Then let me keep you warm." I parted her thighs and leaned down to kiss her again, positioning myself between her long legs. I pushed the tip into her, feeling the heat surrounding my cock.

She flinched before relaxing again, moving her hands to the grass.

I took both of her hands and pinned them above her with one hand. My other hand lifted one of her legs higher on my hip as I lowered my hips down, sinking farther into her.

"*Silas*," she breathed shakily. Her thigh was trembling under my touch as I began to move.

"Say it again," I breathed against her cheek, leaving a trail of kisses down to her jaw, then following it to the front of her throat to wrap my lips around the skin there.

"*Silas!*" she cried for me. The vibration of my name in her throat was like honey and sweet cream against my lips as I sucked at her sensitive skin.

I shivered as I thrust into her, feeling her warmth surround me and hitting the sweet spot when bottoming out, letting me know I filled her completely. It would only be me for as long as I was alive. My cock throbbed, dedicated to the single task of pleasing her.

"*Alina,*" I whispered, "tell me what you want." I picked up my pace, burying myself in her as deeply as she would allow.

"I…want you," she breathed, unable to focus on speaking as I became rougher with my movements. She bucked her hips upward, attempting to move with me.

"You have me." My hand on her thigh scooped under her, holding her hips up as I thrust.

Her skin glowed in the night, like moonlight. The dewdrops scattered through her midnight hair, the stars in the sky. The blue in her eyes softened just for me, my very world as I knew it.

I let go of her hands and placed both of mine on her hips. I sat back on my heels as I did so, taking in the view of my cock sliding in and out along with her body on display for me on the ground.

She was *mine*. All of her.

If I had any claim to anything priceless, it was her.

"*Alina,*" I gasped, the sounds of her moans flooding my senses with an intoxicating edge that made me crave more and more until it would be the last deadly dram of opium.

She laced her fingers in the grass. Her long torso arched as I lifted her hips higher, sitting up on my knees as I pushed as deep as I could. She relaxed enough for me to reach the hilt this time, but I knew I would not last much longer.

She suddenly leaned up, kissing me as she pushed me back to

lay on the ground, straddling my hips and effectively switching our positions. She bit my lip roughly, drawing some blood. I kept our lips locked to prevent a similar situation to the botanical gardens. My tongue slipped over the cut on my lip and over her own.

She rolled her hips on my cock, desperately trying to bring it deeper, to use it to derive as much pleasure as she could. She moaned against my mouth before I pulled away, wanting to hear it. Her sweet sounds made it hard for me to hold anything back. I would wait for her to finish, let her use me for whatever she wanted. I would give her anything, body, mind, and soul—if I had one. It was all hers to take.

I leaned up on my elbow, one hand on her hip, entranced with her movements. If she let me, I would worship her like this every day for eternity. Her body rose confidently as she moved her hips, her hands resting on my chest as she used me. I tried to stay still, not wanting to disrupt her. She closed her eyes, tilting her head to the side as she shifted forward on me.

"Alina...I can't much longer," I gasped, subtly moving my hips to her rhythm.

"Then do not hold back," she whispered, leaning forward against my chest as she bit my neck playfully.

As long as I had permission.

I flipped her over and put one leg over my shoulder, the other between my legs. I leaned over her as she lay on her side in the grass. I grabbed her by the face, turning it toward me.

"You are *mine*," I whispered against her lips, a smirk forming as I slammed into her as hard as I could. "You will never be rid of me."

Those blue eyes looked up at me pleadingly before they occasionally rolled back.

That's right. This is how you like to feel.

I gasped as I watched her. The force of my thrusts was making it hard to hold her face at the same time, so I grabbed her hair and pinned my arms to the grass on either side of her, twisting her upper body as I forced my length fully into her with every thrust, making her take it all.

It was useless to hold anything back any longer as I reached orgasm and the spines dug into her flesh inside.

She flinched when the spines pierced her. It brought me no joy that it had to hurt, but it felt so good to be inside her like this. Even the involuntary parts of me ached to sink themselves into her. Not only could I feel my cock pulsing, but I could feel the spines latch on to her, filling her with venom.

She made what sounded like a whimper. I tried to comfort her by kissing her hot skin, the coolness of the air conflicting with our burning bodies. Her leg slipped off my shoulder and hooked around my waist, pulling me closer.

I never thought I could reach the point of craving someone aside from a simple hunger. Starving for her would be more painful than any true hunger. I would rather perish. I was whole-heartedly, pathologically addicted to her.

CHAPTER FORTY-THREE

THE POISONER

I was close. *So* incredibly close.

Our visit to the Den gave me a new perspective on what I was dealing with. Impulsive, abusive, messy pests with no control over themselves and no place in society. They were unnatural, earning them the fitting title of *corrupted*. While Silas insisted that there was a difference between the corrupted and the true born, I did not believe it. I thought one had just had more time to perfect their craft.

My working hypothesis was that they were all like that deep down. I imagined that young Vipera and corrupted humans shared a similar level of impulse control. It would only make sense if both were experiencing these things early on, but as young Vipera aged, they at least had the privilege of mentorship within these "Nests" that Silas spoke of.

I was almost relieved when I remembered him saying how difficult conception was. That was the only reason they must not have been as prevalent as they already were. Many lists of connected family names had been drawn up, but I only grouped them by region and kept to the B and C class names with generational wealth, but without infamy. That was the only way I thought they could skate by without at least one person realizing. If they stayed mostly confined to these Nests, then it would not be difficult to go about surviving without drawing attention.

Which brought me to the Mellifluous Hosts. It was a critical part of how they kept themselves fed in a somewhat civilized manner, unless you were Silas and left bodies in your wake, seemingly for the fun of it.

Then there was the other shadow that watched my every move, the dark specter that stood in my kitchen, who fed from me without me even knowing. The only discomfort from that time period would have been sleep paralysis, unless it was just the side effect of the venom while the man fed on me. He must not be corrupted, but someone like Silas who had had plenty of practice at getting by without raising suspicion.

The hair on the back of my neck stood up, and I tried to rub the feeling away. Flipping through the pages of the textbook, I jotted down notes and composed hypothetical reactions for my newest rendition of my poison. I would ensure that it worked this time, for my own sake and for everyone else's sake who might come across these sick offenses to nature.

"I think almost every time I've seen you, you've either got your nose buried in a book or a glass." A charming laugh rang in my ear. Viktor slid into the chair across from me at the library desk. "You'll hurt your eyes if you do that." He flicked on the desk lamp next to us on the long table. The library had just installed a dozen of these recently. I had not thought to turn it on, as I had arrived when it was light outside.

"Thank you." I glanced at him out of the corner of my eye.

"What is that bright mind of yours working on now? Chemistry?" He propped his elbows on the table and leaned forward, resting his chin in his hand.

"Yes, just working on something small." I tapped my pen against the paper. "You wouldn't happen to be good at reactions, would you?"

"I could try my best." He lifted a shoulder indecisively, dragging my notebook toward him and plucking my pen from my hand. He studied it for a minute before looking at me over the rim of his glasses. "Still working on the toxin and antidote?"

"Yes."

"The structure is unstable," he pointed out. "With this, the antidote would cause a bigger reaction than just breaking it apart. It would destroy the poison and possibly surrounding matter. What are you trying to do with it?"

"Precisely that," I said plainly.

"So you are weaponizing an antidote?"

"I want to see every possibility," I explained.

He nodded with a smile as if he was amused.

"What?"

"Nothing, just admiring your mind." He shrugged. "Have you tested any of this?"

"Some of it. It's just not finished yet." I pulled my notebook toward me and stole back my pen.

"What happens when it's finished?" His voice had lost its curiosity. It sounded more like a challenge.

"I don't know," I answered honestly, closing my book and notes before standing.

"Are you not staying in your town house?" he asked suddenly. "I went to give you some literature, but I noticed the mail was piling up."

"No, there is maintenance to be done," I lied. "I am staying with a friend."

"A friend," he repeated, letting the words hang. I knew he wanted to ask, but he was too polite. He did not press me further.

"Yes, maybe for about a week or two. I am unsure how long the repairs will take."

"I see." He paused. "So where can I leave some papers for you?"

"I am unsure—it is best that you hold on to them unless you can bring them to the shop this week."

"Will you be going to the gala in a few days?"

"If no act of God prohibits me, then yes." I rolled my eyes. "Phoebe prefers that I come. She thinks she is socializing me like a newborn hound."

He chuckled at my remark. "She is a good friend. Even if her methods are tedious. From what I have seen, she only hopes the best for you."

"She does have an unusual way of showing her love."

"That kind of love is always the purest kind."

"I wouldn't go as far as to say that."

"Well, let me walk you home." He stood and held his hand out to me.

"I don't think that's a good idea."

"Why not?"

"I just—"

"Is it because of him?" There was a tinge of venom in his tone.

I hesitated to answer, but he had already drawn his own conclusions.

"Don't worry, I understand." He nodded. "This is just a gesture, nothing more. Let me escort you home. If you got up and disappeared like so many do at night, I wouldn't forgive myself."

His words left me uneasy, sounding vaguely threatening. Maybe it was jealousy I was hearing or bitterness toward the fact that I was with Silas now. Whatever it was, it slipped away faster than it was brought up.

CHAPTER FORTY-FOUR
THE POISONER

The poison had consumed my entire evening and carried into the morning. I had been tweaking and testing until the sun came through. I convinced Viktor to get me a coach to my shop instead of Silas's home to avoid an altercation. There was too much work to do, and I needed to get my hands on my tools while the ideas were fresh in my mind.

I had gotten it to the point where I added the solution to blood and it made most of the cells combust from a chemical heat. It was not perfect by any means and incredibly unstable, but it was enough for the purposes it was intended for. Sometimes it would make all of the blood cells combust. Other times, it would only make them clot. Any reaction was better than nothing.

I had five small vials in my purse. I could test it if my second shadow showed itself tonight.

Butterflies formed in my stomach as I fantasized about finally feeling less helpless around these creatures. Now I had an edge.

"Alina!" a high-pitched voice called out, and pulled me from my deep thinking.

I held the pen still as if to mark my place in my book, glancing up at the red-haired manic in front of me.

"You weren't at the shop, and we have to be at our appointment for our fitting!" Phoebe stopped in front of the coffee shop table where I was posted. "Do not make this a habit. You didn't even call this morning! Just because you have a new shiny toy to play with doesn't mean you get to ignore your best friend!"

"I didn't notice the time," I explained, looking up at the fractious nymph before me. I checked the small watch face on my wrist. "We still have thirty minutes."

"Yes! But we didn't get to have our morning walk!"

"We are going to walk together now."

"It's not the same type of walk!" She threw her hands up in frustration. "Let's just go. The clock is ticking." She hurried me out of my seat, collecting my book and dragging me away.

"What's gotten into you, Phoebe?"

"The more important question is *who* is getting into *you?*"

"That's not fair!" I bit back. "It's none of your business."

"Alina!" she snapped, stopping in the middle of the walkway to face me. "You are allowing a *man*, of all things, to cut you off from the life you've built around you. Four months ago, you would have called me insane if I told you what has become of you." She poked the corner of my book into my chest.

I had never seen her so consumed with anger.

"Phoebe—"

"No! Don't 'Phoebe' me!" She raised her voice, and pedestrians glanced briefly at us upon hearing the commotion as they passed.

We looked at each other in silence. Phoebe's chest was heaving from her bout of anxiety.

Slowly, I wrapped myself around her, squeezing her tight with my head resting on top of hers.

Her body was tense but gave way slightly with her head on my chest.

"I'm sorry," I whispered softly to her. "I would never abandon you, and I didn't intend it to look that way."

She was silent, which meant I needed to give her some sort of reassurance.

"My absence isn't because of Silas. I won't even let him see me while I work," I told her. "I am working on something big. Something new. It will help a lot of people." I moved away to hold her shoulders at arm's length. "It is my fault for shutting myself in. I promise I will not do it again."

She mumbled something under her breath before reluctantly nodding.

I would take that as an acceptance of my apology.

"WILL YOU CONSIDER VERMILION?" Phoebe asked as she looked up at me on the block. The seamstress was pinching and pinning a dark-green dress around my body in the places that needed to be hemmed and taken in.

"Won't that be too flashy?"

"That's the point! It's a gala. It's the best time to flaunt bold patterns and colors!"

"Are you going to wear something other than pink?" I arched my brow.

"I will be wearing yellow!" She gleamed.

I stepped down from the small podium and looked at myself in the mirror. I liked the way the dark green brightened my eyes.

It was the only color I was comfortable in besides black, though a shade so grim would be too bleak for a gala. I would not have cared before, but now I knew I needed to blend in a little more than usual. Nothing stuck out quite like mourning clothing.

"What set you off earlier? Why do you hate Silas so much?" I asked her suddenly, speaking to her reflection in the mirror.

"Why does anyone hate the flashier breed of men? I am tired of him getting involved with things he shouldn't," she mumbled, a blush creeping up her fair cheeks.

Phoebe was not allowed many friends in childhood, keeping a small circle even in adulthood. She had me, but that was it when it came to fraternizing with people who were not some sort of blood relative. We were only allowed as friends because of our fathers' business relationship and how often mine was at their estate.

A guilty swell of my heart clutched my chest when I realized she might have thought I was abandoning her. I understood the hatred she held for anyone who tried to take me away. Her panic was making more sense to me as I thought about it.

"Tonight will be fun. We can stop by and pick up the dresses after tea. How's that?"

She grinned at me and nodded. "Sounds like a plan."

The rest of the preparations were done at Phoebe's place. We wanted to arrive together, and she would lend me some jewelry for the occasion.

My dress had a square neckline and no sleeves. The silhouette was kept close to my tall figure and cinched around any curves, emphasizing the waist and hips. The dark-green fabric was decorated with small hints of black and gold along the hemlines and through the design. There was a subtle train in the back that was fitted with an elegant bustle, letting the fabric fold and drape its way down to the floor. I wore black gloves to match, and Phoebe let me borrow an emerald necklace with matching earrings. This time, I kept my hair up, extending my long neck and figure. I was a bit hesitant with the bite scars on my neck, but they had healed enough that they would not be too noticeable under a velvet ribbon tied neatly at the back.

Phoebe's outfit was a lot brighter than mine, to say the least. It was a warm yellow gown with a matching square neckline to mine. The sleeves were long, and there were many buttons down the front. The yellow fabric bunched before draping down the sides, exposing a lavender underskirt that went to the floor. The trim of the yellow train behind her matched the soft purple. A nice fashion-forward piece—it was suitable for her. The yellow complemented her strawberry hair. She wore gold earrings with amethysts dangling about. She was currently adjusting her white gloves.

"What catalog is that one from?" I circled her to ensure that there was not even a hair out of place.

"I picked from a few and just told the tailor to combine them in some way." She beamed. "Do you like it?"

"It's very bright, very you." I smiled. "Do you think we are ready?"

"Should be!" She shrugged on an overcoat before handing one to me.

I pulled the black overcoat on and followed her toward the door. I paused before leaving, grabbing my small purse that held my knife and tinctures from the coat hanger. The most important items for a night out.

CHAPTER FORTY-FIVE

THE CREATURE

One might think having so many valuable items in one room would be a liability. I guessed no one thought of that when they organized this circus.

There must have been enough paintings and pieces of art to add up to millions in value, yet they sat here without even so much as a rope barrier to keep nosy patrons from touching them.

The museum had closed off most of the rooms and kept the event contained to just one wing, but it still baffled me how much they trusted these guests with their precious items just because they were paying for them. The only redeemable quality about this overly pretentious display was the complimentary liquor.

I took a long sip from my glass. The liquid only burned, though I could taste the peppery whiskey notes as I drank. Events like these were so boring. I did not know why my father insisted I come. I know he disapproved of my time away from the Nest, so attending this frivolous thing was the least I could do to get him off my back. I was not looking forward to the next family gathering.

A thick Russian accent cut through the noise. "You know that you really should smile more. You're scaring away the food."

I tilted my head to the side. The elusive Fixer himself had decided to make an appearance.

"I guess they really let anyone in these days," I sneered, turning my attention back to the crowd as it grew in attendees.

"Can't you just enjoy one evening without being so sour?" Luka studied a passing group of women, lowering the rim of his glasses before taking them off and tucking them in his vest pocket. "So many pretty little snacks. Do you think they taste better or worse after liquor?"

"Luka," I warned.

"Actually, I rather like Viktor." He gleamed, a crazy spark in those blazing eyes. The amber gave off a red glow in the lighting without the presence of those ugly glasses. "It will sound so much better falling out in a clumsy mess from your pet's mouth."

My hand snapped out and grabbed him by the throat, my fingers digging into his skin. "Lay a finger on her and I promise you there will be no body for them to find when they look for you."

"Oh, you are comical. Your father didn't tell me you were funny." He grinned. "I am afraid you are too late for that. Besides, she has such a delightful kick to her." He laughed, leaning in closer. "I haven't had this much fun since—" He tapped his chin, pretending to think about it. "Well, since 1476."

"You will have no hands to touch her with if you choose to go down this path," I threatened.

Luka plucked my drink from the bar top. "Then take them." He let the remaining liquid slip down his throat with a single tip of his head and then slid the cup down the bar to the tender. "I don't need them to do what I have in mind."

He pulled away from my grip and winked before retreating through the crowd.

I ran my hand through my hair, scraping along my scalp in frustration. By the sound of that conversation, I did not have long. I'd cut off his access to her by moving her around, making her stay with me, or distracting her with enough samples that she would disappear for hours on end. She was lucky she had me, truly, because there would be nothing stopping him from gutting her the minute she stepped out of her meticulously planned schedule.

I scanned the crowd, losing track of him when he moved through the sea of people. Instead, my eyes landed on a different dark-haired figure. My beautiful shadow was adorned with an expensive green dress next to that babbling *fool* of a friend.

Is she trying to kill her?

I pushed past the bodies of people. I lost sight of Alina.

That flash of a yellow dress moved through the crowd. I grabbed Phoebe's arm and yanked her with enough force that I wondered if I'd pulled it out of the socket by the way she glared at me.

"Why must you be so feral?" Phoebe hissed at me, clawing at my hand on her arm.

"What is Alina doing here?" It was less of a question, more of a demand.

"I invited her. Why else would she be here?"

"The Fixer is here," I started.

"Yes! I heard he was in town. I know things too, see?" She rolled her eyes. "He's here about a poisoner. That's why Father called us home. I hope he makes an example out of him."

"Phoebe"—my voice strained as I pinched the bridge of my nose—"Alina *is* the Poisoner. How can you be this blind?"

Her face could not have gotten any more pale. "I didn't—"

"Think? You didn't *think*? Oh yes, I am well aware of that," I scoffed. "How do you not know she's been making poisons out of her shop this whole time?"

"It's not my fault that she doesn't tell me anything anymore now that she's so busy with you!" she seethed, jabbing a finger at my chest. "You could have told me!"

"I thought you knew!" I raised my voice at her. "Maybe she would have told you if *you* had told her the truth!"

"She would hate me."

"She's never going to forgive either of us if Luka gets to her first—" I paused to look around. "Where is she?"

Phoebe chewed her lip and looked around but could not see over the horde.

"If you find her before me, bring her to your home, and don't let her leave," I instructed, releasing her arm to push past the crowd of people, frantically looking for that deep-green fabric.

CHAPTER FORTY-SIX
THE POISONER

"I t seems like fate that we keep running into one another," Viktor murmured. "I love such pleasant coincidences."

"Ah, I don't believe in coincidence in that way." I took a sip from my cup as I hung back in the corner.

All night, I was bombarded by people I did not know who clearly knew me. There were more questions about my "romantic" life than about my work. It was nice to see someone who would not interrogate me, at least.

"Maybe you should. You never know." He shrugged.

"Where are your glasses?"

"I didn't think they fit the look tonight." He looped my arm through his. "Come with me. Silas told me to fetch you."

"Fetch?" I frowned at his wording but followed anyway. "Why wouldn't he just come get me himself?"

"Because he's a dog and needs things done for him, of course." He smirked.

Viktor led me to a different wing that contained medieval

examples of bedchambers belonging to some important figures whose names were littered in the historical texts.

"You know, you're lucky." Viktor slid my arm out of his and turned toward me. He took my hands and led me through the closed-off wing, walking backward so he did not have to break eye contact with me.

"Why would you think that?"

"You're going to get to live your life comfortably, which is more than most can say." He sighed. "Most would beg for that position, kill for it, even, as long as you fall in line."

"What are you referring to?" I glared. "Do you mean the rumors about my romantic endeavors?"

He tilted his head at me. "Oh no, but I am sure he will get to see you be a good Host if he ever decides to visit home." A wicked smirk cracked across his face. His eyes held such a fierce fire that the man before me was almost unrecognizable.

As his grin widened, I could see a flash of long teeth.

That was the moment it all clicked into place. He was never there for my company. He walked me home that first night to find out where I lived. That was why, for weeks after, I was in so much pain. This monster snuck into my house, and I practically thanked him for it by inviting him back.

"Viktor—" I said, a hint of panic in my voice, but his grip on me tightened.

"It really does sound better when you say it like that." He leaned close, backing me against the wall. "But it feels disingenuous. It is Luka—I'd rather hear my real name when you scream it."

My eyes widened as he slapped his hand over my mouth.

"Listen closely, *dorogaya*." He leaned close. "This will hurt. If you scream, I'll make sure it's worse," he whispered, his fangs flicked out. They looked different from Silas's. Both sets were fairly long and thick, like some nightmare come to life.

Before I could find the time to react, two sets of eager needles plunged into my shoulder.

I screamed into his hand, and a burning pain tore through my body. There was no numbness to follow, just my muscles and consciousness fading, failing me. The last thing I remembered was the feeling of teeth biting down into my flesh as my vision went black.

CHAPTER FORTY-SEVEN
THE POISONER

The rough path of the carriage slowly rocked my consciousness back to the surface. Even when I opened my eyes, I was blind. Scratchy wool fibers brushed against my face and got in my mouth. A hood was over my head, but I could not feel any other clothing on me.

Rope bound my wrists and elbows behind my back, as well as my knees and ankles together. I was now certain that I had been stripped of my clothes. A heavy boot rested on my hip as I lay on my side.

Is he using me as a footrest?

The coach stopped, jolting my body and eliciting a whimper from me due to the pain in my shoulder. More awareness of my body came with the register of pain as I slowly came to full consciousness.

After a moment of stillness, the cold air whipped at me when the door opened. The pressure of the boot was removed only for me to be yanked up into strong arms by the ropes that restrained me. Nothing could stop the wince as I was hauled up into someone's grasp.

"Ah, so glad you could join us from the dream realm," Luka's muffled voice rang through the wool.

I wished I had some witty response, but the energy was not there.

It was like I was in some kind of fever dream. Paralyzed.

When we entered the inside, the sickly-sweet smells of florals overwhelmed my senses, and I lurched. It was *too* sweet. Like it was masking some other smell.

"Throw up on me, and I will drop you," he threatened.

He carried me up some stairs. I counted thirty-five steps, a plateau, then twenty-five steps. He pushed open a door with his hip before kicking it shut behind him.

I swiveled my head, desperate to see. He let go, and my back smacked against the floor with a hard thud.

"Hell!" I shouted, my body stiffening. The air was knocked out of me when I landed on my restrained arms.

"Whether this is or isn't hell will be entirely up to you." He yanked the wool cover from my head.

It took a second for my eyes to focus on the dark, looming figure above me. I leaned up, but he placed a boot on my chest.

"Good morning," Luka said sweetly. "Welcome to the Nest."

I refused to answer him.

He leaned down, grabbing my face and forcing me to suck in my cheeks. "I said *good morning*. What do we say back?"

I stared silently.

"*Alina*"—his tone was sweet, but tinged with venom—"I don't think you want me to be your trainer. It never ends well."

"I am not a dog, you devil."

"Wrong answer." He dragged his boot forward to my injured shoulder before pressing down.

I yelled out in pain, tears forced out of my eyes.

"Let's try again. *Good morning, Alina!*" he said enthusiastically, a carnal delight in his expression.

"Good...morning," I struggled to breathe out.

"Good girl." He removed his boot and tilted his head at me innocently. "Oh, don't be discouraged, little one. You'll get used to the way things are around here soon," he said, then the door swung open.

Three maids fluttered in with bowls and fresh linens.

He reached down and pulled a knife from his waistband, placing it under one of the ropes. "I'll reward you by taking these off, but I have no problem wrapping you in knots if you can't behave," he warned.

I nodded reluctantly.

He cut the ropes, and they slipped off my limbs. He picked me up and sat down on the edge of the bed with me between his legs.

"Unhand me."

"This is for your own safety and others'. I have to make sure you don't hurt the staff, you feral thing." He hummed, tapping my nose playfully.

Unamused was the most polite way I could describe how I must have looked. He just laughed, positioning me so my back was against his chest, and I faced the maids.

They started to use wet cloths to wipe my body down and clean me up. A bowl of milky liquid was placed off to the side. It smelled like vanilla and was soft on my skin. One of the maids had some type of liquid that she spread over my skin after they scrubbed it. I looked at my arm where she had put it and studied the oily substance. It smelled floral. When they were finished, two maids left, and one remained, but this time she pulled out something that clinked together in the box before her. She reached in and pulled out what looked like a gold *collar.*

My eyes widened, and I moved to get up, but Lukas's arms wrapped around my waist and placed me firmly back down in a seated position.

"Let go!" I yelled, turning and smacking him in the face.

He grabbed the wrist that swung, and squeezed. "What did we just say about your behavior?"

His grip made my panic fester, and my eyes darted toward the maid, who brought over a few metal pieces.

"What is this, the Middle Ages?" I growled.

"Oh, don't think of it like that. Think of it as decoration."

The maid snapped the flat collar around my neck. The metal was a flashy gold, and on the collar, there were sharp fleur-de-lis patterns decorating the top and poking upward. It was designed in a way that didn't let me lower my head too far without it jabbing into my skin. It was more decorative than practical, like a way to ensure I could easily be secured or grabbed. There was a loop at the front of the collar as if to secure a lead to it. When she finished, she handed the key to Luka before gathering her things and leaving us alone.

I could feel his hungry eyes, so I refused to look at him.

"You can't be mad at me forever. I am your only friend here," he breathed against the bruised punctures on my shoulder.

"You lied to me."

"Lie? No, you must be thinking of a different man," he retorted. "I meant everything I said to you. Could he say the same?"

I picked at my nails, unsure if I could answer that honestly. If Luka could fool me, I was sure Silas could too.

"I meant it all," he whispered, his fingers tracing the front of my hips.

"You pretended to be a student to get close, learned about the things I was studying just so you could betray me in the end." I glared. "How is that fair?"

"Well, I didn't lie, like I said," he explained plainly. "I was once a student, and I've been a doctor since before they studied medicine in schools." He took my hand in his and studied my red-stained fingertips. "So you can imagine that it wasn't hard to piece together who you were, though I wasn't expecting you to be a woman, I will admit that."

I pulled my hand away in disgust.

"You were never in danger. You never have been in your entire life," he said flatly. "Mr. Astor—or I suppose you know him as Mr. Aston—kept you hidden away. Imagine his surprise when I told him the infamous Poisoner he had been hunting is his hidden gem."

"What are you saying?" My voice wavered.

"Did your little friend not tell you?" he mocked. "Now I feel special that I get to be the one to tell you!"

"Tell me what?"

"Mr. Aston kept you close all these years because he knew that you were a Host. Why do you think his daughter was only allowed one single friend? Do you think a social butterfly like her didn't keep other friends as a child out of personal preference? She begged for a single friend. It was the perfect place to keep an eye on you."

"That can't be true. She and I grew up together. We are the same age. She isn't one of you," I practically bit out. "You are lying."

"That's because even though we have to be born and grow, we just happen to stop at year twenty-five." He laughed. "She's just his recent child."

"Recent?"

"Yes, well, you've met his eldest."

My brow raised as I waited for him to continue.

"The golden boy didn't tell you either? Today is not a good day to be Alina, is it?" He shook his head.

As the pieces clicked in my mind, I was internally punishing myself for being so blind. What I thought was simple rivalry and distaste was actually just *siblings* interacting with each other. Their familiarity with one another was making more sense than ever. How could I not have seen through their banter?

That would explain her hesitancy with he and I spending so much time together.

They both knew and did not tell me a thing.

"She couldn't have known this would happen." I tried to at least make an excuse for Phoebe.

"But he knew." He traced little circles down my arm. "He knew who I was since the exhibition."

My gut flipped on itself and pinched my insides. I could feel the anger rising in me with each new revelation. Every memory became corrupted with what I knew now, exposing everything in a new light. Why must everyone hide things from me as if I were a child in need of protection? I could have protected myself if I had known these important details beforehand. Now, they were useless to me.

Luka slipped me off his lap. "Well! That sums up my duties for the day. You'll be staying in here tonight—food will be brought to you," he explained, looking back at me as he paused before the doorway. "Welcome home," he chirped before closing the door, locking it once it snapped in place.

With the room to myself, I finally looked around. It looked more fitting for a spoiled pet than a person. There was very little furniture, one of which was a lounging chaise in front of the large window, but it did not look like it could open. Aside from that, there was the bed, and many pillows and folded wool blankets were neatly placed on the chaise. I was not even afforded the decency of a mirror.

The walls were blank and gray with a few cracks in the paint, a testimony to their forgotten state. This was a haphazardly organized prison.

I moved sheepishly toward the window and looked out. I saw a field surrounding the property until it hit the tree line. Luka walked out the front door with someone while he smoked. I recognized the other man as Nikolai, his alleged *peer*. He spotted me from the corner of his eye and gave me an innocent wave before returning to his conversation.

My face twisted in disgust when I saw him, turning back toward the room. Snatching a wool blanket neatly folded on the chaise, I wrapped myself in it. My mind tried to retrace my steps. Where were my clothes? I needed my purse with the poison in it. There was no knowing what they were planning, but I could not stay unarmed for long.

I crawled onto the bed, staring at the small cracks in the paint as I tried to think.

What is real? What do I know now?

Viktor's real name was Luka. Luka was a psychopath for hire. Silas and Phoebe were siblings. Phoebe had been a Vipera this whole time, though she was young. I was being added to a collection of Hosts in a Nest. I was at a Nest now. I was in the countryside. I was at one of Mr. Aston's properties, who was also their father. Mr. Aston had also been grooming me to prepare me for this fate, either out of mercy or malice.

I groaned and gripped my throbbing head. This was all a lot for me to absorb, but I was trying my best to screw my head on straight before I had to face it head-on.

The only thing that kept me comfortable was knowing that

they weren't going to kill me based on what Luka had explained, though that did not mean they would not take turns breaking me. The worst part was that everyone I thought would look for me I could not trust to come for me at all.

Everyone I knew had been keeping things from me.

I did not know any of these people anymore.

WHILE THE SITUATION was less than ideal, the mattress was expensive and I slept better than the dead. I had been asleep from the minute they left me alone until the next morning, embracing sleep as the depression wrapped around my limbs and sucked all the energy out of me. It was useless to ignore the helpless feeling. My wick was extinguished at the end of my metaphorical candle—no more wax to burn. I might as well use the opportunity to rest.

As I lay there quietly, the maids came in and out to collect the uneaten trays of food. I never moved from my spot on the bed, and the maids did not disturb me.

A sharp sting suddenly bloomed on my wounded shoulder, and I whipped around, snagging the pale hand.

She yelped at the sudden movement.

"Phoebe." My eyes widened.

"Alina—"

"What have you done?" My expression twisted painfully.

She avoided my gaze.

I yanked her arm to pull her toward me. "Did you hear me?" I shouted.

She looked pathetic. Like a dog that was caught doing something she was not supposed to. How weak could she be to let them do something like this? After everything I had done for her, she could not find it in her to trust me? To tell me the truth? My emotions were getting the best of me, but I had less empathy for her now. I squeezed her wrist tighter.

"Y-you're hurting me," she said tightly.

"Good. You deserve it," I sneered. "Since you think yourself *so* capable that you neglected to warn me of any real danger, you are going to get me out." My words cut like a cold blade.

I could feel her holding back her judgment.

"I can't," she whispered, having difficulty looking at me.

"What do you mean you can't?" I hissed at her, sitting up.

"I don't know what to do. They're watching. Listening," she said quietly, and looked at me sympathetically.

"I need you to find my purse." I leaned close and spoke lowly.

"You're worried about your *purse* right now?"

"No, I have something inside it. Small glass tubes a half-inch long," I instructed, showing her the size between my fingers.

"All right, fine. I can try. I don't know where they put it—"

"Figure it out," I snapped, throwing her wrist back at her.

"Alina," she began, "you can't pretend I was the only one keeping secrets."

"Don't think for a moment that Silas isn't going to find a knife in his chest when I get my hands on him. Rest assured."

"I am not speaking of him." She frowned. "Why didn't you tell me you were a poisoner?"

"For the same reason you didn't tell me you were one of those *things*. Or that Silas is your brother!"

"*Half* brother," she corrected. Her eyes found the bruised bite mark on my shoulder. "I could have helped you."

"You're going to help me now. That's the least you can do after what you've done."

She wanted to protest, but didn't. The tension between us was thick, like chilled tallow.

"Why wouldn't you tell me? Do you think so low of me that I couldn't be trusted?" I asked.

"Alina, I didn't know."

"We have known each other for as long as we could retain memories. How could this have never come up?"

"I was told that you would abandon me if I did. Father said that it was for your safety." Her lip quivered. "He said if I told you, you would be hurt, and it would be entirely my fault. It was too late to tell you by the time we were older."

"I would have listened."

"I know you would have." She sighed. "But you were too important to risk losing. I thought I wasn't hurting anyone by keeping it to myself." She took my hands in hers. "You must understand, because of Silas, I was not allowed to have friends outside the Nest—I didn't even live in the Nest full-time. I begged Father for just one friend, and he allowed me to see you. I couldn't lose you. You are all I have."

I could see it in her eyes, but her shame was too great, and it pushed down everything she wanted to say to me. My arms wrapped around her, and she squeezed me back. The wet tears landed on my shoulder, and she sniffled. "I am so sorry, Alina. It was never supposed to end like this."

"I know, I believe you," I said softly, holding her tight. "We will get out together. Start over. Get far away from here." It was impossible to stay angry at her. I would not admit it out loud, but we'd kept our secrets for similar reasons. Everything I did was to protect her and those like her, the lighthearted good of the world.

She quietly got up after a while and let me go. "I will be back once I figure out where your things are. Just…don't draw attention to yourself for now." She approached the door. She looked back at me before she closed the door behind her.

Sleep was not something I was able to turn to after that. Picking at my nails again, I assembled a plan in my head. My only weapon was poison, which might or might not be as effective. Did I have to poison everyone to get out of this mess? Could Phoebe arrange for us to run? I had to think, but it was impossible to do on an empty stomach, and I was running on what was left of my adrenaline.

My mood was becoming irate. I was coming off of my newest self-medication, which might not have been the wisest choice, not that I could have anticipated my current situation. Another thing I would not have done if I'd known the bigger picture.

CHAPTER FORTY-EIGHT
THE POISONER

T he walls closed in more every day.
I swore the room had been bigger upon my arrival. Seven days had passed since then. It was like someone moved the walls an inch every time I closed my eyes. It had also been seven days since I last saw anyone familiar. The only ones who kept me company were the maids, and it took them several days to trust me enough to talk to me.

I was shuffled between three rooms throughout the day—the bedroom, a small room with a table for dining, and a bathroom. This morning, they served me pomegranate, berries, aged cheese, biscuits, and some eggs.

They still had not given me clothes.

"So, you are saying Host positions are voluntary?" I picked at the pomegranate on my plate, rubbing the irritated skin on my neck from the collar.

"Yes! Hosts are approached to serve a Nest or individual. They are paid very well and get to live their lives comfortably," the maid answered.

"Why is it that I am here, then?" I watched the blonde-haired maid seated neatly across from me.

"Unfortunately, that is something I cannot answer. Not due to any reluctance, but because I simply don't know. It is unusual."

She was nice enough to join me for meals when I requested her. They all seemed a bit ignorant to most of the happenings. It was like she was reciting from a guidebook on how to answer my particular queries.

"Why haven't I seen anyone? It's been a week."

"We were told we are not allowed to let anyone see you while you heal and acclimate to the routine." She sounded rehearsed.

I nodded in acknowledgment of her answer as if convinced.

"My appetite is no longer here. I am ready to go back." I smiled at her, cupping the small cheese knife in my palm as I rested it on my lap.

Once I was escorted back to my room and the door was closed tight, I slipped the knife inside the pillowcase. It gave me some relief knowing I was not completely helpless, though I knew they were keeping me locked in here for my own safety and theirs.

From what I'd gathered from the maids, the Hosts and the Vipera were on strict schedules. They rang a dinner bell to indicate when they were allowed to feed on Hosts, and if even one was damaged, it could mean exile from the Nest or losing a finger or two, depending on the damage.

It made me feel better knowing that, while I was still a hostage, my title as a Host meant I was afforded some protections.

The edge from the venom I'd used on myself had long worn off, but it left me feeling like I was sinking into a void. My reliance on substances was not something I was forced to reckon with until now. Life was extremely blunt when you did not use anything to soften the blow.

I threw myself on the bed and buried my face in the softness. A scream ripped through my throat, muffled by the lush pillow. All I could do was follow the routine, as simple as it was. I was confined by four walls for however many hours until the next time they fed me, bathed me, and repeat.

A sharp noise cracked through the air and jolted me awake.

"Welcome back to the land of the living!" Luka chirped.

With a screech, he dragged a wooden chair across the floor to the corner.

"You're not supposed to be in here." I sat up quickly. "I know you're not allowed. The maids told me."

"Is that right?" He did not pay me any attention as he examined the chair placement. In his hand was a thin braided riding crop. He swung it in an upward position, whistling as it cut through the air. He inspected the flat leather tab at the end.

"You can't feed on me. You can't even touch me without permission. I'm a Host now, correct? You'll lose a finger."

"And who do you think is the one in charge of taking fingers, hmm?" He turned on his heels to face me. I noticed his outfit was a bit equestrian as well. Tall, shiny leather riding boots with dark trousers and a loose shirt.

"Is this a ruse?"

"What makes you think this is a ruse? It's time for a lesson."

"Lesson?"

"Well, you were half right about being a Host. You're also a hostage. A hostage that might need some...breaking." He smirked.

"You're sick. Why do you smile when you say it like that?"

"Because this will be more fun for me than it will be for you."

He moved over to the edge of the bed, his knee sinking into the edge of the mattress before crawling slowly toward me.

"You're a sadist."

"You say that like it is something I should be ashamed of," he said slowly. His movements stilled briefly before he lunged.

I whipped the blade out from under the pillow and cut him across his cheek as I stumbled to the other side of the bed.

He stilled, smoothing his finger over the fresh cut. Blood beaded in a neat line, and he inspected the fresh droplets on his hand. A slow grin crawled across his face before his eyes snapped at me, narrowing on their prey. "You are making all the most terrible, *delightful* decisions today."

He lunged again, sweeping over the bed and to the other side, grabbing me by the collar, and making the sharp points of the design dig up under my jawline.

"Luka, don't—"

"Too late for that." He gleamed as he pulled me over to the corner with the chair.

A soft click was heard, and the pressure relief from my neck followed, the collar clamoring onto the floor. I glanced at him through my lashes as I rubbed my neck.

"Don't look so hopeful," he said flatly. "I need you to focus on this exercise. I simply cannot have you getting overstimulated from anything other than the task at hand."

"What do you mean?"

He picked up a mason jar from the floor and dumped the contents out in front of the chair. Hundreds of grains of rice scattered onto the floor, mimicking the sound of soft rain. I suspected that sound would be the only comforting thing about this activity.

"Kneel."

"Kneel?"

"Yes, Alina, you heard me correctly. On your knees, on the rice," Luka instructed.

I looked down at the rice scattered along the floor. What was this?

Before I could think too hard, Luka kicked the back of my knees one by one until they landed on the rough surface.

I cried out, shaking at the shock of the movement. The little bits of rice dug into my skin from my own weight on top of it.

Luka stepped around me and sat in the chair. I was not facing him in this position. He had a nice view of my side profile from where he sat. He rested that long crop across his knees, watching me.

"Stand up on your knees, nice and straight," he ordered, giving a light tap to my behind with the end of the crop.

As I went up on my knees, I could feel the rice grinding against the bony parts of my knees. I stumbled forward slightly, and my hands landed on the ground.

Fwip!

His crop slapped my hand, and I flinched away from the ground.

"I said straight, not forward or backward." He tilted his head mischievously at me. It was like he was waiting for all the wrong moves without telling me the rules—I had to figure them out as I went.

"You can't just punish me when I don't know what you want me to do," I gritted through my teeth, staring forward at the wall and refusing to look at him.

"I gave you pretty clear instructions."

I stood on my knees as straight as possible, but the rice made it hard not to waiver. I leaned back slightly to adjust my position on the coarse surface.

Fwip!

He whipped the back of my thighs, eliciting a yelp from me. I could feel the burning continue in a straight line where the crop had hit me.

The same would happen if I leaned too far forward.

Fwip! Fwip!

Back and forth, he would hit the back and front of my thighs to keep me straight. When I glanced down at my thighs, I could see red lines appearing in the places he hit, searing into my skin so it remembered.

After a while, I got *really* good. I kept myself straight, still, calm. If I just focused on the wall ahead and let myself drift, I forgot the pain digging into my skin, burning my flesh. Breath control was paramount when trying to tune everything else out. He stopped hitting me with the crop. There was nothing to critique until he decided to change the rules again.

While I got him to stop smacking me with the crop, it did not stop the lashing in my head. The pain was the only thing to focus on unless I dissociated from it, which risked my posture faltering. The lightheadedness crept up on me slowly. Soon, I could no longer ignore the pain, but with it came another feeling. It was like my body was making up for my situation by sending endorphins. The pain and numbness bloomed in small increments and became more intense the longer I waited. During the first half, maybe I was running on adrenaline, but now it was all melting together, and I could not tell pain from anything else I was feeling.

"You are doing so well, Alina," Luka praised.

I looked over at him. He blurred in and out of my vision as my eyes became glassy. I could not bring myself to talk. It would break my focus.

"Do you want to get off the rice?" he asked, almost kindly.

I nodded slowly.

"How do we ask for things?" he crooned, standing from his seat and circling to the front, kneeling in front of my face. His riding crop traced gently over the red marks on my thighs, making even my skin twitch at the touch.

"Please," I barely made out in a breathy voice.

"Please what?" he asked, tilting his head like there was something to be confused about.

I shifted desperately. "*Please* let me off the rice." My voice shook.

"Do you think you've earned it?"

"Yes." I nodded. "Please, I have done all you asked!"

"Not everything." He grinned. "I will reward you, but you are staying on the rice."

"No!" I trembled. "Please, I will do anything. Just let me get up!"

"Dangerous words, Alina," he warned, getting up and walking around me to the back. "I will ask one more thing, then you may get up."

"Anything." I shook, my hands clenched against my thighs.

I heard two knees dropping to the floor, and then he shoved me forward.

My voice hitched as my palms hit the rice-covered wood.

"Luka?" My voice trembled. "What is the last thing?"

A warm, hard object pressed between my legs, moving between my thighs in steady, teasing strokes.

"No…" I whimpered.

He leaned forward and placed his hands on top of mine as his body hung over me from behind.

My entire body was losing its grip, trembling like a trapped animal.

"Let me in," he whispered in my ear. "Don't you want your reward for being so very *good* for me?"

I trembled harder, my head light, and I could only focus on the rice under our hands, scattered across the wood.

He ran his tongue over my neck, seeming to relish the taste of sweat and endorphins that raced through my body.

"Promise...no more," I breathed.

"No more after this, I promise," he said against my skin, moving the warmth from between my legs and pressing against my vulva. "Tell me when you're ready."

I nodded, swallowing hard as I became too aware of the friction around me. The heat of his hands, the rice grinding against my knees, his soft lips trailing over my skin, everything was too much.

"No, I need you to say it," he said, his voice lowered, nipping at my shoulder where he previously left his mark.

"I-I'm ready."

"For what?"

"Your cock," I choked out. "Please just put it in."

"That's a good girl." His words came out needy, hungry.

He jerked forward, and it pushed inside. The sultriness coming from his body and the friction from being utterly unprepared felt *different*. It was like this type of pain was sweet in comparison to the coarseness I had been enduring for what seemed like hours.

I clenched my hands into fists, but he laced his fingers through mine, squeezing them tighter. It was too intimate. It was *wrong.* Yet I wanted to cry into anyone's arms who could make this stop.

Soft kisses were scattered along the back of my neck. The tenderness made my skin shudder and flush. My elbows buckled, and I lowered my chest to the ground, letting go of Luka's hands, trying to ground myself.

He chuckled and leaned forward, smoothing his hands up my spine with one resting on the back of my neck and the other on my waist as he thrust forward, jolting my body every time he went deeper inside me. My knees and chest scraped along the floor, the grains digging into my skin.

"How does it feel, Alina? Is it what you hoped for or were you looking forward to the virgin act?" he teased.

I shook my head, refusing to answer.

His hand at the base of my neck smoothed forward, his fingers combing up the back of my head before taking a fistful of hair, yanking me upward until my back hit his chest.

"I asked you a question," he whispered. "But since you won't say it out loud, allow me."

He moved his other hand on my waist to slide it to the front, resting it on top of my lower stomach. "You hate yourself right now because you know that it feels good. You feel me deep in here." He pressed down on my abdomen, pushing himself deeper inside. "The worst part is you want me here, buried in your womb, and you would beg for me to mate with you, sink whatever I could into you, but you are too stubborn to let the thought manifest as pleas on those sweet lips of yours," he gasped, thrusting faster as he slammed into me.

I cried out, my nails digging into his thighs as he fucked me like some animal.

He pulled my hair tighter, pressing his cheek to mine as he held me against him. "Oh, Alina…you are so soft. Your flesh is so supple and sweet, inside and out. I will take great pleasure in ruining you," he moaned, biting my neck as he pushed down on my abdomen roughly, sitting back on his knees and making me sit down on him as he throbbed, filling me with his seed.

I was shaking, worse than I ever had in my life. Tears fell endlessly from my eyes, but I would not dare make a sound. When I looked down, I could see his spines flexing against my thighs, itching to be inside, just out of reach from my flesh. It brought me some comfort knowing he spared me the pain and embarrassment, but I felt guilty for praising him for the minimum after what he put me through.

He let go of me, and I slipped off his lap when he finished.

I curled up on the floor. The shame of feeling even an ounce of pleasure from what had just happened made it feel like I was having an experience outside of my body. Every part of my body felt disgusting and vibrated with thrill simultaneously. It was Issac all over again. I could not bear it. It was my fault.

"What a lovely sight." His arms looped under my legs and waist as he gathered my limp body to his chest. He brought us to the bed, and he settled against the headboard. He was gentle now, returning that familiar feeling I used to get when I was around…well, Viktor. It felt like he died, a friend that was never real, left behind in my memory. In my head, it registered like Luka had killed off Viktor, making me miss him more. But my body didn't know that, making it all the more confusing.

I stared down at a frayed piece of thread on the blanket as Luka…licked me?

He bent my leg up, licking over the red cuts and scrapes on my knees, delivering that numbness to the wounds as he worked along my body. He kissed my palms softly before licking along the crosshatch cuts, irritating my skin. It was odd finding comfort in the action as he cradled me close.

My head rested against his chest. It was like I had been running, completely exhausted mentally and physically. My body did not even have the spare energy to shake, tremble, or pull away from his touch.

The creaking of the door did not even bring my attention fully back. All I wanted to do was close my eyes, and I did.

"Ah, you're a little late to join, but maybe next time?"

There was a long pause, but he did not need to speak for me to know who had walked in. It made me want to sink into the mattress like quicksand, weighed down by my humiliation.

"You have...exactly thirty seconds...to explain." The words sounded painful in Silas's throat, like he was holding back the rage of something so formidable that it could be biblical in scale.

"Training the new pet, of course. We had a great time— right, Alina?"

I shook my head, and the heat rose in my neck and ears.

"Twenty seconds..."

"Don't be foolish, Silas. We both know that you would not lay a finger on me while I hold your prized possession. One snap of my wrist to her neck and she's gone," Luka said with a chipper tone, like he was telling a lighthearted joke. He then shifted me in his lap so my back was against his chest.

I squeezed my eyes shut as he pulled my legs apart, spread eagle to show Silas what he had done. I shivered as the hot semen leaked from between my legs. All I could manage was a whimper, and then I slapped my hands over my mouth to muffle the sob.

"The garden, ten minutes."

"Sounds like a date," Luka purred, closing my legs for me.

There was a thick tension in the air as the words ran out. Either they had nothing else to say or did not want to say it in front of me. It felt like an eternity. I wanted to be alone. For both of them to leave me instead of using me for their own idiotic games.

I got my wish as my mind slipped into darkness, not remembering even the door slamming before I was lulled off to the back of my mind again.

CHAPTER FORTY-NINE

THE CREATURE

E very single long-lost method of torture flashed before my eyes. Taking fingers or severing his cock from his body would not be enough to satiate the rage I felt when I saw what he did to her.

My poor Alina was made to endure that *beast*. I physically recoiled at the memory of their scents mingling, filling that room and burning my nose and throat like chlorine.

I wanted to find a way to make him feel like he was dying many times over without relief—like Prometheus when a bird of prey ate his entrails every day of his miserable, eternal suffering that he called a life.

No matter how violently I imagined Luka's death, it did not satisfy me. Nothing calmed me. I was seeing red, and it would not end until reality matched my rage-colored lenses.

"This is all quite romantic. Are you sure you aren't flirting with me?" Luke teased as he stepped out into the garden from behind a neatly trimmed hedge.

My fist was already meeting the side of his face, and I heard a crack that could either be his jaw or my knuckle. I was too numb to differentiate. My limbs were moving on only instinct now.

I swung again, but he put his arms up for my fist to smack his forearms.

"Already hot and bothered." Luka laughed.

"I am going to rip your limbs from your body and beat you with them," I growled. "Do you hear me? I will ensure that you are only alive enough to feel everything I do to you."

"Now you're really getting me excited. This is more my pace." He smirked. "What on earth could have you so bothered? It couldn't be our new pet, could it?"

"She is no pet," I hissed, grabbing him by his throat and backing him against the hedge. I could just yank his head and pull it off right here, watering the garden plenty with his blood.

"Uh-uh." He clicked his tongue in disapproval. He gripped my wrists and squeezed. "You forget yourself, Silas." He yanked my hands from his neck and shoved me roughly backward. "Why are you getting so worked up over a meal?"

"You wouldn't have fucked her if you really thought of her as a simple meal," I spat at him.

"You are right. I admittedly have grown attached to that odd little raven of ours, but I was not the one foolish enough to have mated with her," he sneered. "What were you thinking? That you would live happily? She would make you breakfast in the morning and dinner when you came home?"

"Of course not, but she has the potential to be greater than the two of us combined. I know that you see it." I circled him as he mirrored my movements. "Her blood is even more potent than anything Father kept hidden away here. Can you imagine what she would be if she turned?"

"Possibly, but for what purpose? It has been whispered for a long time that you planned to take your father's Nest. Were you planning on starting with her?" he asked amusingly. "Would you build an army from scratch?"

"Don't pretend you have any loyalty to my father. As long as the money comes, you will follow," I sneered, lunging again, and my knuckle buried into his gut.

He grabbed me by the shoulders and fell backward. We wrestled along the neatly trimmed grass, kicking up the lawn and dirt as we fought.

"While that is true, I do not have a reason to have any loyalty to you either." He grabbed my hair and bit my neck.

I hissed and bore my fangs at him, attempting to bite back, but he held me at arm's length once his teeth let me go.

I scratched at him, but he bit my hand and kicked me again.

Biting, scratching, kicking, clawing—we were going to tear each other limb from limb. None of it could come to any conclusion due to our equal match of strength and vigor. By the end, we stood there, battered and bloodied. The sun had disappeared by then. All we could do was glare at each other and observe the wounds we had traded. We sat in silence on opposite sides of the garden, surrounded by foliage that trembled in the cool breeze, neither of us having the energy to continue this useless struggle.

"I will make sure you never know peace," I promised.

"I have never known such a thing," Luka replied.

I WENT to see her that morning, not that she was conscious enough to know. I had never seen her so dejected, so detached. Even at rest, she looked like she'd lost something. Something was breaking inside of her. The maids said she was not eating, which looked to be true based on how pale she was getting. The soft rosy pink of her lips and cheeks was pale and dull. This place was poisoning her. I needed a way to get her out, but Luka was watching me—waiting for a reason to tear into me like I wanted so desperately to do to him.

I sat on the edge of her bed as the morning light crept into the window, slowly moving across the floor as the hours passed. I just wanted to see her, to bear witness to her being alive and that she would not fade away, though she was certainly fading. She could not take much more of being in a place like this. It was unnatural.

I ran my fingers through her hair, lying face-to-face with her. She would not wake, but she was breathing. Whatever Luka did to her drained her enough to send her into a deep sleep.

I cherished my moments with her, even this one. Someday perhaps we could look back on this time and be proud that we made it. Go somewhere far away, where no one would ever find us, and we could live out what time I had left with her in peace. Those would be my favorite years.

It would not be long before Luka realized my company was missing from the main floors. I had to return sooner rather than later.

"It will all end soon, I promise," I whispered, cupping her face before kissing her forehead. "Just a little longer... They will all suffer."

THE BOTTOM FLOORS of the Nest were stuffy. It was like an Easter gathering every day. All wearing light and expensive clothing, giving the impression of purity and cleanliness despite the morbid reality of this congregation. How frivolous must it be to have human meat stuck between your teeth while you wore your Sunday best?

There were flowers in every corner, elaborate displays on tables, vases along hallways and by the door—all to mask the metallic scent of blood.

It smelled more horrid than if they just kept the stench of bodily fluid. Besides, there was no need to keep up appearances for anyone out there. Pretending to be civil creatures was useless.

Servants bustled about preparing food, though most of it was not for the Vipera. Aside from Hosts, there were other imports prepared. Human meat was a booming trade for less developed tastes, but the Hosts were the staple. I suspected there were around twenty girls littered throughout the estate.

The house was bright, with lots of creams and light colors. It gave it an almost sterile feel.

This Nest held twenty families, including my own—though only my father remained within the walls. As modern as he liked to pretend the Nests were, they operated like courts of the romantic period. Maybe I would like the idea of a Nest more if it was not so callous. They pretended that their treatment of Hosts was fair and progressive, but they turned a blind eye to my Father and his usual cruelties. *Cowards.* Everyone was supposedly on the same side—except the only side they took was their own.

I entered the kitchen intending to make a cup of coffee, but a particular dark-haired feral was taking up the room.

"Silas! Did all that roughhouse last night build up an appetite?" Luka grinned, his bruised face bringing a brief moment of joy to the bitter moment.

"Yes, now move," I mumbled, moving beside him to pour some of the coffee from the siphon brewer on the counter. I could still feel the scratches and bites he'd left on my shoulder when I moved my arm.

"How did she look this morning?" He smirked. "Did you see all those pretty marks I left on her? You should have seen her. She was magnificent."

"Another word about her and I will be removing your tongue."

"You want to put *what* in my mouth?" He raised his voice and caused a few eyes to glance our way.

"Be quiet," I hissed, shoving him in the chest.

Some of the other Vipera looked our way, wary of us.

"Careful—you have no loyalists here. You are surrounded by some of the oldest Vipera you've ever known. Don't give them a reason to get rid of you." He raised his hands in surrender.

I backed down and returned to my cup of coffee, leaning against the counter as I sipped it. Focusing on the bitter taste was easier than trying to interrogate Luka with so many eyes on us. He was safe as long as the Nest was focused and intact.

"When is Father returning?"

"A fortnight, possibly." Luka shrugged, leaning against the counter next to me. "Why? Nervous to see Pop?"

"No," I said simply, becoming lost in thought.

"I am sure he will be delighted to hear that his son was sleeping with his Host *and* the Poisoner. It really should earn you some points with him," he chimed sarcastically.

"He can't possibly expect me to keep track of what things he thinks are his."

"No, but it makes sense how you did not find her sooner." Luka laughed. "Maybe he hid her away to protect her from *you*."

"Nonsense."

"He hid her in plain sight, right next to your fair sister."

"Speak any more about either of them, and I will not hesitate to make a scene." My eyes snapped to him. "Phoebe is off-limits. Father will have your head if you meddle with his favorite."

"I am sure the Sire will understand. Maybe he will give her to me as a reward if I slay you now."

"She does not enjoy the company of men," I said plainly. "She is a bit of an invert, quite Bostonian. You will not find as much joy in the conquest as you may think."

"Ah, here I thought you didn't visit your youngest sibling, as you couldn't see the gem by her side this whole time."

"That is not true. I know my sister well, and I visit her often alone. She banned me from her parties because she did not like me 'womanizing her guests,' as she would say. Besides, it is easy to miss a shadow like Alina when she rarely decides to attend in the first place."

"You thought your sister did not have friends?"

"I knew she had one friend." I sighed. "She told me outright that she kept her hidden from me. How many men did Phoebe eat because they simply upset her friend? It took my sister years to quit the habit of meddling in her friend's love life. They are more alike than they care to admit. I did not know that Alina was *the* friend until after."

"All I heard is that you and your sister have the same taste in women."

I rolled my eyes at him and walked away. There was no point in allowing him to taunt me. He was only there to instigate, banking on some sort of conflict so he had an excuse to gut me. I had a new plan to get out of this mess, one that I could use Luka for.

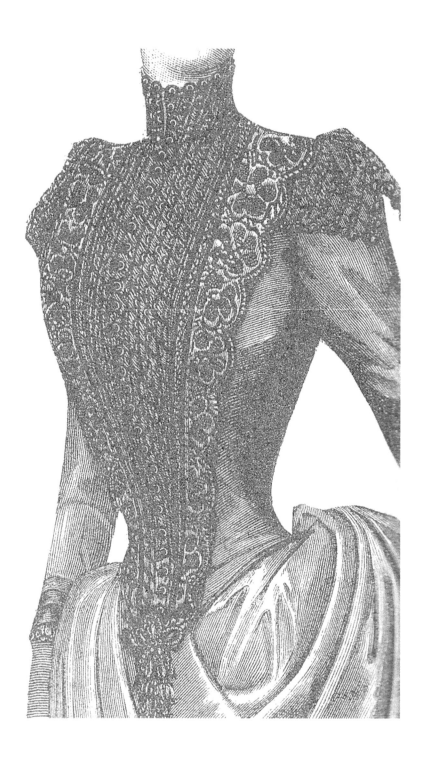

CHAPTER FIFTY

THE POISONER

The routine was so rigid that it made it hard to tell the days apart.

Was it a week later or a few days? The only distinguishing part was the menu. Everything else was wash, rinse, repeat.

They still limited me to the second floor. Sometimes I would hear people downstairs. Sounds of celebration, storytelling, drinking, eating, dancing, music, everything.

This must be how bears felt in hibernation. Every day was bland and covered in white, with nothing to tell the days apart. The only thing to do was sleep.

They did not allow me any objects. Nothing to comfort me. I was just waiting for my next guest, though it was rare that I had visitors. It was like a lethal game of chance. Would I get Phoebe, the maids, or one of the two creatures that tortured me?

As I lay curled in the middle of the bed, the night was like any other. Quiet, drifting through my thoughts and dreams until they bled into one another. Every once in a while, I would have dreams that I'd escaped, running across that elongated field, the wind whipping my hair against my face and my legs taking over for me as I fled to freedom.

Then I awoke, cried, and slept again. This happened many nights.

Amid my slumber, the bed dipped on one side, then the other.

Hands, one set—no, two.

As I lay on my side, two bodies pressed me between them.

I could feel lips against mine, soft and familiar. I kissed him lightly, knowing that it would be Silas. He was so real, so warm against me. His fingertips left hot trails across my skin that made me shiver.

The body behind me could be none other than Luka. The soft curls of his hair tickled my neck as he left kisses across my skin, letting his bottom lip drag as he moved to my shoulder. Could this be a dream? Or was I just hoping it was?

Silas moved from my lips down to my breasts, gently taking my nipple between his teeth before wrapping his lips around it. Electricity shot through me when he nipped at me.

Luka's hands wrapped around my waist, holding my hips closer as he sucked on my neck. His hand reached down, touching between my legs. In that moment, Silas hissed at Luka.

My eyes snapped open. This was no dream.

Their touches were becoming rougher and more possessive as the moments passed. It was like they were both playing a game of territory, and I was stuck in the middle, their hands marking what was theirs.

"Stop—" I barely got the word out in a whisper before Luka sank his fangs into my shoulder.

The pain was like no other. It was like he did not possess the venom necessary for numbing or did not care to use it. Knowing the sadist he was, it was most likely the latter.

I blinked away the blur of my vision, staring at Silas.

How could you let this happen?

"I'm sorry." Silas cupped my face, a pitiful expression plaguing his features. Then, his needlelike teeth pierced the other shoulder, granting me some relief from Luka's bite.

The sound that came from me was pitiful, a whine like some injured kitten as the ravens plucked at its wounds. To feel utterly helpless and at the mercy of not one but two animals was enough to bring tears to my eyes. My situation just kept getting worse and worse the more days that went by.

"Get off me," I cried, though I had no more tears. I had cried for days alone in my prison cell of a chamber. I tried to sit up.

Luka's jaws clamped down harder as his arms wrapped around me.

They let me sit up, one to my front and one to my back, but they did not relieve me of their deadly grasp. I swallowed and stared up at the ceiling. The cracks and indents were subtle against the eggshell color of the paint that attempted to cover them.

My arms covered my bare chest and whatever I could.

Nothing was mine anymore. Not my body, not my words. I tried to curl up, but they wouldn't let me become any smaller than I already was.

Luka's hand ventured too close to Silas. He pulled away only to bear those bloody, twitching fangs at Luka as he hissed. Luka let go of my neck to hiss back, making me flinch between the two.

Their greedy hands grabbed me and held me between them as they drained me. I started to see stars against the ceiling, my vision narrowing until all I could see was blackness, but I could still hear the sounds of them consuming me, their teeth in me, their hands on me.

I AWOKE in that small room while the maids buzzed about cleaning me up and putting me back together that morning. This fussing over the Host bodies made more sense to me as I thought about how sick or injured livestock would harm the consumer's health. I realized now that they were indispensable, which meant I might have leverage on those two animals. From what I could tell about the dynamic, feeding was a privilege, not a right, in this Nest. Which was why they had no issue keeping me from the others. Who were they saving me for?

Why did everyone look so panicked? They were shocked I was awake. When I tried to sit up, the maids all jumped at the action and insisted I stay still.

I brought my hand to my shoulder and flinched. Both of them were so tender.

What happened the night before came rushing back to me. I could feel my face grow hot with anger and embarrassment. Those *selfish* animals.

The creak of the door brought my attention back down to earth.

"I am not interrupting, am I?" An older man entered the room, tall and lanky like a scarecrow.

I wanted to cry.

"Dr. Hayes?" I whispered.

"Ah, Alina, I wish I could say it's a pleasure to see you again." An awkward smile tightened across his face. "Leave us be," he instructed the maids, and they filed out one by one.

"You knew," I snapped. "You knew this whole time, and you did not tell me."

"Please get a grasp on your emotions. I know it's an adjustment for you." He pulled over a stool and sat at my bedside. "I heard that you had a rough night."

I ignored him. "Why wouldn't you warn me? Why didn't you tell me?"

"I tried to run you off your train of thought, but you were too stubborn," he stated matter-of-factly. "I even tried contaminating your little experiment. You are the reason that you're here. You chose to poke around." He glared before moving my hair to check my neck. "I see that you got quite the welcome."

"You're just as bad as them." I pushed his hand away. "You willingly work for them."

"They pay me to make sure their food source isn't in pain, won't be injured, and is in the best health possible," he explained, ignoring my protests and checking the other side of my neck. "I am curious to see what you define as cruel."

"They kidnapped me."

"You're the only one, Alina." He sighed, sitting forward and placing the buds of his stethoscope in his ears. "These Hosts are here because they chose to be," he explained, placing the cold piece of his instrument on my chest. "You should have stopped poisoning people when Luka nailed the madam to your door," he continued. "Now breathe in and out," he droned on.

I complied with his request.

"Alina?" a small voice piped from the doorway. "Oh, apologies. I didn't realize the exam was still going," the red-haired nymph bumbled.

"No need for apologies. We are done." Dr. Hayes plucked the stethoscope from his ears and wrapped it up, sticking it in the black medical tote. "Keep her within eyesight. Solitude wouldn't be wise in case she receives any more visitors. Best have a maid sit with her." He rose from his seat.

"No need. I will do it." Phoebe smiled awkwardly at him as he left, closing the door behind him.

"Did you find it?" I cleared my aching throat, rubbing my face in frustration.

"Yes," she whispered, coming up beside me and placing a small vial in my hand.

"Where are the rest?"

"I have them hidden. I figured you should keep one in here just in case." She held my hand. "What do we do next?"

"I don't know."

"You don't know? What do you mean you 'don't know'? I thought you had a plan?" she pressed, squeezing my hand anxiously.

"I didn't think that far. All I know is I am going to have to use it. You'll know when I do." I looked from the tincture to the hand she was squeezing. "It won't be safe for either of us. We will only have a small window of opportunity to flee. I say draw up the route. You're the one who's good at planning things."

"I don't know where to start."

"Figure it out. If you can plan elaborate balls and galas, you can plan an escape route for us. Pick anywhere, far away from this place."

"All right," she said softly. That worried look on her face made me nauseous. Could I pull this off? I just hoped she could put together a good plan for when the time came.

CHAPTER FIFTY-ONE
THE POISONER

B eing watched like a pet was worse than solitude.
We moved down the stairs, and several men and women in their finest tea dresses and informal wear were sitting at tables and lounging around the general areas. Their voices hushed when I was brought into view. As I glanced at them, their eyes looked ravenous. The men and women looked at me like I was some circus animal they'd paid handsomely to see. It took everything in me not to shout at them in my already irritated state.

The only bright side to this seemed to be that I was so graciously granted clothing. They let me wear a simple white tea gown but kept the abrasive gold collar.

Before they sat me in a chair in the corner, I was already taking a mental inventory of how many wine bottles were scattered around the lounging room. I also took notice of not one but two particular creatures in my midst. They both looked surprised that I was down there, probably wondering what I did to convince them to let me out of my neat little box.

They made my skin itch. I needed something. I stared longingly at the other figures, drinking and laughing with one another in this casual gathering. Hesitantly, I slunk toward a small ornamental table that held some small bites of fruits and cheeses set out for the Hosts.

The other Hosts wore the same white dress, minus the elaborate restrictions.

I stared down at the spread of fruits, plucking an apple slice and inspecting it.

"Need something stronger?" A hand with a glass appeared before me.

I slowly took the glass and looked at the man next to me, who could be nobody other than Silas.

"Do you think my forgiveness can be bought with liquor?" I sneered. I could feel my brow twitch with the anger I harbored. I was beginning to loathe him. He was selfish and hungry above all else.

"Possibly." His eyes trailed over me, assessing the damage from the other night.

"Oh, I am so elated that you asked! I am doing much better after the doctor stitched me up after those two animals attacked me in my own bed! It is so kind and gentlemanly of you to ask," I said sarcastically, turning away from him to look at the happenings of the parlor.

"Alina," he started.

"I hate you, Silas. I want you to know that for whatever comes next." I let the fruity wine disappear down my throat before I decided that it was time to breathe again.

"I know you do." He leaned in. "Luka wouldn't let me into the room unless he came too."

"Have you thought maybe you shouldn't have come?" I

snapped my head to him. "Have you considered that if you hadn't been so selfish, I wouldn't be here?" I raised my voice.

"Alina, please lower your—"

"My what? My voice? Are we afraid of public perception now? Like I was afraid of being seen with *you*?" I yelled at him.

Luka approached out of the corner of my eye.

"No!" I screamed, throwing the glass at his head, though he moved just in time for it to shatter against the wall behind him.

The parlor guests gasped and muttered. How dare they act *surprised*? Why would no one help me? Why was it not alarming to them that a battered and bruised woman with a collar was locked away upstairs?

"Enough," Luka spoke lowly as he grabbed one of my arms.

"Apologies! We have it handled!" Silas addressed the gathering as he grabbed the other arm.

The two dragged me toward the back of the estate, bringing me to the garden.

The garden looked like a maze of tall hedges. It was a perfectly private place to tear these two to shreds.

"What? Sorry, is this embarrassing for *you*? How do you think I feel being treated like livestock in captivity?" I shouted, pulling my arms away from their grip and backing away. I stood in the middle of the grass, the two creatures eyeing me cautiously.

"Alina, the Nest is full of very old, very strong Vipera that would not hesitate to slaughter you if you step out of line like that. If we weren't there, there is no telling what they would have done to you," Silas said calmly, stepping toward me.

"If you weren't here, I wouldn't be here either! See how that works? Both of you are currently the source of all of my problems."

"Well, technically, I am only involved because you were

poisoning the Nest," Luka corrected. "You're *here* because it was a step below *killing you*."

"You can't just lash out like that. They think you are feral. If a Host becomes dangerous, they will put them down," Silas scolded. "You need to cooperate."

"Like I did last night? Was that not enough cooperation for you? Even when I trust you, you nearly kill me by feeding on me too long!" I spat at them. "You are both fools."

"The meal was worth it." Luka smirked.

"You are not helping," Silas snapped at him.

I could not stand them. Their presence alone was grating against every one of my senses. I took a deep breath and let out the most bloodcurdling scream I could rip from my throat.

Silas rushed to me and clamped his hand over my mouth.

"Go calm the Nest. I'll handle this," Silas instructed Luka, and began dragging me into the hedge maze.

I thrashed against his grip, pulling and biting at his hand until he let me go, pressing me against the prickly hedge.

"Alina, I can't help you if you keep acting like this," he pleaded.

"Like what? Like an animal?" I glared.

There was something in his eyes that looked genuine. Like he was worried for me. I did not believe one bit of that act.

"I need more time. Please just trust me," he whispered, resting his head against mine.

"How much more time? How many more hours of torture will you subject me to while I wait for my golden knight to break me free?" I mocked him. "Will you let Luka fuck me again? Or feed from me while you stare at your hands and wonder what to do? I'm done waiting."

"It's complicated."

"For you maybe," I scoffed. "I'm getting myself out of this, and when I do, I never want to set eyes on you again."

"You don't mean that."

"Oh, but I do." I laughed. "I will kill myself if that is the only way to get away from you and this awful place."

"You wouldn't."

"I would do whatever it takes." I pulled away from him. "You know that."

He yanked me back. "You are just saying these things because you are angry."

"Unhand me, you unnatural thing!" I screamed at him. "I will not be told what I can and cannot do by a creature so abominable that he must keep me here in chains to keep me at all."

"You don't mean it." His jaw clenched. "Say you don't."

"I should have dissected you and sold your corpse to the museums," I seethed. "They would applaud me for slaying such a beast. The world, in turn, would have been brighter if I had removed your stain earlier. That is where my mistakes started when it comes to you, *Creature*."

The pain in his eyes was like nothing I had ever seen. It was how I used to fantasize about how maybe he would look if I sunk the blade through his heart. This was for his own good as well as mine. We simply could not exist together while I made it my purpose to destroy these things that surely were unnatural. *We* were unnatural. If I made it out alive, I needed to sever *everything*.

CHAPTER FIFTY-TWO

THE POISONER

"Alina, wake up," Phoebe whispered, lightly tapping my face.

I moaned and rolled over in bed, wrapping my arms around her warm body as she lay next to me. She refused to let a maid stay with me so she could keep my company to avoid more feeding accidents.

"Are you well?" She rested her head on my chest.

"For now, I am fine," I mumbled, rubbing my face against the soft pillow.

"You resemble a barely animated corpse." Phoebe pulled off the sheets and inspected me.

"I think that is the greatest compliment you've given me in my twenty years of knowing you." I laughed weakly.

I had not seen my reflection, though I was sure I looked as grim as Phoebe described. Tired, fatigued, sore, bruised, and an always healing wound. I had endured much these past few months. This was the last limb. I could feel it.

"You are requested downstairs tonight." Phoebe traced her

finger around the bruising on my shoulder. "I think it'll be the best time to act. Everyone will be drunk, feeding, or on some other substance."

"If you say so, I trust you," I said as her worried face studied me. "We will be fine. Don't look at me like that." I tried to comfort her, though I was barely convinced myself.

THERE WAS a wide assortment of fruits and colorful vegetables. Sliced pomegranate and berries. Cooked sweet potatoes and greens. There were two platters of meat: one was lemon haddock, and the other sliced red meat. It smelled like heaven. Then, my eyes trained on the beautiful pile of oranges in a bowl. I could understand why the girls did not want to leave. It really was heaven if you came of your own accord. There was also a large decanter of red wine in the middle.

Finally, something to numb myself with.

I had not realized how hungry I was until now. I poured a generous amount of wine into my glass before eating. There was so much food around me I was overwhelmed with deciding what to eat first. I decided to stick to red meat and wine. My orange was going to be saved for last. I downed the wine fast, and the lightness in my head hit me like a train. However, it did make my mood slightly more enjoyable. Overall, my body was relaxed. I was well rested and ready to depart this dreadful place.

My eyes slowly looked down at the deep purple in my cup. Wine was a blood thinner. I realized the entire spread before us was made up of ingredients that increased blood volume.

I plucked a few peeled orange slices from the table. A tingling at the back of my neck warned me of eyes watching.

I checked behind me to see Silas with three Hosts around him, but his eyes were only on me. They held such hatred in them, I could sympathize.

There was a girl on each of his legs as he sat there, then a third between his legs, touching his chest. They fawned over him, begging for him to take a bite.

As the scene unraveled, I wondered what he was getting at. Was this supposed to make me feel something?

He gave me a sly smirk before turning his attention to one of the women in his lap. He grabbed her neck and made her expose it for him. He licked his lips and glanced in my direction, not breaking eye contact as he sunk his teeth into her.

She gasped and clutched onto him.

What is his point?

I looked at the other side of the room and saw my other secret admirer, who watched with amusement as he sipped wine.

Two can play this silly game.

I grabbed a bowl of cherries from the table and walked off to the other side of the room.

"Is this seat taken?" I asked Luka sweetly.

"That depends. Do you have anything sharp on you?" He looked me up and down before he focused on my bowl of fruit, a curious look on his face as his eyes returned to mine.

"I will take that as a no." I hummed, sitting across his lap.

Luka looked down at me before glancing over at Silas across the room. "What do you want?"

"Let's not pretend that you care about the answer to that question as long as you get something in return." I plucked a cherry off its stem with my teeth. They had a rich sweetness and didn't have any pits, making them even more enjoyable.

"You caught me there." He laughed. "You're quite the exhibitionist, then?"

"Would that put you off?" I held another cherry at the front of my mouth.

"Quite the opposite." He leaned close and grasped the cherry between my lips with his teeth, snaking a forked tongue in before closing the distance and rolling the small red fruit between our tongues.

I could feel the burning stare of a particular set of blue eyes across the room. Silas was not the most subtle. He had no one else to blame. He started this.

If I could get these two at each other's throats, it would be killing two birds with one stone, and I would be free of them both. I just needed to endure it a little longer.

Luka let out a low chuckle as he stole the cherry from me, pulling away to chew and glance at Silas. He gave an amused laugh when he saw his face. "You were right. It is more fun when you have a voyeur."

"I am not wrong about many things," I whispered, nibbling playfully at his earlobe.

"Don't get cocky," he warned, looking back down at me. "You're already poking two bears at once."

"Well, what fun is being a captive when you can't play with the keepers?" I asked innocently.

"The difference is that one of us could reduce you to only ribbons of flesh on the floor. Imagine what *two* will do," he retorted. His eyes narrowed dangerously at me, but he kept a handsome grin on his face.

I ignored him, putting another cherry in my mouth and scanning the room. Silas was gone. I slipped off Luka's lap, plucking the wineglass from his hands to drink from it.

"I don't respond well to threats," I mumbled. "When you hear a rattle, you don't walk farther into the brush."

Luckily for me, I spotted Phoebe, her back turned to me as she stood by a small cocktail bar.

"Phoebe!" I whispered as I approached her, turning her around by her shoulder.

She flinched, and my eyes widened.

There were red marks around her neck, as well as some other bruising that disappeared under the hem of her pink dress.

"He knows," Phoebe choked out, her eyes red. "He found the other samples." She was trying her best to hold back a sob.

"Shh." I hugged her, resting her head against my chest. Out of the corner of my eye, I saw Luka approaching. I quickly turned my face down to her.

While my face was covered, I pulled the small half-inch vial that she gave me earlier from my sleeve, placing it in my mouth.

"How touching is this?"

I craned my neck to see Luka standing over us.

"You know the rules," Silas warned, leaning against the common area entryway.

"Don't pretend you care about rules now, Mr. Forbes," he scoffed.

I closed my eyes. I needed to close them for a minute, clutching onto Phoebe. I hesitated to let her go, taking in the perfume she was wearing, the softness of her hair, and the temperature of her body against mine. There was no knowing if this would be the last time I saw her.

"This way!" Luka roughly yanked me by my arm toward the other room, settling on the red couch with the mahogany trim. "You sit over there. You know the rules, one at a time," he directed to Silas.

Silas sat across from us. Phoebe was hovering by the door.

Other guests were preoccupied with their Hosts, too busy to notice any commotion, though I suspected brash characters were nothing new at a party involving alcohol and blood.

"You've been up to mischievous things, haven't you?" Luka pulled me onto his lap, positioning my legs on either side of his hips.

I stared silently.

"Cat got your tongue?" He played with a piece of my hair between his fingers. "You seemed happy enough to take this position moments ago. What changed?"

I turned my face away from him.

"It's disappointing. I thought we were all bonding, no? How about we share some things about ourselves?" He glanced at Silas. "Did she tell you about what happened at the country estate?"

I remained silent, though I did look in Silas's direction. He looked intrigued, but his expression held something else. Was it contempt? Jealousy? Something worse?

"Yes," Silas said.

"Even the part about her father?"

Silas was silent.

"I must be the delegated bearer of bad news." Luka cringed. "What did your father's coroner's report say? Arsenic?"

My eyes snapped angrily at Luka. I had to keep it together. Just wait a little longer. My bottom lip trembled, and I shook my head.

"It was interesting to find that you poisoned your father and his assistant. Were you jealous he finally had a son?" Luka teased. "I thought your journal entry from that day was quite interesting too. 'Thirty-five hours, twenty-nine minutes, and fifteen seconds.' I couldn't believe you tracked how long it took him to expire! How morbid."

I stared off in the distance, though I saw the look on Phoebe's face. Her expression was nothing short of petrified, frozen in a state I had never seen. I did not want to see the look on Silas's face.

"Playing with poisons before a storm wasn't very bright of you, was it? Truly careless, Alina. Though I assume that it was a beginner's mistake." He laughed. "Oh, I found your little collection. Your friend did a poor job at hiding them." His eyes were locked on me, interrogating me. "Tell me—which one of us would you have poisoned first? Me or Silas?"

I could feel the anger building up, the tears clouding my vision.

"Oh, don't be so glum. You should learn to be thankful that I didn't snap that pretty little neck of yours after that stunt." He smiled, moving my dress up and unbuttoning his trousers.

"Luka!" Silas shouted, standing up. "That's enough!"

"Uh-uh! Stay there!" Luka grabbed me by the back of my neck, pulling me closer against his chest.

I shook my head subtly at Silas, and our gazes lingered.

Then, he remembered I was *silent*.

"Ah!" Luka scolded, and grabbed my face to look at him again, a fire burning in the embers of his eyes, his smile showing off those deadly talons for teeth. "Don't look at him. Look at me."

Silas hesitantly sat back down, eyeing me nervously.

"I have to know your methods, Alina. He's quite obedient," Luka said smugly, holding my face gentler than before. "Now, where were we?"

He slid the skirt of my dress higher, exposing some of the leftover bruise marks on the back of my thighs from the riding crop. It was all a disgusting display designed to make Silas angry because Luka knew he was safe behind my flesh as a shield.

His craving for power over others was his unfortunate vice. It was precisely why he was perfect for this particular stunt.

I leaned forward, holding the fabric of his shirt gently between my fingers. My lips timidly brushed over his chest, the front of his throat, then the crook of his neck.

"That is a much better attitude." He leered, believing he had won some sick victory. I knew that his focus was on Silas though. I could assume that the pain he was inflicting on him was a bigger turn-on than the body in his lap.

Predictable.

I clenched my teeth around the glass, making it shatter in my mouth with a crack.

"What was that?"

I sank my teeth into his neck, letting the glass and poison mix with the fresh wound I was creating as I clenched my jaw harder, his blood filling my mouth as I held on.

A purely animalistic shriek came from him as he shoved me onto the floor, a patch of skin being taken as he did so.

The wind was knocked from my lungs as I tried to regain my breath, spitting out the glass pieces and flesh while black blood dripped from my lips.

Luka let out a harrowing yell. It did not sound even remotely human. He charged at me before Silas's body crashed into him, both of them baring their teeth and tearing at each other violently.

The burning in my mouth told me I did not have much time. My throat was closing, and my breathing was becoming more labored as I tried to focus and steady my spinning head.

In the commotion, other patrons clamored around us, mainly crowding around the two animals in the middle of the room.

The last thing I saw as I was dragged across the floor was the two figures slashing at each other. Luka's face was burning. His eyes filled with blood as it came in tears down his face, the skin around my bite dying and turning red as it spread across his face. I had never wondered what burning flesh smelled like, but I remembered it from that night.

I was not sure if it was the lack of air in my brain, the lingering venom, or the satisfaction of my poison working, but I took comfort in that scalding monstrosity possibly being my last masterpiece.

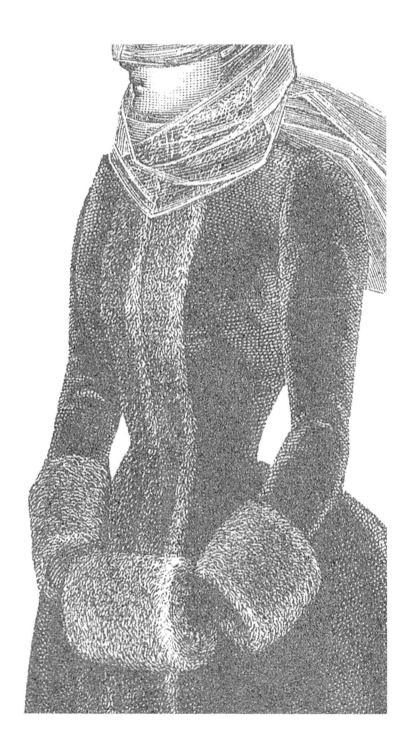

CHAPTER FIFTY-THREE

THE POISONER

W ho knew what became of the two creatures? It mattered
little to me now. They would just be one of many things
I left behind. If luck would have it, both men would have
perished.

The tip of my cigarette cherried with each breath as I
watched the boat push away from the dock. The wrinkled paper
with my new destination was clutched in my hands.

WHITE STAR LINE
From Liverpool to New York

New York. A fresh start.

Well, as fresh as it could get from here. I had a new purpose
now. Not only did I have new subjects to play with, I had a new
poison to perfect.

For Silas's sake, I hoped he would assume me dead. It was

best for both of us. Would he feel betrayed if he knew I was alive? *Betrayal.* I wondered if he was capable of feeling even that after all this time.

"Are you coming inside?" Phoebe asked, pulling her wool shawl closer around her as she approached me at the back of the deck.

I sighed and tilted my head back, letting the smoke push through my nose, watching it disappear into the gray sky, giving me snowflakes on my lashes in return.

"Yeah." I sighed, flicking the cigarette overboard. "Let us go."

The land behind me slowly turned into an endless horizon of water, disappearing with the memory of my old life.

It was good to disappear for a while.

I was heading west.

END OF BOOK I

ACKNOWLEDGMENTS

There are so many people to thank that made this book possible, none of whom are a therapist.

First, thank you to my partner, Ryan, who has supported me through many nights of manic rambling about this story in particular. I also appreciate his contributions as *logistics coordinator*.

I owe a huge thank you to Grace and Brooke, my Alpha readers who gave me the confidence to finally publish. Same goes for every Beta reader who gave my story a fighting chance!

Thank you to Vanessa, who was present for the conception of this story after we started buddy reading together!

Thank you to my editor, Tiffany, there would be way more commas if not for you!

Thank you to my parents (whom will *never* know this book exists) for your blind support about my author journey despite the fact I refuse to tell you my pen name.

Lastly, thank you to all the readers that took a chance on this story and I look forward to making more for you!

AUTHOR LORE

Now, on to the author lore.

I'm a New England-born, New York City-based author. My career, aside from writing, is a full-time artist and photographer. I started my education as a pre-med biology student due to my adoration of nerdy things, but I finished my schooling with a BBA in Marketing.

My writings will always encompass romance, the complexities of relationships, and their more significant meanings. I gravitate towards gothic historical romance and deep symbolism is a staple in the genre. I know an ungodly amount about Victorian plant symbolism to let it go to waste.

I have always been supportive of erotica, the kink community, and the importance of expression through art.

I'm a mother of three beautiful, poorly-mannered animal children: Boba, Sigma, and Lana. Sigma passed when I finished this book. She was the best dumb, deaf, blind cat, and I bet she's playing that mean pinball game in the sky.

I have never had to write an "about the author" section before, so I will list some random lore about myself. I worked for the largest reptile distributors in the States, I collect authentic gowns from the 1850s-1910s (I own 9), I restored a 200-year-old camera for fun during the plague of 2020, My real surname is one of 30 in the world, I have been on the news twice because of my photography work, I own a 60 drawer apothecary cabinet (this will impress the antiquers), I was a reserve champion equestrian in my state when I was 12.

I am proud that **_The Poisoner_** was my debut novel and I'm itching to weave more tragically beautiful stories.

instagram.com/ophallic

tiktok.com/@ophallic

goodreads.com/ophallic

Milton Keynes UK
Ingram Content Group UK Ltd.
UKHW020646300424
441966UK00014B/213/J